GIRL ON FIRE

Also by Eden Hart

The complete *Girl on Fire* Series:

Girl on Fire Book 1

Ashes Falling Book 2

Embers Burning Book 3

Phoenix Rising Book 4

GIRL ON FIRE

EDEN HART

PHOENIX FLAME
PRESS

GIRL ON FIRE

Copyright © 2022 by Eden Hart

All rights reserved.

For more information, contact: EdenHart77@outlook.com

1st Edition 2024

ISBN 978-1-922838-00-1 (paperback)

ISBN 978-1-922838-04-9 (ebook)

ISBN 978-1-922838-13-1 (hardcover)

Cover Design: Covers by Christian

Edited by Clio Editing Services

PHOENIX FLAME PRESS

For my husband, Peter,
whose love and support made this possible.

KASSIA

An ordinary girl
An extraordinary destiny

1

DAY ZERO—Thanksgiving

NEW YORK

On my sixteenth birthday, I was condemned to death—twice.

My first death sentence was calmly delivered in a sunlit room.

A few hours later, my second death sentence exploded from the night sky as the apocalypse began.

Five hours before the arrival of the red mist, my cousin and I were in New York's Central Park, watching some boys from school engaged in a tug-of-war match. In the grassy Sheep Meadow, picnickers enjoyed the unusually warm Thanksgiving weather and the rare opening of this field in November. Families gathered around baskets of food. Music drifted through the air. Children laughed as they played.

No one knew that this was humanity's last normal day.

Restless as usual, my cousin brushed some crumbs off her lap and onto our blanket. "When's your appointment, Kass?"

"Three o'clock." I checked the time on my phone. "I'll have to go soon."

"Why's Dr. McKay working on Thanksgiving?"

"He's off to Scotland tomorrow and wants to see me before he leaves."

Charlotte shot me a sharp glance. "Are you sick again, cuz?"

"I'm fine."

"Sure?"

I hesitated, then nodded. After four years, I was used to people fussing over my health. Being sick wasn't much fun, but the alternative—being dead—was worse, so I put up with it, hoping I'd eventually go into remission. Lately, I'd been feeling healthy. Almost normal. Maybe today I would finally receive the good news I'd been craving.

First, though, I had to survive Charlotte's birthday ritual.

"I'm glad you're okay, Kass." She tucked a stray lock of red hair behind her ear. "That means it's time. Truth or dare?"

I sighed. "Do we have to play this game every year?"

She frowned, her brief concern for me forgotten. "Are you wimping out?"

Charlotte loved challenges, the wilder the better, but I had enough challenges with my illness and would've preferred celebrating my birthday with a cupcake and a candle.

Still, classmates weren't exactly lining up to spend time with "the sick girl." In the past month, my circle of friends had shrunk when Amy and Beth had moved away. Since my cousin was now my only friend left in New York, I couldn't bear to lose her too.

I turned as a youth shouted to someone across the grass. Nearby, two girls laughed at videos on their phones. Mothers played with giggling babies. An old woman read a fairy tale to three wide-eyed kids.

Simple, everyday sounds …

… soon to be forever silenced.

"Truth or dare, Kass?" Charlotte's question held impatience and an unspoken demand that I honor her birthday tradition.

"Fine," I reluctantly said. "I pick truth."

With the hint of a smile, she looked at the boys in the tug-of-war match. Since group sports were banned in this area, the teams were waging their battle in the shadows of some trees. Muscled arms layered with sweat, they heaved on a thick rope, each side trying to topple the other.

My gaze lingered on the tall, brown-haired leader of one team. Jase Harris. Class president. Star quarterback. Popular. Good-looking.

And Charlotte's boyfriend.

"Are you ready?" She watched me closely. "Truth: which boy at school do you like the most?"

I turned away, hoping my suddenly flushed cheeks wouldn't reveal the secret I'd been hiding for months.

My gaze shifted to a nearby boy scrolling through his phone. Medium height. Nice smile. What was his name again? Brett? No, Brendon.

Charlotte narrowed her hazel eyes like a cat about to pounce on a bird. "I'll know if you're lying, Kassia Jane Madison."

Uh-oh. My cousin only used my full name when annoyed. I swallowed, already feeling guilty. All our lives, I'd been unable to slip a lie past her. "I've changed my mind. I'll take the dare."

"Are you certain?" she asked, pretty face alight with mischief. "Last chance to back out."

"No, thanks."

"Okay, I warned you." She pointed to a boy standing in the shade of a nearby tree. We'd seen him here a few times before, always at the edge of the grassy area. Always alone. He never spoke to anyone; he just studied people, his eyes hidden behind dark sunglasses. "For your dare, you have to kiss Loner." Our nickname for him.

I felt the blood drain from my face. "You're kidding."

"Am I laughing? If you don't complete your dare, it permanently reverts to truth."

A chill shot through me. My cousin was everything I wasn't. Popular. Athletic. And fiercely possessive. If she knew how I felt about her boyfriend, our relationship could shatter under the strain. I would end up friendless. Alone. Rejected. Again.

"What's your problem with kissing Loner?" Charlotte gave a knowing smile. "He's drop-dead gorgeous."

"So you've seen him up close?"

"Yep. He's our age. Maybe a bit older." When I still hesitated, she said, "Ticktock, ticktock."

Reluctantly, I stood.

I'd never kissed a boy before. Sure, I'd daydreamed about it, imagining a romantic setting where I melted into the arms of a boy who cared about me. I had hoped my first kiss would be slow, passionate, and memorable.

Instead, I was about to hurriedly kiss a stranger in a noisy, crowded park.

I winced. This would definitely be memorable—for all the wrong reasons.

As I moved toward Loner, I ran a hand over my wavy auburn hair, glad it had remained thick and healthy despite my illness. I wished I'd worn blush on my pale cheeks, along with eyeshadow to highlight my green eyes. And why had I picked today to wear boring jeans and a white top instead of a pretty dress?

Loner ignored my approach. On past occasions, I had seen girls try to talk to him, but he had ignored them all. He'd just kept studying people in the park, his focus so intense that I'd wondered if he was looking for someone—or waiting for something.

The closer I got to Loner, the more my anxiety grew.

He was tall, with the erect posture of a soldier on duty. As usual, a black baseball cap and dark sunglasses hid most of his face, shadowing his features. His rolled-up sleeves revealed lightly tanned skin, and his lean body hinted at strength and discipline. Strangely, his clothes didn't match his alert, military-like posture. His red plaid shirt, faded blue jeans, and scuffed cowboy boots suggested a laid-back country boy visiting New York.

From the way he held himself—confident, distant, intense—he seemed miles out of my league.

With each step, I could feel Charlotte's gaze boring into my back, waiting for me to chicken out.

The tug-of-war match ended in a pile of toppled boys. Some lay on the grass, watching as I approached Loner.

Knees suddenly weak, I trailed to a stop. What was I doing? No way would this boy let a gawky, pale-faced girl kiss him. He'd turn away with such open scorn that my watching audience would roar with laughter. Did I really need any more humiliation and rejection in my life?

But if I didn't kiss him, my challenge would revert to "truth." And Charlotte, with her built-in lie detector, would become suspicious if I tried to pretend I wasn't interested in her boyfriend, Jase.

I forced myself onward and stopped before Loner. His head moved a fraction in my direction, barely acknowledging me.

Good, I thought. Let him stand there as motionless as a statue, practically ignoring me. One quick kiss and I'd be done. Free of Charlotte's challenges for another year.

Another year ...

How blissfully unaware we all were that day. No one knew that eight billion people wouldn't have another year. Most had only days left to live.

Taking a deep breath, I stepped toward Loner. He smelled of pine trees and earth and rain, as though he'd been born in the depths of a forest.

Somehow, I forced myself to lean up and press my lips to his mouth. His body stiffened and the muscles beneath his plaid shirt tightened into iron. Flushing with embarrassment, I began to move away—but his arm suddenly encircled my waist and he pulled me against him. The warmth of his body blazed through my own as though we were both on fire.

My heart pounded.

His mouth crushed my lips as he kissed me with an intensity that both shocked and excited me. The world receded: the drone of traffic, the cries of playing children, even the sound of blaring music all faded into silence. Nothing existed except the burning sensuousness of his lips and the strength of his arm holding me against him.

Then, abruptly, he pulled away, releasing me. And even though the noisy world rushed back again, I felt as if I were plunging through the cold emptiness of space.

Face still shadowed, Loner tilted his head to the side as if inspecting a newly discovered insect.

"Interesting," he said and walked away.

I stared after him, my bruised mouth gaping in disbelief.

Interesting? We'd shared an incredible kiss that had left my body on fire and my heart racing—and all he could say was *interesting?*

Dazed, I returned to Charlotte, who was staring open-mouthed in shock.

Gathering my gear, I said, "Gotta get to my appointment. Thanks for my birthday lunch, cuz."

I headed for the bus stop, aware of Charlotte's gaze on my back once again. Only this time things were different. For once, I wasn't a loser. I was no longer the poor little sick cousin. I was a girl who had kissed a mysterious, good-looking boy—and had been passionately kissed by him in return.

As I crossed Central Park, I didn't just walk tall. For a few brief minutes, I soared.

I felt as if I could do anything. Be anything.

Live forever.

An hour later, I received my first death sentence.

2

"I'm sorry, Kassia. You have only three or four months left."

Dr. McKay delivered his grim prognosis from behind a gleaming oak desk. A wall of windows bathed his high-rise office in sunlight and, through the glass, I numbly watched birds wheeling in a glorious blue sky. In the city below, millions of people lived and worked and loved with the carefree attitude of those whose lives stretched reassuringly before them.

But I was no longer one of them.

The doctor's death sentence coiled around me like a snake, its grip cold, hard, terrifying.

I could barely breathe.

"Four months?" My father's protest emerged in a croak. "That's impossible." His gentle eyes were wide with shock behind his thick glasses. "She's been feeling good. She hasn't had a symptom for ages."

In a brisk, professional voice, Dr. McKay explained what was going on. Although my new meds had suppressed my symptoms and allowed me to feel better, the effects were only temporary. The latest tests had confirmed that my acute myeloid leukemia was getting worse. It was entering its most aggressive stage. Its last stage. I was in my final months.

Dad clutched at a straw. "What about another bone marrow transplant from Kass's twin, Olivia? It might work this time."

"That's very expensive."

"I don't care." My father struggled to support us on a cab driver's income, but I knew he would sell everything he owned, if necessary, to save my life.

"We've tried that procedure twice, Mr. Madison. Both times it's failed. It's high-risk and very painful. I'm reluctant to put your daughters through that again." Dr. McKay turned to me. "I'm sorry. There's nothing more we can do."

The rest of the afternoon passed in a daze of tears and disbelief. Promises. Anger. Despair. Fear.

After my birthday dinner in our small Bronx apartment—a meal neither of us ate—my father and I went up to our apartment building's flat roof. We were desperate to escape the music of a neighbor's twenty-first birthday party, a milestone we both knew I'd never reach.

There, beneath a starlit sky, Dad and I tried talking about my condition, but our conversation quickly faded into silence.

My heart twisted with pain at the thought of leaving my father all alone. Three years ago, Mom had taken my sister, Olivia, and had left Dad and me behind. Now I would be leaving him too. Forever.

I leaned on the concrete parapet that edged the rooftop and gazed down at the street four stories below. In the bliss that is ignorance, I was unaware this was the last view I'd ever have of our normal world ... the world before the apocalypse.

Kids played on the sidewalk. Two lovers embraced beneath a glowing streetlamp. A family sat on a stoop, chatting and laughing.

Everything was so sharp with beauty that my chest ached.

It seemed utterly cruel and unfair that I'd soon cease to exist. I would never graduate from Stowe High or experience the joys and wonders of boyfriends and love and getting married. I'd never have kids, write a novel, hike the Grand Canyon, grow old.

At sixteen, I had no future ...

... only a life about to end.

I didn't know this would soon become the dark fate of nearly every other person on the planet. Only a tiny percentage would survive the oncoming red mist.

On the night-draped rooftop, Dad struggled to hide his grief and fear. "Don't give up, honey. You must fight. Doctors can be wrong, you know."

I shook my head. "Dr. McKay is one of the top oncologists in the country. That's why we moved to New York, remember? So he could save my life."

Instead, the move had destroyed my parents' marriage. My mother, non-maternal at the best of times, had claimed that she didn't have time to care for a sick daughter plus write her screenplays. She'd barely lasted a year in New York before she'd fled back to Los Angeles, taking a protesting Olivia with her.

Since then, I'd only received the occasional call from Mom. Over time, my grief at her rejection had shrunk to a tiny stone that lodged itself in my heart. There it remained, just one more thing I'd learned to live with.

The loss of my twin, though, remained sharp and painful.

For most of our lives, Olivia—Via—and I had looked identical. That had changed when I'd fallen ill. She'd remained popular, fit, healthy, and beautiful, while I'd become the opposite.

Lately, we didn't even look like sisters. A few months ago, a tanned Olivia had straightened her hair, which now streamed in a shiny auburn fall to her waist, while I remained pale and thin, with shoulder-length wavy hair.

One thing stayed the same. Nothing could break our bond and the sisterly love we shared ... except death.

Voice cracking, I said to Dad, "Via called earlier to wish me a happy birthday. I couldn't tell her that I've only got a few months left. She's having a big party tonight, and I didn't want to ruin it for her."

"I spoke to your mother before dinner. She's going to break the news to Olivia tomorrow." Gently, Dad squeezed my shoulder. "Don't give up, honey. Your future isn't written in stone. Things can change at any moment, so be prepared. Be alive. Don't ..." He paused, unable to say the word *die*. Blinking back tears, he went on, "Don't go quietly into that deep night. Promise you'll always keep fighting."

I wanted to tell him that fighting was useless. Death had been stalking me for years, and Death always won in the end.

My father's tear-filled eyes stopped me. At the love and despair on his face, I sighed. "Okay, Dad. I promise to keep fighting."

He hugged me in relief.

A moment later, the night sky exploded.

3

I GASPED, FEARS OF terrorism and another 9/11 flaring in my mind.

"It's okay." Dad put a comforting arm around my shoulder. "It's just Thanksgiving fireworks."

"I don't think so." I pointed up.

Hundreds of red meteors were streaking downward from the infinity of space. High above the buildings, they exploded into sparks that threw a blood-red glow over the city.

People rushed onto the sidewalks. Traffic ground to a halt. Everyone stared at the sky in awe and confusion.

No one had any idea that this dazzling display was the start of an apocalypse.

The Night of the Red Mist had begun.

Within minutes, some of the red sparks had drifted onto our rooftop, where they glowed on the concrete like slumbering fireflies. Dad stomped on the sparks, snuffing out most of them. When he lifted his shoes, though, a few red dots remained attached to the concrete, still gleaming.

"Oww!" A sizzling spark stung my hand like a wasp, and I flicked it away. Blood oozed from a pinprick in my skin.

"Are you all right, honey?"

"I think so. What are these things, Dad?"

"I'm not sure."

An acrid smell wafted around us and the air felt thinner, as if we were on a mountaintop where breathing required more effort.

The glittering red dots were everywhere. They speckled the surrounding rooftops and clung to the sides of buildings. I could even see them flecking the street below. Bright. Beautiful. And strange.

Something slammed onto the concrete in front of me, and I gaped at a pile of bloodied feathers. Another thud sounded behind me. Then a third. A fourth. More.

Dead pigeons were dropping onto our rooftop and onto the street below.

"What's happening, Dad?"

"I don't know." He pulled me beneath a canvas umbrella beside an outdoor table.

Dozens of explosions continued to spray the air with bright red droplets, as though the sky were a body being riddled by bullets.

Dad frowned at the dead pigeons. "It looks like they were flying and got caught up in the explosions."

I shuddered at the small, battered bodies.

Those poor doomed birds were the first victims of the apocalypse.

4

The sky was still bleeding when I woke up the next morning.

Everyone was talking about the strange event. The internet, television, and newspapers were filled with reports about the red dots that had showered the planet.

No country was spared. And, later, we realized that no one was safe.

I sprawled in front of our TV, pretending to watch the news. In reality, I was trying to forget my death sentence from Dr. McKay yesterday.

I had no idea that last night's red "meteors" had condemned me to death—again.

When Dad entered the living room, I asked, "Is Elizabeth coming over today?"

Recently, my father had started dating. While I had little in common with the middle-aged teacher, Elizabeth was warm-hearted and kind, and I liked the way she'd made Dad smile again.

"She's spending the Thanksgiving break with her parents. She'll be back tomorrow."

"Good." I hoped things worked out between them. That way, Dad wouldn't be alone when I was ... gone.

An hour later, my mother called and awkwardly offered her sympathy at my leukemic death sentence. Two minutes later, she passed the phone over to my sobbing sister, and I found myself comforting Olivia instead of vice versa.

I made my father promise not to tell anyone else about my worsening medical condition. At least, not yet. I didn't want Charlotte, my classmates, or the teachers at school to look at me with even more pity in their eyes than they did now.

Throughout Day 1, a bloodied mist blanketed New York and the rest of the planet. It hovered in a foul-smelling haze that coated people's clothes and skin. Winds didn't disperse the thick vapor. The midday sun didn't burn it off. And sealed entryways, blocked vents, and filters couldn't totally prevent it from entering buildings and homes.

On Day 2, the strange red mist remained. Like parents everywhere, Dad continued to keep me indoors, afraid the stuff outside was even more dangerous than the diffused red mist inside our apartment. However, when scientists tentatively announced that the air was safe, most people slowly resumed their lives.

Not Dad.

As the mist lingered over the following days, he refused to let me leave the apartment, worried I'd get sicker. His concern was heightened by reports of brief bouts of weird behavior in some animals across the globe.

Finally, on Tuesday—Day 5—I'd had enough.

Using my most pitiful voice and my best puppy-dog eyes, I said, "Dad, if you keep me cooped up any longer, I'll go crazy. Is this how you want me to spend my last few months? Stuck inside this apartment? Bored out of my brain? No friends, no school, no life?"

My pathetic plea worked. When Charlotte knocked on our door a few minutes later in a well-planned arrival, he reluctantly allowed me to go outside.

As my cousin and I walked down the block, I gazed around in shock. The air inside our apartment had been a watery red mist, filtered by the towels that Dad had stuffed in vents and at the bottom of doors. Outside, though, it was much thicker. A sickly red haze veiled the roads and buildings. At 10 a.m., cars and trucks still had their headlights on, and the streetlamps glowed like small moons.

Everything looked weird and creepy.

A siren wailed and across town another siren answered it, their shrieks eerie and foreboding.

Charlotte and I wandered toward Harriet Beecher Stowe High, a couple of blocks from my home. In this strangely unfamiliar landscape, we both needed the comfort and reassurance of a familiar place, even if it was our school.

Thousands of dots speckled the roads, sidewalks, and buildings. Five nights ago they'd been tiny. Now they were as large as confetti. Most were green. Others were red or yellow or blue. A few were black or white.

At the school—still closed because of the red mist—I peered at a cluster of spots on the sidewalk. "What are all these dots?"

Charlotte crinkled her freckled nose. "No one knows for sure."

"They're bigger than before. They're growing."

"Yeah. Some science guys on the internet think they might be mold. Or a fungus." Charlotte's hazel eyes glittered, excited at this break in our regular lives. "Maybe they're a fungus that'll get into people's brains and turn them into zombies. Imagine that! This might be the start of a zombie apocalypse."

"Yeah, sure."

Further down the misty sidewalk, a boy in a red plaid shirt, blue jeans, and cowboy boots stood in front of the deserted school. Arms folded, he studied the building.

It was Loner. For once, he wasn't wearing sunglasses or a baseball cap, but I still couldn't see his face clearly because his features were blurred by the mist.

I blushed, recalling our passionate Thanksgiving Day kiss ... the heat that had flooded me ... the feel of his soft lips ... his firm body ...

Charlotte blinked in surprise. "What's Loner doing here? Does he even go to our school?"

"I don't think so."

Someone cried out.

A few yards away, a girl from our English class had dropped her grocery bag and was gaping at her blood-splattered hands. Rivers of red poured from her nose and streamed down her yellow top.

She stumbled forward. "Help me." Then, with a whimper, she collapsed like a marionette whose strings had been cut.

We raced to her side.

"What happened, Amanda?" I sat on the pavement and cradled her head in my lap, wincing as her warm, sticky blood seeped through my jeans.

Charlotte pressed a wad of tissues to the girl's nose, trying to stop the bleeding.

At school, Amanda had been one of the few classmates who'd been kind to me. She suffered from epileptic fits, and I suspected that she saw me as a kindred damaged soul. We'd never been actual friends, but still, she was friendly, and that meant a lot to someone as lonely as me.

"Charlotte, call 911," I cried.

"Can't. I forgot to charge my phone. Where's yours?"

"I'm sitting on it." I cradled Amanda's head, watching her blood flow onto the sidewalk. "If I move, I might make her worse."

Frantic, I looked around and saw Loner watching us.

"Hey," I yelled. "Call an ambulance. Hurry."

He made no attempt to pull out a phone. Maybe he didn't own one, but I doubted it. Every teenager I knew had a cell phone practically glued to their hands.

Again, I yelled, "Call an ambulance. Help us."

He jotted something in a notebook. Then he turned and walked away.

Stunned, I watched him disappear into the red mist. How could he just leave? What was wrong with the guy?

"Jerk!" I shouted after him.

I managed to pull my phone from my back pocket, and Charlotte babbled details of our location to the emergency operator.

As we waited for the ambulance, we tried to comfort Amanda, who lay limp in my arms. Her blood had spread across the sidewalk, and her face had turned white. By the time help arrived, she was unconscious, and when they loaded her onto a gurney, I had the strangest feeling that we'd never see her again.

The ambulance had just been swallowed by the mist when my phone rang. I groaned when I saw Dad's name. I'd been outside for less than an hour, and even my father wasn't paranoid enough to order me home after such a short time.

He had to be calling because something was wrong.

5

THE NEXT MORNING AT the airport, I fought back tears as I hugged my father goodbye.

"Try not to cry, Kass." Dad nudged his wire-rimmed glasses up his nose. "Your mother will be fine. She's in the best hospital in Los Angeles, and she has great doctors."

My tears weren't for my mother.

Although my love for Mom had faded after years of being ignored, I didn't want her to die. Clearly, she was a better mother to my twin, Olivia, than she was to me. And maybe my father still felt some remnants of love for her. For everyone's sake, I hoped she'd be okay.

Today, my tears were for my father.

I was worried about him.

I understood why he was leaving me with his girlfriend, Elizabeth. He had to fly to LA to be with my mother during her sudden illness and to take care of Olivia.

Still, I was scared for him.

Earlier, as we'd passed through the crowds at the airport, I had noticed lots of people holding bloodied handkerchiefs to their noses. At the odd sight, an unease spread through me: Dad had suffered a nosebleed while shaving this morning.

When I'd tried talking to him about it a few minutes ago, he'd brushed off my concern. "People have bleeding noses all the time. I'm more worried about your mother."

The doctor in LA had told him that Mom had fallen into a strange, coma-like sleep. They couldn't awaken her, and her vitals were fading each day.

She was dying.

In the airport terminal, I gave my father's girlfriend an apologetic glance as I said, "Dad, don't make me stay here in New York with Elizabeth. Let me come with you. I want to see Via." I missed my sister, Olivia, so much that it was like a physical ache. "And I want to see Mom."

To my surprise, I realized I meant that last bit too. After all, she was still my mother. Maybe, like my father, some remnant of my previous love for her remained in a corner of my heart.

"You can't come, honey," Dad said. "Every flight to LA is full for the next two weeks. I only got a seat today thanks to a buddy who works for the airline."

Since the arrival of the thick red mist, planes had been grounded everywhere. Some people had claimed it was like 9/11 all over again, only this time it was worldwide.

Today, the mist was finally thinner. With the reopening of New York's airports, thousands of delayed passengers had rushed to fill all departing flights.

Dad gave me a hug. "I'll call you when I land." He turned to Elizabeth and said, "Please take care of my daughter. And yourself."

The woman's kind face creased with a reassuring smile. "Don't worry, Joe. We'll be fine." She rested a soft hand on my shoulder.

As blood trickled from my father's nostrils, I cried, "Dad, you're bleeding again."

"It's nothing." Handkerchief pressed to his nose, he hurried toward the security checkpoint, turned a corner, and disappeared.

Anxiety clawed at me. The same sensation I'd had yesterday with Amanda returned, only stronger this time: I had a feeling that I'd never see my father again.

I shook off my fears. Thousands of people had nosebleeds every day. No one died from them, did they? Dad wasn't worried, so why should I be?

Comforted by my own assurances, I relaxed a little. One of my father's birthday gifts hung from my neck—a large crystal starburst on a gold chain—and I fingered the necklace, as though holding it would keep my father safe.

Beside me, Elizabeth asked, "Isn't that the actress you and Olivia like so much, Kass? Willow something?"

A familiar couple stood nearby. The seventeen-year-old girl was Willow Grace. Breathtakingly beautiful, she had long blond hair, porcelain skin, and stunning violet eyes. Her acting had already earned her two major awards and countless fans; her strong activism on behalf of animals and the disabled had won her even more admirers.

The boy embracing her was Asher Weston, also seventeen. Son of an Australian billionaire, he was every bit as stunning as Willow in his own masculine way. Athletic build. Blond hair. Handsome features. And an incredible, melt-your-heart smile.

His hands cupped Willow's face as they gazed at each other, clearly in love. I'd read they'd been dating for a year, with a devotion and exclusivity rarely seen in privileged celebrities these days.

My heart twisted.

In the few months I had left to live, the leukemia would burn away my flesh, leaving my body gaunt and my eyes sunken. With Death casting its shadow over me, no boy would ever look at me with the love on Asher Weston's face. No boy would ever touch my cheeks the way he was gently touching Willow Grace's cheeks.

"She's so beautiful," Elizabeth said, awed. "What's she doing here?"

"I heard she's making a new movie in Hollywood."

"You mean she might be on the same plane as Joe? How exciting."

"Yeah." I doubted they'd run across each other, though. Willow would probably be in first class while Dad always flew coach.

Asher bent and tenderly kissed Willow goodbye.

My fingers tightened on my crystal starburst necklace, and my eyes welled with tears of regret and longing.

Last week, I'd been kissed by Loner—a thrilling, passionate kiss that had set my body on fire.

But Asher's kiss for Willow was soft, gentle, and filled with love.

I would never experience such a kiss, the kind that goes beyond mere physical sensation or lust.

Asher's kiss was the kind that makes a soul soar.

Heavy-hearted, I followed Elizabeth from the terminal.

6

"For real? You saw Asher Weston at the airport this morning?" Charlotte's hazel eyes glowed with excitement.

In an attempt to cheer me up, Elizabeth had dropped me at my cousin's place for the afternoon, promising to pick me up at 5 p.m.

The red mist no longer blanketed the city, yet the sky remained an ominous scarlet that floated overhead like a giant bloodstain.

As Charlotte and I walked the few blocks to our local shopping mall, I'd told her about seeing Willow Grace, but Charlotte was far more interested in details about the actress's boyfriend, Asher Weston. She had followed his life online for years and was thrilled to hear that I'd seen her idol in the flesh.

"Tell me again what happened, Kass."

Patiently, for the third time, I repeated every detail of the incident. Yes, Asher Weston was even more handsome in real life. Yes, he was deeply in love with his girlfriend. Yes, his lips were perfectly formed.

His tenderness. That kiss. The love it conveyed.

And yes, his clothes were as perfect as the rest of him. Crisp white shirt, tailored pants, expensive shoes, and flashy watch.

I was glad to feed her addiction. Talking about celebrities was easier than answering her earlier question, which I'd fobbed off: *What did Dr. McKay say last week, Kass?*

How could I tell Charlotte that I was going to die in a few months? In a crazy, flippant part of my brain, I wished Hallmark had a card for such a bleak announcement. That'd be easier than telling her in person or—

A siren shredded the air.

At an intersection down the block, an ambulance streaked past. A moment later, two more ambulances screamed by, as though chasing the first one.

I shivered, unnerved by the urgent shrieks. In the past half hour, I'd heard at least twenty sirens.

Weird. And worrying.

On our way to the mall, we stopped in front of Stowe High. No sign of Loner. Pity. If he'd been nearby, I would've told him off for not helping our classmate, Amanda, when she'd collapsed yesterday.

Charlotte looked at the dried blood on the sidewalk. "Have you heard how Amanda's doing?"

"I've called around, but no one knows anything. Her parents aren't answering her phone."

"Maybe they're at the hospital with her."

Which would mean she was still alive.

I remained silent, reluctant to say what we were both thinking. Maybe they weren't answering their phones because Amanda had died, and they were too grief-stricken to talk to anyone.

No. They were at the hospital. They had to be.

People—*Dad!*—didn't die from nosebleeds. Did they?

Pushing my dark thoughts aside, I bent down to the clump of bright dots near the school gates. Overnight, the confetti-sized things had grown into small objects, each half an inch tall.

I frowned at Charlotte. "They're plants?" The tiny stems supported even tinier leaves.

"Yep. They're all over the place."

Standing, I surveyed my surroundings. Tiny plants dotted the roads, clung to the sides of buildings, and nestled in dark corners. Most were green. A few were red or orange or yellow.

As we continued walking to the mall, I noticed that the strange plants were everywhere: Sprouting from the tops of bus shelters. Sticking to lampposts and street signs. They were even growing on the roofs of parked cars.

"What's going on?" I asked. "How can these plants grow so fast? And how do they grow on metal and concrete?"

"I don't know." Charlotte's phone rang and she checked her screen. "It's Jase."

I tried not to feel envious as she spoke to her boyfriend. The only male who ever called me was my father. I sighed, wishing a gorgeous boy—*Jase Harris*—would call me. *Huh! No chance.*

After a brief conversation, Charlotte hung up. "You'll never guess what Jase just told me."

That he's going to ask me out? Yeah, sure.

"What?" I asked in a deliberately casual tone.

"Apparently, it's just hit the internet and TV."

"What has?"

"Scientists have figured out where all these plants came from."

"Where?"

"Well, they're not local yokels." She paused for dramatic effect.

"So what are they?"

"Non-terrestrial plants."

"*What?*"

"Remember those exploding red 'meteors' on Thanksgiving night?" Charlotte asked. "And the thousands of red sparks in the sky? Scientists think the sparks were actually seeds from another planet. Tough seeds too. My mom and I tried squashing some seed-sparks that landed outside our building, but most of them survived."

I looked at the tiny plants scattered everywhere. "They've sprouted in concrete and bricks and roads. Even without soil, they've grown. How's that possible?"

"Because they're non-terrestrial plants. They're from another planet where they do things differently than Earth plants. Anyway, they can grow in soil too. On the internet, people say the ones in the countryside are already bigger than the ones in the city."

"How did they get here? What do they want?"

"They're not intelligent, silly. They can't talk to us or make demands or anything. They're just plants. Jase said that scientists think they travel through space in gigantic clusters, randomly seeding planets in their path."

"How big will they get?" I asked.

"No one knows."

"Are they dangerous?"

Charlotte regarded a patch of small plants on the path. "Not yet. But let's make sure." She stomped on the patch, grinding them beneath her boots. When she stepped away, some yellow and white plants lay crushed—but the green, red, gold, and blue ones remained unbroken. I wondered if the different colors were different varieties. Were some tougher than the others?

I surveyed the unbroken ones. "Not good. Some of those dots are strong."

"They're not called dots anymore," Charlotte informed me. "Jase says they're called *terras* now, short for *non-terrestrial plants*." She turned into a shadow-clogged alley. "Let's cut through here to the mall."

"Okay."

The alley stank of rotting garbage and urine and other disgusting odors. It held four dumpsters and a pair of tents that housed two old alcoholics. Jeff and Tim were Army veterans who survived on handouts from local restaurants and stores.

Last winter had been extra cold, so Dad and I had brought them some thick blankets, which they had eagerly accepted.

Now, as we walked down the alley, I expected to hear Jeff snoring like a buzz saw or Tim playing his harmonica. While one was off foraging for food, the other would stay with their tents, protecting their possessions.

Today, there was no snoring or music.

Instead, a hush filled the alley. The only sounds were the echoes of Charlotte's and my footsteps—plus the increased thudding of my heart.

7

Charlotte and I stared at a bucket-sized pile of gray dust outside Jeff's tent. It was odorless and fine-grained, like flour.

The dust itself wasn't the problem. What creeped me out was the artificial limb poking from the gray matter. Nearby were a pair of battered sneakers, a cheap watch, and a vinyl belt.

Charlotte gasped, "Why would Jeff leave his artificial leg out here? Someone could steal it. And how's he walking around without it?"

"Maybe he's got a new one."

She peered inside Tim's tent. "There's another pile of dust in here. It's got shoes and stuff in it too."

I picked up a stick and poked through the mound outside Jeff's tent. A row of false teeth grinned from the dust like a severed smile. *What?* The man wouldn't leave his false teeth behind.

My heart pounded at a sudden realization. "I ... I think Jeff's still here."

"Where?"

"*Here.*"

Confused, Charlotte asked, "He's in the dust?"

"I think he *is* the dust."

The police thought I was crazy.

That evening, I called them from Elizabeth's apartment in Brooklyn.

"Are you saying, Miss Madison, that a person has been burned and reduced to a pile of ash?" The officer on the other end of the line sounded interested. "You're reporting a murder?"

"No, I don't think so. It wasn't a pile of ash. It was dust."

"Dust?" His interest turned to annoyance. "You're reporting a pile of dust?"

"*Two* piles of dust. Like I told you earlier, there were things in them like dentures, shoes, watches, and a fake limb. No clothes, though. I think the clothes turned to dust too."

"Thank you, Miss Madison. I have all the information I need, along with your contact details. We'll look into it."

I knew he wouldn't.

And maybe the officer was right. Maybe the whole idea was ridiculous. Once I'd settled into Elizabeth's apartment with its TV, furniture, and central heating, the conviction I'd felt in that shadowy alley began to waver. I'd read about people being reduced to ashes by spontaneous combustion, but that hadn't happened with the two homeless veterans. It seemed like their bodies and clothes had been turned into dust. Bucket-sized mounds of gray floury matter. How could that happen? Surely it was impossible.

When my father called a few hours later, I forgot about the dust.

Elizabeth put him on speaker.

"How's Mom?" I asked him.

"She's getting worse, honey." He hesitated, then said, "I'll be home in a few days. I'm bringing Olivia back with me."

Elizabeth frowned. "If Gemma's getting worse, Joe, why are you and Olivia coming home? Don't you want to stay with your ex while she's in the hospital?"

"We're not allowed to visit." Dad's voice tightened. "She's in quarantine, along with scores of other patients with the same condition. They've all fallen into comas and their blood pressure keeps dropping. Dozens have already died."

I struggled with my shock. "Dad ..."

"It's too dangerous to stay in LA, honey. All afternoon, there have been reports of people across the city falling into comas. Doctors think it's some new disease, very contagious, with a high mortality rate. I'm getting Olivia away from this place tonight."

"Good," Elizabeth said. "Get the first flight out of there."

"I can't. Every seat on every airline is booked for the next week."

"What about a train or bus, Joe?"

"Nothing available there, either. I need to try and rent a car."

"What?" I cried. "You want to drive back to New York, Dad? That's three thousand miles. It'll take you days."

"It doesn't matter. At least Olivia and I will get home to you and Elizabeth. Plus we'll be far away from whatever's going on in LA."

"Is Via there? Can I talk to her?" Our sisterly chats on the phone, plus brief get-togethers during summer breaks, weren't enough. Our separation remained like a pain in my heart.

"She's cried herself to sleep back at her home." Home for Olivia was a multimillion-dollar, architecturally designed mansion in Beverly Hills. In the past two years, Mom's movie scripts had graduated from B-grade to A-grade. Obviously, not splitting her time between her career, a cab driver husband, and a sick daughter had benefited her work. "Best leave her be, Kass. She's pretty upset."

I felt guilty at not being more upset. Then again, I barely knew my mother anymore. My heart ached for Olivia, though, and I wished there was some way I could ease her grief. But there was nothing I could do right now. However, when she got back to New York, I could hold her as she cried, listen to her talk about Mom, and try to support her through this terrible time.

"Where are you, Dad?"

"Standing in a long line at a car rental agency. People everywhere are trying to get out of LA. We'll call you tomorrow when we're on our way home. Meanwhile, stay with Elizabeth and give her a hand with the chores, okay? She sounds tired."

He was right. Elizabeth had been dragging herself around the apartment all evening. When she'd struggled to put together a stir fry for dinner, I had taken over preparing the meal. And when she'd gone into slow motion while folding a basket of laundry, I'd steered her to the couch, placed a magazine in her hands, and folded the sheets and towels myself.

She had rallied a little when Dad called. Still, I suspected she was coming down with a cold or something.

On the phone, Dad said, "I need to go. My battery's almost dead."

A niggle of worry made me ask him, "How's your nose? Did the bleeding stop?"

"Mostly. Don't fret about it, honey. I'm okay." He addressed his next words to Elizabeth. "Please take care of my daughter."

"I will, Joe."

After a couple of mushy comments, they ended their call.

That night, my dreams were full of dead people dropping from the night sky like battered pigeons.

8

WHEN I AWOKE THE next morning, the apartment was silent.

Dad and I had stayed at Elizabeth's place before. Each time, I'd awoken to the smell of coffee, the rattle of pots and pans, and the sound of off-key singing.

Today, the kitchen was quiet.

Perhaps Elizabeth was still tired.

Keeping the volume low, I watched a news channel as I started eating a bowl of cereal—but I quickly lost my appetite.

Overnight, the world had changed.

Across the planet, thousands of people had fallen into comas. In New York, hospitals were overcrowded, with wards overflowing and gurneys clogging corridors.

Piles of gray dust were appearing in homes, offices, subways, everywhere and anywhere. Some reports on social media claimed that people fell asleep and, hours later, turned into piles of dust. Others reported actually seeing people dissolve into dust, along with their clothes. Strangely, certain items didn't dissolve: watches, buckles, shoes, belts, and other things—like false limbs and dentures.

Oh no. Poor Jeff and Tim. Had they become tired, lain down, and drifted into an eternal sleep?

Tired!

I bolted to the main bedroom.

"Elizabeth!" I banged on her door. "Are you awake?"

No answer. No sound of a shower from her bathroom.

Outside, a siren wailed, its drawn-out notes hovering like a cry of mourning.

Gingerly, I entered Elizabeth's room. No sign of her. Just a lump under the bedclothes.

Pulse racing, I drew back the blankets.

A pile of dust lay on the sheet, with a ruby ring in it. I'd seen that ring on Elizabeth's finger before. It was a family heirloom passed down by her mother. She never took it off.

And she hadn't now.

It was still with her.

I ran into her bathroom and threw up.

I called the police. Then my father. When he didn't answer, I phoned Charlotte and told her what had happened.

"I'm coming over, Kass."

My cousin arrived at the apartment a few minutes after the police left.

Charlotte gazed at the gray pile on Elizabeth's bed. "Why didn't they take … her … away?"

"They just took a sample, asked me questions, and left. The officer said they're getting hundreds of calls every hour from all over the city. They're stretched thin."

She nodded grimly. "I've seen the news. I tried to make Mom stay home from work today, but they need her at the hospital." Charlotte's father—Dad's half-brother—had died a few years ago, and Aunt Suzanne struggled by on a nurse's salary. "Mom made me promise to stay indoors today."

"So what are you doing here?"

"Helping my cousin." She glanced around the apartment with a faint smile. "Besides, I'm indoors, aren't I?"

"I guess."

I blinked back tears of gratitude. Sometimes, Charlotte could be too wrapped up in boys and clothes and makeup, but when I needed her, she was usually there.

"Get your stuff together," she said. "You're coming home with me."

I heaved a relieved sigh, glad to be away from Elizabeth's dead ... dust.

After packing a duffel bag, Charlotte and I headed to the station. I called my father again, and this time he answered.

"I couldn't rent a car anywhere," he told me.

"Does Mom have one you could borrow?"

"No. She took cabs. So I had to buy a used one."

"Oh." Money had always been tight in our family. If Dad had bought a car just to get out of LA, he was really worried.

I was worried too. Last night, Elizabeth had been healthy. Hours later, she was a pile of dust. Bracing myself, I told Dad about his girlfriend.

"*No!*" He fell silent, struggling with the news. After a few questions, he somberly asked, "Are you staying with Charlotte and your Aunt Suzanne tonight?"

"Yes. Charlotte's with me now."

"Good. How are you girls getting back to the Bronx?"

"Train."

"No way. Use the emergency credit card I gave you. Take a cab to Aunt Suzanne's place."

"That'll cost a fortune."

"I don't care. You're already sick, honey. I don't want you and Charlotte crammed on a train with people who might have some new infectious disease. Catch a cab, okay?"

"Okay." Relief shot through me. A comfortable cab ride to the Bronx would be much better than a crowded, smelly train.

A short time later, I wished we'd taken the crowded, smelly train.

9

HALFWAY ACROSS THE BROOKLYN Bridge, our cab veered into the neighboring lane.

Jolted from our chat in the back seat, Charlotte and I yelled to the Indian driver:

"Watch out."

"That van—"

Our cabbie jerked in his seat, wrenched the steering wheel, and swerved back into his lane. A van missed us by inches, horn blaring as it whizzed past.

"Sorry, missies," our driver said, adjusting his turban with one wrinkled hand. "I know not what happened."

I peered at the ID card on display—Amar Singh—and then checked the Sikh's reflection in the rearview mirror. His eyes were half-closed, as though struggling to stay awake, and his face was saggy and tired.

Oh no! Elizabeth was tired last night. And then she died.

I rapped the transparent partition between us. "Can you pull over and let us out, please? I'll pay what we owe you."

Singh's hooded eyes abruptly widened. "Are you crazy, missy? I cannot stop here. Please, you wait until we get to Manhattan."

Around us, traffic roared by. The cabbie was right. There was no place to pull over. He changed lanes until he was in the furthest one near the side of the bridge.

"Is he drunk?" Charlotte whispered to me.

"Worse. He's tired."

Our gazes locked in cold fear.

In the front seat, Singh suddenly slumped over the steering wheel. The side of our cab slammed against a metal rail and scraped along it with a loud screech.

Charlotte and I screamed. Covered our faces with our arms. Hunched in our seats.

The cab veered to the other side. Whammed into an SUV. Swerved back. Hit the rail again. With another squeal of tortured metal, it started slowing down.

A car smashed into the back of our cab, jarring every bone in my body. I flew forward, headed straight for the driver's partition. At the last second, my seatbelt yanked me back, and a band of pain blazed across my chest, but at least I was in one piece.

The cab slowed as it scraped along the guardrail. The second it stopped, my cousin and I scrambled out and huddled together.

"Are you okay?" I gasped.

"Y-Yeah." She shoved a fall of red hair from her face. "You?"

"Yes."

The cabbie, Singh, hadn't been wearing a seatbelt. He was slumped behind the wheel, his face a bloodied mess; his neck was bent at an unnatural angle, and his eyes held a fixed gaze.

He was dead.

Traffic whizzed past, uncaring.

The car that had rear-ended us had stopped further back. Its driver, an overweight businessman, climbed out and glared at the steam escaping from beneath his crumpled hood. Swearing, he punched a number into his phone and barked orders at someone on the other end.

I hit 911 on my phone. A recorded message told me that all lines were busy and to try again later.

"Try again later?" Charlotte squeaked at me. "How much later?"

"I don't know. Five minutes?" I bit my lip, anxious. Emergency services throughout New York were probably drowning in calls for help. Charlotte and I could be stuck here for hours, breathing in stinking exhaust fumes, being buffeted by wind from the passing cars, and almost deafened by the din of the traffic.

"What happened to our cabbie?"

"Maybe he had a heart attack or stroke ..." My voice trailed away. Had Singh died from the Red Fever? That's what the police officer had called it back at Elizabeth's apartment earlier this morning.

The Red Fever.

According to the news, many doctors linked this lethal new illness to "the Night of the Red Mist." This was the media's nickname for the red explosions that had lit the sky on Thanksgiving night.

The president's science advisor, Professor Blake Doylen, had offered a theory. He believed humans were fatally allergic to something produced by the non-terrestrial seeds and plants. Doctors across the planet agreed with him.

Had our cab driver died from this Red Fever? Was he going to turn into a pile of dust like my father's girlfriend?

Singh's body lay slumped in the front seat, blood dripping down his face, and I half-expected him to disintegrate in front of me.

When Elizabeth had died during the night, how long had it taken her to turn to dust? Had it happened quickly? Or over a few hours?

It was barely 10 a.m., yet the morning was already filled with death.

Desperate for a brief distraction, I looked past the concrete-and-metal bridge to the view beyond. It was beautiful.

Although the sky was stained red, its fluffy clouds were comfortingly familiar, and the warm sunshine was welcome after the chill of the cabbie's death. Mixed with the stench of exhaust fumes was another smell. Vanilla. As I inhaled the pleasant scent, some of my tension ebbed away.

Beyond the horror of the cab crash and its dead driver, people were going about their lives. Small vessels worked their way up the East River, carving white-frothed wakes in the smooth waters. At the northern end of the Brooklyn Bridge, the skyscrapers and buildings of Manhattan rose proudly into the red sky, their windows gleaming in the sunshine.

Above, a large bird cruised the warm thermals, and as it soared through the air, I envied its joyous, carefree flight.

Breathing deeply, I reveled in the vanilla-scented air. "I'm going to miss this city when I'm gone."

"Why?" Charlotte glanced at me. "Where are you going?"

I suddenly realized that I hadn't told her about my death sentence from Dr. McKay. "Er, to visit my grandmother in Kansas." I hated lying, but now wasn't the time to hit her with the truth.

"Really?" She tossed her long red hair in disdain. "Kansas sounds *bor-ing.*"

Maybe. Still, it was better than dying. The leukemia burning through my body was going to rob me of everything: my family, my home, my future ... my life.

I thought of my mother and Elizabeth and the cab driver—and shame flooded me. I had to stop worrying about my own death, which was still months away. Right now, people all over the world were dying from this Red Fever. These people weren't being given a few months to say goodbye to their loved ones and their lives, like me. They were dying within hours or overnight.

Then again, maybe I didn't have a few months at all. This Red Fever could infect me at any moment, and I could be dead within hours too.

Sheesh. This day just kept getting better and—

"Ouch!" I jumped back, gaping at my hand, which I'd absently run across the metal guardrail. Bright blood seeped from my freshly scraped palm.

"Yuck." Charlotte crinkled her freckled nose. "Did you hurt yourself in the crash?"

"No. I just touched the guardrail."

Had its surface been rough enough to sandpaper my skin?

I peered at the railing.

What the—?

10

A THIN LAYER OF gray fur covered the metal railing, the coating as fine as velvet.

I leaned closer. The "fur" was actually a layer of tiny gray plants. Each was only a fraction of an inch long, clustered so tightly together that they looked like gray fur.

This vegetation covered most of the bridge, growing on the structure's pylons and beams. Even the deck was mottled with gray patches; despite being run over by countless cars, they appeared undamaged. The plants must be incredibly strong, I thought. Were they also dangerous? Was this stuff eating the metal like rust?

I bent toward the grayish mat and sniffed. Vanilla. This was the sweet scent I'd been smelling. Gingerly, I poked the mat—and yelped. The plants had scraped off the top layer of my skin, leaving my fingertip as raw as my palm.

"Are you okay, cuz?"

"Don't touch the railings." I wrapped a handkerchief around my bleeding hand. "They're covered with some really sharp plants. I think they're non-terrestrial plants."

"Terras?" she asked, using the shortened version of their name.

"Yeah." In the week since the Night of the Red Mist, the non-terrestrial plants—*terras*—had spread with alarming speed. Plus there were reports that some had vicious defense systems that, when they grew bigger, could become lethal.

Lethal plants. Great. Just great.

A large bird with a red beak swooped down and landed on a railing a few feet away, seemingly unharmed by the mat of gray terras. Although its wings and body had black feathers, its head and long neck were as bare as a plucked chicken. It looked around, its eyes an unnaturally bright silver color.

What an ugly vulture. What's it doing in New York?

Wings folded against its body, it stared at the sky. I followed its gaze and saw a midsize jet flying low.

Strange.

"Why's a plane flying over the river?" Charlotte asked, watching the same jet.

"I don't know."

"I didn't think they were allowed around here."

"They're not." Only small tourist planes could use this air space, not commercial jetliners.

The plane kept coming, engines roaring.

I drew an invisible line between the aircraft's approach and the bridge. Pure terror clutched my heart. "*Run!*" I pushed Charlotte toward the Manhattan end of the bridge. The plane was closer. Bigger. "It's going to hit!"

I waved my arms at the passing cars. Gestured frantically toward the plane. Screamed warnings.

My words were drowned by the roar of the oncoming jet. On the bridge, vehicles screeched to a halt. People gripped their steering wheels, too shocked to move. Others fled, weaving between the cars.

Charlotte remained frozen to the spot, gawking at the plane.

I shoved her again. "*Run!*"

Finally she ran.

I followed.

We raced along the narrow gap between the guardrail and the cars. Glancing back, I saw the plane barreling onward. One wing was tilted up, as though beseeching the sky for help; the other was tilted down, as if grasping for something below to delay its fate.

Its thunderous roar chilled my blood.

Hell was about to be unleashed.

11

THE PLANE SLAMMED INTO the Brooklyn end of the bridge.

A massive fireball erupted, gushing flames and black smoke. Pieces of metal shot in all directions, and a huge wheel crashed down, flattening cars like plastic toys. The aircraft's wings severed some thick steel cables that had supported the bridge. As the snapped wires fell like guillotine blades, they sliced through cars and vans.

Charlotte and I reeled back, even though we were a safe distance from the crash site. I gaped at the fiery scene. Had a terrorist flown the plane into the Brooklyn Bridge? Was this the start of a new 9/11?

At the crash site, the fire roared with the fury of a blaze from hell.

People screamed.

Sirens shrieked.

More supporting cables snapped with loud twangs, and metal groaned and growled.

"What's happening?" Charlotte cried.

"I'm not sure." I climbed onto the roof of an abandoned postal van for a better view.

The road around the burning jet was twisting and breaking apart ... and with a series of tortured bellows, the far section of the bridge collapsed into the waters below, along with the burning plane and dozens of cars. This world-famous bridge was now in two pieces, separated by a gap over a hundred feet wide.

Emergency services personnel ran past us, shouting orders.

"Leave the bridge. Hurry!"

"Get to safety!"

"Move! Now."

These first responders wore fire-retardant uniforms and carried the latest rescue equipment, but I knew they couldn't save the people at the bottom of the East River.

Heartsick, Charlotte and I ran toward the Manhattan end of the bridge. With every step, I fought back a nausea that swelled within me.

No, I can't be ill. Not here. Not now.

The moment we reached solid land, I rushed to the curb. "I'm going to be sick."

"It's okay," Charlotte murmured, holding my hair back as I threw up. When I began to shake uncontrollably, she held me until my body stopped trembling.

We thought the worst was behind us.

It wasn't.

I fought back my growing panic.

Rescue vehicles roared past Charlotte and me, sirens shrilling. The *whomp-whomp-whomp-whomp* of helicopters added to the din. Police cars screeched to a halt. Officers yelled at people to leave the area immediately.

Charlotte and I hesitated.

Where could we go?

An officer shouted at us, "Move it, girls! Now." His face held the same grimness that shadowed the other first responders.

Fear filled the air, and the bloodstained sky seemed like a shroud for the chaos and death below.

Charlotte and I hurried into Manhattan, where we hailed several cabs. None stopped. On our phones, all the rideshare apps were frozen. At the subway entrance, a large sign hung on the closed gate: "Due to technical difficulties, all Manhattan trains have ceased operations until further notice." Buses had also been canceled.

"What's going on?" Charlotte asked. "Why would a plane crash mess up the trains and buses in the city?"

"It wouldn't." Worry began spreading within me. "Something else must be happening."

Her voice dropped to a whisper. "Terrorism?"

"Maybe."

Around us, people were staring at their phones. Two fire engines raced north, streaking to other emergencies in Manhattan. My shoulders hunched in dread, half-expecting to see another plane drop from the sky or feel another car crash into us. I felt confused. Helpless. Vulnerable.

Charlotte pulled out her phone. "We can't walk all the way to the Bronx. I'm calling Jase."

"What about asking your mom to pick us up?"

"She's working a double shift at the hospital. Besides, I can't tell her that I went to see you in Brooklyn and nearly got killed when a plane crashed into the Brooklyn Bridge. She'd ground me until I was thirty."

For over an hour, we waited for Jase in a small park. Across Manhattan, the cries of sirens became an endless wail as ambulances rushed the injured and dying to hospitals. Rescue vehicles raced from disaster to disaster, shrieking urgently.

We could've used our phones to check the news online. Or we could've stopped some passersby and asked them what was going on.

Instead, Charlotte and I sat on a park bench, doing nothing. Neither of us could deal with any more bad news right now. We both knew that when Jase arrived, he'd fill us in on the terrible events happening across New York—and we guessed his news would destroy our peace forever.

So we deliberately chose the temporary bliss of ignorance.

In silence, we waited in the park. We watched squirrels squabble in the trees. Watched children play ball on the grass. Watched flowers sway in a breeze.

Watched the last shining moments of our world as we knew it.

12

A WHITE CHEVY SCREECHED to a halt alongside the park, and Jase slammed his hand on the horn.

Above the buildings, plumes of smoke gushed into the red Manhattan sky.

Quickly, Charlotte and I piled into the Chevy.

I studied Jase from my rear seat. In profile, his handsome face looked strained, and his square jaw was tight with tension as he accelerated into the traffic.

"What's happening?" I asked Jase. "Is it terrorism?"

"Worse." He wove from lane to lane, detouring around gridlocked streets. "It's all over the internet. The planes have been grounded."

"Why?" Charlotte cried.

He explained that over the past day, countless pilots around the world had fallen asleep in midflight, causing hundreds of aircraft to crash. Other accidents had soared in numbers too. Drivers of trains, buses, and cars had fallen asleep as well, leading to the suspension of all public transportation.

The death toll was in the tens of thousands and climbing.

Private vehicles were only allowed on the roads if they had a passenger who could take over if the driver fell ill.

We drove past a bus that had crashed into some parked cars, rolled across them, and ended up lodged like a cork in a second-floor window. Police officers stood on the crumpled cars, helping passengers climb from the rear of the sloping bus. Five bloodied bodies lay on the sidewalk.

Had this been an accident? Or had the driver fallen asleep behind the wheel?

Our cab driver, Singh, had seemed okay when he'd picked us up in Brooklyn. Yet minutes later, he'd slumped unconscious behind his steering wheel.

I cleared my throat. "Um, how are you feeling, Jase? Are you tired?"

"I'm okay."

So far.

"Besides," he continued, "I have the required backup driver." He patted Charlotte's knee, but his deep voice held a thread of worry. My cousin had only taken three lessons since getting her learner's permit a month ago.

She shook her head at him. "Steering's about all I can do. I can't reach the brake pedal from my seat, so you'd better stay awake."

"Jase," I said, "what's the treatment for the Red Fever? If someone falls asleep or unconscious, what can we do to help them? What do the doctors suggest?"

"No one's found a treatment. Nothing works."

"*Yet,*" Charlotte added, voice unsteady. "Nothing works *yet*. They'll find a cure. They have to."

I bit my lip. Years ago, I had hoped for a cure for my leukemia, and the doctors still hadn't found one. Still, maybe a cure would be found someday, long after it had killed me.

How many people would die from this Red Fever before the doctors found a cure for it?

"How do we stop ourselves from catching it?" I asked.

"By not breathing." Jase swung the car in a sharp right turn.

"It's airborne?"

"Yep."

Shocked, I fell silent.

We drove down Fifth Avenue, one of my favorite streets in Manhattan. I loved the dress stores with their promises of beauty, style, and glamour—as long as you weren't me. No matter what I wore, I still looked thin and frail, with green eyes too large for my pale face.

On the sidewalks, pedestrians hurried by, ignoring the glittering window displays. At the surgical masks they wore, I muttered, "Useless." The non-terrestrial seed balls had traveled immense distances through space. They had probably survived asteroid belts and meteors and other "spacey" dangers. I doubted that a flimsy mask would stop their Red Fever.

My phone rang and I raced to answer it. "Dad, are you okay?"

"I'm fine."

"How's Mom?"

"I'm so sorry, honey. She didn't make it."

"Oh no!" My mother hadn't loved me enough to stay in New York when I was ill. She'd virtually ignored me for years. Had made me feel unimportant and irrelevant. And yet, at my father's words, a piece of my heart crumpled in grief.

Mom's dead.

"Everything's going to be okay, honey. But I can't talk for long. I've been having problems with this phone all morning."

"Okay. Just quickly tell me how Via is." She'd be taking the loss of our mother much worse than me.

"She's in the back seat, trying to stop a nosebleed."

"*What?*"

"It's just a nosebleed, honey. It doesn't mean anything. I've had a few myself over the past couple of days. They always stop. Lots of people have had them."

He was right. Nearby, several people on Fifth Avenue were holding bloodied handkerchiefs to their faces.

"How bad is she, Dad?"

"Not too bad. I think she'll be okay."

Jase turned into Central Park, taking a detour to the Bronx. Despite my shock at Dad's news, I noticed hundreds of small, weird plants growing everywhere. Corkscrewed blue stems dotted the fields. Skinny black vines hung from tree branches, their surfaces covered with thorns. Yellow flowers the size of baseballs sprouted from garden beds. Other weird vegetation grew on statues, rocks, benches, and trash cans.

They were all non-terrestrial plants.

I shivered at the eerie sight. "How far are you from New York, Dad?"

"Days away."

"I can meet you and Via somewhere in the middle. It'll be quicker than waiting for you to drive here."

"No. Stay in New York, honey. Wait for us at Aunt Suzanne's place."

"But—"

"Promise."

"I—"

"Kass!"

"Okay. I promise."

"By the way, how are you feeling, honey?"

"Fine."

"Good. I'm sure Olivia will be fine too, like you. After all, you're identical twins and share the same DNA." He sounded like he was trying to convince himself as much as me.

Further in the park, a woman screamed and a man shouted in fear.

"Hang on, Dad." Lowering my phone, I asked Jase, "What's going on?"

"I don't know." His hands tightened on the steering wheel.

"Shouldn't we go and see—?"

"Nope." Jase kept driving through the park.

I hesitated, then turned back to my phone. "Where exactly are you, Dad?"

"About a hundred miles—" His phone went dead.

"Dad!" I tried calling him back a few times. Nothing. No voicemail. No dial tone.

I gripped the phone. Willed it to ring.

Silence.

Okay, okay, no reason to panic. Dad's phone is acting up, that's all. He'll buy another one and call me back.

When I called Olivia's phone, I heard the same nothingness.

Trying to stay calm, I told Charlotte and Jase about my conversation with my father.

When I finished, my cousin said, "I'm sure Olivia and Uncle Joe are fine."

"Really?"

"Yes. They're probably in a dead zone. They'll call back as soon as they can."

"I hope you're right." Breathing deeply, I looked out of the window.

A construction worker staggered toward a park bench, a handkerchief clasped to his nose. He collapsed on the bench, head lolling, blood trickling down his face. A woman rushed over to him. She shook the limp man with one hand and pulled out her phone with the other.

Jase ignored the scene outside. "Your sister will be okay, Kass."

I tried to reply. Couldn't.

He continued, "People don't die from nosebleeds."

I wanted to believe him.

He drove out of the park and turned onto a street that looked like a set from a disaster movie. A fire engine had its ladder stretched up the side of a ten-story building. Flames roared from shattered windows, belching black smoke and orange death. People leaned out of other windows, waving and screaming for help.

Firefighters trained their hoses on the flames, their shoulders slumped; others climbed the ladder, moving slowly. All seemed weary.

Had these first responders been dealing with other fires today? Were they tired? Or was it something else? Something like the Red Fever?

Fear chilled my body.

At an intersection, an old guy in a tattered overcoat held up a cardboard sign: "The End of the World is Nigh." His clichéd warning was common in disaster movies and often used as a joke. Normally, I would've smiled.

Except today it felt like he was right.

13

A FEW MILES FROM home, Charlotte's nose started bleeding.

One moment she was fine. The next moment, thick blood poured from her nostrils. Tissues pressed to her nose, my cousin's frightened gaze swept to Jase. "What's happening? Am I going to be all right?"

"Yeah," he replied without conviction.

"Of course you will," I told her with false confidence.

Turning in her seat, she studied my face. "You're lying, Kass. I can always tell."

My mind raced. What should we do? How could we help her? "Charlotte, I'm calling your mother. She'll know what to do."

It took a few minutes to get through to Aunt Suzanne, a nurse at a hospital in the Bronx. Quickly, I explained the situation—how Charlotte had picked me up from Brooklyn when Elizabeth died, and how her nose had started bleeding a few minutes ago.

Voice trembling, she ordered us to bring Charlotte to her immediately.

"She'll be okay, won't she, Aunt Suzanne?" I whispered into the phone. "It's not the Red Fever, is it? It's just a bleeding nose."

"I hope so. But the doctors here think the bleeding is another symptom of the Red Fever. We've been getting reports from all over the place about people with nosebleeds."

"What happens to them?"

"Th-They … usually die too."

I couldn't speak. Couldn't breathe. Dad. Olivia. Charlotte. The three people I loved most in the world all had bleeding noses. "Usually. You said they *usually* die, Aunt Suzanne. Not all of them, right?" I clutched at the faint thread of hope.

"I don't know. Get Charlotte to me ASAP." The line went dead.

Charlotte slumped in the front seat, as though … tired. My cousin had always awed me with her athletic ability and energy. Cheerleading, dancing, hiking, roller-skating—she'd embraced them all with relentless enthusiasm, as though determined to cram as much into life as possible.

Now, all the life seemed to be draining from her.

It took Jase over an hour to get to the hospital, thanks to accidents and road detours. Charlotte sat with her head back, tissues pressed to her nose; when they became saturated, she used an old T-shirt from the back seat and then a ratty beach towel.

Ten minutes from the hospital, she fell unconscious.

Jase drove those last few miles like a maniac, swearing constantly. Finally, the Chevy squealed to a halt a block from the hospital, the closest we could park. Ambulances and cars clogged the streets and sidewalks as desperate people sought medical help.

Jase scooped up Charlotte's limp body and rushed toward the emergency department.

I followed.

The place was bedlam. People everywhere. Shouts. Alarms. Cries of despair.

Fear.

At the entrance, my aunt waited with a wheelchair. After Jase lowered Charlotte into it, I brushed a lock of damp hair from her face and stroked her hot forehead. "Please get better, cuz."

Aunt Suzanne pressed a key into my hand. "Use this to get into our apartment. And stay there, okay? I'll call later to let you know how Charlotte's doing."

"No, I want to stay with her." I turned to Jase. "You want to stay too, don't you?"

He remained silent, fear shadowing his face.

"You need to leave," my aunt told us firmly. "All nonessential personnel are banned from the hospital. There's no room inside. You need to go now, Jase, or your car will be towed away. And, Kass, stay inside our apartment. It'll be safer there than outside."

"All right," I reluctantly replied.

"Good. I'll call you later, dear." Aunt Suzanne wheeled Charlotte through the crowd on the sidewalk, toward the emergency department.

A white-coated doctor stopped her. "Put her on there," he ordered, pointing to a bus loaded with patients. "We're sending our overflow to Brooklyn Grace Hospital."

"This is my daughter."

"Sorry, Nurse Jenkins. They're all somebody's daughter or son. There aren't any more beds here, and no doctors to treat new patients. She'll have both at Brooklyn Grace."

"Okay, but I'm going with her."

"Very well."

I stood on the milling pavement, watching as Charlotte was carried onto the crowded bus. Aunt Suzanne gave me a brief wave, then climbed on board.

Jase tugged my arm. "Let's go. There are too many sick people here."

I regarded him with a wisp of distaste. "Afraid of getting infected?"

"Of course I am. I've got more to lose than you."

"What do you mean?"

"I'm fit and healthy. I've got decades ahead of me. You don't." He didn't mention my illness, but I got the message loud and clear. "Let's go."

Shocked into silence, I followed him to his Chevy.

Jase grudgingly agreed to a detour before we headed to Charlotte's apartment. Since my duffel bag was in the crashed cab back on the Brooklyn Bridge, we stopped by my place. I packed another bag with clothes, toiletries—and all my meds, almost a month's worth. I wanted the drugs safely with me, not vulnerable in an empty apartment.

I packed a second bag with fresh and canned food. If I was going to stay with Charlotte for a few days until my father arrived, I wanted to contribute to the meals.

Jase dropped me outside Charlotte's building, tossed me a hurried "Bye," and sped off. Feeling abandoned, I stood on the sidewalk, watching his car disappear around a corner. I understood his haste and lack of concern for me. He was worried about his own family. And Charlotte. I was just his girlfriend's cousin.

Sighing, I gathered my bags and hauled them up to the apartment. After unpacking, I set up the sofa bed in the living room and made a pasta dinner for three people.

Later, I sat down and watched the news on the TV.

It was all bad.

Everywhere, emergency services couldn't cope. People were dying in the thousands, including doctors, nurses, police, firefighters, and other essential personnel. The armed services had been hit too, along with members of the government and, of course, ordinary citizens.

Since the Red Fever was airborne, no one was safe. And no one knew what to do.

Fires raged in the city. Supermarket shelves were stripped bare. Overcrowded hospitals turned away new arrivals. Schools, halls, and community centers were transformed into makeshift medical centers—but with no doctors or nurses to staff them, these places simply became holding areas for the dying.

The Red Fever was ruthlessly efficient. People fell unconscious, then died; others had bleeding noses, then died. Several hours later, the victims' bodies and clothes decomposed into bucket-sized piles of gray dust called "decomp-dust."

On TV, scientists and doctors speculated and argued and offered theories.

No one knew anything for certain. No one could offer a solution.

Exhausted from the day's traumas and grief, I forced myself to stay up watching the news as I waited for my father or Aunt Suzanne to call.

I waited. And waited.

Eventually, exhaustion won, and I fell into a restless sleep filled with nightmares.

The next morning, I awoke with a start and rushed to check my messages. Maybe I'd been so tired that I'd slept through a call.

No messages.

A cold shiver slid down my spine.

No messages.

The two words were a terrible, ominous sign.

I'd never felt more scared.

Or more alone.

14

Over the next three weeks, humanity headed for extinction.

No one knew it, of course. We all hoped we'd somehow pull out of this death spiral. We hoped the Red Fever would burn itself out. We hoped our lives would eventually return to normal.

We humans are like that. We hope. And that hope can be both our salvation and our downfall.

The morning after Charlotte's nosebleed, I tried calling Dad and Aunt Suzanne over and over again. Each time, I hoped they would answer.

They never did.

I paced the apartment, lying to myself that Dad hadn't been able to buy another phone. No, that didn't make sense. Cell phones could be purchased almost anywhere these days. Even if he couldn't buy another one, he could call me on Olivia's phone.

Maybe they were in an area with poor reception.

Definitely possible.

Whatever, he'd contact me as soon as he could.

I lied to myself that Dad and Olivia—*please be alive*—were still driving to New York. They'd be here in a few days. I just had to wait. And Aunt Suzanne wasn't answering her phone because she was busy with hundreds of patients.

I thought about going to Brooklyn Grace Hospital to see Charlotte. Three things stopped me: there were no buses, trains, or rideshares working; I didn't have a car; and I couldn't drive.

Then it struck me. Jase. Maybe he'd already gone to the hospital to see my cousin.

By the time I tried calling him, the phones were dead. All of them. Landlines and cell phones. Even the internet was down.

I searched for Jase's address. When I couldn't find it anywhere, I realized that Charlotte and Aunt Suzanne probably used their cell phones and computers—both password-protected—to store people's details.

I switched on the TV, desperate for news. Every channel was a blank screen or a test pattern.

Agitated, I headed up to the flat rooftop of the tall apartment building. From there, I could see large sections of the Bronx and the suburbs beyond.

Smoke gushed from scattered buildings in the distance. However, the chorus of ambulance and police and fire sirens, so earsplitting yesterday, had thinned to a few wails. Traffic had thinned too. People were too scared to go outside. Or too sick.

Overhead, an eagle wheeled in the red sky.

Red.

How I'd grown to hate that color.

Red, the color of the mist that had started this catastrophe. Red, the color of the sky that had shrouded the planet for the past week, harboring the Red Fever. Red, the color of the blood from the injured and dying.

I knocked on the doors of other apartments in the building. A few people yelled, "Go away." Others cracked open their doors and tersely told me they had no news either. Many apartments remained silent, as though their owners were huddled inside, too scared to even talk to me—or too dead to answer my knocks.

Finally, I returned to Charlotte's apartment and sat in front of the blank-screened TV, forcing myself to eat in order to keep my strength up. A quick survey of the kitchen showed that I had enough food for ten days. If I skipped breakfast and ate smaller meals, I could probably double that to twenty days.

I slept. Read books. Played Solitaire. Paced the floor. And waited.

I waited for Dad and Olivia to arrive. For Charlotte and Aunt Suzanne to come home. For the phones to work again and the TV programs to resume.

For the Red Fever to kill me.

Over the following days, a great silence descended on the city. First, the power stopped. It wiped out the music that had blared from a neighbor's apartment, and although the music had been annoying, the sudden silence was much worse. Outside, the shrieking sirens eventually faded to an awful hush. The once-busy streets gradually became deserted.

The hush spread to my apartment building. Earlier, I'd heard voices murmuring behind thin walls, doors slamming, footsteps in the hallway. Eventually these sounds faded away, like warm summer days retreating before the advance of an endless winter.

Every now and then, the silence in the Bronx was ripped by a volley of gunshots or an outburst of shouts filled with menace and aggression. Clearly, there were other survivors in the city, just not ones I wanted to meet.

On Day 21, a sudden roar of motorcycles brought me racing to the living room window. Huddled behind the heavy drapes, I withdrew a pair of binoculars from my pocket and peered through a thin gap.

A couple of dozen Harley-Davidsons slowly cruised down the street.

The leader of the pack was a bald, tattooed man in his forties. He wore a leather jacket blazoned with the name of a biker club: Wilders. As he rode, his gaze swiveled from side to side, scanning for trouble—or scanning for loot.

Some of the men swigged on bottles of alcohol. Others hollered and yelled in drunken glee. Half of them had beards and mustaches; the rest were unshaven. Most had guns stuck in belts, rifles slung over shoulders, and knives thrust into boots.

A couple of the bikers had young women passengers on their Hogs, and as they rode by, I frowned. Something was wrong. The women didn't match these rowdy thugs. One wore a pretty cream dress, and her shiny brown hair streamed behind her. The other wore a lacy pink top and white jeans. Neither seemed to be the kind to associate with drunken louts like this gang.

Both women appeared terrified, and I quickly understood why. Their arms were wrapped around the waists of the riders—and their hands were bound with rope.

They weren't willing passengers.

They were captives.

Helpless prey.

Horrified, I stared at these women. What could I do? How could I help them?

The answer to both questions made me sick to my stomach. I couldn't do a thing. The bikers were a strong, well-armed, and ruthless pack. I was a single, weak girl.

One man threw a bottle at a parked Ford. When it ignited into a fireball, the thugs cheered wildly and cruised away.

I grabbed up a fire extinguisher from the kitchen, paused, and put it down again. If the Wilder bikers returned and saw the Ford only partially burned, they'd know someone had put out the flames. And they might decide to go searching for that survivor.

If they discovered me, it wouldn't matter that I was a thin and sickly girl.

I'd become their prey as well.

I wished Aunt Suzanne owned a gun. But she didn't. She hated the things.

From the kitchen, I took a sharp carving knife and placed it on the coffee table. If anyone broke into this apartment, I'd use it to protect myself.

Then I returned to the living room window.

On the street below, the car burned. Thankfully, the fire wasn't close enough to spread to the other parked vehicles. After a while, the raging flames died down and the smoke thinned into oblivion.

I stared at the Ford's blackened metal skeleton, feeling as burned out and broken as the car. Over the past two weeks, my previous desire to live had been eroded by the increasing deaths across the city and the cold loneliness of my existence. Like the smoke outside, I could feel my need to survive thinning into nothing. Life had become empty. Joyless. Frightening. And now, after being unable to help those two captive women, it was also riddled with guilt.

I felt lost and alone. I longed to lie on the couch and slip into the same oblivion that had swallowed the flames and the smoke.

But what if Dad or Olivia or Charlotte came back and found my lifeless body?

I had never entertained millions of people like that movie star, Willow Grace. I had never provided work for thousands of employees like Asher Weston's wealthy family. In my sixteen years of being alive, I'd made no real contribution to society.

Yet I still meant something to the people who loved me. In a world filled with death, my own death would still shatter them. The thought of adding to their pain and grief was unthinkable.

I needed to survive—not just for myself, but for them as well.

And so, reluctantly, I forced myself to endure.

15

By Day 25, my food supplies had dwindled to zero.

I wandered the silent corridors, knocking on my neighbors' doors. "Hi. My name's Kass Madison. Are you okay in there?"

No one ever answered.

Stomach growling from hunger, I went outside.

Avoiding the firebombed Ford, I tried the doors of the other cars. In an unlocked one, I found a tire iron, which I used to open the door to the building manager's apartment. In the man's bedroom, a pile of decomp-dust lay on the top blanket.

I swallowed. Hurried out of his tomb. Went into his office.

My tire iron snapped open a locked key safe on the wall. Master key in hand, I went to every apartment in the building and knocked on each door again. If no one answered—and they never did—I entered, calling out a loud "Hello" in case the owner was waiting with a loaded shotgun.

It never happened.

Instead, I found only mounds of decomp-dust, each a painful reminder of a stolen life.

Many apartments had stacks of food in their kitchens; some even had crates of bottled water. At first, taking the food felt like looting. Then I reminded myself that the owners were dead. The supplies belonged to whoever found them.

Along with food, I collected every packet and bottle of vitamins and medicine I could find: painkillers, penicillin, antibiotics, or anything else that might be needed in the future.

Unfortunately, I didn't find any leukemia meds. My own supply was dwindling, and when they ran out …

I'd worry about that problem later. For now, I had work to do.

Over the next few days, I brought cans, bottles, and bags of food back to my apartment. Carefully, I stored them in boxes and crates stacked along the walls, feeling like a crazy doomsday prepper—except doomsday had already arrived.

I listened for the roar of motorcycles, fearing the return of the Wilders, and wrestling with the fact that the world had changed almost overnight. I wondered if the bikers' earlier fire-bombing of the Ford would still be regarded as a criminal act. After all, the vehicle no longer belonged to anyone.

And what about my own actions? For days, I'd been breaking into apartments and taking dead people's food and bottled water. Were my quiet thefts more moral than the Wilders' loud violence?

Maybe our world was becoming grayer and grayer—but one thing was still certain. The Wilders' capture of those two young women had definitely been criminal.

With memories of the bikers haunting my thoughts, I gathered up weapons from the other apartments, alarmed and relieved at how many people owned guns. Eventually, I built up a pile of pistols, revolvers, even an Uzi.

Previously I'd hated guns, along with the death and destruction they inflicted on countless victims. Now, my collection of weapons gave me a sense of security and comfort—plus an unexpected, angry regret.

I wished I'd been standing on the street a week ago, holding a revolver when the Wilders and their two terrified captives had roared past. Would I have used it to try to save the women? Could I have shot those men in cold blood?

Maybe I couldn't have killed them, but I suspected I could've wounded them without feeling too guilty.

The world was changing in ways I didn't like. And so was I.

By the time I finished searching the apartment building, I had enough food to last Dad, Olivia, Charlotte, Aunt Suzanne, and me for months. The odds of them all surviving were slim, but maybe some were still alive. Or at least one.

It was an increasingly fragile hope. Yet hope was all I had left.

Hope got me up in the mornings. It drove me through the days of collecting supplies and weapons. It sat with me at the window for hours as I scoured the streets below, looking for signs that someone—other than drunken bikers—was still alive.

However, even the bikers had vanished.

A heavy silence lay across the city. Thick. Permanent.

And then on Day 39, a winter's day swathed in the same soul-destroying silence of the previous ones, a sudden thunderous sound made me jump.

Shocked, I dropped the book I'd been trying to read.

Someone was banging on my door.

16

I PULLED BACK FROM the peephole. I was hallucinating. I had to be.

I drew in a deep breath.

Waited.

Another knock thundered on the door. This time I wrenched it open, afraid he'd vanish if I waited a moment longer.

"Jase!"

I couldn't help myself. I threw my arms around his neck and hugged him. His body was hard. Muscular. And real.

When he didn't respond to my embrace, I flushed with embarrassment and stepped back.

Charlotte's boyfriend just stood there, wearing a thick jacket and dirty gray jeans. His face was thinner than when I'd last seen him a few weeks ago. His brown eyes were glazed and distant.

When I'd first heard the knock, my emotions had splintered. Part of me had feared it was a drunken biker or some other thug. Another part had hoped and prayed it was Dad and Olivia, or Charlotte and Aunt Suzanne.

If it couldn't be one of those four, then I was glad it was Jase. At least not everyone I cared about was gone.

He peered over my shoulder, into the dim apartment. "Where's Charlotte?"

"She and Aunt Suzanne never came home from the hospital."

"Did Mrs. Jenkins call you? Tell you how Charlotte was doing?"

"Not a word," I replied, returning to the living room. "Didn't you go to the hospital to see her?"

"I couldn't." He followed me inside. "My mom got sick. Then my dad. Later, my brother and sister …" His voice faded, and I guessed the rest.

"I'm so sorry."

"The last of my family went two weeks ago. Little Katie. Four years old. She'd never hurt anyone." His shoulders slumped, as though bending under the weight of his sorrow. "She didn't deserve this."

"No one does."

It was strange seeing Jase so subdued and beaten. Before the Mist, he'd been a force of personality. His good looks, friendly nature, and sporting prowess had ensured his popularity with his classmates, while his good grades had endeared him to his teachers.

Once, his glittering future had held promises of a fulfilling career, a family, love, and a long life. Now everything had changed.

"Have you been alone for the past two weeks, Jase? Why didn't you come here sooner?"

"I wasn't sure if I was infectious, so I waited."

His answer didn't ring true. The Red Fever had been in the air for weeks. By now, everyone had been exposed to it, and any survivors were probably immune.

I suspected Jase had been protecting himself, not me. Had he been worried that Charlotte's nosebleed meant she was infected? At school, Jase had been a charmer and an athlete, but apparently that didn't mean he was brave or selfless. And being class president didn't automatically mean he was strong enough to be a leader in real life.

He headed for the door, walking slowly and stiffly, like an old man who had lived too long.

"Where are you going, Jase?"

"Brooklyn Grace Hospital."

"Hold on. I'll come with you."

After weeks of living alone, I craved human contact—plus I needed to know what had happened to my cousin and Aunt Suzanne. And maybe, just maybe, I'd find enough leukemia meds to keep me alive for a little longer.

I left a note for Dad and Olivia, in case they turned up while I was out. Then I grabbed my backpack and followed Jase from the building.

He seemed indifferent to my presence, but I didn't care. After being stuck indoors for weeks, it felt good to be out in the sun, despite the cold breeze.

I frowned at the cloudless red sky. Would it ever be blue again? Or would it remain forever red?

Two blocks later, we arrived at Jase's car. He opened the Chevy's trunk, which was crammed with clothes and supplies. Rummaging through the stuff, he found a couple of flashlights and passed one to me. "We'll need these when we search the hospital. With the electricity off, it'll be dark inside."

"Good idea." I climbed into the front passenger seat. "Why didn't you park outside Charlotte's apartment building?"

"Things have changed, Kass." His brown eyes narrowed. "There aren't many survivors around. But you still don't let anyone know where you live, or where other people live. It's not safe." The Chevy's engine growled into life. "Not every survivor is a nice person."

"Yeah." I remembered the drunken Wilders and their captive prey. Were those two women even alive anymore?

And if they were, did they wish they were dead?

17

We headed toward Brooklyn.

Jase drove in silence, scanning the roads and side streets, alert for trouble. When I withdrew a revolver from my backpack and placed it on my lap, he eyed it, surprised. "You have a gun?"

"You don't?"

"Just a large knife."

Satisfaction flickered through me. At least I was well-armed.

"Have you cleaned it?" he asked.

My satisfaction evaporated. "Was I supposed to?"

"Of course. Otherwise, it might not work."

"Why would someone keep a broken gun?"

"They don't usually break. They just need cleaning every so often."

"Oh." I paused. "Why don't you have a gun instead of a knife?"

"Because my parents never allowed them in our home. I'm surprised Mrs. Jenkins owns one."

"She doesn't," I said.

"Where did you get it?"

"From one of her neighbors."

"You stole it?"

"I took it. They didn't need it. They were dead."

He gave me a grudging smile. "Way to go. I never thought you'd steal a piece of candy, let alone a gun."

"I'm not a thief. I'm a survivor."

Jase lapsed into silence again.

As he drove toward Manhattan, I studied our surroundings.

The apocalypse had struck so quickly that the city was still intact. Sure, there'd been lots of car accidents, but most of the smashed vehicles had been pushed to the curb, leaving the roads reasonably clear.

Markets and delis had been stripped of supplies, their broken windows and gaping doors showing looted interiors.

New York's streets were bare of traffic, and the buildings held a silence that echoed the morgue-like hush of Charlotte's apartment complex. I didn't see a single person, just a few horses, rabbits, and dogs. These animals only emphasized the absence of people in a city once home to millions.

"Where are the other survivors?" I asked.

"They exist, but they keep out of sight."

Just then, I caught sight of a familiar figure standing on the sidewalk down the block.

Loner.

He looked the same as when I'd seen him back in Central Park on Thanksgiving Day. Same baseball cap, dark sunglasses, faded blue jeans, and red plaid shirt. As before, he was alone, surveying his surroundings. What was he looking at? The desolate city? The emptiness?

Or was he hoping to spot other survivors?

At the sound of our engine, he turned.

Saw us.

And stiffened.

"Stop the car! I know that guy." Well, I didn't really know him. I'd just kissed him once—a long, passionate kiss that had set my body on fire. Did that count as knowing someone? Doubtful.

By the time Jase screeched the Chevy to a halt, we'd passed Loner.

"Wasn't that the guy from Central Park?" he asked. "The one who always kept to himself?"

"Yes."

He backed up the car to the office building.

The sidewalk was bare. Loner was gone.

Jase's brows furrowed. "Why did he take off like that?"

"No idea." I had assumed that most folks would've been happy to see a familiar face after surviving a horrific apocalypse. Didn't people need to band together for protection and support? "Maybe he thought we were dangerous. Out to attack him or something." Like the bikers.

"Yeah." He accelerated again. "Let's keep going."

My thoughts lingered on Loner. "Or maybe he doesn't like staying outdoors for too long because of the Red Fever."

"I think the Fever has run its course." Jase wove the Chevy past a bus and a truck that had collided at an intersection. It had only been a few weeks since the Mist, yet the smashed vehicles appeared almost ancient, like relics of a lost age.

"I wonder how many people survived."

He shrugged. "Our apartment building had an epidemiologist living in it. He was in contact with doctors all over the world, exchanging details with them about death rates and possible treatments."

"And?"

"When my parents got sick, I asked him what I could do to help them. His answer was 'nothing.' He told me that only a fraction of humans were immune to the Red Fever." He scowled. "I can't remember the exact percentage. According to him, about four hundred thousand people would survive."

"In New York?"

"Across the entire planet."

"Four hundred thousand out of eight billion!"

"Yep. Before he died on Day Nine, this guy said that a place like New York City could have about four *hundred* survivors. It's not many, but hopefully it's enough to find a group to join somewhere. Safety in numbers and so on." He scanned the street, as if looking for other survivors.

"Statistically," I asked, "isn't it highly unlikely that two people from a school of three thousand students would both survive?" I was referring to him and me.

"That's not how statistics work." Jase had always been good at math.

"What do you mean?"

"Let's say only one person survives out of every twenty thousand. That means, out of a million people, you might expect about fifty survivors."

"Right."

"But not necessarily accurate. Statistics are far more random, and many different factors can effect the survival rate in each city. If you line up a million people in New York, and another million in London and Paris and Tokyo, each city wouldn't have the same number of fifty survivors. There might be one hundred and eighty-three survivors per million in New York versus twenty-six per million in London, or three in Paris."

"So, statistically, it's possible for several people who lived in the same area before the Mist to all survive."

"You and I are living proof of that. We're both from the Bronx. We must have certain genes that allowed us to survive while others died. And since Charlotte is your cousin, I'm hoping she has the same survival gene as you, Kass."

"And Dad," I added. "Plus Olivia. My sister and I have identical DNA."

"I guess it's possible they're still alive too."

"You don't sound too sure."

"They were in LA during the Night of the Red Mist. If the terra seeds were thicker there than here in the Bronx, that might alter their chances of survival. Many different factors can effect survival: altitude, temperature, wind, density of terra seeds, and so on."

"I get it, sort of."

Ahead, a flock of large birds circled in the air. Something about them seemed odd and, peering through my binoculars, I tried to identify them.

"They're vultures, Kass."

This was the second time in weeks that I'd seen a vulture. A few days after the Night of the Red Mist, one had perched on the Brooklyn Bridge just before a plane had crashed into it.

"Something must be dying," I said. If the animal or human was already dead, the vultures wouldn't be circling overhead, waiting. They'd be on the ground, eating. "Maybe we should check and see what's going on."

"No way. There are flocks of vultures all over the city. If we check out every possible problem, it'll take forever to get to the hospital."

"What if someone's hurt or dying?"

He laughed, a dry and brittle sound like winter leaves being crushed. "Billions of people have been hurt or dying since the Night of the Red Mist. We can't save them all. We can only try to save the ones we care about. Even that's impossible most of the time." He kept driving.

Wherever I looked, the non-terrestrial plants were flourishing. Green patches dotted the roads and buildings, their oddly shaped leaves several inches long. Larger varieties grew in parks and playgrounds. Fat vines snaked down the sidewalks, fed by the weak wintry sunshine and, apparently, the concrete beneath them.

"Are these terras everywhere?" I asked.

"I hope not." He slowed the car as we crossed a patch of brown terras, and the plants crunched beneath our tires like broken glass.

In silence, we continued through the deserted city, swerving past smashed vehicles.

Thankfully, the Manhattan Bridge was still intact, allowing us to cross it safely. To our right, the severed remains of the Brooklyn Bridge hung limply over the East River, a tombstone for the hundreds of people who'd died when a plane had crashed into it weeks ago.

I turned away from the awful sight.

Finally, we arrived at Brooklyn Grace Hospital.

After parking, we exited the Chevy and paused outside the multistoried building, as wary as soldiers about to enter hostile territory. The hospital appeared empty and unnaturally silent, and—

A dark shape moved in an upper-floor window, then darted out of sight.

Jase's grip tightened around his knife. "Someone's inside."

"Yeah." I withdrew my revolver. Held it before me. Reveled in its comforting feel.

"Give me the gun, Kass."

"Why?"

"Have you ever used one?"

"No."

"Do you even know how to use it?"

"Point it. Pull the trigger. It's not rocket science."

"I've been target shooting. I'm a better shot than you." He held out his hand.

I knew he was right. His skill would increase our chances of survival.

Reluctantly, I passed him the weapon and received a large kitchen knife in exchange. I grasped the lightweight implement, already missing the solid feel of the revolver.

Next time, I'd pack *two* guns in my backpack.

"Ready?" he asked.

I nodded, my throat dry.

Quietly, we crossed the sunny sidewalk. At the gaping front doors, we drew in deep breaths and entered the shadow-filled hospital.

18

THE CORRIDORS BEYOND THE reception area were thick with shadows, and we hastily switched on our flashlights.

Mounds of decomp-dust lay everywhere: on top of the metal gurneys that cluttered the reception area, on the plastic seats in the waiting rooms, on the tiled floors.

I knew the doctors and nurses would've struggled to save their patients, but their efforts had clearly been in vain. Each silent room was a testament to humanity's failure and the triumph of the Red Fever.

We moved down the hallways, calling Charlotte's name but keeping our voices low, unsure who'd been at the upper-floor window. And why had this person ducked out of sight when we'd seen them?

A strange scraping sound echoed down the hallway.

We froze.

Listened.

Jase put a finger to his lips, then pointed upward. The sound had come from the floor above us.

Who was up there?

He held the revolver in front of him. Nodded at me to keep going.

As we cautiously moved forward again, I saw sweat beading on his forehead. Was he perspiring from stress? Or because it was sweltering inside the hospital? Strangely, the air in here was moist and hot, as though we were in the tropics instead of a wintry New York.

Even stranger, and far more disturbing, were the terras.

Layers of green-gray vegetation grew across the floors, up the walls, and over the furniture.

I picked up a metal dish covered in leaves and watched it crumble in my hand. Shocked, I studied the shattered pieces. How had this happened? Had the terras eaten the metal, causing it to break apart when touched?

I held my hand a few inches above a bench smothered with green vines, and I flinched at the warmth rising from the vegetation.

Incredible.

"These plants are giving off heat!" I whispered.

He shrugged. "So?"

"That doesn't worry you?"

"Nope."

We entered a large room crowded with more gurneys topped with decomp-dust. Blinds covered the far windows, shutting out all sight of the post-apocalyptic world beyond.

I skimmed my beam across the gurneys, still fretting about the hot plants. How could plants produce heat? Earth plants couldn't do that. Then again, these plants weren't from Earth. Hopefully, though, we'd figure out how to kill them and—

"Get away!" The shout boomed from the far end of the room.

Startled, we aimed our flashlights at a middle-aged man crouching in a shadowy corner. Lank-haired and overweight, he clutched two cans of soup to his chest.

"I found the cans first," he cried, glaring at us. "They're mine."

"Hey, buddy," Jase said, "we don't want your stuff. Keep it."

"They're mine. Mine."

"Okay, buddy, the cans are yours. Promise."

The man's glare hardened as he gestured to Jase's revolver. "You're going to kill me and steal my food, aren't you?"

"No." Jase lowered his gun. "Seriously, buddy, we're just looking for someone. A sixteen-year-old girl. Slim. Long red hair. Hazel eyes. Have you seen her? Is she here?"

"No one's here," the man screamed. "They're all dead. You can't have my food." He wrenched a blind from a large window, flooding the room with sunlight. Enraged, he slammed a chair into the glass pane, leaped through the broken window, and ran off.

Jase gazed at me, mouth open. "Was he crazy?"

"A little."

"So that's who was watching us from the upstairs window."

"Maybe," I said, confused by the incident. "Didn't the epidemiologist in your apartment building say that about four hundred New Yorkers would've survived the Red Fever?"

"Yeah."

"This city has hundreds of thousands of empty apartments and homes. Most have cans of food in their kitchens. That's hundreds of thousands of cans. I know they only last for a few years but—"

"I get it. There's enough food for us all, at least for the next four or five years."

I nodded. "Right. So why was that guy worried about his two cans of soup?"

"He was crazy."

"I guess."

A chilly wind gusted through the broken window. It raced around the room like an invisible entity, snatching up handfuls of gray decomp-dust from the gurneys and throwing them into the air. Caught by surprise, Jase and I breathed in some of the spreading cloud.

I gagged in disgust. This stuff was the remains of dead people!

Appalled, holding our noses, we rushed from the room.

"Gross," Jase spluttered, brushing down his jacket and jeans, which were coated in the fine particles.

As I slapped the powder off my clothes, a wave of nausea hit me. Desperately, I fought down the bile that rose in my throat. I'd been feeling unwell for the past few days. Was a lack of meds allowing my leukemia symptoms to return? Or was I feeling nauseous from the billowing decomp-dust?

My stomach settled, and I gulped in steadying breaths. "I don't remember seeing any piles of decomp-dust during our drive here."

"Well, duh. We had a storm a few nights ago, remember?"

I nodded. The howling wind and pelting rain had been so loud that I'd lain awake for hours.

He continued, "The storm would've washed away the remains of anyone who died outside."

"Oh. Right." But the wind and the rain wouldn't have touched the millions of mounds of decomp-dust lying inside buildings across New York. There, these pitiful piles of once-lives would wait, sealed within rooms until time broke the buildings and exposed them to the elements. Then they would be freed—flung to the winds, deposited in rivers and oceans, and eventually returned to the ever-waiting earth.

"Come on." Jase strode down the hallway. "Let's check upstairs for Charlotte."

"And for some leukemia meds."

I waited for his usual reaction to the word *leukemia*.

In the year that he'd been dating Charlotte, I'd often caught him watching me warily, as if afraid I'd infect him with my disease. I'd wanted to tell him to stop being paranoid, that cancer wasn't contagious. In the end, I had kept quiet. My classmates at school knew I was ill, but most people no longer mentioned it to me, much to my relief. So, reluctant to talk to Jase about my condition, I'd simply pretended I was normal. Healthy. Not dying.

And for a few precious months leading up to my sixteenth birthday, that had seemed true.

Another wave of nausea swept me. Again, I fought it back.

This time there was no decomp-dust around to blame. The symptoms of my illness were definitely rearing their ugly heads again.

"I need more leukemia meds, Jase. I'm out of them."

For once, he didn't wince at the mention of my leukemia. Maybe with everything happening in the world, worrying about my illness was low on his list of problems.

"Fine," he reluctantly said. "We'll find you some meds. And Charlotte." He uttered the last two words in a softer almost hopeless tone. Like me, he was fighting the growing conviction that Charlotte wasn't alive, that she was one of these piles of gray dust.

I couldn't bear to dwell on that possibility.

Floor by floor, we searched wards and offices and supply rooms. Almost every area in the hospital contained mounds of decomp-dust. Sometimes there was just one; other times there were multiple piles.

All the stockrooms and storerooms had been stripped of medicines and supplies, leaving empty shelves and cupboards.

Every so often, I heard scrapes or rustles coming from a room, and I wondered—*hoped*—that someone was still alive. Someone like Charlotte. Each time, it turned out to be an animal. A stray dog scrounging for scraps. Rats foraging in the litter. A bird.

In an open-plan office, a chimpanzee bounded across desks. When it spotted us, it shrieked in surprise, jumped onto a tall cabinet, and disappeared through a narrow window in the upper wall.

I gaped at Jase. "What's a chimp doing in a hospital?"

"It must be from a lab or zoo. Weeks ago, I heard that animal lovers were releasing animals from zoos, sanctuaries, farms, labs, and so on. They figured that humanity was heading for extinction, so they decided to give the animals a chance to live. Better than letting them die in their cages, I guess."

I agreed. I loved animals and hated the idea of them starving to death. Freeing them was the right thing to do.

However, releasing them had created one slight problem.

Humanity wasn't extinct—yet.

Some of us still survived.

I wondered which animals had been released from the city's zoos. Elephants and rhinos would probably be okay, but my skin crawled at the thought of sharing the streets with lions, tigers, and other ferocious predators. They'd be hungry. And we'd be prey.

A low, savage growl from behind prickled the hairs on the back of my neck.

Jase looked around. His face paled.

Swallowing, I slowly turned.

Oh no! Sometimes I hated being right.

A huge grizzly bear blocked the office doorway. Black eyes glinting, it stood upright on its hind legs. Nine feet tall. Several hundred pounds of pure muscle.

Throwing its head back, the grizzly opened a mouth lined with sharp teeth and roared.

I couldn't move. Couldn't breathe.

This beast was an apex predator.

And Jase and I were its prey.

19

THE MASSIVE GRIZZLY DROPPED onto all four paws.

It pounded through the maze of desks toward us, sharp claws clacking on the vinyl floor like knives.

"Shoot it, Jase!"

Snapping out of his daze, he aimed the revolver at the oncoming beast.

Click. Click. Click.

He stared at the gun. Shook it. Pulled the trigger again. Nothing. "You should've cleaned it, Kass!"

The floor trembled under the weight of the pounding bear.

What could we do? Play dead? No way. We'd *be* dead within seconds.

Frantically, I scanned the room for another weapon. Could I throw a monitor at the animal? No. It would shrug off the equipment like a tossed flapjack and keep coming.

High in a wall, sunlight streamed through a window, the one the fleeing chimpanzee had exited through. The opening was wide but narrow. Too small for humans to fit through.

Besides, we were on the eighth floor.

The bear barreled down an aisle, headed straight for us.

Escape was impossible.

Our lives were ticking down to seconds—and another wave of nausea was rising within me. I fought the bile back down.

The beast stopped a short distance away and rose onto its hind legs again, its roar promising agony and spurting blood. The furred mass of death raked the air with long, curved claws that would slash our stomachs open, gutting us like fish. If we were lucky, we'd be dead before it ate us.

Jase snatched the knife from my hand.

Arm shaking, he held the blade out, protecting himself.

What the—?

Weaponless, I grabbed a chair and swung it up like a shield, metal legs sticking outward.

Abruptly, my stomach gave a forceful heave, and I threw up.

The stench of vomit wafted through the air.

The grizzly stopped roaring, as though disgusted by the smell.

"Jeez," Jase snapped. "You're being sick here? Now? Are you expecting me to fight this thing alone?"

"No." I wiped the spittle off my mouth and raised the chair again. My makeshift shield seemed to weigh a ton, and my arms trembled as I struggled to hold it up. "I'll fight too." But the massive creature would still slaughter us in seconds. At least it'd be quick—I hoped.

The beast lumbered a couple of steps forward, savage eyes fixed on us, threads of saliva trailing from its jaws.

We backed away. Felt a wall behind us. Knew there was nowhere else to go.

This was it.

Jase whispered, "Charge on the count of three. Right?"

I wondered who was going to charge the bear. Me? Or both of us?

"Ready, Kass?"

"Okay."

A shriek sounded from our right.

Startled, Jase and I—and even the grizzly—glanced over.

A huge eagle powered through the open window high on the wall. Wingspan over six feet wide, it shot across the office, dived at the bear's back and ripped its hooked talons across its flesh.

The bear bellowed. Whirled to face its attacker.

The eagle flapped off. Darted around. Dived in for a second attack. Then another. Another.

Jase and I watched in stunned disbelief, trapped against the wall by the battling animal and bird.

The bear dropped onto all fours. Bleeding from multiple slashes, its right ear ripped, it bolted from the office, charged down the hall, and pounded down a stairwell.

The bird landed on a desk a few feet away. Stretching its brown wings, it blocked our exit as it stared at me with silver eyes.

Was it going to attack us next?

Please no.

Warily, we watched it.

"Careful, Kass. We need to show that we're not threats." Jase slowly lowered his knife, and I followed suit by putting my chair down. A moment later, he gasped in recognition. "WindLord."

"What are you talking about, Jase?"

"It's WindLord, the golden eagle from the Bronx Zoo."

The eagle was beautiful. Golden feathers on its head and neck. Chocolate brown feathers on its body. Hooked blue-gray beak. Yellow feet. And—strangely—bright silver eyes.

"Why are its eyes silver?" I asked.

"No idea. They used to be black. Maybe they've turned silver from eating terra plants or something."

"Are you sure this is WindLord?"

"Positive. One of my buddies worked as a volunteer at the Bronx Zoo. A couple of times, I watched him clean WindLord's aviary." Addressing the bird, he said, "How are you doing, eagle? Listen, I need to get out of this room. Take off, bird, so I can leave."

I noted Jase's use of the word *I*, instead of *we*, and I felt sick again—emotionally this time.

Wings still outstretched, WindLord ignored the boy. Instead, its silver eyes studied me with a quiet intensity that goosebumped my skin. Eagles were skilled hunters that could easily snatch up weak, slow prey. Did this one see me as weak and slow? Did it recognize Death's shadow on me?

No. I was imagining things.

With a sharp squawk, WindLord launched itself into the air. I grabbed the chair and swung it up again, expecting a beaked-and-taloned assault.

Instead, the silver-eyed eagle flapped across to the narrow window, swooped through it, and disappeared.

Dumbfounded, I stared after it. Why had it attacked the bear? Had it been trying to save us? Or did it simply hate grizzlies for some unknown reason?

I had no answer; I suspected I'd never have one.

Jase and I didn't stop to discuss our extraordinary rescue, aware the bear could return at any moment—injured and enraged and dangerous.

He fled.

I followed.

20

A BLEAK WINTER GRIPPED Manhattan.

Over the next week, the tension grew between Jase and me.

At first, we tried to ignore it by focusing on our daily routine.

At Jase's suggestion, he started each morning by giving me a driving lesson, and within a couple of days, I was skilled at navigating the empty, icy roads in a car.

After our near-death experience with the grizzly bear, we went everywhere fully armed. Guns, knives, pepper spray. Heck, we would've packed the Uzi that I'd found, except it had turned out to be a stage prop. Disappointing.

We stopped by my old apartment in case Dad and Olivia had made it back to New York. But there were no signs of them.

Then we swung by the new places marked on our paper map. Dressed for warmth, we searched hospitals and drugstores for leukemia meds, but didn't find any. Next, we headed to Charlotte's favorite movie theaters and malls and boutiques. Jase clung to the possibility that she was still alive somewhere. Although I suspected she was dead, I went along with his searches anyway, since it was better than doing nothing.

We ended each day by checking the homes of people we knew.

No meds. No Charlotte. No signs of any friends or family members ... alive.

Loner had also vanished from the streets. Was *he* still alive?

There were other survivors in the city, of course. Occasionally, we glimpsed them darting into buildings or down alleys as we drove by. We tried pulling over to talk to them. However, after a couple of survivors shot at us, we stopped approaching them.

People were afraid of strangers.

We understood their fear. The distant sound of motorcycles and gunshots showed that the pack of Wilders was still around. And still dangerous.

During the day, Jase and I were so busy searching places that the tension between us wasn't too bad.

But at night the tension stretched like a frayed, taut rope about to snap.

We turned Charlotte's apartment into a semi-fortress. We cleared out Aunt Suzanne's craft room and moved most of our food and bottled water into it. We hung double layers of drapes across the windows, hiding our candlelight at night. We placed a variety of weapons at strategic points and slept with the apartment door barricaded.

I took Aunt Suzanne's bed, while Jase bunked in Charlotte's room.

Jase and I shared a bond of grief. Even though we went through the motions of searching for loved ones, we both knew our families and friends were dead. They were among the billions of piles of gray dust scattered across the world.

Yes, we shared a bond of grief.

But there it ended.

At night, after a canned-ingredients dinner, and after we planned our next day's search, Jase would wrap himself in blankets in an armchair and read a book until bedtime. Whenever I spoke to him, he either grunted or ignored me.

After several nights of this treatment, I'd finally had enough.

"Jase." I had to say his name four times before he looked up.

"What?" He lowered his paperback.

"Why do you keep ignoring me every night?"

"Do you want the truth?"

I had a feeling that I didn't. "Yes."

"I don't want to be here."

"Oh. No problem. We can move. There are some great penthouses on Fifth Avenue that—"

He interrupted me. "I don't want to be here with you. I want to join a group. I don't want to be alone."

I felt like he'd punched me in the stomach. "I don't want to be alone either." I struggled to understand his words and the reasons behind them. "Look, I know I'm not Charlotte, but we're all we have. We need to watch each other's back."

"Then what?" he demanded, snapping shut his novel. "You talk about watching your back. What I'm actually doing is watching you get sicker and sicker."

It was true. Since my meds had run out, I was growing more tired each day. Stairs had become harder to climb, and I needed to take frequent breaks. I thought I'd hidden my slow deterioration from him. Obviously not. "I'm sorry."

"It's not you, it's me."

This was feeling more and more like a clichéd breakup. Except we'd never dated. "I don't mean to be a burden."

"You're not. Yet."

Yet. How could one little word hurt so deeply?

He continued, "I watched my family die. First my mother went. A few days later, my father got ill. My brothers were next. Last of all, my sister. I couldn't do a thing to save them. I could only watch them die. Before the Mist, I thought my family and friends would be part of my life for years. But they're all gone. Their early deaths were wrong. Real wrong."

"I'm so sorry for your loss."

"But with you, Kass, your early death was always expected because of your leukemia. And yet you're still here. Every day, I look at you and wonder why you're alive while other, healthier people are dead. It's not fair."

"Life's not fair."

"Exactly. So why the heck should I hang around while you take your time dying?"

How could he utter such brutal words so casually?

"I ... I don't have the Red Fever," I replied, barely able to speak.

"You've got leukemia. That's worse. You'll take longer to go, and it'll be painful and ugly. Do you really want me to watch you die?"

My protest emerged in a whisper. "My leukemia's not about you. It's my problem."

"One that affects me. I know I should be saintly enough to sit at your bedside for the next few months. You'll need someone to hold your hand, wipe your butt, feed you like a baby." He drew in a sharp breath. "I can't do it."

As much as I wanted to block out his words, the anger and self-pity beneath them rang through the room with deafening clarity.

I stood, trying to gather the shreds of my dignity together. Tears welled in my eyes but I blinked them back. The thought of being alone was terrifying. My worst nightmare.

Part of me wanted to cry.

But another part—the eternally optimistic kernel essential for survival—hoped Jase was just having a bad day. Maybe he'd change his mind once he realized we had no one else. Surely he wouldn't ... he couldn't ... pick being alone over being with someone, even a sick someone.

"I never expected you to take care of me if I got really sick," I told him. "I'd never put anyone through the agony of watching me die. Down the road, when I reach the point of no return, I plan on simply leaving a note and then checking out in my own way." Alone. "I promise I'll leave before I get to that stage. Until then, I can't talk about it. Okay?"

"Look, I'm not trying to be cruel. We just need to face facts here."

"I get it. You want to go your own way. I understand."

I hoped he would argue with me. Or tell me that I'd misunderstood him and that we'd continue having each other's back for a while longer.

"Okay." He returned to his paperback.

Numbly, I walked into my bedroom and closed the door.

21

THE NEXT MORNING, NEITHER of us mentioned last night's painful conversation, but I felt Jase constantly watching me.

At breakfast, I became nauseous and, ten minutes later, threw up my cereal. Fortunately, I felt better afterward, although weak.

Jase heard me vomiting. When I left the bathroom, his face was tight. Closed down.

I sensed him distancing himself even further from me.

Aware of this, I tried to hide the growing despair in my eyes by wearing a pair of huge sunglasses.

At my request, we stopped by my old apartment. The place had been ransacked, but only the cans of food had been taken, probably by other survivors. Shrugging, I gathered some clothes, photos, and mementos. I also packed my *Lakmé* CD and my crystal starburst on a gold chain; these birthday gifts were the last things Dad had ever given me.

After braiding my hair and pinning it up, I pulled on my father's old aviator hat and leather jacket, gaining a bit of comfort from the familiar and much-loved items.

In our storage area, I wheeled out my father's well-maintained Honda motorcycle and insisted Jase teach me to ride it.

"Why?" he asked, puzzled by my sudden demand.

Stalling for time, I tucked the items gathered from my apartment into the bike's saddlebags.

My father had promised me lessons for my sixteenth birthday; we had dreamed of traveling along country roads with the wind in our hair and the sun on our faces. That would never happen now. I knew Dad was gone. Still, if I could race down a few city streets on his Honda, through the cold wind and wintry sunshine, maybe I'd feel a little closer to my father, if only for a short while.

Again Jase asked, "Why do you want to learn to ride a motorcycle?"

I couldn't share my private thoughts with him. Not anymore. Instead, I quietly answered, "So I can have another way of traveling around the city when you leave."

Avoiding my gaze, he quickly explained the Honda's instruments and controls. Two hours later, after a couple of solo rides, I felt confident with the bike.

"I think I'll ride the Honda today." I couldn't bear sitting in a car with him.

He seemed relieved. "Okay. Good." He nodded at a dusty Harley-Davidson at the curb. "I'll take that."

Barely looking at each other, we rode our motorcycles to Central Park, which topped the day's list of places to search.

I used to love the park. It had been my second-favorite place in New York, after the Statue of Liberty with its symbolism of freedom, equality—and hope.

Leaving the bikes, we silently walked through the overgrown grounds and stopped by the Pond. A wide ring of pink flowers floated around its edges, and the air was heavy with a scent similar to gardenias. Breathing deeply, I inhaled the perfume, reveling in its beauty after the distress of last night's conversation with Jase.

The floating blooms resembled peonies, with feathery petals that waved and beckoned as though longing to be caressed. In the past, some people had released their tension by stroking their pets' fur. With no cats or dogs around, I sought comfort in these flowers, and I bent to pick one.

Jase shoved me away.

"Ouch!" I cried. "What are you doing?"

"Look." He gestured to a white dog floating among the flowers. Strangely, it didn't have the agonized expression of a drowned animal. Its muzzled face appeared relaxed, as though the dog had simply drifted into a gentle, eternal sleep.

Bewildered, I asked, "The Red Fever?"

"The Red Fever doesn't kill animals."

We walked along the edge of the Pond and saw more bodies floating on the pink blossoms. Most were animals. The others were two old men and a middle-aged woman. All had relaxed expressions on their dead faces.

"It's the pink flowers." I shivered. "They're terras."

"Highly poisonous and fast-acting, by the looks of it. None of the people or animals seem to have struggled at all."

Had the three people deliberately chosen the quick and painless death of the flowers over the harsher battle to stay alive?

I'd almost touched the deadly plants. How could I have been so stupid?

In the past, my fingertips had been bloodied by the tiny razor-sharp plants that had coated the Brooklyn Bridge, and I'd felt the heat generated by the small plants in Brooklyn Grace Hospital. Not every terra was dangerous, but until I knew which ones were safe and which were deadly, I needed to be more careful.

I muttered to Jase, "Thanks for saving—"

Terrified shouts rang from further up the park.

22

JASE AND I WITHDREW our guns. Gripped them in our gloved hands. Glanced at each other.

"This could be a trap, Jase."

"Yeah." He avoided my gaze. "Or some people are in trouble. We should check it out."

I wondered if he wanted to help them out of the goodness of his heart—or because he wanted to find a group to join.

Quietly, we ran through a grove of trees. We dodged terras that dangled from the branches like twisted snakes, and we skirted rocks and statues infested with bizarre outgrowths.

A few minutes later, we paused at the edge of a massive field.

Sheep Meadow was covered by large patches of saucer-sized flowers. A few inches high and tightly packed together, the blossoms resembled lotuses, and their intoxicating fragrance filled the air.

They were terras. Amazingly beautiful terras.

Although a cloud-clogged sky now muted the day's sunshine, the blooms were luminous, as though glowing from small internal lights. They rioted across the ground in sapphire blues, iridescent reds, glittering golds and greens and violets.

At the edge of the field, four people huddled together, staring at a child lying on the flowers.

Shoving our guns into our waistbands, we ran across to them.

"What's going on?" Jase demanded. His gaze flickered to a pretty teenager with flowing black hair. Tears trailing down her cheeks, she trembled as she gazed at the fallen child.

A gray-faced man in his forties wheezed in distress. "It's Melanie, my niece. They got her."

"Who got her?" I asked.

"The flowers." A woman in her twenties turned to us. She wore a necklace with the name *Sophie* on it, and she fidgeted with the piece of jewelry. "We were cutting across the park," she told us, agitated. "The kids saw these flowers and got excited. Rebecca tried to stop them." She gestured to the black-haired teen who was still trembling in shock. "But they just ran into the field."

Confused, I looked at the child lying on the blossoms.

Had this little girl, Melanie, fallen over? Was she hurt?

I moved forward to help her.

The fourth person, a little boy about ten, shoved me back. "You can't go in there, lady. You'll die, just like Danny. Rick tried to help him"—he glanced at the middle-aged man—"but it was too late."

"What are you talking about?" I asked.

He pointed.

I turned. *Oh no.*

Another child lay nearby. His small body rested on the blooms like an Indian raja on a flowered deathbed.

The luminescent plants threw off so much light that the boy, Danny, appeared lit by colored globes. From his blank eyes, frozen face, and the blood around his mouth, he was clearly dead. A couple of dozen blossoms lay on his body, like clods of dirt thrown onto a coffin by mourners at a funeral.

The man, Rick, gestured to the little girl lying nearby. "Melanie's dead too. They kill you within a couple of minutes."

I thought of the peony-like pink blooms on the Pond. Beautiful but lethal. Just like these lotus-like flowers.

"Hey. Get away from those things." A youth with a backpack hurried across to us.

Behind my large sunglasses, my eyes widened in surprise.

It was Asher Weston. Not the Asher Weston I'd seen at the airport weeks ago, kissing his actress girlfriend, Willow Grace. That boy had been smartly dressed in an expensive white shirt, tailored pants, flashy watch.

This Asher Weston wore crumpled chinos, a torn brown shirt, and battered boots. A rifle hung over one shoulder, a machete over the other. He had a pistol and a large hunting knife strapped to his thighs, and I guessed that his bulging backpack contained other weapons.

Asher Weston's clothes may have changed for the worse, but he seemed even more good-looking and dynamic than before.

The scene from the airport flashed through my mind.

His tenderness. That kiss. The love it conveyed.

I glanced at Jase, a tiny knife twisting in my heart. For over a year, I'd daydreamed about Charlotte's boyfriend, guiltily imagining scenes where he would realize I was the only girl in the world for him. Recently, he'd made his own feelings quite clear. Even if I were the only girl left in the world, he still wouldn't want me.

And I no longer wanted him—not romantically, at least. Jase's shining image as a popular athlete and class president was just that: an image. Now, he seemed weak, selfish, even a little cowardly.

However, being with him was still better than being alone.

Jase watched Asher Weston with the wariness of a dog sizing up a potential rival. For the past couple of years, Jase had ruled the social scene at our school. With the arrival of this attractive stranger, some of his old sense of entitlement had resurfaced.

Asher dropped his backpack on the ground and leaned his rifle and machete against it.

He strode to the edge of the flowers and assessed the situation. Then he ran his fingers through blond locks that seemed more sun-streaked than when I'd seen him a few weeks ago.

"Are the kids dead?" he asked Rick.

Gee, zero points for subtlety, I thought.

The man, Rick, nodded. "Yeah."

"You sure?"

"It's been six minutes," Rick replied.

"It only takes two," Asher said.

"I know."

"Good." He spoke with a sexy Aussie accent, and I remembered his Australian roots. "At least you knew enough not to walk into the flowers."

The little boy shot me a pointed look. "Most of us did."

The teenage girl, Rebecca, finally spoke. "It's not her fault," she said, referring to me. "She might not know about these plants and how they kill." She shook her head, and her long black locks gleamed in a stray sunbeam.

Jase stepped forward, squaring his shoulders. "There was nothing I could do. I got here too late."

I, not *we*. He was continuing to distance himself from me.

"Well, you can do something now. All of you." Asher rummaged in his pack and withdrew several long sticks topped with clumps of rags. "You can help me turn this field into a scene out of that old war movie, *Apocalypse Now*." He gave a dry laugh. "Fitting title."

He withdrew a small can of gasoline and poured fuel over each stick, saturating the rags. All evidence of the teenager I'd seen at the airport—the loving and tender boyfriend of Willow Grace—had vanished. The boy in front of me was serious, focused, intent.

Jase and I shucked off our backpacks and dropped them on the grass.

"What do you do?" I asked Asher Weston, curious. "Roam the city, searching for strangers to help you burn terras?"

He looked at me without the slightest trace of recognition on his face. Not surprising. Why would he remember someone from a crowded airport terminal several weeks ago? Besides, my auburn hair was now bundled inside an old aviator hat, and a huge pair of sunglasses hid half my face. Even my father would've had trouble recognizing me.

"Nope," he replied. "My colleague, Harlem, usually helps me burn them."

"Oh." I pointed north. "If you're after dangerous terras, try the Pond. It's got these floating pink flowers that look poisonous."

"I know. They're on my list, along with dozens of other terras."

Dozens? The city was even more dangerous than I realized.

Asher's blue eyes narrowed as he surveyed us. "I'm always looking for newcomers to join my group. I especially need fighters."

The man, Rick, shook his head. "We're not interested."

"Are you sure? You haven't even heard what I can offer: a place to live and food to eat. You just have to pass a short interview."

"Interview?" Rick snorted. "What are you? Some sort of elite community?"

"I've built up a small community, but we're not elitist. I'm just careful who we accept. We're—"

"Not interested." Rick turned away.

"What about the rest of you?" Asher asked, swiveling his gaze. "Anyone want to join my group?"

I longed to say yes, but I was too sick to be a fighter. If Jase was going to abandon me, I'd need to find a group of ordinary people to join. People like Rick and his friends.

I expected Jase to jump at Asher's offer. To my surprise, he remained as silent as the others.

Asher gave a disappointed shrug. "Fine." He turned to the little boy, who was eying the gasoline-drenched sticks. "You're too young to handle fire, kid."

"My name's Corey and I'm not a kid. I'm ten and a half."

"Still too young. Wait over there. It's safer." Asher pointed to a grove of oaks.

Shoulders slumped, Corey stomped to the trees.

Further along the tree line, I noticed a familiar figure. Baseball cap, dark sunglasses, blue jeans, black jacket over a red plaid shirt.

Loner.
Still alive.
Still watching.
And still living up to his name.

23

Loner watched us, arms folded.

I didn't bother calling out to him and suggesting that he help us burn the terras. For whatever reason, he avoided other people and refused to get involved, no matter the situation.

Before the Mist, keeping to oneself was okay. Hermits and other antisocial citizens could survive with the assistance of welfare organizations and charities. But the world was different now. More dangerous. These days, people needed to band together for survival.

I wondered if Loner had ever heard of the John Donne quote: *No man is an island, entire of itself; every man is a piece of the continent, a part of the main.*

Asher handed the sticks around. As he ignited our torches, he told us what to do, finishing with, "Be careful. Those glow-lotus terras are lethal."

Glow-lotus?

I held the flame-topped stick away from my face, fighting off another attack of nausea. Lately, without my meds, my leukemia symptoms were getting worse.

Asher zeroed in on me. "You okay?"

I gulped down the foul taste that rose in my throat. I couldn't throw up now, not in front of everyone. How embarrassing.

Jase's lips tightened. A muscle twitched at the corner of his eye.

"I'm fine," I lied. Another gulp. Another lie: "The smell of the gasoline's making me ill."

"Really?" Asher said. "It's not that strong."

Talk about being perceptive.

And brave.

This son of an Australian billionaire, this rich and pampered teenager, clearly hadn't broken when his privileged world had disappeared. Instead, he'd gone into fight mode. It sounded like he'd studied the invaders, prepared lists—and then set about destroying the terras.

His David-and-Goliath battle with the invaders seemed to have changed him. In the past few years, whenever Asher Weston had given interviews on TV and social media, he'd looked unhappy and passive.

Now he appeared confident, determined, and in charge.

Like the rest of us, he had probably been devastated by the loss of his loved ones, including his girlfriend Willow Grace. Unlike the rest of us, he was the first person I'd seen who was actually fighting the terras.

The world had become a far more dangerous place. No doubt the terras threatened Asher's life every day, but at least he had the courage to fight back. And for that, I admired him.

I just wished I were well enough to join his battle.

"Take your positions," he ordered us.

The expanse of glow-lotuses had grassy trails between them, which we used to safely reach the middle of the large patch. Here we stood in a circle, facing outward. Each of us had an assigned section to burn.

"Start from the center," Asher told us. "Be careful. Use the grass trails as you head to the edge. Don't step on any flowers. Make sure you burn the plants on both sides of the trail. Wait for my signal ... *now*."

As I hurried to the outside of the field, I swept my burning torch from side to side, over the blossoms.

Once clear of the terras, I turned to watch the destruction.

Waves of flames began racing across the multicolored flowers. The fires dazzled in brilliant blues and yellows, glittering greens and reds, vivid purples, scarlets, pinks, and golds. Crackling and shimmering, they writhed upward like living blades of heat.

Fascinated, I watched the glow-lotus terras burn beneath this rainbow of flames. How could something so poisonous die so beautifully?

And then—

—the gates of hell suddenly cracked open.

The egg-shaped balls in the centers of the flowers exploded, expelling pockets of air that sounded like the tiny screams of doomed souls. Across the burning field, tens, hundreds, then thousands of little screams pierced the crackle of the fires. The hairs on my arm prickled and, suddenly anxious, I looked around, seeking the comfort of Jase's presence.

Was he still here? In all the racket of the fires and the glow-lotuses' screams, had he slipped away, abandoning me to these strangers?

Through some gaps in the flames, I saw him standing on the far side of the inferno.

I breathed a sigh of relief.

A scream—human—came from some glow-lotus terras near me.

The woman in her twenties, Sophie, was standing between some blazing flowers and an unburned patch. Arms flailing, almost hysterical with fear, she tried to beat off a cloud of brown embers.

I moved to help her.

A vague, queasy sensation wafted through me, and beads of sweat popped across my forehead. Ignoring the warning signs, I ran around the edge of the flaming field toward Sophie.

When I reached her, I realized that the cloud wasn't made up of embers after all.

It was a swarm of brown locusts.

The insects must've been sheltering under the flowers, and the flames had driven them from their hiding spots. They were attacking Sophie—or maybe they were trying to land on her, a safe place amid the growing flames.

"Get them off me," the woman cried. "I hate bugs! Get them off!"

I brushed the locusts from her clothes.

New ones landed on her.

Dozens of small hard-shelled bodies began crawling over me as well. Their thin barbed legs clung to my skin and hair, and I wanted to scream, but I was afraid they'd dart inside my open mouth. I'd heard that people in some cultures regarded these insects as delicacies and ate them—*Eww!*—but probably not alive.

More and more tiny bodies skittered over me, their stench drowning out the smell of smoke. I jerked in a circle. Brushed the things off. Wrenched them from my hair.

My nausea grew stronger.

Abruptly, the insects launched themselves into the air. They swirled in a brown swarm above the gushing smoke, then flew away. Only dead locusts remained, scattered on the ground.

Stunned, Sophie and I looked at each other as—

My stomach heaved, and I clasped a hand to my mouth. More nausea surged within me.

I stumbled forward, dizzy, and crashed into Sophie.

24

SHE STAGGERED. TOPPLED BACKWARD. Landed face-up on a patch of unburned glow-lotus terras.

"No!" I lunged for her.

A pair of strong arms darted from behind and wrapped themselves around my waist. "Stop!" Asher cried, pinning my body against his own. "It's too late."

Sophie's friends shouted as they raced toward us.

She lay motionless on the blooms, winded by her fall. Seconds later, her body jolted as though an electric shock pulsed through her, and she sank into the blossoms.

She screamed. Tried to sit up. Couldn't.

Something was pushing her down. No, *holding* her down.

I struggled in Asher's grip, but his arms seemed made of iron instead of flesh and bone.

Twisting around, I shouted, "Help her, Jase!"

But Jase turned away.

Asher tightened his hold on me. "No one can help her. We'd die too."

By the time the others arrived, Sophie's screams had stopped. She appeared dead—glazed eyes, gaping mouth—yet her bloodied body was still trembling.

My voice emerged in a croak of despair. "The plants poisoned her."

"Not poisoned." Asher unfurled his arms, slowly releasing me. "They speared her."

"What?" I looked down. Numerous pointy stems were sprouting from Sophie's torso, arms, and legs. Each stem opened into a spray of fat petals with an egg-sized center. The glowing flowers sprinkled her body, as though scattered by a careless wind.

I glanced at the bodies of Danny and Melanie.

Blossoms adorned the children's corpses as well.

The truth hit me with the impact of a hammer.

Hidden beneath the exquisite petals, the spearlike stamens lurked ... waiting. When someone stepped on them, the pressure triggered them into action, and they would shoot through the shoes, into the flesh. With the victim's feet suddenly pinned to the ground, the person would fall over. Other stamens would then spear the body, pushing through flesh and organs with incredible speed. Moments later, leaves and petals would sprout from the corpse, blooming like plants in a garden.

Oh no. I knocked Sophie into the deadly flowers.

Turning away, I vomited up my lunch. Again and again I heaved, until there was nothing left in my stomach.

Never had I felt so empty—physically and emotionally.

"How did this happen?" Asher asked.

Wiping flecks of vomit off my mouth, I faced him. I no longer felt empty. Guilt filled me, burning with the intensity of the nearby fire.

"I did it," I blurted out. "I felt dizzy. I stumbled and knocked her onto the flowers."

"You did this?" Asher gasped.

Jase snorted. "She's been feeling rotten all day. She's in the final stages of leukemia."

Aghast, I stared at him. How could he reveal my greatest secret to complete strangers? The next moment, shame flooded me. I'd just caused a woman's death. Who cared if they knew about my illness or not?

"I'm so sorry," I cried. "I never meant to hurt her." My gaze slid across the faces of the others, reading their shock and grief for Sophie.

The teenager, Rebecca, stood with her eyes closed, as though trying to block out the sight of her dead friend.

Asher's frown softened as his gaze swept over me. My thin body was clad in baggy pants and my father's leather jacket, which was too big for my slight frame. An old aviator hat hid my hair and ears, and a pair of huge sunglasses dominated my pale face.

"I'm sorry you're ill," he said gently. "What are you doing here if you're sick?"

"I ... I thought I could help."

"Well, you didn't." His voice held a strange resignation. Had he seen so many terrible things over the past few weeks that death no longer surprised him? After a last, sympathetic nod at me, he addressed the others. "Are you sure none of you wants to join my group?"

Silence.

"Fine." He glanced at his watch. "I have to meet my team." He passed his lit torch to Jase. "Make sure you burn this last patch of glow-lotuses."

Jase glanced at Sophie's body. "What about her?"

"It's too dangerous to move her. Burn her as well."

Asher's words sounded harsh and heartless, yet I suspected he was simply being practical. He slung the rifle and machete over his shoulders, shrugged on his backpack, and hurried away.

Jase gripped the burning torch. He'd told me that he wanted to belong to a group. Would he run after Asher and ask to join his team of fighters? At seventeen, he was strong, fit, and healthy. He'd be a perfect candidate.

Scowling, Jase used Asher's flaming torch to ignite the last patch of flowers. When he finished, he threw the burning torch into the fire.

That gesture was his decision.

Jase didn't want to battle terras every day. He didn't want to enlist as a soldier in a growing war.

Was he being smart? Or a coward?

He refused to look at me.

In silence, we watched the blazing funeral pyre. The multicolored flames snapped and crackled as they devoured the little boy Danny, the girl Melanie, and the woman Sophie.

I took off my sunglasses and brushed off a locust crawling across the lenses.

"There are two bugs on your hat," Rebecca told me.

I removed my aviator hat, swept the locusts away, then jammed my hat and sunglasses back on. Automatically, I pushed my shoulder-length auburn hair back beneath the hat, out of sight.

When Rick, Corey, and Rebecca began to walk away, Jase called to them, "Wait."

Rick turned, his middle-aged face creased with sorrow. "What?"

"Where are you going?"

"To meet some other survivors. We've got four vans waiting on the far side of the park. A group of us—fifteen now—is heading south to Florida. We've heard it's better down there; not as many of these freaky plants." Rick watched Jase with an appraising stare. "You're welcome to join us."

My heart leaped. Florida sounded much safer than New York. Plus we'd be with other people.

Jase asked Rick, "What about her?" He jerked his head in my direction.

The middle-aged man regarded me sadly. "Girl, I know you didn't mean to kill Sophie. It was an accident. You've got leukemia, and for that I'm sorry. But I've got folks to take care of, and not enough meds as it is. We just don't have room for someone as sick as you. Thing is, you'll be a burden and a danger to us."

Dismayed, I searched for some words to argue with the truth. Found none.

I swallowed. Blinked back my disappointment. Nodded.

Rick flicked a glance at Jase. "Coming?" Without waiting for an answer, he took the little boy's hand and set off across the park again.

Rebecca lingered a few steps behind. She twirled a lock of her long dark hair as she tilted her head at Jase, her lips parted in a silent question.

He shouldered his backpack and turned away from me. "Sorry, Kass." Without a backward glance, he ran to catch up with Rebecca.

Stunned, I watched the pair walk away from me. Maybe they'd change their minds and wave for me to join them. *I'll leave before I get really ill*, I mentally promised them.

When they disappeared into a group of distant trees, I knew they weren't coming back.

I looked around.

Loner was gone too.

Trembling, I stood next to the field of blazing glow-lotus terras.

Alone.

25

PINK DEATH FLOATED ON the Pond, seductive in its promise of eternal peace.

Standing on a footbridge that crossed part of the Pond, I gazed down at the pink flowers on the water below.

After Jase had left, I'd forced myself to return to our parked motorcycles. I'd wanted to take another ride on Dad's Honda, cruising down empty streets, through the wind and the sunshine.

Except clouds had smothered the sunshine.

And the Honda's saddlebags had been ransacked.

Someone had tossed my stuff onto the ground, smashing most of my mementos. The glass in my picture frame was cracked and, hands shaking, I pulled out the photo of my family and tucked it into a pocket.

I searched the sidewalk for my father's last gifts to me: a CD of the opera *Lakmé* and my crystal starburst necklace.

Both were gone.

In a city cluttered with millions of ownerless items, a passing survivor had thought my possessions were fair game. Abandoned. Like me.

Numbly I returned to the Pond and wandered onto the Gapstow Bridge, thinking about the events of the past few weeks—and my future.

It was bleak.

A little while ago, I'd applied a John Donne quote to Loner. *No man is an island, entire of itself; every man is a piece of the continent, a part of the main.*

But the quote also applied to me with brutal force.

I wasn't an island.

I needed people in my life, but they no longer wanted or needed me.

My illness had caused Sophie's death by the glow-lotus terras, a tragic accident whose guilt would haunt me for the rest of my life. Since I was clearly sick, any other groups I met in the coming weeks would fear they'd have to nurse me, and they'd reject me too.

All my family and friends were dead.

I was sixteen. Terminally ill. Weak.

And alone.

My future loomed dark and bleak.

My leukemia felt like an ugly fire that was slowly searing my body. I knew I could go back to the apartment and live off my canned food for months, waiting for the disease to burn through me until I died.

Or I could force myself to search New York for more meds.

My oncologist, Dr. McKay, was old school, and his paper files would probably contain the names and addresses of other patients in the city. Their meds might extend my life for a few more weeks. All I had to do was drive around New York and search each of their homes and offices—by myself.

In the distance, a volley of gunshots and shouts splintered the silence. Elsewhere, a lion roared in response.

I looked down at the pink flowers floating on the Pond. Soft. Enticing. Lethal.

Sure, I could drive around the city searching for meds. But I'd be prey for the Wilder bikers ... the hungry animals ... the dangerous plants ...

If any of them got me, my death would be violent and painful.

Or I could end it all now. Quickly. Painlessly. Permanently.

I climbed onto the side of the Gapstow Bridge and sat on the wide parapet. My legs dangled over the pink flowers that waited below, their petal-mouths open and inviting.

Jump, I told myself.

Jump.

I hesitated as the hairs at the back of my neck prickled. Was someone watching me?

Turning, I scanned the trees but didn't see anyone.

I was still alone.

Taking a deep, trembling breath, I began to lean forward and—

Music poured through the air. Not just any music, but the "Flower Duet" from the opera *Lakmé*.

I straightened with shock as the two sopranos' voices blended in a joyous celebration of life. The magnificent piece wrapped me in its beauty, and I sat on the side of the bridge, listening to the angelic singing. Transfixed, some of the tension leached from my body.

Was this the *Lakmé* CD, the one my father had given me? The one taken from my saddlebag?

It had to be.

I guessed how the opera was being transmitted: someone must've used a back-up generator to power the emergency loudspeaker system across the city.

I didn't know who was playing the music. Or why.

The unknown person played the song over and over again, as if mesmerized by the music. And as I listened, I finally felt the icy weight of my despair melt as my soul began to soar. Mixed with this euphoria was a sharp sense of loss. *Dad. Olivia. Charlotte.*

As the song faded into silence, a squirrel raced along the edge of the bridge's parapet. It paused a couple of feet from me and sat on its haunches. Fluffy tail curling upward, it regarded me with bright silver eyes.

"Hello, little cutie," I murmured. "What are you doing here?"

It chittered a squirrel response.

"Huh! Your eyes are silver, too, just like that eagle, Wind-Lord. Weird."

Another chitter.

To my surprise, the small creature sat beside me for a few minutes, as though enjoying the view and my company. Finally, it whirled around and scampered off. I smiled, comforted by its brief visit.

At a squawk, I glanced up.

The sky was still red, but this time the color wasn't a bloodied stain. The clouds were brushed from a palette of scarlet, gold, and pink.

I exhaled in wonder. A real sunset. The first one we'd had since the Mist.

Overhead, a large eagle wheeled against the brilliant sky, then dived toward the Pond and glided past me—and I caught a glimpse of silver eyes. WindLord. This was the golden eagle that had saved Jase and me from a grizzly bear. As I watched the bird disappear into a nearby clump of Earth trees, I finally realized that my world still existed in many places.

Life was still beautiful.

But was it worth living?

My father's words echoed in my mind.

Keep fighting, Kass. Your future isn't written in stone. Things can change at any time, so be prepared. Be alive. Don't go quietly into that deep night.

I had promised Dad to keep fighting, no matter what. He'd be so disappointed in me if he knew I'd given up.

With a sigh, I slowly climbed down from the parapet.

Standing on the Gapstow Bridge, I watched the spectacular sunset, knowing I'd be seeing more of them in the future. And more sunrises, too—although I had no idea that so many of those future red dawns would be blood-soaked.

On my left, someone was hurrying down a path that led to my bridge.

I stiffened, alert for danger.

Something about the way the person moved caught my attention. My heart pounded in my chest.

The person stopped. Stared at me. Raced forward—to me.

Frozen, I stared back.

And then I was running. Running for my life, for reborn hope, for the sense of belonging ...

... for my sister.

26

WE MET IN A joyous embrace at the end of the bridge, our hug filled with happiness and relief and tears.

"Via!"

"Kass!"

I peered down the path behind her. "Dad?"

She shook her head. "It was quick."

"Good." I blinked back fresh tears and looked at my sister.

Olivia was no longer the image of a sun-kissed Californian beauty.

A dark woolen beanie hid her hair, except for a long auburn braid that hung over one shoulder. Streaks of grease marred her face. Baggy navy coveralls camouflaged her figure. A rifle dangled from her right shoulder.

What had happened during her trip across the country?

She grabbed my hand and pulled me down the path. "Hurry. We've got to go."

"Where?"

"A friend of Dad's used to work at Grand Central Station. He was a doomsday prepper. Before he died of cancer last year, he told Dad about this abandoned bunker hidden in the subway. Apparently, he'd stocked it with survivalist stuff like a generator, oil, bunks, blankets, even boxes of canned food." She swung onto a track that veered left. "Dad drew me a map of its location."

"Why can't we just stay at Aunt Suzanne's place?"

"So Aunt Suzanne and Charlotte are okay too?"

I swallowed. "No. They're gone."

"I'm sorry," she said, increasing her pace. "Is that where you've been staying? At their apartment? I've been looking for you for three days."

"I left a big note on the fridge at home, saying I was with them."

"I didn't find it. Every apartment in your building's been ransacked. I had Aunt Suzanne's address on my phone but it's been dead for weeks."

The wind howled across the park, battering branches into frenzied swaying.

"Why are we going into a bunker?" I asked, hurrying beside her. "There are millions of empty apartments in New York. We can stay in any of them."

"Dad made me promise to take you belowground."

"But it's winter. It'll be cold down there, Via."

"It'll only be winter for a couple more months. Besides, there's an oil heater in the bunker and a barrel of oil in a nearby cutting." She glanced at me. "Dad thinks we'll be safer there, away from the red mist."

"But the red mist's gone. There's even a normal sunset today."

However, when I looked at the sky, all traces of the glorious sunset had vanished. Greeny-yellow clouds stretched overhead in weird, bubbling layers, like massive pustules ready to burst.

My skin prickled.

I sensed something terrible was about to happen.

Still gripping my hand, Olivia ran. In my weakened state, I struggled to keep up with her.

"We need to get belowground." Fear filled my twin's voice. "The red mist has gone, but something else has arrived. He told me it was coming."

"What's coming? Who told you? Dad?"

"A boy. I met him a few minutes ago when I was looking for you. He knew things. Terrible things." Olivia turned onto a path that led across the park. "He warned me to get to safety immediately."

And yet my sister had stayed outdoors, searching for me.

We dodged cabbage-sized terras on the ground and avoided sharp-edged orange vines that snaked between branches.

"What boy?" I asked. "What did he look like?"

"Some guy named Rock. White T-shirt. Old jeans. About our age. He was from Canada. Do you know him?"

"Rock? No, I don't think so."

She withdrew a couple of flashlights from her pocket and shoved one at me. "Come on. We need to get to safety."

By the time we reached the nearest subway entrance, the roiling greeny-yellow clouds appeared to be boiling and the air vibrated with a hidden threat. My pulse quickened in dread. This oncoming storm promised to be strange and savage.

A fierce wind sprang up. Screaming, it rampaged down the street, vicious in its bitter chill. It shook parked cars in fury, swept books from a sidewalk stall, and tossed debris high into the air.

Above, the putrid clouds whirred and buzzed. Something was inside the weird bubbles. And it was about to break free.

Heart thudding, I threw one last look at the empty, battered city. Then, switching on my flashlight, I trailed Olivia down the steps of the subway entrance.

I paused in the mouth of an old tunnel, my nose crinkling at a foul smell.

Ignoring the stench, Olivia studied a hand-drawn map in the beam of her flashlight. She pointed left. "This way, Kass."

I hesitated. How could we live in an old underground bunker? How would we survive in a place of shadows and foul air and whispered sounds?

Shivering, I followed Olivia into the cold darkness.

ASHER

A life lived looking back
Is a life half lived

27

DAY ZERO—Thanksgiving

NEW YORK

THERE WAS NO HINT that an apocalypse was about to start. No shiver of warning to spoil the moment.

Instead, as Asher Weston gazed across the underwater lounge of the luxury yacht, he had a sudden realization. This laughing girl sitting cross-legged on a Persian rug, playing jacks with his little brother, was not simply his girlfriend.

Willow Grace was the love of his life.

Kind and gentle, she was using her acting skills to convince the delighted eight-year-old that he was beating her, even though Asher knew she was skilled at the game.

She glanced over and saw him watching her.

"Are you okay, Ash?" she asked softly.

"I'm fine." He smiled at the violet-eyed blonde.

Last week, his girlfriend had been voted Most Popular Teenage Actress. To her adoring public, seventeen-year-old Willow Grace was the beautiful and talented star of *Pandora*, a hit paranormal series. To disabled persons and animal lovers, she was a tireless crusader for their causes.

To Asher, she was love, joy, and warmth. Wherever she went, she seemed to bring a glow to the air, as though she were reflecting sunshine.

And to his amazement, this incredible girl loved him as much as he loved her.

His smile vanished as his father stormed into the lounge, wearing his usual scowl.

Asher tensed, alert for trouble.

"What are you three doing down here?" Rufus Weston snapped, his eyes shark-cold. "Get upstairs and join our guests. Everyone's on deck waiting for the fireworks to begin."

Asher glanced at his watch. "I thought they weren't starting for another half hour." The yacht had dropped anchor in the ocean a mile east of Staten Island. By now the crew would be preparing to launch his father's Thanksgiving fireworks.

"They'll start whenever I give the order." Rufus shifted his glare to Tommy. "Your nanny's been looking for you for ten minutes, you little brat."

The small boy sat frozen, jacks in hand, face paling.

Asher saw Willow's lips press together as she fought to remain silent. She hated cruelty of any sort, whether to people or animals. However, she'd learned that springing to Tommy's defense would only make things worse.

Violet eyes shadowing, she wrapped a protective arm around the child's shoulders.

Asher stepped forward, hoping to turn his father's focus onto himself.

"We were just admiring the view." He gestured to the immense window in the submerged hull. "It's incredible." Stroking his father's ego sometimes deflected his rage.

This time it worked.

"It should be incredible. That bloody thing cost me a fortune."

Despite the man's harsh tone, Asher knew his father was proud of the underwater lounge.

On the other side of the clear glass, powerful lights flooded the saltwater with brightness. Hundreds of fish darted through a vivid blue world, attracted by the food a crew member was covertly dropping overboard; the Australian billionaire didn't want his guests looking through his enormous submerged windows and seeing only empty water.

Beyond the brightness, Asher glimpsed a shape darting through the shadows. Large. Dark. Fast.

A second later, it was gone.

Had he imagined it?

Rufus Weston snatched up a box of Cuban cigars from a marble coffee table. "I want you three on deck now." He focused on his older son. "There are some CEOs you need to meet."

Asher suppressed a sigh. His father's parties were always the same—full of ruthless people clawing for money and power. He loathed these events. Loathed his father's business world. Loathed the blackmail responsible for chaining him to this life.

If it wasn't for Tommy, he would've fled this nightmare years ago. Instead, he'd stayed to protect his little brother.

From the corner of his eye, he glimpsed another dark shape flashing through the water. His skin tingled, sensing something unseen. Unknown. Deadly.

Turning from the window, he calmly met his father's glare. "We'll be there in a few minutes." He knew he was playing with fire. His father wanted him on deck *now*, not in a few minutes. Still, he'd had enough of the man's bullying for today. He needed to stand up to the thug, even if only for a short while.

Rufus Weston's scowl deepened, but to Asher's relief he simply took his box of cigars and stomped from the lounge. Perhaps the presence of his guests had stopped him from launching into another barrage of shouts and ugly promises.

However, Asher knew he'd be punished later. At least he no longer owned any pets. He'd given away his beloved Labrador two years ago, after learning that his father had planned to kill the dog as Asher's punishment for missing an annual shareholders' meeting.

Tommy's face tightened with a familiar anxiety. "I'd better find Ella before Father fires her." He loved his nanny, the latest in a long line, and he fretted at the thought of losing her.

Tommy hurried from the room and closed the door behind him, putting a barrier between his big brother and their father. Asher smiled sadly; in his own way, his little brother was trying to protect *him*.

Muffled explosions came from above.

Surprised, he looked up, toward the deck. "Sounds like the fireworks have started, Willow."

Thud-thud.

Startled, he turned to the hull window. "*What—?*"

Outside, the hundreds of small fish had vanished.

A great white shark loomed beyond the glass.

28

The underwater window was huge, yet the shark seemed to fill it. Asher guessed it was about eighteen feet long and over two thousand pounds.

Willow gasped and rushed to his side. Instinctively, he stepped in front of her, shielding her as she peered over his shoulder. "Are we safe in here, Ash?"

"Definitely. The window is unbreakable."

According to a documentary he'd seen during Shark Week, the great whites' teeth, muscles, and strength had helped the species survive since the age of the dinosaurs. Scientists regarded these predators as triumphs of nature.

Asher regarded them as white death.

At the sight of the great white shark, his first instinct had been to run.

But he refused to flee.

He forced himself to face the terror born of his recent near-death experience.

A month ago, he had visited Willow at a film set in Cape Town. While there, he'd decided to try an extreme adventure, hoping its adrenaline rush would help reduce his stress and his growing resentment of his father.

Cage diving off the coast of South Africa had seemed perfect.

But the experience had almost killed him.

A great white shark—attracted by the natural electrical field given off by Asher's metal cage—had smashed through the thin bars and wedged itself halfway into his enclosure. There it struggled in fury, its razor-toothed jaws inches from his body. Since sharks couldn't swim backward, he'd realized that he needed to escape before it destroyed the cage and ripped him in half.

The moment the flailing mass of white death had twisted away, he'd scrambled through a gap in the bars and shot to the surface.

Asher still had nightmares about the incident—and how helpless he'd felt.

Every day he worked with his father, he felt that same helplessness, that same sense of being trapped in a cage with a savage shark.

Outside the hull window, four more great whites swam into view. He'd heard that scientists called this gathering a "shiver" of sharks. Excellent description, he thought, his skin prickling.

"What are they all doing here?" Willow whispered.

"Feeding on the fish that my father, in his wisdom, has lured to the yacht."

"I didn't think sharks came this close to New York."

"Sometimes they do. According to a documentary I saw, great whites are common along the East Coast. Scientists believe they occasionally follow schools of fish much closer to the shore than anyone ever suspected. In fact, they—"

He paused.

Dozens of red dots were falling through the water, sparkling like stardust.

Willow stood beside Asher, watching the sharks swim among the sinking red dots. "Are those sparks from the fireworks?"

"I don't think so. They would've gone out the moment they hit the water."

The liquid blue world was speckled with hundreds of dots, each glittering as it drifted past the hull window and sank into the depths.

One by one, the sharks began thrashing and flailing. Some whirled around like mad dogs chasing their tails. Others slammed against each other or darted through the water in wild zigzags.

"What's wrong with them, Ash?"

Again, he drew on his hours spent watching the Shark Week documentaries. "Great whites have special glands on their snouts that can detect electrical fields as small as one-billionth of a volt. If those red dots are giving off even the tiniest amounts of electricity, it could be enough to screw up the sharks' senses and drive them wild."

Growing more violent, the great whites churned the water in a riot of thrashing bodies.

Asher's heartbeat raced.

His girlfriend buried her face in his chest. "They're going crazy."

"I know." As he wrapped his arms around Willow's slim waist, his racing heartbeat began to slow. Her mere presence was always enough to calm him and make him feel better.

He hugged her a little closer, wanting to hold her in his arms forever.

They'd been friends since they had met in kindergarten. Over the years, his feelings had slowly deepened into love, but he'd remained silent as Willow's acting career had soared. Then, last Christmas, she'd confessed her love for him, and they'd dated ever since.

The past year had been the happiest of his life.

"Ash!" she gasped, staring at the hull window.

A great white had ripped a chunk of flesh from another shark. As blood gushed from the gaping wound, it triggered a mass attack by the other sharks.

The blue world beyond the window quickly became a bat-tlefield.

Amid this bloodbath, the strange red dots still glittered as they passed by, uncaring of the chaos around them.

The wounded shark slammed against the glass, leaving a hideous red smear.

Willow shuddered.

"Come on. Let's get out of here." He hurried her up the stairs that led to the deck, away from the bloodied world below ...

... and into a world where the night sky was bleeding from thousands of red dots.

29

Something was wrong.

Asher could feel it. It was more than the acrid smell that had lingered in the air since the Night of the Red Mist last week. The media's name for the strange event was less frightening than his own description of it: the Night of the Bleeding Sky.

Following the mist's arrival, governments everywhere had grounded their planes across the planet. His father had spent days trying to reorganize business meetings and conferences.

Finally, the red mist had cleared.

The US government believed the phenomenon had been caused by billions of non-terrestrial seeds that had floated through space in huge balls; as they'd entered the atmosphere, the balls had broken up, releasing the seeds.

Now, five days later, the planes were flying again.

And Willow was leaving for Los Angeles this morning.

As Asher accompanied her through the crowded airport terminal, he noticed a strange sight. Dozens of people were holding bloodied handkerchiefs to their noses.

He frowned. Why were there so many nosebleeds today?

Nearby, a mounted screen showed images of an African village destroyed by a locust swarm. Sixteen dead. Twenty-seven injured.

His frown deepened. How could locusts kill people?

Willow paused near a food court, worried. "Do you think Tommy will be okay?" Two hours ago, they'd waved goodbye to his little brother, who was on a flight to a language camp in Europe.

Asher already missed his brother, and he hated the thought of the boy being stuck on a plane with their father. Fortunately, Rufus Weston was traveling in first class, while Tommy and his nanny were in coach; Asher knew the pair would happily play games, watch movies, and snack on forbidden junk food for the entire flight.

"He'll be fine. His nanny will stay with him in Germany, and they'll fly home in ten days, when Tommy's language camp is over."

"Why's your father flying commercial? I thought he'd take the jet."

"It's got engine troubles. Normally he'd postpone his trip, but he has wall-to-wall meetings in England for the next two weeks."

"That sounds terrible. And this is the life he's grooming you for?"

"Unfortunately, yes."

Until five years ago, Asher's older brother, Dylan, had been slotted to take over the business. When Dylan and their mother had died in a plane crash, Rufus Weston had presented Asher with a harsh choice: give up his friends, sports, interests, and start learning about his father's empire. If he refused, his little brother would have to start learning the business in a few years' time.

Asher couldn't bear the thought of Tommy being forced into such a grueling life, so he'd reluctantly bowed to his father's demands.

His attention strayed to a strange scene in the airport terminal. A couple of sniffer dogs—sweet, docile beagles—were huddled together, refusing to obey their handlers' instructions. The animals whimpered in fear as they sniffed the air.

He glanced around uneasily. Hundreds of people were in the terminal. Everything seemed normal.

What was spooking the dogs?

Softly Willow said, "I'm going to miss you."

His gaze shifted from the frightened dogs to her. The tender words he'd planned for their parting suddenly vanished as he gathered her into his arms.

"Don't go, Willow. Stay here today and leave tomorrow."

He sensed something was wrong ... or about to go wrong.

Or maybe, since the Night of the Red Mist, the world just felt ... wrong.

"I can't stay. I have two important meetings in LA this afternoon. Later, I'm having my hair dyed red for my new movie."

Sighing, he looked around, searching for the source of his unease.

At the far end of the terminal, a tower of scaffolding stood below a hole in the high ceiling. Patches of green non-terrestrial plants covered the ceiling tiles, and a maintenance worker stood on the scaffold's metal platform, scrubbing at the strange vegetation with a long-handled brush. On the floor, another worker scraped patches of non-terrestrial plants off the tiles.

He walked his girlfriend to the edge of the security area. Trying to ignore his unease, he said, "Promise you'll be careful. I'm a bit worried about these terras."

"Terras?"

"That's what people are starting to call these non-terrestrial plants."

"Oh. Shorter name. I get it. You be careful around them too." She glanced at a digital clock on the wall. "I'd better go. My assistant's probably pacing the departure lounge, ready to send out a search party for me."

He cupped her face with his hands. "I'll try to visit you in LA next week."

"That'd be great."

After a final tender embrace and a kiss goodbye, he watched Willow walk down a corridor and disappear around a corner.

As Asher turned to leave, he noticed a teenage girl standing nearby. Over the years, he'd become used to members of the public staring at him in awe or envy, impressed by his family's fame and money. Most of the time, he ignored the unwelcome attention.

But this girl was watching him with a soft, wistful expression. Absently, she touched a large crystal starburst that hung around her neck.

She looked about sixteen years old. Shoulder-length auburn hair. Large green eyes. Pale skin. Her slender figure held a strange fragility—and he had the curious notion that she was a delicate blossom struggling to survive in a fast-paced and uncaring world.

All thoughts of the girl vanished as another news report flashed across a mounted screen. This one showed areas of green vegetation growing inside a skyscraper.

He shook his head in disbelief. How could these plants—these terras—grow in concrete and carpets? He'd always thought seeds needed soil to grow. Yet these things were flourishing everywhere, and they'd grown incredibly fast in the six days since their arrival.

Willow's flight was scheduled to leave in an hour, so he decided to wait in one of the terminal's cafés, drinking sodas while catching up on news stories about the terras. One channel featured multiple reports of strange behavior in animals across the planet. His brow knotted, remembering the battling sharks outside his father's yacht last week. Had the red seeds caused their weird behavior?

A few minutes before 11 a.m., he crossed to the wall of windows that overlooked the runways.

He raised a hand in farewell as Willow's plane thundered down the tarmac and lifted into the air.

A surge of loss filled him. Her two months on location already felt like an eternity. Would his father allow him to copilot one of Weston Enterprises' small private planes to LA next week? After all, he'd earned his helicopter license over a year ago, and by his seventeenth birthday he'd clocked over a hundred hours of flying and—

He froze.

Stepped closer to the glass.

Stared at a darkness in the distance.

30

A BLACK CLOUD HAD appeared at the far end of the runway.

The strange mass spread across part of the hazy red sky—directly in the path of Willow's plane.

Asher's heart skipped a beat. What was the cloud? Smoke? No, it was too grainy. It seemed composed of thousands and thousands of ... what?

Birds?

Please, no.

He knew that birds flying into a plane's engines could cause a crash, a deadly event known as a "bird strike."

Willow's plane arrowed toward the growing cloud.

Cold fear swelled within him.

He pictured scores of birds being sucked into the powerful engines. The engines stopping. Willow's plane plummeting downward. Slamming into the ground. Cartwheeling. The cabin exploding in a fireball of heat and flames. People screaming. Burning.

Horrified, he pressed against the glass wall, his attention riveted on the departing plane. The aircraft soared upward, tucking its wheels into its metal belly. Any second now, the plane would hit the dense flock of birds and its engines would stall.

How could he face life without Willow?

He watched her plane, heartsick, following its doomed path as—

—it veered sharply left, away from the cloud.

The plane soared into a clear section of the red-hazed sky.

Relief coursed through him. Shaking, he leaned his forehead against the glass, fighting to slow his racing heart.

Further down the field, a small passenger jet emerged from the black cloud of birds. It dropped. Slammed onto a grassy area. Exploded. Oily smoke gushed skyward, heating the air. Flames roiled in a savage blaze, as though erupting from hell.

His face paled.

Sirens wailing, four emergency vehicles raced down the runway, lights flashing.

The cloud of birds swept along the tarmac in a huge billowing mass that pulsated and shifted and churned. It smothered the rescue vehicles in a dark veil that blotted out the sunlight.

The massive flock was about four hundred yards from the terminal.

A fire engine swung left, trying to dodge the birds, and it collided with an ambulance with such force that Asher staggered back a step, almost feeling the impact. The two vehicles exploded into a fireball. These flames stretched upward and ignited dozens of birds, dropping them like red sparks to the earth.

The cloud was now only three hundred yards from the terminal.

A rescue truck veered across the runway. It plowed into another vehicle and flipped over, rolling twice before coming to a crumpled halt.

The cloud barreled onward.

He studied the window in front of him. Was it as unbreakable as the glass in his father's yacht? He knew he should retreat, but he couldn't leave until Willow's plane was completely out of sight, far from this oncoming mass.

Two hundred yards from the terminal.

Behind him, people cried out as the black cloud loomed like an enormous living entity. Nearby, the beagles barked in agitation, and Asher remembered their earlier whimpering. Had the sniffer dogs' incredible sense of smell detected the approaching flock before it was even visible? Or had they just sensed a ... wrongness ... to the air caused by the terra plants?

One hundred yards.

As Willow's plane shrank into a distant dot, he breathed a sigh of relief. She was far from the airport. Safe.

Fifty yards.

He could hear the birds now: thousands of cries and squeaks that formed a multi-voiced shriek. Wings beating in frantic flight, they swarmed forward and slammed into the terminal's windows.

He stared at the tiny bodies slapping the glass. Ugly faces stared back at him. Beady eyes, piglike noses, fanged jaws.

Hairs prickled at the back of his neck.

They weren't birds at all.

They were bats.

Thousands of black bats.

31

ASHER GAPED AT THE mass of bats swarming outside the windows.

Where had they all come from? What had driven them from their dark sleeping spots and into the daylight?

On the tarmac, he saw a large commercial jet roll to a halt. Moments later, its passengers began fleeing the cabin via inflatable slides as bright flames gushed from two engines that had suffered a ... no, not a bird strike. A bat strike. Was that even a term?

Again he studied the huge terminal windows overlooking the runways. The glass was probably strong enough to withstand the bats' assault. And if the automatic doors stayed shut, the people inside this building should be safe and—

Shouts rang behind him.

He turned.

A flood of black bats was pouring from the ceiling hole above the scaffolding. Swarming inside the terminal, they filled the air with their leathery wings, shrill cries, and stomach-churning stench. They darted everywhere in a whirl of fluttering wings and shrieks. People screamed. Tried to cover their heads. Knocked over chairs and luggage in their rush to escape.

Above the chaos, Asher heard a crash and shouts of fear. He spun around.

Cripes!

A maintenance worker was bolting across the terminal, beating back the bats that darted around his head. At the scaffolding, another worker had fallen off the metal platform; the terrified man hung upside down, his ankles snagged in plastic cables, and his head dangling twenty feet above the floor.

"Hang on!" Asher called. "I'm coming." He raced to the scaffolding and scrambled up a side access ladder. Above him, a black man in Army dress uniform was already climbing from the top of the ladder, onto the metal platform.

A bat swooped down and anchored its hooked feet in Asher's hair. He grasped the wriggling body and dragged it from his head, wincing as it ripped strands of hair from his scalp. Swearing, he threw the thing away.

He pulled himself onto the platform. Thankfully, the flood of bats inside the terminal had now eased to a trickle. But outside, the small creatures continued thumping and fluttering against the glass windows, and they still darkened the runways with their numbers.

Inside the building, people flailed at their airborne attackers.

The Army officer ignored a bat flying around his head and turned as Asher joined him. The black man was in his fifties, with strong features, gray hair, and the trim physique of someone who'd spent most of his adult years in the military. A name badge on his shirt read "Colonel Powell, Recruitment."

"I could use your help, kid," the black man said.

"Asher," he replied, bristling. He hated being called a kid, even by a man old enough to be his father.

"Excuse me?"

"My name's Asher Weston."

"Fine." Powell pointed at the dangling worker. "We need to haul him up here. First, though, we have to secure him. I want you to climb down the far side of the scaffolding—you'll be closer to him from there—and stop when you're level with the guy's waist. Be careful." His deep voice was firm with confidence and authority. "Once you're in position, I'll toss you a rope."

Asher's irritation rose. He'd spent years taking orders from his father, and he resented the way this Colonel Powell was ordering him around. Besides, he didn't trust the man. What were his credentials? True, he'd heard of Army officers who, after their period of active duty was up, had transferred to the recruitment sector instead of retiring.

But if this guy had spent his entire career behind a desk, he might have no idea how to mount a rescue.

Then he realized he had no basis for his mistrust, other than years of being let down by the males in his life. His teachers and his private tutors had always obeyed his controlling father. Even his uncles and grandfathers had been too scared to stand up to Rufus Weston.

"What's your plan, Colonel?" he asked warily.

Powell blinked, as though not used to people questioning his orders. Kneeling, he reached for a rope attached to a suspended container of cleaning supplies. "We'll use this, kid," he replied, hauling up the rope. "We'll tie one end around the worker's waist and anchor the other to the side framework. That way, if the cables snap, he'll still be secure."

Asher looked for the flaw in the plan. Couldn't find one. Time was running out. The cable could break at any second, plummeting the maintenance worker to his death. He needed to take a leap of faith. "Okay."

Asher climbed down the far side of the scaffolding, waving away some bats that seemed intent on attacking him.

Powell pulled the supply bucket closer, checked to make sure no one was beneath the scaffolding, and emptied the container. Plastic bottles, sponges, and brushes rained onto the tiles far below. He unclipped the bucket from the rope and dropped it as well. "Ready, kid?"

Something in Powell's voice—a tone, a confidence—eased Asher's misgivings. Maybe this guy could be trusted after all.

He wrapped an arm around a metal support and stretched out his free hand. "Ready." He caught the end of the rope tossed to him.

Still kneeling on the platform, Powell addressed the worker suspended several feet below. "What's your name, sir?"

"M-Mike."

"Okay, Mike, you're going to be fine," Powell said calmly. "But you must keep still. Can you do that?"

"Y-Yes."

"I'm going to drop you a rope. Wrap it around your chest and knot it three times."

Mike gave a quick upside-down nod. "Okay."

Asher reached for the thickest beam on the framework. "Oww." He jerked his hand back, staring at the blood on it. When he'd grasped the beam, it had felt like broken glass. What had ripped the skin on his palm and fingers?

"Problem, kid?" Powell called from the platform.

No time to worry about his hand. The worker, Mike, could fall at any second. "No. All good." Warily, he knotted the rope around another beam, then shouted up to Powell, "Ready."

"Hang on. I need to tie the end of this guy's cables to a brace. They seem secure, but I don't want to risk it."

"No worries." Waiting, Asher peered at the beam that had scraped his hand. The metal strut was covered in a fine gray substance similar to the velvet on a buck's antlers. His blood drenched a patch of the stuff.

He peered more closely at the coating. It seemed to be made up of tiny plants.

Terras.

Several beams were also covered with the same stuff.

He frowned. These plants—these terras—were growing on metal. Even worse, despite being only a fraction of an inch tall, they could already scrape the skin off his hand, leaving the flesh raw and weeping. What would these terras be like when they grew larger? How dangerous would they become?

"Okay, kid," Powell yelled to him. "Climb back up here."

Wrapping a handkerchief around his bleeding hand, Asher rejoined the colonel. Together, they began hauling Mike up.

When they finally pulled the maintenance worker onto the platform, the man thanked his rescuers, untied himself, then scrambled down the ladder and rushed off.

Asher and the colonel returned to the ground.

The terminal was now almost empty. Most of the crowds had disappeared—and most of the bats. Only a few winged stragglers remained, plus scores of dead ones.

Scattered people rose from their huddled positions on the floor, while others emerged from restrooms where they'd taken refuge. Stunned shopkeepers wandered around their damaged stores.

"Where'd all the bats go?" Asher asked. "Why did they attack the terminal?"

Powell shrugged. "In life, much is unexplained—until it is made clear."

"Thanks for that, Yoda."

"Yoda?"

"Don't tell me you've never seen *Star Wars*."

A corner of Powell's mouth twitched in amusement. "Of course I've seen it, kid. I've been in the Army, not on another planet. I'm just not used to being compared to a weird midget with pointy ears."

"Again, my name's Asher, not *kid*. FYI, I'm seventeen." This time, Asher's reproach was milder and less annoyed. He liked this man and admired his calm, take-charge attitude.

"Right." To his surprise, Powell clasped him on the shoulder. "Good work up there, kid. You did well. If you ever decide to join the Army, I have a feeling you'd make a fine soldier."

Unused to praise, Asher stumbled over his words. "Th-Thank you ... sir."

It had been years since his father had complimented him on anything he'd done, no matter how well performed. Until now, he hadn't realized how much a few words of praise—even from a stranger—could warm him.

Powell crossed to an old woman with a deep gash on her temple. Murmuring comforting words, he bandaged her forehead with her scarf.

Asher hesitated, then hurried to the officer. "How can I help, sir?"

Powell regarded him with approval. He pointed to an overweight woman with a bleeding nose. She sat on the floor, shaking, blood running down her face. "You can start with that lady, Asher."

"Yes, sir." He felt a brief flash of pride. Powell's use of his name felt like another gesture of approval.

He helped the overweight woman to her feet. "Is your nose broken, ma'am?"

"No." She pressed some tissues to her nostrils. "It started bleeding just before the bats arrived and ..." Eyes rolling back in their sockets, she began slumping to the floor. He caught her.

As she lolled in his arms, unconscious, he struggled with her weight. "Colonel, I need help."

Desperately, he looked around for Powell.

The officer was hurrying across to a little boy who had blood streaming from his nose.

With difficulty, Asher lowered the woman to the floor again. He gazed around the terminal. A dozen people lay unconscious, blood from their noses flowing across the tiles.

The internal alarm he'd earlier felt now returned, only louder and stronger this time.

What was going on?

32

OVER THE NEXT FEW days, Asher's question remained unanswered. No one seemed to know what was going on. And no one could halt the downward spiral.

He was stunned by how quickly civilization began breaking apart.

Thousands of planes crashed across the planet. Closer to home, a Boeing 737 cut Manhattan's Brooklyn Bridge in half, killing hundreds of people.

Quickly, all air traffic was grounded again.

Trains, buses, and cars kept operating for a little while, despite numerous accidents. However, as the death rate skyrocketed, the tracks and streets eventually grew as silent as the skies.

Asher's personal world also began shattering.

First, his brother's nanny called with the news that Tommy had been hospitalized in Germany with a bad nosebleed. Asher's stomach twisted in dread, and he longed to fly to his little brother's side, but the grounding of the planes made that impossible.

Next, a secretary called to say that Rufus Weston had passed away. Asher's father was one of countless people across the planet who'd perished from the Red Fever. Victims fell unconscious, died, and crumbled into something called "decomp-dust."

Moments after Asher hung up, the phones at Weston Tower stopped working. Telecommunication systems everywhere were failing.

He'd barely had time to absorb the news of his father's death when Willow called.

"My cell phone's not working," his girlfriend told him, "so I'm using my satellite phone."

"Where are you? Are you okay?"

"No. I'm still in LA." Her frightened voice rang from his cell phone. "So many people are dying here. I'm heading back to New York."

"I'll come and get you. We have four small planes at a private airfield outside of Manhattan. I'll fly out to you."

"Too risky and too far," she told him. "You'll need to stop at least once for refueling. What happens if the electricity fails and the fuel can't be pumped? Or what if there's no one to refuel your plane and the equipment is locked down? You'll be stuck in the middle of nowhere, alone, with no way to fly out."

Loud crackles interrupted their conversation, and for a heart-stopping moment, Asher was afraid Willow's call had dropped out.

To his relief, the crackles stopped.

Willow spoke with a rare firmness. "Please listen to me, Ash. I've heard that things are going from bad to worse everywhere. It's only a matter of time before all phone lines break down. If you get stuck at some tiny airfield in the middle of nowhere, without a phone that works, you won't be able to contact me. We'll never find each other." She stopped, as if shaken by the terrible possibility of them losing each other forever.

"Willow—"

"You need to stay in New York, at Weston Tower. You'll be safe there. I'll come to you."

He looked around his plush office with its panoramic views of Manhattan. "I'm in Weston Tower now." He desperately wanted to fly to California to get her, but she was right. It would be an incredibly stupid move. "I've got a better idea! Wait at your hotel. I'll *drive* to LA and get you." Even if gas stations along the way stopped pumping fuel, he should be able to siphon supplies from abandoned cars.

"No. I can't stay here. I'm leaving in a few minutes."

"You can't drive from LA to New York by yourself."

"I'm not going to. I'm getting a lift with a woman and her children. They're heading there."

"Do you know these people?"

"No."

"So you'll be traveling with complete strangers?"

"At the rate people are dying, there'll only be strangers left alive. Or no one at all. You need to be careful. I don't know what it's like in Manhattan, but the terras are bad in parts of LA."

His grip tightened on the phone. "They're bad in parts of Manhattan too."

The line crackled again, and her voice shook with urgency. "Wait for me at Weston Tower."

"I will. Everyone's already gone home, so I'll be locking the building down today. You know the code to get in, don't you?"

"Of course." She paused. "I love you, Ash."

"I love—"

The crackle became a deafening squeal.

Then nothing.

Dead silence.

Panicked, he tried calling Willow back again and again, using his cell phone, landlines, and finally his satellite phone. Each time, he heard a hollow emptiness instead of a dial tone. The silence held a cold finality, as though the lines were permanently severed.

Asher gripped his satellite phone, wanting to hurl it across the room in frustration. Instead, he carefully placed the handpiece back in its cradle, hoping it would start working again soon.

Numbly, he sank into a leather chair in front of the window. Thousands of buildings stretched to the hushed horizon, and the streets below were almost bare of traffic.

He had the soul-chilling feeling that he'd never see Willow again.

33

AFTER ASHER'S PHONE CALL with Willow, the days passed with heartbreaking emptiness.

He waited for her at Weston Tower, his pulse racing every time he heard a car or motorcycle on the increasingly cold and deserted streets.

But the cars belonged to other survivors. And the motorcycles belonged to a gang of drunken men led by a bald, tattooed guy who wore a leather jacket blazoned with a biker club logo: Wilders.

None of them had pulled up in front of Weston Tower.

The days passed in a blur of hollow hope. Grief and fear churned within him, from the moment he awoke to when he finally fell asleep after hours of tossing in bed. He knew he'd never see his little brother again—was Tommy even alive?—and he feared he'd lost Willow forever.

He tried to ease his grief with lies and self-deception.

Maybe Tommy had recovered from his nosebleed and had been taken in by a kind family in Germany. With planes and ships no longer running, Europe was as impossible to reach as Saturn. All he could do was pray his little brother was okay.

And maybe Willow was alive as well. Even though she was thousands of miles away, at least she was on the same continent. Eventually, she'd make it back to New York. She had to.

He was tempted to retreat from the world. Wallow in his grief. Wait for his girlfriend.

But he couldn't.

If Willow was still alive, *he* needed to be alive—physically, mentally, emotionally.

Slowly, he emerged from his despair and buried his fears beneath layers of action.

He tended to the crops grown in the massive farms inside Weston Tower, weeding out any terras that sprouted in the garden beds. He listed the hundreds of cans and bottles of water crammed into the storerooms of the building's eateries; hopefully, these fresh vegetables and canned food would feed him and Willow, when she arrived.

Next, he armed himself and drove around the winter-chilled city, checking the homes and offices of every person he knew in Manhattan. He was desperate to find a friend, a colleague, or an acquaintance alive.

He found only the hush of death and more piles of de-comp-dust.

As the silence in the city grew heavier, Asher turned his attention to the survivors scattered throughout the city. He saw them scurrying down the sidewalks, and he heard their vehicles in distant streets. Most were jittery or wary of strangers.

These people—alone and frightened—needed help.

One by one, he invited them to join forces with him.

Some refused, preferring to take their chances alone.

Many were interested.

He wanted to vet these people. Years of his father's tyranny had taught Asher one important lesson: people could hide their true natures behind friendly smiles. But with the internet down, vetting these strangers was impossible. Unfortunately, only time would reveal who was actually a bully, slacker, weirdo, or psy-chotic axe murderer.

So far, all his recruits seemed okay, at least at face value.

Taking a leap of faith—similar to the one he'd given Colonel Powell that day at the airport terminal—he invited all the interested survivors to live in Weston Tower and to work in the skyscraper's farms. They accepted, eager to escape the loneliness of life in a dying city; his new companions craved company, a renewed sense of purpose, and the wonders of fresh fruit and vegetables.

He ended up offering work and lodging in Weston Tower to twenty-two people. The youngest was an eight-year-old boy. His oldest recruit was a seventy-four-year-old history professor, whose wild gray hair earned him the nickname Einstein; this kind, grandfatherly man appointed himself their cook and proceeded to produce a variety of delicious meals.

Asher heard rumors that billions of people across the planet had died from the terras' Red Fever.

In New York, millions had died. The evidence was everywhere. It lay in the deserted buildings and streets, in the soul-numbing silence of Manhattan, and in the spread of the terras across the city.

He feared that humans were headed for extinction. Each day, this possibility increased as the terras multiplied. The plants seemed so unstoppable that he suspected resistance was not only futile but also laughable.

However, he didn't feel like laughing. He needed to focus his energy, grief, and anger on something.

So he decided to fight the invaders.

This battle would be unwinnable.

He didn't care.

The terras had brutally destroyed his life and the lives of billions of people—*Willow and Tommy*—across Earth.

On a paper map, he marked the location of several dangerous terras. Then, carefully, he explored ways to kill them.

Fire burned the orange plants that grew along a pavement near Weston Tower; unfortunately, the flames were difficult to control, so he shelved that method. He used a machete to cut down the terras beside his building, but it took hours and left him exhausted; hacking these plants wasn't an efficient solution. He poured oil on other terras, killing them; but oil was a limited resource that he needed to save, not waste on plants.

He pressed onward, refusing to abandon the fight.

Early one morning, he and a recruit were cruising the streets in a whisper-quiet hybrid Lexus, the vehicle recharged with electricity provided by the self-sustaining Weston Tower.

As usual, his sixteen-year-old passenger, Tyson "Harlem" Jackson, was fiddling with an iPad. In the past two weeks, the boy had collected eleven tablets, eight Game Boys, and six smartphones from various homes and buildings.

Thin, with tight curls, the black boy had been living on the streets since he was thirteen. When Asher had come across him three weeks ago, the kid had been as skittish as a mistreated puppy and reluctant to trust anyone.

"We've got food at Weston Tower," Asher had gently told him that day.

Silently, the boy had huddled in the doorway of an electronics store.

"We also have a warm place to live," Asher had continued. "You'll be safe there."

Harlem stirred, his voice as thin and pathetic as his body. "I don't trust White Breads."

"White Breads? Do you mean me?"

A hesitant nod.

"I promise you can trust me."

Silence again.

Asher noticed an iPad mini sticking from the boy's filthy jacket. "We've got electricity. You could charge your tablet, if you like."

The boy's sad eyes widened with hope and longing, again reminding Asher of an abused puppy. "Really? I can charge it?"

"Sure. We have lots of electricity."

"No way."

"Let me show you."

Half an hour later at Weston Tower, the skinny black boy had turned his suspicious eyes on Asher. "You own this place?"

"It was my father's."

"Wow. Sure beats sleeping on the sidewalk in a cardboard box."

"Well, now you can sleep in a real bed."

On a floor recently transformed into a dormitory, the boy had picked a dingy bedroom cubicle in a dark corner, as though afraid he wouldn't be allowed a better room.

Initially assigned to Weston Tower's farms, he'd finally shown a spark of defiance by refusing the job.

"I've lived on dirty streets for three years. I hate dirt."

"In this building, we can grow our own food. Our farms are safe and away from the terras. Do you know how incredibly lucky we are?"

Before the internet and television stations had shut down for good, Asher had heard an interview with the president's science advisor. According to Professor Blake Doylen and other scientists—all probably dead by now—only a tiny fraction of humanity was immune to the Red Fever: about four hundred thousand people scattered across the planet. Professor Doylen had predicted that most survivors would live on canned food for a while, but eventually the cans would run out or become toxic. The survivors would then have to adopt hunting-gathering-farming lifestyles. These new ways of life would be riddled with terras, wild animals, diseases, and other dangers.

Some groups would endure. Most would struggle to survive. Others would perish. And so the gap between the fed and the hungry would continue to widen.

"I don't care if I'm lucky." Harlem crinkled his nose at the indoor garden. "I'm not putting my hands in that dirt."

And yet Asher noted that the boy tolerated dirt on himself and refused to take regular showers.

Gritting his teeth at Harlem's body odor, Asher began bringing him along on his missions, telling himself it was safer to have a partner when fighting the terras, anyway.

As the Lexus cruised down the empty streets, a string of cries echoed through the chilly air.

The black youth in the passenger seat stiffened. "Were those shouts, Rich Boy?"

"Yep. Probably those bikers again. Wilders."

"Wilders." Harlem placed a protective hand on his iPad, as though afraid the unseen bikers would snatch it from him.

After a lifetime of poverty, the boy now had his pick of the city's riches, but the only things he wanted were electronic devices. Even though the internet no longer worked, most of Harlem's devices were downloaded with enough games and music and e-books to last for years, as long as they were regularly charged.

"What's that name you call the bikers, Rich Boy? Scuzzballs?"

"Ultra-scuzzballs."

Lately, Asher had heard rumors of Wilders roaming the city streets, snatching up girls. He'd even glimpsed some bikers with girls seated behind them, but he hadn't been able to tell if they were willing or unwilling passengers. And since no one knew the location of the bikers' hangout, he couldn't take a team to investigate the rumors of kidnapped girls.

But today, he and Harlem could definitely check out those shouts.

He parked the Lexus on Rosen Street, an area of factories and warehouses mixed with a few trendy restaurants.

A biting wind pawed at them as they exited the vehicle, and they zipped up their jackets. The warm Thanksgiving weather had retreated weeks ago, but so far the winter had been mild. Cold days, colder nights. No signs of the snow that sometimes blanketed New York around mas Day.

Christmas.

Asher sighed. The streets this year were empty and bare. There were no festive decorations, twinkling lights, crowds of shoppers, or selfie-snapping tourists. Instead, many buildings seemed to hug their new leafy coats around them, as though huddling against the cold weather and the even colder emptiness.

Ignoring the harmless terras on an adjacent building, he listened.

Several men were whooping and shouting with wild glee.

He crept alongside a warehouse, trailed by a reluctant Harlem. At their approach, a grazing antelope bounded away and several rabbits scurried beneath an abandoned delivery truck.

Near the corner, three gray plants sprouted from the sidewalk.

He jerked to a halt. "Crawlers!"

Harlem's eyes rounded with alarm. "Gross!"

Asher hated every terra he saw. Hated them with a passionate anger that could only be eased by destroying them.

The black boy had a different attitude. Harlem was okay with the harmless terras and wary of the dangerous ones, but he absolutely loathed crawlers, regarding them as "evil and dangerous fiends from hell."

The tall terras vaguely resembled fountains, with long ro-pelike growths that arced outward from a central stem. Each "rope" was covered with hundreds of thorns that glinted in the sunshine like knife tips.

Asher's left leg and Harlem's right arm still bore the scars of a recent battle with them.

Nearby, an unseen man gave a triumphant shout edged with menace.

Asher's stomach knotted.

He peered around the corner of the warehouse—and at the scene down Barr Street, his brow furrowed.

"What the heck?" he muttered.

This was a new low, even for ultra-scuzzball bikers.

34

Barr Street was lined with small shops and restaurants.

In the center of the road, a blazing car was ringed by a dozen men clad in dirty jackets and ripped jeans. All hollered gleefully as they danced around the flames.

A dark-haired teenager hung upright over the burning vehicle, his arms above his head. His roped wrists were tied to the platform of a boom fire truck: a fire engine with a long armlike crane topped by a small platform.

Asher estimated the soles of the hanging teenager's boots were about twenty feet above the burning car. Good. Not in immediate danger.

He pulled back from the corner, swept by déjà vu. Weeks ago, he'd helped a black officer, Colonel Powell, rescue a man dangling from some scaffolding during a bat swarm. And now a youth was hanging above a fire lit by drunken bikers. Cripes! Where were all the easy rescues?

He recognized the victim's red plaid shirt, faded blue jeans, and cowboy boots.

Lynxx.

He'd seen this boy on the streets before. Three times, Asher had invited him to join his group at Weston Tower, sure the country boy would jump at the chance to work on the indoor farms. But Lynxx had simply stared at him with those unusual golden eyes, muttered "No," and walked away.

Asher had written him off as a loner.

Judging from the boy's behavior today, he was also ... strange. Despite hanging by his wrists above a roaring fire, Lynxx didn't seem worried. His eyes were closed, as though taking a nap—or perhaps he was merely showing scorn for his tormenters.

Did Lynxx think the men were only messing with him? Possibly.

Asher knew the thugs enjoyed getting drunk, setting cars alight, and smashing shop windows. But surely they wouldn't burn a person alive ... would they?

He scanned the area with his binoculars, pausing at a small restaurant named Fire and Ice. Memories flooded back, sharp with grief. He'd taken Willow to this Mexican hotspot last year. He could still remember her shocked gasps as she'd tried to eat a chili-laden burrito drenched in pepper sauce. Eventually, laughing, she'd admitted defeat and had settled for mild nachos washed down with icy colas.

"Ultra-gross," Harlem whispered, pointing across Barr Street to a three-story building.

On the roof, a large bird sat as motionless as a stone gargoyle, staring at the rowdy bikers. Something long and black dangled from its beak.

Asher focused his binoculars. "It's WindLord," he muttered. "The golden eagle from the Bronx Zoo." For the past three years, the zoo had used the bird's image on promotional and educational material. But the eagle's eyes had always been black in the posters—not silver.

What was going on? Were WindLord's silver eyes due to it eating terra plants?

"What's it doing out here?" Harlem murmured.

"Not sure. I heard that, a week or so after the Mist, some animal rights activists went around releasing all the animals from zoos, labs, and other facilities across New York."

"*All* the animals?" Harlem gasped. "Were they crazy?"

"They wanted to give them a chance to live."

As if to back up his comment, a distant roar split the air. The bikers stopped dancing and glanced around, uneasy.

"What was that noise?" Harlem whispered, trembling.

"Lion. Their roars can be heard for blocks. That one doesn't sound nearby."

Was it Zimba? Shortly after the Red Fever's death count had begun to soar, Asher had checked on his "fur-brother." To his surprise, the lion enclosures at the Bronx Zoo had been emptied, along with every other pen and cage. If the lion roaming the streets was Zimba, he wasn't worried; his furred friend would never harm him or another person—he hoped.

However, if it was a different lion, all bets were off.

Another roar echoed through the streets.

"Yay, crazy animal lovers." Harlem nervously looked around. "Go ahead, dudes. Release all the critters from the zoos, including the really dangerous ones. Wish them luck in surviving. Watch them hunt down lots of tasty humans." He peered at the silver-eyed WindLord, who remained perched on the roof, still dangling a long black object. "Oh my gawd. What's that eagle holding?"

Asher saw a scaly serpentine body wriggling in the eagle's beak. "A snake. Big one. Fifteen, maybe sixteen feet long."

"No way! What kind is it?"

He sighed. "Where are your binoculars, Harlem?"

"Back in the car."

"Next time, carry them in your pocket."

"Yessir, Boss Man."

Asher gritted his teeth but remained silent.

His friend, the elderly Chef Einstein, had casually chatted with Harlem, getting him to open up. Later, he'd filled Asher in on the black boy's life in the ghetto: dead mother, alcoholic father, constant physical and mental abuse.

Moved by Harlem's terrible life, Asher tried to be patient with the boy.

He trained his binoculars on the black snake again, noting a telltale hood that flared below the scaled head. "It's a cobra."

Harlem's face sagged in horror. "Is it from a zoo too?"

"Probably. Cobras aren't native to the US."

"What's WindLord going to do with it?"

"Eat it, I suppose."

"Mega-gross!"

The silver-eyed eagle sat on the roof, casually dangling the reptile as it watched the bikers. Or maybe it was watching the burning car. Or Lynxx. Whatever, Asher hoped WindLord didn't drop the cobra onto the ground near Harlem and him.

Whoops and shouts erupted again. The drunken bikers had resumed circling their makeshift bonfire with its human chandelier.

A man in his forties stood apart from the revelers. He wore jeans, a brown shirt, and a black jacket with a biker club logo on it: Wilders. Tattoos covered his arms and neck. A huge swastika marred his bald head, and a red bandanna hung around his neck. A ragged scar stretched across his forehead.

From the way the man was ordering the others around, Asher guessed he was the leader.

The tattooed man gestured to someone operating the boom fire truck. Its engine grumbled. The crane vibrated into life. The metal arm creaked and moved down a little.

The rope dropped.

Lynxx now hung nineteen feet above the flames.

The tattooed man gave a twisted grin as his gang whooped even louder and danced like savages at a campfire.

And maybe that's what they were, Asher thought. Savages.

He doubted the Red Fever had left an existing gang of bikers alive. These survivors had probably joined forces after the Mist. Perhaps most had once been law-abiding citizens. Now, for whatever reasons, they'd become a band of misfits, thugs, and arsonists.

Harlem nervously tugged the sleeve of Asher's denim jacket. "Let's blow this place."

"Not yet." He rubbed his chin, studying the scene on the road. "If we try to talk to the bikers, we'll probably end up hanging next to Lynxx. And we can't shoot our way in. They're armed and outnumber us five to one."

"We need to get going." Harlem was skinny and brave but not stupid. Clearly, the idea of dealing with a pack of drunken well-armed bikers wasn't high on his to-do list.

"Retreat isn't an option," Asher said, regretting it wasn't. He didn't want to put Harlem in danger—and yet he was about to do exactly that. "We have to help Lynxx."

"Why? We've tried talking to him three times, remember? He didn't want anything to do with us. And you called him a loner. No way would that guy help us."

"We have to try anyway."

Harlem huffed in disgust. "You remind me of the dude in that old movie last week." The Weston Cell ran movie nights every Friday, a mixture of classic films and more recent blockbusters. "The Spanish dude wore an old suit of armor and rode around the countryside, looking for dragons to fight. Like you, he believed in truth, justice, and the American way."

"That's Superman. You said the guy was Spanish."

"Whatever. Anyway, this Don-key Hoh-tee was all noble and caring and stuff, just like you."

"Don-key Hoh-tee?" Asher's eyebrows rose. "Oh, you mean *Don Quixote*. The last name—Quixote—starts with a *q* not a *k*."

"Whatever. But yeah, that's it. In the end, though, it didn't matter. The Don-key man couldn't save the whole world. It was impossible."

"I'm not trying to save the whole world today. Just Lynxx." He stared at the fiery scene. "I need to get to that truck. Then I need to knock out the driver and lower the platform so you can cut him down."

Harlem lifted his chin, eyes flashing. "I lived on the streets for three years, Rich Boy. You lived in a luxury penthouse with your father's billions. I've met idiots like those Wilders before. You haven't. Believe me, they'll get mega-mad if you spoil their fun."

"I agree. We'll need a distraction." Asher pulled back from the corner. Down Rosen Street, a firehouse lay as quiet and abandoned as the rest of the city, its garage doors open.

His gaze shifted to the patch of fountain-like crawler terras.

An idea sprang to mind but, shivering, he rejected it. Surely he could figure out a better plan, one that didn't involve those disgusting plants.

Another rumble of engine. Another creak of metal.

Asher stole a glance around the corner.

Lynxx had been lowered again. He was now only eighteen feet above the flames.

No time to waste. He'd have to use the disgusting crawlers.

35

Harlem's eyes widened as he listened to the plan.

When Asher finished, the black boy whispered, "No way. I hate crawlers. They're evil and dangerous fiends from hell."

"Fiends from hell?" Asher tried to hide his smile. This street kid from the ghetto had an interesting way of occasionally mixing slang with cultural references. "Did you used to watch *Buffy the Vampire Slayer*?"

"Just for a few months. Then one night my dad took a baseball bat to the TV—and me."

At the pain on Harlem's face, Asher hurriedly changed the topic. "I know you hate crawlers, but we have to use them. We don't have a choice."

"That's what that Don-key Hoh-tee dude said in the movie last week."

"Don Quixote."

"Whatever."

"Like I said, we're not saving the world today, just one person."

He saw Harlem's shoulders slump in defeat, as though he knew he couldn't win. Had the boy's rough life on the streets crushed his spirit? Or had his mother's death and father's alcoholic rages done the job?

"You're the boss, Don Q," muttered Harlem.

Asher pushed down his guilt.

They gathered some equipment from the Lexus and returned to the gray terras that sprouted from the sidewalk.

He passed a burlap sack to Harlem. "You hold the bag open while I cut them."

"This job sucks."

"I know."

"Crawlers got both of us a week ago. My arm still hurts."

"So does my leg. We'll be more careful this time."

Asher used a long-handled pole with a clawed tip to grip one of the ropelike crawler stems. Holding it tight, he swung his machete and slashed the thorny stalk from the main plant. Then he dropped the three-foot offcut into Harlem's bag.

Quickly, he filled two bags with pieces of the crawlers. After tying the necks of the bags with rope, he placed them beside the warehouse, ready for use.

"Okay," he said, "the clock's ticking. The cut crawlers will only be still for a few minutes."

"If any of those evil fiends from hell grab me, I'm blaming you."

"We'll be fine. I hope." He hid a smile at Harlem's annoyance. It had taken three weeks, but today the boy had briefly emerged from his wounded cocoon. Asher had loathed his own ruthless father, but at least the man hadn't physically beaten him in drunken rages.

Another creak of metal.

He checked again.

Lynxx had been lowered a little closer to the flames.

Things were definitely hotting up for the plaid-loving, cowboy-booted loner.

He and Harlem raced to the firehouse in Rosen Street and quickly outfitted themselves. Black heatproof suits with yellow markings. Heat-resistant ski masks over most of their faces. Tinted safety goggles. Helmets with clear face guards.

Asher shifted uncomfortably in the firefighting gear, already feeling ten degrees hotter. Beads of sweat trickled down his face and his breathing began to labor.

He noticed two piles of decomp-dust on the garage floor. He supposed there could be more upstairs, but he doubted it. Most of the first responders had probably died in the field trying to help others, while scum like those bikers had survived. It didn't seem fair.

Life sure had a warped sense of justice.

"I'm suffocating," Harlem puffed, the thick ski mask muffling his words.

Asher pulled on boots and gloves. "This gear should protect us from the crawlers and from recognition by the Wilders."

"So you've used this gear before? We'll be safe from the hell fiends?"

Asher shrugged.

Harlem groaned.

They returned to the bulging bags at the corner and took another peek.

Lynxx was still suspended over the burning car.

Asher scowled. Would the boy be dead before he could carry out his plan? "Wait five minutes, Harlem. Then empty your bags of crawlers."

"Are you sure about this?"

"No."

Another groan.

"Keep out of sight." Asher inspected both their suits for gaps. "Stay alert and stay alive."

"Count on it." Harlem's gaze returned to the golden eagle on the building in Barr Street. The enormous cobra was still dangling from its beak. "That snake's freaking me out, man."

"Same here."

"Let's go." Asher grabbed his bag of crawlers and hurried down an alley behind Barr Street. Rounding the corner, he moved along a line of parked vehicles, crouching to shield himself from view.

At a green van, he paused to check his watch.

Two minutes until release.

Metal rattled as Lynxx was again lowered.

He imagined beads of sweat popping across Lynxx's forehead. Why wasn't the boy begging for his life? How could he just hang there, eyes closed, face blank?

Another roar sounded, this one nearby.

Asher froze. That wasn't a lion.

He peered around the green van.

A massive grizzly bear lumbered into Barr Street. Its furry back bore long scars, and its right ear was ripped and tattered. Growling, it rose onto its haunches, towering nine feet tall. Throwing back its head, it gave another roar and its sharp claws raked the air, as if preparing to shred flesh and spill organs.

He looked at Lynxx again. The boy hadn't even opened his eyes at the roars. Was he already dead?

Further down the street, the biker leader shouted, "Don't shoot unless that bear attacks us. Grizzlies can rip you to pieces, even with a dozen bullets in them."

A skinny man with stringy hair looked at the tattooed biker leader. "I vote for running, Fang."

The bear fixed its beady eyes on the drunken men and uttered another bellow of rage.

"No one moves, Viper," ordered the biker leader, Fang. "That thing can outrun us."

"So what do we do?"

"Yell real loud. That'll scare it off."

The men erupted into shouts and yells and swearing. The bear answered with roars.

Asher smiled grimly. This racket gave him the perfect cover.

The bear was a hundred yards away. The Wilders were only seventy.

He glanced at his watch again.
Time to unleash the crawlers.

<h1 style="text-align:center">36</h1>

ASHER CREPT TO THE front of the green van and emptied his bag. The cut terra stems fell to the ground.

He held his breath. Prayed his heat suit would protect him. Watched the crawlers.

The cut stems twitched on the road. From painful experience, he knew they were working out the closest source of animal heat.

Then, like something from a horror movie, they set off. Fast.

Using an up-down humping motion similar to the way caterpillars moved, they rushed along the road—away from Asher.

Within his heat suit, he heaved a relieved sigh.

He still couldn't get used to the idea that crawlers could move. He knew many Earth flowers would turn their petals toward the sunlight each morning and turn away at night. Plus Venus flytraps could snap shut with amazing speed, trapping insects and small frogs in their jug-like flowers.

But these thorny crawlers were drawn by the heat and smell of animals. And they could cross distances much faster than any Earth plant.

Through his binoculars, he watched the crawlers scurry toward their targets, their skinny gray stems blended into the road, almost invisible.

The bikers were still trying to scare off the bear down the block, and their shouts drowned out the crawlers' thorny clicks.

The terras zeroed in on their targets with the accuracy of heat-seeking missiles.

Beyond the burning car, Asher saw faint threads of movement. Good. Harlem had emptied his bag as well.

Like a coordinated pincer movement, the two packs of crawlers attacked.

Some lunged at the bikers' jeans, their thorns unable to pierce the thick denim. Others slid beneath the bottoms of the pants and impaled themselves in their targets' hairy legs.

The men shrieked. Frantically tried to rip the crawlers off. Couldn't.

More crawlers lassoed their arms.

Asher remembered his own pain last week. A single crawler had plunged a dozen thorns into his calf, each a needle of agony.

Down the street, the grizzly bear uttered an angry snort. It dropped onto all fours and lumbered away, as though bored by the unfolding drama.

At a flap of wings, Asher glanced up.

WindLord flew overhead, its beak empty.

His eyes widened. No way could that golden eagle eat a sixteen-foot snake. It must've dropped the cobra before taking flight.

Nervously, he checked the surrounding ground. No sign of a massive black snake with a hooded neck slithering toward him ... yet.

Harlem was right. Their jobs really sucked.

The moment the grizzly was gone, Asher leaped to his feet. Still scanning the ground for the cobra, he darted forward in his heat suit and wove between the screaming men as they battled their thorny attackers. No biker grabbed for a weapon as he passed by. No crawler tried to climb his legs.

He wrenched open the fire truck's door, jumped onto the step, and swung a fist—

—at thin air.

The cabin was empty. Its far door gaped open.
The driver had already fled.
He peered up at the crane.
Tattered rope hung from the platform.
Lynxx was gone too.

37

Confused, Asher glanced around. Down the street, a long black snake was slithering into a cafe. Good. At least the cobra was far away from Harlem and him.

Lynxx stumbled around the front of the fire truck, rubbing his wrists. "Looking for me?" he asked, voice weak and unsteady.

Asher gasped, "How did you get down?"

Pain glazed the boy's unusual golden eyes, and his sentences tumbled out in broken fragments. "Once you distracted bikers ... with *Ransilien exTerrus* ... I pulled myself up rope ... onto platform." He gave a weary sigh. "I cut myself free, climbed down the crane ... punched out the driver." He flexed his reddened knuckles. "Punch felt ... strangely satisfying."

Asher noted Lynxx's trembling body and the sweat glazing his forehead. "Are you okay?"

"Not really ... but will be fine ... by tomorrow. Need rest."

"You can't rest yet." Asher studied the fallen bikers. Some had crawlers wrapped around their legs, others around their arms. "I need your help for a few minutes, Lynxx."

"Why?"

He lifted his empty burlap sack. "We have to collect their guns and keys."

"Why?"

Asher frowned at Lynxx's cluelessness. No wonder the Wilders had tagged him as a victim. "*Why?* So we don't get shot in the back. And so we don't have these thugs chasing after us on their motorcycles."

"Oh. Logical."

The groaning bikers didn't resist as they were stripped of their weapons and keys.

Lynxx gestured to the thorny terras. "Fascinating, aren't they?" he said to Asher.

"No! They're hideous plants."

"Really? I rather admire their efficiency." Lynxx wiped his sweating forehead. "When offshoots drop from the main plant ... they proceed to the closest source of animal heat. Once the *Ransilien exTerrus* have found their targets ... they'll stay there for days, feeding on the flesh. Not a pleasant experience for the host."

"Yeah, I found that out the hard way last week." Asher lifted the face guard of his helmet, leaving the ski mask and tinted goggles in place.

"So you're acquainted with them, are you?" Lynxx asked.

"Well, I haven't had them over for dinner or anything, but I've certainly had a close encounter of the thorned kind."

"I'm confused. Are we talking about ... the *Ransilien exTerrus*?"

"I call them crawlers."

"Really? Hmm ... I suppose it's an appropriate name."

Asher flinched at the sight of a terra wrapped around the biker leader's neck. "I hope those things aren't poisonous." He'd wanted to free Lynxx, not kill a dozen scuzzballs.

"Not exactly. Eventually, the flesh decays around the thorns. Once infection sets in, usually after ten hours or so, the hosts will die in three days." Lynxx paused, as though considering the scenario. Then, reluctantly, he said, "Perhaps we should help these gentlemen." He crossed to the groaning Fang, who was lying on the ground, pulling at the crawler twisted around his neck. "You need vinegar."

"What?" the biker croaked.

"Vinegar. You pour it over the ... crawlers ... and they release their grip." Lynxx pointed to the restaurants and stores on Barr Street. "Some of those places should have bottles of vinegar in them."

"How we gonna get it?" Fang's breath came in agonized gasps. "We can't move."

Lynxx threw a glance at the fire truck. "Your driver is lying on the far side of that vehicle, knocked out." He rubbed his reddened knuckles. "He doesn't have any crawlers on him. Once he regains consciousness, I'm sure he'll assist you."

Fang groaned. "Why are you helping us, after what we did to you?"

"The breakdown of civilization has obviously brought out the worst in you and your cronies. While I dislike your savage behavior, I dislike terras even more, despite their fascinating properties." Lynxx turned away from the fallen man, hesitated, then turned back to him. "If you need any assistance in dealing with terras in the future, you may ask for my help. I've been experimenting with ways to kill them."

"What?" Fang gaped at him. "Oh. Okay."

Asher's brow knotted. Was Lynxx being stupidly noble in helping these thugs survive the terras? Or was he being smart? By offering valuable information about the terras, he was essentially protecting himself from future attacks by the bikers.

Fang shifted his glare to Asher. "You set these crawlers on us, didn't you?"

Asher adjusted his ski mask, making sure it still concealed his features. "Sure did."

"Who are you?"

"Adolf Jewman." Probably the world's most unlikely name. "Why do you want to know?"

"So I can kill you, Adolf Jewman."

"Good luck with that."

The biker leader pulled at the thorny plant wrapped around his neck. "Hey, you," he snapped at Lynxx. "Is there something else we can use besides vinegar? That stuff's gonna hurt like crazy."

"Sorry, vinegar's the only thing that works," Lynxx coolly replied. "Any other liquid, including water, makes them double in size."

"Freakin' heck!"

38

As they hurried away, Asher murmured to Lynxx, "I used cola on a crawler around my calf last week. It was painless."

Lynxx cast a glance back at the groaning, fallen men who'd partied as he'd hung above the burning car. "I'm aware that cola is a pain-free way to remove the *Ransilien exTerrus*."

"Huh! Getting a little revenge, eh? Good. I was beginning to think you weren't human."

At the end of the block, Harlem shouted, "I'm ditching this sweat suit, Don Q."

"Put it in the car," Asher called back. "Then grab as much gear from the firehouse as possible. We might need it someday. And don't call me Don Q."

"Whatever." Harlem disappeared around the corner.

As they turned into Rosen Street, Asher peeled off his ski mask.

Lynxx grunted in recognition. "It's you. Asher Weston."

"Who else did you think was rescuing you?"

"I had no idea. And I didn't care."

Asher sighed. Lynxx was a real loner, doomed for an early death if he didn't change a few things. "You need to become a less obvious target, pal. Start by ditching your bright come-beat-me-up clothes."

Lynxx regarded his red plaid shirt. "I've always thought red was a cheerful, friendly color. You don't agree?"

Asher thought of the Night of the Red Mist, the scarlet blood that had streamed from victims' noses, the strange red sky. He shuddered. "No, I'm not keen on red anymore."

"Really?"

"Try darker clothes," he advised. "They'll help you blend into the background. And start carrying a gun for protection."

He removed his heat suit and shoved it onto the back seat of the Lexus, next to the sack containing the bikers' weapons and keys.

At the rear of the vehicle, Harlem was stuffing armfuls of gear into the trunk, clearly eager to leave. When he finished, the boy withdrew a cell phone from his pocket.

Thanks to Chef Einstein's explanation, Asher finally understood the boy's obsession with the phones. A life of poverty had left Harlem a bystander to life. Longingly, he had watched people use their phones to talk to people anywhere and everywhere.

Now, since the Night of the Red Mist, Harlem owned a dozen phones, all as uncommunicative as their dead owners. Every day, Asher would see him turning on a couple of screens, hoping that someone, somewhere, had revived a cell tower network; his fingers would always hover over the call buttons, eager to punch in a random phone number.

Today, as usual, Harlem's cell phone remained silent. Dejected, he slipped it back into his pocket.

Lynxx stood near the Lexus. "I ... appreciate ... your attempt to save my life."

"*Attempt* to save your life?" Asher shook his head. "Wow. Talk about gratitude."

"They weren't going to burn me alive, you know."

"It sure looked like they wanted to."

"I had things under control."

"Really? It didn't seem that way."

"Appearances can be deceptive."

Asher rolled his eyes. "Sure." He paused. Should he again invite Lynxx to join the Weston Cell? *Naw.* The guy's first three refusals had been firm. No point in collecting another one. "Well, even though I only *attempted* to save your life, you still owe me." Bartering and favors had become the new currency in this changed world.

"Of course." Lynxx withdrew a shiny, fat wallet. "How much?"

Asher regarded him with disbelief. How could someone so clueless ever survive? "Are you kidding me? Money's useless." With Rufus Weston's death, Asher was technically worth billions, but no amount of money would buy him a fresh apple these days. The apocalypse had been a ruthless financial equalizer. Nowadays, people needed physical and mental strength, intelligence, and resourcefulness to survive—plus luck.

"If my money's useless, how do I repay you?"

"By doing me a favor one day."

"When? I have a calendar and can mark the date."

With difficulty, Asher kept his incredulity under control. "I don't know exactly when, Lynxx. Just whenever I ask for it. Okay?"

"Oh. Very well."

Harlem nervously glanced around before he slid into the front passenger seat. "Let's go, Don Q. Those thugs are meaner than alley rats." He flinched, as though remembering fists beating him in the past.

Lynxx squinted at the sky, where thick dark clouds were gathering like soldiers massing for an assault. "There's a bad storm coming. You should get indoors before it hits."

"Okay," Asher said. "Do you want a lift to wherever you ... hermit?"

"Is that even a verb?"

"It is today."

"Interesting." Lynxx's golden eyes shaded with fatigue and pain. "I don't require a lift. My car is close by. However, I do have a suggestion."

"What?"

"I was going to investigate a building in Brooklyn this afternoon. But it'd be better if you did it instead. I'm feeling unwell and need to rest. My efficiency is compromised."

"What do you want me to investigate?"

"Hillsend High."

In the first week following the Mist, the government had turned schools and community centers into makeshift hospitals in a futile attempt to handle the increasing numbers of sick and dying.

"Earlier today," Lynxx continued, "I was collecting terra specimens outside the school when I saw a woman at a window. She was grubby and possibly ill." He paused as a huge locust landed on his arm, wings outspread. "Interesting. You don't see these beauties in New York very often."

Asher stifled his annoyance. Who cared about a locust? "What woman? Why didn't you help her?"

"I was about to, but something important came up."

Asher didn't even bother asking what could be more important than a sick person in trouble. He already knew that this country boy, this loner, marched to the beat of his own drum.

Lynxx lifted the locust onto his palm and scrutinized its hard-shelled body and transparent wings. "So, will you go to the school?"

"Sure."

"The girl appeared rather confused. Sooner might be better than later."

"Girl? I thought you said woman."

"She was about seventeen, so she could be regarded as either."

Asher's heart beat a little faster. Hope shivered within him, a slender thread that the slightest breath could break. "What did she look like?"

"Um, average height, slim, dirty fair skin, long greasy red hair. She looked familiar." Lynxx watched the locust launch itself into the air, joining a small swarm whose multiple wings hummed as they flew past. "I need to go." He walked away, his gait unsteady.

Asher's heart pounded against his rib cage. A wild hope left him breathless. Everything matched except for the hair color.

Then he remembered his last few minutes with his girlfriend at the airport. Just before she'd flown off to LA, she'd said something that now boomed in his mind: *Later, I'm having my hair dyed red for my new movie.*

He knew it was a long shot, but Lynxx's description almost matched.

Maybe Willow was still alive and back in New York.

39

BEHIND THE STEERING WHEEL, Asher fought down his growing frustration.

He longed to drive straight to Hillsend High School in Brooklyn, to find the girl that Lynxx had seen.

However, Harlem had suffered an allergic reaction to some terras growing alongside their parked Lexus. A red rash had spread across his neck and arms, and he kept wriggling in the passenger seat, struggling not to scratch or infect himself.

He needed immediate treatment.

Cursing all terras, Asher drove back to Weston Tower. The infirmary nurse, Maria Ortiz, was a middle-aged Hispanic woman with twenty years' experience. When he brought the scratching Harlem in, she took one look at the rash and declared, "Poison ivy. Mild case."

"Are you sure?" Asher asked, surprised. "I thought terras had poisoned him."

Nurse Ortiz rummaged through her supplies for a tube of calamine lotion and a bottle of corticosteroids. "We have some nasty plants of our own, you know."

"True. But at least they're ours, not warped imports."

By the time Asher returned to the first floor, the storm had struck the city with full force. He stood in the entrance to Weston Tower, watching swords of lightning slash the darkening sky. Howling winds roared down the Wall Street canyons, flinging trash everywhere. A windborne plank of wood smashed into a parked car, spearing the driver's seat.

Traveling in these conditions would be extremely dangerous.

He couldn't risk another person's life in this storm. But maybe he could make the journey to Brooklyn by himself ... through a blackened city in a savage thunderstorm ... dodging deadly wind-driven debris ... battling the pelting rain ... and struggling to see in the wild conditions.

His shoulders sagged. If he crashed and injured himself, it might be days before anyone found him. And that meant days before anyone went to the school to help the girl ... to help Willow?

He couldn't risk it.

He'd have to wait until morning.

The night passed in an agony of frustration. He listened to the shrieking wind and the rain battering his apartment windows. At dawn, the storm still raged furious and strong. *Are the spreading terras changing the weather?* he wondered. *Or is this just a bad storm?*

He checked on Harlem in the infirmary. The lotion and steroids had kicked in and his rash was starting to clear. The boy sat up in bed, happily playing a game on his favorite iPad.

Finally, midmorning, the wind exhausted itself into a breeze, and the deluge shrank to a drizzle.

Asher gunned his Lexus from the underground garage and drove toward Brooklyn, dodging trash that littered the streets and bridge. By the time he screeched his vehicle to a halt outside Hillsend High, a midday sun had scattered the clouds, and the wet streets steamed in the heat.

He surveyed the school. Dozens of abandoned ambulances, police vans, and trucks were parked everywhere. Still, the place looked like most schools in the area. Multistory brick building. Hall. Lunch area. Gym. Other facilities.

Nothing special.

Nothing alarming.

And yet, as he crept up the front concrete steps, he felt goose bumps prickle his skin.

Pistol in one hand, flashlight in the other, Asher worked his way through the main building first, going from the classrooms to the science labs and teachers' lounges.

He fought an impulse to run down the corridors yelling Willow's name. Living in this new world had taught him to move carefully and quietly in unknown situations.

In the main building, the admin offices and classrooms were dotted with piles of decomp-dust, maybe a couple of hundred in total. Except for some rats, spiders, and terra vines on the walls, the buildings were silent and dead.

He scoured the rooms, fighting memories. If he half closed his eyes, he could almost see the classrooms filled with chattering students and teachers. He could almost hear music and laughter. Smell the rotten egg gas whipped up in the science labs.

It was all a painful illusion, of course.

Hillsend High School was a graveyard. There were no tombstones, crypts, wreaths, or angel sculptures, but the air held the same lifeless hush of cemeteries, the same sense of loss and quiet grief.

Even the enormous gym was a graveyard. It had been converted into a makeshift hospital and was littered with abandoned medical equipment, trays of used bandages and syringes, and discarded latex gloves. Hundreds of camp beds crowded the floor, each topped with a mound of gray dust. Similar mounds dotted the chairs, desks, and the tiered benches along the walls.

He estimated the gym contained at least a thousand mounds.

A thousand people, once full of plans and dreams, had been reduced to piles of gray dust. This number was just a drop in the ocean of deaths, a horror repeated countless times in countless cities and towns across the planet.

Numbed by the terrible scene, he moved down the rows of cots. Sunlight seeped through the windows near the ceiling, diluting the shadows within the gymnasium, except for the corners, where darkness still huddled.

He circled the gym, shining his flashlight into every corner. In the furthest one, someone lay on a cot, facing the wall. A girl in a dirty hospital gown. Long, lank red hair. Slender body. Bare arms and legs greased with sweat and grime.

Asher's heart stopped. He froze, unable to move. To believe. To hope.

And then he was racing forward, stumbling over cots, hitting his shins on the corners of camp beds, almost slipping on the empty cans and water bottles on the floor around the girl.

"Willow."

Pocketing his gun, he gently touched her shoulder, moving her so that she lay on her back.

The girl looked up at him ... no, *through* him, her dazed eyes gazing into the distance.

Her dazed hazel eyes.

Not violet.

Not Willow's.

Disappointment crashed through him.

He staggered back. Sank onto an adjoining cot. Sat there staring at this not-Willow. This stranger. This death of hope.

The world seemed to fade away. Nothing existed except his overwhelming pain and disappointment.

Finally, after a few minutes, the girl's soft groans penetrated his misery and he crossed to her cot.

She looked about sixteen or seventeen. The sole inhabitant of a school cemetery. Somehow she'd survived for the past month by herself. Alone. And sick.

She wasn't Willow, but she needed his help.

Kneeling, he pulled on a surgical mask and a pair of latex gloves.

"Hello. Can you hear me?" No answer. He repeated the question several times.

Finally her gaze flickered to him.

"Y-Yes," she groaned.

"What's your name?"

Her lids fluttered as though she was struggling to stay conscious.

"What's your name?" he again asked.

Another groan. Another flutter of eyelids. Two words slipped through her lips like a tired sigh. "Charlotte Jenkins." With an effort, she partially opened her eyes. "Is my mother okay?"

"I don't know. You're the only one I've found alive in this place."

"What … what about my boyfriend? And my … cousin? They … in car with me . . . are okay?"

"I don't know." But he did.

He was almost certain that her mother and cousin and boyfriend were among the billions of mounds of decomp-dust dotting the world.

Just like his Willow.

40

WILLOW WAS DEAD.

Asher couldn't deny it any longer or hide his fears beneath lies and self-deception.

He had to accept the unacceptable. Live with the unlivable. *Willow was dead.*

The three words tolled like a funeral knell as he drove back to Weston Tower. The phrase echoed in his mind as he carried Charlotte Jenkins to the infirmary on the fourteenth floor.

He briefly explained how he'd found the girl.

"Leave her with me," Nurse Ortiz said, tucking the sick newcomer into a bed. "She needs a sponge bath, meds, and food."

"What's wrong with her?" He asked the question mechanically, not really caring about the answer. Inside, he felt dead. He was merely going through the motions of breathing.

"It's too soon to tell." Nurse Ortiz studied him. "Are you okay?"

"No."

He turned. Left the infirmary. Caught the elevator to his penthouse apartment.

And sat.

He stayed in his room, not eating, and sleeping too much. Sleep was his only escape from the pain that gnawed at his soul. Waking was pure agony.

Memories of Willow lingered like ghosts in his apartment. In the home theater, they had snuggled together, watching movies and eating popcorn. In the games room, they'd battled each other on the crazy arcade game he'd imported from Japan. In the gourmet kitchen, they'd laughed at her awkward attempts to cook—and he'd eaten her meals anyway, happily, because she had prepared them.

Willow was dead.

When the apartment became unbearable, Asher took the elevator to the rooftop farm and sat on a bench near the vegetable beds. He banned Harlem and all the others from the rooftop. Trays of food were sent back to the kitchen, mostly untouched. He only returned to his apartment at midnight, to sleep.

On his third day among the garden beds, the sound of footsteps penetrated his misery. He looked up as an elderly man joined him on the bench.

"I don't want to talk, Einstein," he said, using the man's nickname.

"That's fine." The chef buttoned his thick jacket, closed his eyes, and tilted his face to the wintry sun. "You've occupied this place for three days, son. Surely you wouldn't deny an old man a little Vitamin D, to stop his bones from getting brittle." The words were spoken kindly, but they held a firm note, and Asher knew his protests would be dismissed with a stubborn smile.

The seventy-four-year-old bore a striking resemblance to the famous physicist, Einstein. He had the same shock of gray hair, bushy mustache, bulbous nose, and stout physique. In addition, his hooded gray eyes gleamed with a mixture of intelligence, humor, and kindness.

Asher felt too broken and miserable to argue with the chef. Instead, he ignored him. He stared into the distance, lost in his memories of Willow.

In silence, they sat in the cool reddish sunshine for hours.

Asher expected Einstein to crack first by going for a cup of coffee ... or a visit to the bathroom. Didn't elderly men usually have prostate problems?

But perhaps Einstein had skipped fluids that day, for he seemed content to just sit on the bench. Sometimes he closed his eyes and soaked up the sunshine with the devotion of a teenage sun-worshipper. Other times, he gazed around the gardens in delight. He reveled in the butterflies and flowers, the birds, the plants. Everything and anything seemed to bring a smile to his wrinkled features.

After a while, Asher found his companion's presence ... comforting. Almost a soothing balm on the rawness of his pain. Some of his stress seeped away, and the icy fist around his heart relaxed its grip, just a little.

As the afternoon's shadows stretched and darkened, Asher finally told Einstein about Willow. How much he'd loved her. Their happiness together. His recent black realization: Willow was dead.

Einstein listened with the patience of a grandfather, his watery eyes soft with sympathy. His aged head nodded in understanding and concern.

The next morning, Asher found Einstein waiting for him on the rooftop. The chef handed him a plate of whole wheat pancakes topped with canned strawberries, and a glass of canned fruit juice.

"Eat, son," Einstein ordered. "It's been days since your last proper meal."

Asher ate the food automatically, enjoying none of it. When he finished, he pointed to a trio of fountains in the middle of the vegetable beds. Their sprouting waters shimmered like liquid pink diamonds in the reddish sunlight.

"Willow had those installed," he told Einstein. "She loved this place. We used to visit here a lot and work in the gardens for hours. Other times, we'd pack a picnic lunch and eat it while looking at the view."

"This place must be special to you."

"Yes." He swallowed against the grief that burned his throat. "One day, she suggested adding some fountains and flowers." He pointed to the clusters of blossoms that hung on a trellis, their stray petals dancing and floating in the breeze. "She said the farmers up here worked with vegetables all day and needed some beauty for their souls."

Einstein murmured, "She sounds like a wise girl."

"She ... was."

Was.

It was one of the most brutal words in the English language, weighted with a terrible, bleak finality.

How could he bear it?

He drew in a shuddering breath. "Maybe it's for the best that she's gone. She didn't get to see how awful the world's become."

Einstein stared, perplexed. "What do you mean?"

Asher struggled to state the obvious. "Everyone's dead ... almost. Our world has changed. The terras will eventually destroy everything and everyone."

"No, yes, and nonsense."

"Excuse me?"

"*No*, not everyone's dead. We both know there are thousands of survivors across the planet. *Yes*, our world has changed. And *nonsense* that the terras will destroy everything."

"The Red Fever killed most of humanity."

"True."

"The terras are changing our world."

"Also true, son. But it's neither good nor bad. It just *is*." When Asher stared at Einstein, the old man furrowed his brow and carefully explained, "Our planet is over five billion years old, son. Change has been happening for every minute of those billions of years. Humanity has not been present since the birth of Earth. Our species only evolved in the past two million years. Eventually, humans will sink back into oblivion, as every species does, sooner or later. It's arrogant and foolish to think our hold on this world is permanent. It never is."

Through his misery, Asher struggled to comprehend these words and the concepts behind them. "I could probably accept these changes if they'd happened naturally. But these terras aren't from Earth. They're not terrestrial. They don't belong here."

Einstein shifted uncomfortably, as though he had a stiff back from sitting too long. "Earth isn't separate and alone, son. It's part of an immense universe. The billions of planets, suns, meteors, and asteroids are interconnected. Nature is not solely beautiful in our world and ugly everywhere else. Nature is beautiful everywhere and in many different forms."

"Not these terras. They don't belong here."

Einstein sighed. "Try to think of Earth as a single flower—part of an infinite garden that's called our universe, and which contains billions of flowers. None of the flowers exists by itself in isolation. They all exist in the garden together, pollinating each other, sharing resources, growing, and changing." A golden butterfly landed on the elderly man's hand and he studied it avidly, as though aware this might be the last time in his long life that a butterfly would alight on him. "We're all part of a cosmos, son, where nature is infinite. These terras are just an incredibly tiny part of that nature."

"So I should love these terras because they're a part of our cosmos?"

"Of course you can't love them, not when they've caused such death and misery. I lost my entire family too, you know. But you need to understand that the terras are not evil."

"They killed billions of us!"

"The terra plants didn't kill billions. Their Red Fever did." Einstein paused. "The plants didn't deliberately plan to wipe out humanity. It was just our bad luck that most humans were allergic to them. The terras simply behaved as plants do on Earth.

The seeds floated through space, looking for places to grow and flourish." He sighed again as the golden butterfly winged away. "They landed on Earth and, yes, they're changing parts of it. But it's still our home. It's still full of beauty and wonder and possibilities, especially for someone as young as you."

"Not without Willow in it. She was the love of my life."

"I'm sure she was, son. However, you may be one of the lucky ones, a person who finds another soulmate. Often we get more than one, you know. The next girl could be out there right now, waiting for you—and she might become the *great* love of your life."

"Impossible."

Einstein ignored Asher's reply. "But to find this great love, you need to look forward. You can't keep looking back to your past with Willow. If you do that, you won't see the new girl who's waiting for you in the present or in your future."

"Maybe I'm happier living in the past."

"You're too young to trade sixty years of your future for ten years of your past. What if the situation was reversed? What if you'd died and Willow had lived? Would you want her to spend her life grieving for you?"

"Of course not."

"Exactly. So don't dishonor her memory by becoming a shell of a human being. Don't emotionally retreat from the world. You only get one life. Live it to the fullest. If you ignore the beauty and wonder of our world, if you only focus on the bleak and black parts, your soul will die."

Einstein stood. The points he'd wanted to make for a few days had now, finally, been heard. "Think about what I've said, son. Meanwhile, I promised the others I'd prepare one of my world-famous vegetable stews for dinner tonight." His old eyes sparkled as if he were sharing a secret. "My stews weren't really world famous, but somehow they taste better when I tell people that."

Asher remained silent, waiting for the man to leave so he could return to his memories of Willow.

Einstein stretched his aching bones. Then, just before he left, he paused for one last piece of grandfatherly advice.

"Always remember, son, that a life lived looking back is a life half lived."

41

Einstein's words echoed in Asher's mind over the following days.

A life lived looking back is a life half lived.

His grief for Willow remained sharp, but he tried to blunt its claws by focusing on the present and the future.

He ate the meals the chef sent up to him. Stared out at the silent city stretching to the horizon. Visualized people hiding in buildings, alone, afraid. Frowned at the thought of the terras continuing to spread wherever they liked.

At first hesitantly, then with increasing determination, Asher resumed driving around Manhattan. He killed more terras, gathered more survivors, and within two weeks had doubled the community at Weston Tower.

The red-haired girl found at Hillsend High School remained weak and ill.

"I think Charlotte will recover," Nurse Ortiz assured him. "You found her just in time."

"Good."

"She keeps asking about her mother and some other people."

"I didn't find anyone else alive in that school. I'm guessing they're all dead."

The nurse nodded and returned to her patient.

Asher assigned some of the newcomers to the kitchen and indoor farms.

The rest were broken into two-person teams that searched the city. Several collected canned food, meds, and other supplies. On Asher's orders, they only took three-quarters of anything they found, leaving a quarter for survivors who hadn't joined his community. Other teams were tasked with capturing some of the animals that roamed the streets. Horses and camels were stabled for use as transportation. Pigs, deer, cows, and chickens were bred for meat or milk or eggs.

"What about the museums?" Chef Einstein asked Asher one day. "And the art galleries and libraries?"

"What do you mean?"

"It's only a matter of time before those buildings are destroyed by terras, wild weather, or vandals. We need to collect as many of their important pieces as possible and store them in Weston Tower. We must preserve as much of our history and culture as we can. They're an important part of humanity's heritage."

"Good idea, Einstein. I'll assign two teams."

Every scavenging or recovery team that left Weston Tower was equipped with high-tech radios. These allowed them to keep in contact with each other, depending on the weather or their locations. When the groups came across dangerous terras, they added them to Asher's growing list of plants to be destroyed.

Asher and Harlem, plus two other teams, focused on battling the dangerous terras. Asher knew they'd only be able to destroy a few hundred of the millions of non-terrestrial plants on the planet. He didn't care. Einstein might be right about Earth being one flower in an infinite cosmos, but he couldn't let these invaders win without a fight.

In one week alone, he and Harlem destroyed eleven patches of crawlers and eight fields of glow-lotus terras. They also obliterated seventeen clumps of Hades terras—golden plants that burst into flames when their leaves or stems were broken.

A few days later, Asher and Harlem heard music coming from an empty conference room in Weston Tower. Inside, an Asian teenager in a black leotard was practicing ballet.

She pirouetted and whirled to Tchaikovsky's *Sleeping Beauty*, dancing with the grace of a butterfly.

"Who's that?" Harlem breathed in awe.

"Soo-Yun. She joined the garrison a few weeks ago. Haven't you seen her in the mess hall?"

"I eat in my room."

"I wondered why I never saw you eating with the others."

"They're your people, not mine."

"They're *our* community. You need to start getting to know them."

Harlem waved his hand impatiently. "Tell me about this girl."

"According to Einstein, she was on a cultural exchange program when the Mist trapped her in New York. Everyone in her ballet troupe died except her. Poor kid. She's only fifteen."

The girl paused the music and padded across to them on frayed ballet shoes. "I on break from training to be medic. Is okay practice here, Asher?"

"Of course, Soo-Yun." He gestured to his colleague. "This is Harlem."

Mouth open, Harlem stared at the girl, as stunned as if he'd seen a flower in a tutu. "I ... um ... I didn't know they ... um ... had ballet in Asia."

"Once, Korea had many dance troupes," she said.

"Troops? Like soldiers with guns?" Harlem babbled. "Those guys look too mean for dancing."

She blinked at him. "Excuse, please?"

Asher explained to Harlem, "By dance *troupe*, Soo-Yun means dance *group*."

"Oh." Harlem struggled to speak, flustered by the lovely girl with the long black hair. "Er, Soup-Dung ... you speak English real good. You must have good'um teachers in Japan."

Soo-Yun's delicate nose crinkled. Pointedly, she stared at Harlem and sniffed. "Also, we had good bath and shower in *Korea*. Just as in Weston Tower. No?"

Harlem's mouth gaped as she gathered her iPad and sound cube and left. He turned to Asher. "Did she just say I stink, Don Q?"

"Sort of."

Harlem sniffed his armpit, then gagged. "I'm so stupid. She must've thought I was a pig."

The next morning, Asher was surprised when Harlem joined him at breakfast. The boy had freshly washed hair and scrubbed skin and wore a pair of newly laundered jeans and a shirt. From then on, he showered every second day, much to Asher's relief.

The following week, Harlem was isolated to his cubicle room with a cold.

Restless, Asher set off alone to handle some of the less dangerous terras. He had just sliced and diced a cluster of juvenile strangler terras on Fifth Avenue when he heard a clomping sound.

His eyes widened as a full-grown giraffe ambled toward him. The animal had obviously been released from a zoo, yet despite its previous sheltered life, it seemed unworried by the streets and buildings of New York.

Clopping to a halt in front of Asher, the giraffe bent its long neck, bringing its head down to his own. A pair of dark eyes peered at him, and he stood motionless as a blue-black tongue licked his face.

He winced but didn't pull away. The giraffe's licks reminded him of a scene in one of Willow's movies, where a cow had licked her face. The annoyed director had to reshoot the scene eight times, as she'd kept laughing at the tongue slicking her salted cheek instead of recoiling in horror as the script required.

Maybe this giraffe was mooching for carrots, he thought. Or maybe it just missed people. Whatever the reason, he felt an unexpected flicker of happiness as he petted the animal's furry neck. Was this what Einstein had meant when he'd told Asher to embrace the beauty and wonder in life? Was this a way to keep his soul alive?

He stroked the giraffe's soft fur and scratched behind its ears.

"How are you doing, boy? You look healthy. Obviously you're finding lots to eat in the parks and gardens. But stay away from those bad terras, okay?"

The giraffe snorted as if agreeing with him. Its curiosity satisfied, it clomped away, as carefree as someone out for a Sunday stroll.

Asher saw that the surrounding streets and pavements no longer held piles of decomp-dust. In the months since the Mist, the wind and rain had washed away most of the remains of people who'd died outside. Millions of piles, though, still lingered inside offices, apartments, and homes—

A startled cry interrupted his thoughts.

42

GUN DRAWN, ASHER PEERED around the corner of a building.

In an alley, a girl with a waist-length auburn braid was slowly backing away from a grizzly bear. Nearby, a rifle and machete lay on the seat of a muddy Harley-Davidson.

The bear had long scars on its furry back, and its right ear was ripped. Asher recognized the grizzly. It was the one that had threatened the bikers on Barr Street, when Lynxx had been suspended over a blazing car.

Rising onto its hind legs, the creature uttered a ferocious roar.

Pointing his gun at the sky, Asher fired three shots that boomed down the alley. Startled, the bear dropped to all fours and lumbered away.

The girl snatched up her rifle. "Thanks." As he approached, she raised the barrel. "Don't come any closer."

Stopping, he regarded her curiously.

Black grease streaked her face, camouflaging her features. Loose navy coveralls concealed her figure. Fingerless gloves covered her hands. A long auburn braid dangled from beneath a dark woolen beanie.

Although her eyes were hidden by sunglasses, Asher guessed she was in her midteens—too young to be burdened with the weapons she carried. In addition to her rifle and machete, she had a revolver tucked into her belt and a huge hunting knife strapped to her thigh.

She looked as if she'd grown up in the war-torn jungles of Vietnam.

This girl wasn't just a survivor, he sensed. She was a fighter.

Quickly, she stuffed the long braid beneath her woolen beanie, hiding it. Was she disguising herself as a boy? Had she heard the rumors about the gang of Wilders cruising the streets, snatching up girls?

"I won't hurt you, miss." Slowly, he tucked his revolver into his belt, within easy reach.

"I've heard that before."

"My name's Asher Weston."

A flicker of recognition crossed her face. "You look familiar."

"Do I?"

"Aren't you the boyfriend of that actress, Willow Grace?"

"I ... was." *Was.* The word still felt as sharp as broken glass on his tongue.

She lowered her rifle a little, watching him intently. "I'm Olivia." She withdrew a crumpled photo from her coveralls pocket. "I'm looking for my twin sister—" At a growing rumble of motorcycles in an adjoining street, she shoved the photo back in her pocket. "Wilders. They've already tried to grab me once." Hastily, she slung the rifle and machete over her shoulders.

"Wait, Olivia. My car is around the corner. Come with me. I'll protect you."

"I don't need your protection. And I'm not going anywhere with someone I've just met." The roar of the bikes grew louder. "Maybe you're okay, maybe not. I don't have time to find out right now." She straddled the Harley-Davidson, accelerated down the alley, and vanished into a side street.

Great. He'd just lost a potentially valuable fighter.

Asher stepped into the shadows as the Wilders thundered past the alley. There were a couple of dozen bikers, too many to confront by himself.

When the growl of engines had died away, he headed back to his car.

On his belt, his radio squawked, and Harlem's voice crackled from the speaker. "You there, Don Q?"

He rolled his eyes at the nickname. "Nix the Don Q, Harlem. I'm nothing like Don Quixote. That guy thought he was a knight. He fought imaginary dragons and tried to save people in danger. I'm just a guy fighting very real terras."

"And saving real people in danger. Po-tay-toe, po-tah-toe."

Asher rolled his eyes again but merely said, "I thought you had a cold and were taking it easy today."

"I'm feeling better. Luisa needed a couple of people to check out a tip with her, so I volunteered." He paused. "Soo-Yun's here too."

Asher gave a faint smile. Harlem had been smitten by the Korean girl since he'd met her.

"What's the tip?" he asked.

When Harlem told him, Asher's interest quickened.

"Stay put, Harlem. Don't touch anything. I'll be there as soon as I can. Good work, guys." If the equipment they'd found still worked, it might prove highly valuable.

It could even save people's lives.

43

ASHER TURNED HIS HYBRID Lexus into Central Park, planning on taking a shortcut to Harlem's location.

At the sound of shouts, he pulled over. Grabbing his backpack, he hurried through the trees.

A small group of people stood in a field. Nearby, the bodies of two children lay on a large patch of glow-lotus terras.

As he helped the group burn the lethal terras, a swarm of locusts shot up from the blazing plants.

Startled, a sick girl wearing an old aviator hat accidentally knocked a young woman, Sophie, onto the dangerous flowers. Within seconds, their stamens had punctured Sophie's body, and she'd suffered a quick but painful death.

The sickly girl was horrified and guilt-stricken, but Asher had no time to make her feel better. Although distressed at the woman's death, he launched into his usual recruitment spiel, hoping to persuade some of them to join his community at Weston Tower.

They hadn't been interested.

A shame. The teenage boy, Jase, might've made a good fighter.

He returned to his car and drove to the address Harlem had given him. After descending five flights of stairs, he entered a large underground bunker cluttered with computers and other equipment, all powered by an unseen power source.

In the main control room, Soo-Yun practiced a series of ballet steps in a corner, watched by an admiring Harlem.

Luisa sat at a computer console. Petite, with short curly hair, her brown eyes were often dull with misery, as if memories of her former life still haunted her.

Asher suspected that every survivor carried similar emotional burdens: The pain of missing loved ones. Regret for words not spoken. Guilt at being alive, while family members and friends were dead.

"What do you think, Asher?" Today, Luisa's eyes weren't dulled by memories of her past. They were beaming with pride at her latest discovery.

He surveyed the concrete-walled room. The windowless place seemed to be part of a citywide emergency notification center, possibly set up after 9/11. On one wall, a large map marked the location of loudspeakers across the city.

Luisa, a tech enthusiast, pointed to a bank of computers. "I think these control everything." The girl regarded the equipment with the awe of an archeologist discovering an Egyptian pharaoh's lost tomb.

"This is great." He gave a slow smile. "We could use this emergency system to send out warnings or alerts across the city. Every survivor would hear the messages, no matter where they live."

Harlem joined them. "Let's try it out, Don Q." He reached for a keyboard.

"Hang on." Asher pushed his hand away. "People will be terrified if they hear a piercing alarm after weeks of silence. We need to test the system in a way that doesn't frighten anyone."

"I have an idea." Luisa withdrew a CD from her backpack. "How about this?"

He examined the disk, an opera called *Lakmé*. He preferred modern music, but an operatic piece might be more soothing to survivors who were hiding around the city, struggling to live.

Most people were familiar with classical music, even if they'd only heard it in ads and movies. "Good idea. Where did you get it?"

"From an abandoned Honda motorcycle outside Central Park. I was searching the saddlebags for food, but there was none. The CD was the only thing worth taking. Oh, and this necklace." She showed it to Asher.

The crystal starburst on the gold chain looked familiar. A few months ago, he'd seen a pale, fragile girl wearing a similar necklace at the airport. That was the day he'd said goodbye to Willow, who'd been flying to LA to make a movie.

That was the day he'd lost the love of his life.

Pain twisted within him, its claws unblunted by the passing of time.

Face expressionless, he forced his gaze back to the *Lakmé* disk. "I didn't peg you as an opera fan, Luisa."

"My parents used to love this CD." Grief darkened her eyes once again.

"Oh. Sorry." Asher handed a map to Harlem, telling him, "You and Soo-Yun drive to some of the loudspeakers above-ground. See if the system still works. We'll meet up top in half an hour."

"Sure." Harlem eagerly turned to Soo-Yun. "You ready?"

She lifted her delicate chin and huffed, "You no call me Soup-Dung. Okay?"

"What? I would never—"

"Excuse, please. You call me Soup-Dung when we meet."

"Oh. My bad." As hangdog as a naughty puppy, he followed her up the stairs.

Asher turned to Luisa. "Can you see if the loudspeakers on the street upstairs still work?"

"Sure." She showed him how to transmit the music, then left.

A few minutes later, Asher played a random track from the *Lakmé* CD.

As the "Flower Duet" filled the bunker, he sat in a chair and listened to the duet, at first idly, then with growing pleasure. The two female voices were pure and melodic, like angels singing, and as the song rose in glorious harmony, he felt his stress seep away. When the track finished, he pressed replay, needing to wrap himself in the music again and again.

Maybe Einstein was right. Maybe it was still his world, one that still contained beauty and wonder.

For the first time since Willow had gone, Asher felt his spirit finally begin to heal.

And for just a few minutes, as he listened to the "Flower Duet," his soul soared.

44

A PUS-YELLOW TINGE STAINED the sky as Asher emerged from the post-9/11 bunker, onto the street.

Harlem and Soo-Yun were waiting on the cracked sidewalk, which was carpeted with thick terra weeds. A chilly wind howled between the buildings, sending Harlem into a coughing fit.

Soo-Yun passed their map to Asher, with several locations marked in red. "These loudspeaker are much working."

"Great."

He was relieved to see Harlem blow his nose on a handkerchief instead of a scrap of newspaper. He made a mental note to have a dozen more handkerchiefs delivered to his friend's cubicle. Harlem was rough around the edges, but since he'd met Soo-Yun he'd been trying to fit in more with the Weston community. He'd even started having his meals in the mess hall, arranging them to coincide with Soo-Yun's mealtimes.

Luisa winced at the strange sky. "Huh! For a few minutes, we had a normal sunset. I was beginning to think there was hope for the future."

Still stirred by the soaring music of the "Flower Duet," Asher said, "There's always hope. We just have to look for it."

"You're unexpectedly optimistic," she replied.

He knew the music was only partly responsible for his improved mood.

The greater part of his improved mood came from Einstein.

Every day, Asher would wander down to the kitchens and chat with the Weston Cell's head chef. He enjoyed hearing anecdotes about the students the old man had taught in his history lectures. In return, Einstein would listen as Asher talked about Willow or discussed problems with Weston Tower's growing community.

The elderly man was like the grandfather he'd never had, and he always left the kitchen feeling better.

"Einstein doesn't like to complain," Asher now said, "but he needs some more anti-inflammatories for his hands. His arthritis has been giving him a lot of pain lately." He pointed to a skyscraper across the street. "The Cariss Center has a stack of doctors' offices inside. I remember one of my drivers stopping here one weekend to pick up some meds."

"Driver? Wow, Don Q." Harlem gave a faint smile. "Big difference now eh?"

"Totally."

Whenever Asher thought of his previous life, it felt like something from a dream or a movie he'd once seen. The days of jetting around the world were gone forever. No more rafting in the Alaskan wilderness or mixing with superstars at Hollywood parties.

Parts of his previous life had been wonderful, but because of his tyrannical father, it had never been the carefree paradise that people had assumed.

Still, at least he hadn't had to worry about an apocalypse, the Red Fever, bikers, wild animals, and dangerous plants.

And yet ...

He scowled, too guilt-ridden to even allow the next thought into his mind.

It popped into his consciousness anyway.

And yet, despite all the awful things that had happened, he'd never felt freer than he did today. He was finally out of the cage containing the savage shark.

When Harlem coughed again, Asher said, "Your cold's not better, is it?"

"Not much."

"You're sick." These days, a lack of doctors and hospitals meant that simple diseases could turn fatal overnight. "Drive back to Weston Tower and ask Nurse Ortiz for some cough medicine. She has a key to the meds room."

"No can do. I need to go to the doctors' offices with you, Don Q. You're always saying we can't search buildings alone."

"I'll go with Asher," Luisa eagerly offered. "You should get that cough medicine, Harlem. You don't look well." Her face brightened at a sudden thought. "Hey, maybe Soo-Yun should go back with you." When Soo-Yun looked reluctant, Luisa fished a set of car keys from her pocket. "She can practice her driving."

Delighted, Soo-Yun grabbed the keys. "Much good idea."

Asher studied the weird yellow sky. Pieces of paper, leaves, and trash were cartwheeling down the streets, driven by a strengthening cold wind. "It looks like there's another storm coming, Harlem. When you and Soo-Yun get to Weston Tower, stay there. Hopefully, Luisa and I will be back before it hits."

Harlem turned to Soo-Yun, pleased to be spending more time alone with her. "Let's go." They hurried off, bending into the wind.

As Asher and Luisa crossed to the Cariss Center, a trash can barreled past them like a huge bowling ball, and a yellow rubber duck sailed by on a stream of wind. In the distance, an eagle screamed and an elephant trumpeted in response. Asher hoped that all the animals were taking shelter, especially his lion-friend-cum-fur-brother Zimba, and the soft-eyed giraffe he'd met earlier.

He was sure the human survivors were already hurrying indoors, aware of the coming storm.

In the Cariss Center's lobby, a brass directory listed the doctors' offices on the tenth and eleventh floors.

They climbed the stairwell to the tenth floor and searched the rooms for meds. As usual, they only took three-quarters of anything they found, leaving the rest for other survivors.

In an oncologist's office, he paused before a huge window. The sky was filled with greenish clouds that seemed to be slowly bubbling. Strange. The howling wind slammed its invisible hands against the windows, shaking them, and he peered at the fine lines that crisscrossed the glass like snail trails.

"What are you looking at?" Luisa asked.

He gestured to the web of hair-thin vines and tiny leaves on the glass.

She squinted at them. "How can vines grow up ten floors in a few weeks?"

"Maybe they didn't," he said, recalling the red dots that speckled the buildings following the Mist. "We know terras can grow almost anywhere, including concrete, metal, wood, sand. Maybe some terra seeds implanted themselves high on the walls of skyscrapers. And now they're spreading."

He studied the tiny cracks that fanned from the hair-thin vines. It looked like the roots had penetrated the glass, weakening it. The same thing was probably happening in bricks and metal and concrete everywhere; as the terra plants grew larger and thicker, buildings across the city could start developing multiple cracks.

Asher looked around the office.

Thin green lines grew on top of the doctor's expensive oak desk, the Persian rug, and over the walls. The vines even covered a leather couch, weaving a path around two mounds of decomp-dust.

His gaze lingered on the gray mounds.

Who had these people been? Had the cancer specialist died on this couch with a patient? A friend? A loved one?

No one would ever know the answers.

Things had changed almost overnight, he realized. For centuries in cities and towns, deaths had been recorded and people had been mourned, with their possessions handed down to the next generation. These days, most deaths went unrecorded and unmourned, and no one knew if there'd even be a next generation.

Luisa, searching cupboards for meds, awkwardly cleared her throat. "I'm sorry about Willow."

"Pardon?"

"I'm sorry about your girlfriend, Willow Grace. I used to see pictures of you and her on the internet. You looked really happy together."

He hesitated, remembering Willow's smile and the way her face had lit up whenever she saw him. "We were."

"Do you think she made it?"

"No," he replied, surprisingly calm. "She's dead, like nearly everyone else. It still hurts when I think about her, but I'm starting to accept it." He prayed she'd died quickly from the Red Fever. He couldn't bear to think she'd suffered a brutal death at the hands of some crazed person.

"It's hard to believe our families are gone."

"We have to keep going. There's nothing else we can do." He gave her shoulder a gentle squeeze meant to be comforting.

Her longing gaze showed that she'd misread his gesture.

Quickly, Asher pulled his arm away. He wasn't ready for a new relationship yet. When he closed his eyes, he could still smell Willow's perfume, hear the music of her laugh, feel the softness of her hand in his own. "We need to look for those meds, Luisa."

"Oh." She tried to hide her disappointment. "Sure."

They entered a huge admin room lined with desks. Many had enormous potted plants on them, their leaves healthy and thriving despite not being watered for weeks. A moment later, he realized these plants weren't in pots. They were growing in the desks.

They were terras.

At a loud bang from behind, he and Luisa jerked around.

45

HALF A DOZEN WILDERS blocked the doorway, their guns pointed at them.

"Oops," a biker said, kicking away a phone that had fallen to the floor. "I ain't much good at stalking people." He wore a dirty white T-shirt, blue jeans, and a red bandanna tied around his bald, tattooed head.

Asher stepped in front of Luisa, trying to protect her. "Is that what you were doing, Fang? Stalking us?"

The biker leader stared at the girl. "We're not stalking *you*, boy."

His men began crossing the room.

Keeping Luisa behind him, Asher backed toward the window. So the rumors were true: Wilders were snatching up girls. Should he grab the pistol tucked into his belt? No, bad idea. At this distance, and outgunned six to one, he'd be dead before he could even withdraw it.

The gang stopped a few yards away.

Fang's black eyes narrowed. "You seem to know my name, boy, but I don't know yours. Are you Adolf Jewman?" Angry red scars ringed the man's neck from the crawler terras two weeks ago.

"My name's Asher." He hid a grim smile. "Who's Adolf Jewman?"

Fang rubbed his scarred neck. "Someone I plan on killing long and slow."

Good luck with that, Asher thought. Was this guy stupid? No Jew on the planet would name their son after a German psycho who'd murdered millions of Jews in the Second World War.

A sprawling terra on a desk sprayed black goo over a biker.

"Aaargh!" the man cried. "It's one of those squirters that Lynxx told us about. The ones that spew gunk if you break their precious leaves. Stupid terras!"

Stalling for time, desperately trying to figure out an escape plan, Asher asked, "Do you guys know Lynxx? He's a friend of ours." Not strictly true, but maybe it would buy Luisa and him some goodwill with these thugs.

Fang nodded. "The science nerd gives us info about them stinking terras. In exchange, we let him live."

"Mighty big of you."

"My ma taught me to be mag-nan-i-mous." Fang pronounced the word carefully, as though it was one he'd recently learned.

Perhaps, Asher thought dryly, the man had one of those Word-A-Day desk calendars. "How did you find us?"

The biker leader smirked. "One of my guys saw you enter this building. When we seen all the docs' names in the lobby, we figured you were after meds. So we decided to kill two birds with one stone."

"What are you talking about?"

"You collect the meds for us. And we collect ourselves a girl."

Luisa gave a strangled gasp.

Asher stiffened. He couldn't—wouldn't—let them harm Luisa. "Sorry, she's not interested. You're obviously a charismatic and educated gentleman, Fang. I'm sure you'll find other females eager to join your gang."

"Folks are kinda scarce these days, boy. We gotta pump up our numbers."

"Then go on a recruitment drive," Asher snapped. "Offer cookies to entice people to join you. Or maybe some shoe-shine vouchers. Don't kidnap people."

"We're not just after anyone. We need girls so they can pop out brats."

"What?" Forcing teenage girls into their gang was bad enough, but to make them have babies—

"We need brats to take care of us when we're old. Lots of 'em."

Asher regarded Fang with confusion. Then understanding dawned. "Oh. You mean, like in Asia."

"Give the man a cigar."

He would've preferred an Uzi.

A skinny, lank-haired biker looked puzzled. "What happened in Asia?"

"Didn't you never read nothin', Viper?" growled Fang.

"What for? We had TV and the internet."

"To learn stuff," Fang snapped. "Knowledge is power. You should've cracked open a book or two. Or watched a documentary instead of them reality shows. Then you'd know that lots of places in Asia and Africa ain't had pensions or welfare or food stamps."

"Bummer."

"In Asia, the oldies used to brainwash their kids into respecting them big-time. When the parents got old and sick, the kids ended up taking care of them until they died. Sometimes they waited hand and foot on the oldies for twenty or thirty years."

"Yeah?" Viper thought about it. "Hey, you're right. The government's gone. We ain't getting no Social Security or welfare benefits. That ain't fair."

Asher scowled, disgusted at the entitlement mentality of these thugs. "Have you guys ever worked?" he asked. "Invented something useful? Provided a service? Paid taxes?"

Fang glowered. "Not the point." He looked at Luisa, his eyes hard and determined. "We're here for her."

The other bikers shifted their stares past Asher's shoulder. They stiffened. Lowered their guns. Gawked in horror.

Turning, Asher gaped at the roiling scene outside the wall of windows.

46

THE GREEN CLOUDS SEEMED to be boiling in the heavens, as though heated by a celestial fire. Wailing, the wind whipped trash past the skyscraper in an endless stream of debris.

Asher gasped as a huge brown object raced toward the windows. It looked like a dried ball of curved branches, similar to the tumbleweeds that rolled across deserts. Only this one was much larger. It was the size of a "walking ball": an enormous see-through inflatable sphere that people used to climb inside before rolling it down hills or walking it across water.

The massive "tumbleweed" slammed into the office's windows, bounced off, and floated away.

"What's that?" Luisa cried, pointing at a dark shape within the airborne ball-shaped terra.

"I think it was a baboon," Asher said.

The greeny-yellow clouds whirred and buzzed. Something was inside the strange, boiling formations.

Asher's pulse raced. He flicked a glance at the bikers.

They were staring at the storm. Stunned. Confused. Afraid.

Good, he thought. They were distracted.

A brown mass burst from a nearby cloud. Whirling and buzzing, it rushed forward, separating into thousands of tiny objects.

The noises outside the window became louder, and he squinted at the fine cracks in the glass. When the "tumbleweed" had slammed into the window a minute ago, it had damaged the already-weakened panes.

The brown swarm shot toward the building.

Everyone staggered back as the mass struck the windows with thousands of tiny blows.

Locusts. Each several inches long.

The weight and impact of the insects shattered the weakened panes, and glass shards crashed to the floor. A single window remained unbroken on the left, but the rest of the wall was completely open to the air.

The wind gushed into the room in a whirl of chaos and destruction.

So did the locusts.

The chittering insects swarmed everywhere. They snared Asher's hair. Crawled across his face. Tried to push into his mouth.

Panicking, the Wilders shouted and flailed at their tiny attackers. The wind joined the battle, grabbing and pawing everything in its path. Books and office supplies became airborne projectiles. Chairs toppled. Monitors crashed to the floor.

A few feet away, a biker with a Mohawk haircut shrieked and staggered in a circle, frantically brushing at dozens of bugs crawling over him. "Get 'em off! Get 'em off!" Stumbling backward, he slammed into the unbroken window, shattering it.

"Hey!" Asher yelled. He leaped forward. Grabbed the biker's T-shirt. Felt his left shoulder wrenched by the falling man's weight. Tried to hold him. Couldn't. The T-shirt ripped in his hand. "No!"

The screaming man plummeted to the ground, arms and legs flailing.

Sickened, Asher turned away from the death fall.

Ignoring his aching shoulder, he dragged a locust from his nostril. "Luisa," he shouted, scanning the room. "Luisa!"

The girl lay crumpled on the floor, grasping her throat. She uttered a strangled croak, her brown eyes mutely begging for help, her mouth crammed with wriggling, squirming locusts.

She was suffocating.

Asher ripped the bugs from Luisa's mouth and shoved away new ones that tried to push inside. What was going on? Locusts didn't normally try to hide inside people. Had something in the clouds—unseen and unknown—driven them crazy?

He'd removed the insects from Luisa's mouth, but she kept choking. Did she have some stuck further down her throat, out of reach?

He couldn't do anything more in this windswept, locust-filled room.

He snatched an old scarf from a chair and tied it over her nose and mouth, protecting her airways. Covering the lower part of his face with a handkerchief, he tried lifting her, but his wrenched shoulder flared in agony. With a silent apology, he slung her over his good shoulder like a bag of wheat.

The bikers were still yelling and batting at the whirling locusts.

Switching on his flashlight, he bolted from the room. One flight down, he entered another set of offices. In an internal reception area with no windows, he swept folders off a desk, placed Luisa on it, and positioned the beam of his flashlight on her face.

Heart thundering, he dragged the scarf from her mouth.

Lumpy shapes clogged her windpipe, the critters wriggling like something from a horror movie.

He checked for a pulse. Checked again. Again.

Nothing. She wasn't breathing. She was dead.

He was tempted to try CPR, but he knew the locusts clogging her throat would prevent air from reaching her lungs.

He stared at her, numb with shock. Luisa had started this day as a young and healthy survivor of the Red Fever. Now she lay on this desk, lifeless as a stone statue.

Briefly, he stroked her forehead. "I'm sorry. I wish I could have saved you. I wish you'd stayed back at Weston Tower. I wish ..."

He couldn't go on.

There were so many things he wished. If he listed them, he'd be here for hours. Each regret would weaken him only a little—but their combined weight would force him to his knees, crippling him.

A life lived looking back is a life half lived.

Asher rubbed his injured shoulder, biting back a cry of pain. He'd have to leave Luisa's body here and return later, when his shoulder was less sore and he had backup.

He made his way down a rear stairwell to the marble lobby and crossed to the glass walls.

On the sidewalk lay the Mohawk-haired biker who'd fallen through the upper window. His bloodied and broken body crawled with locusts. Thousands more insects whizzed and darted through the green-tinted air.

Asher guessed the bugs would also be covering the side of the skyscraper, their barbed feet scrabbling and grasping at the cement and glass surfaces.

The storm shrieked as it hurled trash through the air like missiles. It pummeled the building with vicious gusts, and it rapped the windows with green hail. Branches flew everywhere. A toppled bicycle scraped past the dead biker, pushed by the savage wind.

Asher watched the wild scene. In the past few minutes, Luisa had died, along with the Mohawked biker and, possibly, other bikers up on the tenth floor. He suspected that most of the surviving Wilders would shrug off their friends' deaths; these savage thugs didn't care about morality and civilized behavior. They thrived in a world of violence and destruction—much like the city outside, where chaos reigned.

Despite Einstein's words of wisdom, despite his own tentative reborn hope, Asher stared in dismay at the dead biker and the weird, raging storm.

His old fear returned, deeper and stronger this time.

Was humanity doomed?

47

THE STRANGE STORM RAGED all night. Finally, by morning, Asher was able to leave the building and drive back to Weston Tower.

The boiling green clouds had disappeared, leaving the usual red sky. He gazed at the clear heavens, relieved. Was the worst over? Were things about to get better?

Thousands of dead locusts littered the streets, and numerous buildings had shattered windows. However, most of Manhattan seemed undamaged. Even the animals had returned outside. Rhinoceroses grazed in a park. A family of skunks padded down a sidewalk. Birds feasted on the dead locusts.

Asher felt a flash of pride. Over the years, New York had endured terrorist attacks, civil unrest, pandemics, and other incredible stresses. It would take more than a wild storm to bring this proud and beautiful city to her knees.

If New York and its new inhabitants could survive, so could he.

He took some painkillers for his shoulder and gave Einstein a bottle of pills for his arthritis. Then he and some others retrieved Luisa's body from the skyscraper.

They buried her in a small park a couple of miles from Weston Tower, marking her grave with a wooden cross.

Asher's shoulder healed, and over the next two months he added more people to his community. He assigned two teams to clean away any terra seeds that sprouted inside Weston Tower or in its gardens. He increased the tower's collection of pieces from museums, libraries, and art galleries. He set up target shooting in an underground parking garage. He fought the terras with Harlem. Talked with Einstein. Organized food and medical supplies. Defused conflicts between people. Arranged for the younger children to receive basic schooling.

He also kept an eye out for Olivia, the girl who'd ridden off on her Harley-Davidson. He needed more fighters to battle the terras, and he sensed she'd be a valuable addition to the Weston Cell.

A couple of times, he thought he glimpsed her in the distance, but she always disappeared before he could catch up to her.

Overall, Asher's mountain of responsibilities was crushing, and once a week he took a few hours off to de-stress. Armed and alone, he would drive around the city checking things out. He noted the location of herds of deer and, incredibly, buffalo. He marked new outgrowths of terras on his maps. He spoke to the occasional survivor roaming the streets.

And, occasionally, he replayed his conversation with Einstein all those weeks ago:

"Willow was the love of my life."

"I'm sure she was, son. However, you may be one of the lucky ones, a person who finds another soulmate. Often we get more than one, you know. The next girl could be out there right now, waiting for you—and she might become the great *love of your life."*

Each time, he'd shake his head in disbelief at the thought of another girl becoming the great love of his life. *Impossible.*

One afternoon, during a drive through Central Park, he noticed something new in the North Meadow. Curious, he parked his vehicle and got out.

A blue sea covered half of the massive field.

Before the Mist, people had played soccer, baseball, and softball there. On warm summer days, the green grass and leafy trees had lifted the hearts of countless New Yorkers craving a natural setting.

Today, the picnickers were long gone, and the handball courts were leaden with silence. The trees around the North Meadow looked stiff and lifeless, with yellow growths clinging to their branches.

A harsh scream rang out.

Asher jerked.

Grasped the pistol in his belt.

Saw a black vulture with a red beak perched in a nearby oak.

Uttering another scream, the bird stretched its long bare neck forward and fixed its beady gaze on Asher. Its bright silver eyes stared at him intently.

Creepy.

He shivered, then looked back at the field.

In the North Meadow, three people stood in the middle of a sea of cobalt-blue flowers. Around them, the blossoms fluttered in a breeze, glittering like thousands of sapphires in the sunlight.

Awed by the incredible sight, he stepped forward.

Stopped.

Withdrew his binoculars.

Peered through them.

The people in the blue sea were two teenage boys and an old man with a thick white beard. The latter held a radio or walkie-talkie. All wore army camouflage outfits. Asher doubted they were military personnel, as they were too young and too old, respectively. Each one was watching the ground, faces worried, eyes wide with fear. Every so often, they clutched at each other and edged backward, as though trying to avoid ... what?

What was worrying them? Was something hidden in the flowers?

The blue flowers erupted into the air, scattering like confetti on the wind. One landed on his arm. Huh! It was a butterfly, not a flower. The insect's wings gleamed an iridescent blue.

The whirling-fluttering cloud of butterflies disappeared into the trees alongside the North Meadow.

Confused, he turned back to the huddled trio. The surrounding ground was no longer a sea of blue butterflies. It was a black and gnarly mass of roots which were slowly moving.

Terras.

A chill slid down Asher's spine. What was going on?

Cautiously, he moved forward, stopping when the three people yelled at him.

"Stay where you are."

"Don't come any closer!"

"You'll die."

What were they talking about?

He studied the black ground.

The twisted roots—some as thick as a man's wrist—veined the broken earth. Their gnarled surfaces were layered with nectar that smelled like heated honey, and he guessed this scent had drawn the cloud of butterflies. Had these three strangers wandered among the thousands of blue insects, marveling at their beauty—and unaware of what lay beneath the shimmering wings? By the time they felt the ground start to shift beneath their feet, had it been too late?

Probably.

What did these terras do?

He frowned at the knotted, veiny plants. Even though Einstein had said that nature was beautiful everywhere, these things were the exception. They'd be ugly in any part of the universe.

In the distance, a thunder of sound swelled louder and louder.

Whomp-whomp-whomp-whomp.

Stunned, he watched a dark shape emerge from the canyon between two rows of tall buildings.

48

WHOMP-WHOMP-WHOMP-WHOMP.

It was an old military helicopter, its blurred blades scything the air as it headed toward Central Park.

Asher stared in astonishment. Where had the chopper come from? Who was flying it? What was it doing here?

It soared over the treetops in the park, crossed to the trio trapped in the middle of the black roots, and hovered above them.

Then it flew toward him in a deafening roar.

A long rope dangled from a landing strut, swaying as the pilot attempted to position the line above his head. The message was clear: *Grab the rope.*

He hesitated. Who were these people? What was he getting himself into?

He glanced at the small group trapped in the middle of the slithering, twisting roots. Obviously, they needed help.

He grabbed the rope and climbed, pushing against the downdraft of air from the whirling blades. *Don't fall*, he told himself. *Don't fall.*

Finally, he pulled himself into the open cabin, where the noise of the blades was still deafening. The pilot thrust a headset with a microphone into his hands, and he clamped it over his ears, reducing the racket to a bearable drone.

He looked at the pilot closer. "Colonel Powell!"

It was the Army officer from the airport a few months ago. Asher had helped the black man save a maintenance worker who'd been hanging from some scaffolding.

So Powell had survived the Red Fever.

Relief washed through Asher. Even though he'd only spent a few hours with the man, at least he was a familiar figure, someone he sort of "knew."

In the weeks following the Mist, all of Asher's family members, friends, acquaintances—*the love of his life, Willow*—had died. Since then, every person he'd met had been a stranger. The realization that his life was now composed of strangers had left him feeling disconnected and empty inside.

But he had met this Army officer a few days after the Mist. This touch of familiarity felt good. Real good.

At the controls, Powell flashed him a strained smile. "I thought it was you, Asher. I need your help again."

"Of course, sir."

He noted the weary droop of the colonel's shoulders, the new lines of stress bracketing his eyes, and the worry shadowing his face. Like every survivor, Powell appeared to be struggling with the changed world. Was he finding this new life to be physically draining and soul-destroying? Maybe this was what Einstein had meant when he'd advised Asher to embrace whatever beauty and wonder he could find, as a way to keep his soul alive.

"What's going on, sir?"

Powell pointed to the trio on the ground. "One of my squads radioed that they were trapped. I didn't have time to wait for backup." He frowned, his dark eyes dull with anxiety and fatigue. "Someone's missing. There are supposed to be four in that squad."

Squad?

"What do you want me to do, sir?"

"I'm fairly new at flying choppers." Powell sighed, as though admitting a personal flaw. "I need you to help me position the rope close enough for them to grab it. We have to hurry. They're trapped in a patch of tentacle terras. There's not much time."

Tentacle terras?

"Okay." Holding a grab handle, Asher crouched next to the open door and yelled directions to the colonel. "A couple of feet left ... go right a bit ... back up ..."

The rope edged closer to one of the boys, who caught it. He knotted it around the waist of the old man and tugged at the line.

"Pull up, Colonel," cried Asher.

Powell lifted the chopper into the air.

The old man rose from the dark roots, swung past them, and was lowered to a patch of green grass. Untying the rope, the man sank to his knees, as if weak with relief.

Asher and Powell repeated the procedure and safely deposited one of the boys next to the old man.

By the time they returned, the remaining teen was in trouble. His ankle was caught in a clump of roots. He tried cutting himself free, but his knife dropped into the tangled terras.

"I need to go down, sir," Asher cried, hauling up the rope.

"Be careful, son. Those things are deadly."

"Deadly how?"

Powell quickly detailed the tentacle plants' properties.

Asher felt the blood drain from his face. Swallowing, he nodded at the colonel, mutely acknowledging his warning.

Powell lowered the chopper until it was a few feet above the grass.

Asher jumped out and knotted the rope tightly around his waist. He held on to it as the helicopter rose, lifting him fifteen feet above the ground. Swinging on the end of the line, he moved through the air, toward the boy.

"Lower me another five feet, Colonel," he said, speaking into his headset.

"Roger."

The chopper slowly descended.

"What's the kid's name, sir?"

"Billy."

Asher yelled to the frightened boy below, "Hang on, Billy." The poor kid looked about thirteen or fourteen. He should've been playing video games or skateboarding with his friends, not battling to survive in a field of tentacle terras.

Leaning down, he shoved the handle of a knife into Billy's outstretched hands. The downdraft of air from the blades pummeled Asher, and he tightened his hold on the rope, wishing he had a harness for the kid. But there hadn't been one in the cabin. "Hurry, Billy."

The boy slashed at the terra gripping his ankle, triggering a spray of brown liquid that splattered his army camouflage pants. A few hacks later, the terra dropped away in pieces.

Holding the rope, Asher reached for the scrawny kid.

A gnarled root, long and ugly, shot from the writhing black terras. It wrapped itself around Billy's legs—and yanked.

49

THE BOY TOPPLED FORWARD, landing facedown on the writhing tentacle plants.

"He fell, Colonel!" shouted Asher. "Get me closer to him."

Billy screamed as dozens of roots burst from the earth and wrapped themselves around his skinny body.

The chopper descended.

"Help me!" The kid's high-pitched plea rose above the racket of the overhead blades. The encircling roots shifted, and he disappeared into the black mass, his screams dying away.

Asher gaped at the slithering terras, searching for Billy. Nothing.

No sign of the boy. No shouts.

"Did you get him?" Powell cried. "Is he okay?"

"I can't find him." Asher fought down the panic that welled in his throat.

"Keep looking, son."

"I am." He scoured the ground. Couldn't see him. "He's gone!"

Amid the pounding downdraft from the rotors, Asher grabbed the rope and hauled himself into a vertical position. Holding the rope with one arm, he squinted at the ground.

Something moved in the blackness below.

Hope flickered within him. Was that a boot near the edge of the roots?

An instant later, the boot was gone. Perhaps he'd only imagined it, but he had to check.

"Head to the edge of the terras, Colonel. Your ten o'clock."

"Roger."

As the chopper moved left, a dark root whipped up, wrapped itself around Asher's left calf—and pulled.

He slid down the rope, almost losing his grip. Somehow, he held on, yelping as the serpentine terra tightened around his leg. The thing felt like coiled steel, squeezing with incredible strength.

"Hold your position!" he yelled at Powell via his microphone. "Hold your position." If the chopper rose up or moved forward, his left leg could be ripped apart.

The chopper hovered in place.

One hand gripping the rope, Asher scrabbled for his spare knife with the other. But the blade was in his ankle sheath, which was squashed by the encircling terra. Impossible to reach.

Another root shot upward and twisted around his other ankle. This second terra tightened. Pulled.

He yelled as pain flared through his body like the upward thrust of a sword. The tightly knotted rope around his waist threatened to cut him in half, and both his legs felt as if they were being dragged from their hip sockets by the two tentacle plants.

According to Powell, if he fell onto the writhing terras, they'd dissolve his body for food. Once they'd finished with him, the things would produce more sugary nectar to attract another crowd of insects. More butterflies would swarm across the mass of roots, their fluttering wings hiding the dangerous terras beneath them. And so the cycle would continue.

Another tug from the plants.

The roots were gripping him so tightly that he thought he'd be torn in two. Across the grass, the old man and the boy huddled together, too scared to help.

Maybe he could untie the rope at his waist and just fall. Hopefully, his death by those shifting roots would be quicker and less painful than having his legs ripped off.

No! He couldn't let these terras win. He couldn't let them steal all the years ahead of him, all the possibilities ... his future. Despite Willow being dead, despite his life changing in so many ways, he realized Einstein was right—joys and wonders still existed in the world.

He wanted to live.

A motorcycle burst from the forest, roared across the field, and screeched to a halt near the terras. A girl jumped off the Harley and ran to the edge of the black patch. A dark woolen beanie covered her head, grease streaked her face, and she wore navy coveralls too big for her slender figure.

"Olivia." It was the girl he'd briefly met in an alley a couple of months ago.

Machete in hand, she slashed at the outstretched roots holding him. The terra roots sprang apart, brown liquid spraying the air like hoses gone wild.

She leaped back, dodging a tentacle plant that whipped toward her.

Around Asher's legs, the severed roots relaxed their grip.

He yelled into his microphone, "Go, Colonel! Go!"

He rose into the air as Powell flew the chopper across to the two remaining members of his squad. After lowering him to the ground, Powell landed the chopper nearby.

The old man with the white beard passed Asher a knife, which he used to saw through the severed roots still clutching his legs.

Powell raced across. "George, where's Ben?"

"He didn't make it," the old man replied.

Powell unleashed a torrent of swearing.

As Asher cut the rope ringing his waist, Colonel Powell hustled the others into the parked helicopter.

Olivia ran to Asher. "Are you okay?"

"I'm good." He rubbed his calf, trying to restore circulation. "Thanks. I owe you."

"No, you don't," she told him. "You scared off that grizzly in the alley, remember? We're even."

Inside the chopper, Powell shouted to them, "I've just received a message from another squad. A pack of Wilders is headed this way. We need to leave."

She raced across to her Harley. "I gotta go."

"Wait," he called after her. "Come with us. We can use someone like you in our group."

"Can't."

As the helicopter rumbled into life, he called out, "Hey, did you ever find your sister?"

The growing noise of the rotors drowned out her response.

"What?" he cried, straining to hear.

"Yes, I found her." Straddling the Harley, she started its engine and roared toward the forest.

Frustrated, he watched her leave. He'd just lost another good fighter again. Sighing, he climbed into the chopper.

At the controls, Colonel Powell shouted over his shoulder, "Don't worry about Olivia, son. She can take care of herself."

"You know her, sir?"

"We've met a few times. She's not interested in joining any community." As shouts came from the southern end of the field, the colonel cried, "Shut the door, son. We're leaving."

The old man sat up front next to Powell, with the young boy in the back.

"Go, Colonel," Asher yelled, closing the door and taking a rear seat.

With a swelling *whomp* of rotors, the chopper rose, swung left, and swept down the field. Below, a dozen motorcycles emerged from the forest and charged across the field in pursuit.

Asher recognized the red bandanna of the rider at the front of the pack.

Fang.

Enraged at the escape of the helicopter, Fang and the other bikers raised their rifles and fired.

50

ASHER PRESSED BACK IN his seat, bracing for disaster.

Would the chopper take a direct hit? Crash to the earth in a blazing inferno? His mind flicked back to the small plane brought down by bats the day Willow had left for Los Angeles.

The military helicopter soared above the forests of Central Park and swung toward the buildings.

Breathing a relieved sigh, he looked out of the window.

The chopper headed down a wide street lined by skyscrapers. This concrete canyon amplified the *whomp-whomp* of the blades, and a herd of grazing deer scattered at their approach. A black vulture winged above the fleeing animals, as though shadowing them. He wondered if this was the same silver-eyed vulture from the North Meadow.

It felt strange seeing wild animals replacing humans on the streets of New York, their presence a powerful reminder of the new world order.

He studied the buildings. Each was a monument to man's past achievements. Some were free of terras; others had plants growing up their walls. Although survival would always be at the top of the Weston Cell's priorities, Asher felt a renewed determination to save as much of this city as possible. He and Harlem and the two other teams couldn't do it alone. He needed to increase the number of people fighting the dangerous terras throughout Manhattan.

A short while later, Colonel Powell landed the chopper on a helipad beside the Hudson River.

Asher climbed from the cabin, glancing at the Statue of Liberty across the dark waters. He remembered standing with Willow on the deck his father's yacht on Thanksgiving night. As the vessel had powered through New York Harbor, they'd seen thousands of red terra seeds drift past Lady Liberty. Those glittering sparks had been a blood-red omen of the future.

Three and a half months ago, he'd been on a luxury yacht with Willow. Today, he was a soldier caught up in a dangerous war. His time with Willow now seemed unreal, part of another life and another world.

He sighed, then shifted his attention back to the parked helicopter. "Is that yours?" he asked as Powell joined him.

"Technically, no. We try to keep it fueled, though, in case of emergencies. Like today." The man gave a tired smile. "Good work back there, son. I knew I could rely on you."

Warmth surged through Asher at the unaccustomed praise, doused a moment later by a chill of guilt. "We didn't save them all."

"We saved some, and that's important. In life, we need to learn from our failures and celebrate our successes."

"You sound like our head chef, Einstein."

"Your chef?" A furrow creased Powell's forehead. "Look, kid, I know you come from a mega-wealthy family, but if you still have a chef—"

"It's *our* chef," Asher rushed to explain. "The man who cooks for our group."

"What group?"

He told the colonel about the dozens of people living at Weston Tower and their various jobs.

When he finished, Powell nodded in approval. "Nice work, son. You've got a good setup there. Much better than mine."

"Yours?"

Powell sketched a similar situation. Over the past two months, he'd gathered seventy-five people who lived in an underground shopping mall. Most spent their days scavenging for food or searching for fuel to power their generators. Only a couple of units were spared to fight the terras.

Asher remembered his brief conversations with the colonel at the airport terminal. Powell was an experienced Army officer used to dealing with battles and strategies. The man was a leader. And the group at Weston Tower needed a mature, experienced leader, not a teenager.

Apart from Einstein, it had been ages since Asher had respected and admired an adult. In the past, his relatives and teachers had pandered to his father. And most of the businessmen he'd met had shared Rufus Weston's greed, his ruthless ambition, his lust for power.

Colonel Powell was driven by different morals. He'd joined the military to serve his country. Protect its citizens. Make a difference to society. These days, the military no longer existed—or the government, the police, and other emergency organizations.

But Powell was still performing his chosen role in life. Still protecting people. Still making a difference.

For years, Asher had breathed in the pollution of his father's vile personality. It felt good to revel in the fresh air of this Army officer. He could learn a lot from him.

Trying to hide his eagerness, he asked, "Why don't we join our two groups together, Colonel? There's room for us all in Weston Tower." He pointed to the military helicopter. "There's even room for the chopper in our plaza. We could block off some streets to create a secured garrison and a huge courtyard for the chopper and other vehicles."

The middle-aged man considered the proposal. Then he fixed Asher with a sharp stare. "Merging is a possibility. But I don't take well to being ordered around by seventeen-year-olds."

He heard the unspoken question. "No worries. I'm very good at taking orders from Army colonels."

With a faint smile, Powell said, "If I'm in charge, I'll want to do things my way."

"You're the boss."

"I haven't agreed yet."

"You will, once you see what we've got." Asher grinned, unable to hide his pride as he announced, "We have farms, water, an infirmary." His grin widened. "And electricity."

Interest sparked in the man's tired eyes. Gruff-voiced, the colonel said, "Next you'll be telling me you have hot showers and working toilets."

"Actually, we do."

A muscle twitched at the corner of Powell's mouth as he struggled to maintain his neutral expression. Finally, his face broke into a wide smile, like baked earth softening beneath longed-for rain. "Shoot. I know I'm supposed to say that I'm fine with roughing it. After all, when I was in the Army, I lived in muddy swamps and bone-dry deserts for weeks on end. But ..."

"But what?"

"I really miss electricity. And showers." Powell laughed, a warm sound that lightened the air. "I'd like a tour of your place."

"How about now? Do you have a car nearby?"

"Follow me."

51

By the time Powell had inspected half of Weston Tower, Asher could tell the man was definitely interested.

By the time they reached the rooftop gardens, the colonel was already making plans. "If we increase our numbers, son, we can expand our areas of operations." Powell's former tiredness had vanished, and his spirit seemed recharged by hope and new possibilities. He crossed to the parapet that edged the roof and gazed at the view of Manhattan stretching northward to the horizon.

"What type of operations, sir?" Asher asked.

"Fishing, for a start. Stockpiling fuel and an arsenal of guns. We also should expand our range of vehicles; I know where we can get some Hummers and Templars."

"Templars?"

"They're like armored SUVs."

"Okay, they'll be useful. But why do we need an arsenal of guns?"

"For protection," Powell told him. "There's a gang of bikers in Manhattan who are pure trouble, son. That girl today, Olivia, has had a couple of encounters with the Wilders."

Asher's attention sharpened. He was still keen to enlist the teenager as a fighter. "What do you know about Olivia?"

"Not much. She always keeps to herself. But I know that she really hates Wilders."

Asher recalled his own dealings with the thugs. He remembered that plaid-shirted country guy, Lynxx, strung up over a burning car, and his team member, Luisa, being stalked as a breeder. "I've had run-ins with them myself."

"We've had a lot of trouble with them. Once the Wilders find out about Weston Tower and all its wonders—and they *will* find out sooner or later—they'll try to take this place by force. We need to start protecting ourselves now."

Asher nodded, relieved to be passing the leadership onto Powell. "Okay. I only want one thing."

"Which is?"

"To continue fighting the terras. We have to keep the ones in Manhattan as under control as possible, especially the dangerous ones."

"No arguments here, son." Powell's voice rang with a conviction and determination that matched Asher's. "In fact, since we're merging our groups, we can increase the number of squads available to fight them. We'll organize a systematic battle plan. Draw up strategies. Figure out ways to kill the terras; fire kills some, so we'll need to train people to use flamethrowers."

Asher felt a stir of excitement. Hummers. Armored Templars. Flamethrowers. Strategies. Obviously Colonel Powell was the right leader in a war. At the moment, there were two looming enemies: the terras and the Wilders.

And there was always the possibility, Asher suspected, of a third unknown enemy emerging sometime in the future.

What was that line? *Be prepared, or prepare to fail* ... or die, in this case.

At least with Powell, they'd be ready.

The colonel continued, "There's this teenager named Lynxx. He's given my group valuable tips on how to kill some dangerous terras. We could use his expertise."

"Lynxx? I've tried getting him to join my community a few times, but he's a real loner."

"True. He's still darn useful, though, and a brilliant scientist." Powell stuck out his hand to Asher. "Let's do it, son. Let's join forces and start a real resistance movement."

"Count me in, sir."

They shook hands.

After Powell left to inform his community of the merger, Asher returned to the rooftop gardens. As he watched the sun slowly sink in a red sky, a wave of emotions washed through him. Relief that Colonel Powell was taking charge. Excitement at having a focus each day: fighting the terras. Hope for the future.

For the first time in ages, he felt happy and fulfilled.

It was time to move on. Live his life.

"Goodbye, Willow," he whispered.

To his surprise, his farewell wasn't sharp and heartbreaking. It was soft with memories and gentle with regret. He would always love Willow, and the pain of her death would shadow him forever. He would never forget her. But she belonged to the past, not the present.

In the sky, the golden eagle WindLord cruised the air in graceful circles. On the streets far below, humans and animals were finding new ways to survive in the strange urban jungles of New York.

Einstein was right, he thought. Despite constant changes—or perhaps because of them—life would continue on.

Asher gave a faint smile.

Maybe Einstein was right about relationships as well.

Maybe there was another girl out there ... a girl who would become the great love of his life.

Maybe.

LYNXX

Great love awakens the soul

52

DAY ZERO—Thanksgiving

NEW YORK

No one suspected a thing.

Lynxx stood in the shadow of an oak, observing the picnickers in New York's Central Park.

Families sprawled on blankets as they ate lunch. Children chased each other across the grassy Sheep Meadow, squealing in delight. Nearby, a group of teenage boys waged a tug-of-war match.

Everyone was enjoying the unseasonably warm and sunny Thanksgiving Day.

No one knew what was coming tonight—except for him and the other Outriders. Only they would survive the First Wave of the apocalypse.

He studied the carefree crowd in the meadow. For thousands of years, humanity had strutted the continents, believing they were the rightful heirs to this planet.

They were wrong.

Humans didn't fully understand that strength could come in all sizes. Weapons could be created in all forms.

And death could sneak in on silent feet like an uninvited guest at a party.

Lynxx wondered what these picnickers, these walking dead, would experience in the coming weeks. What would it be like to feel panic, dread, terror ... grief? He was a hybrid, his alien genes mixed with an equal number of human genes. Technically, that meant he should be able to experience a range of human emotions.

And yet he felt nothing as he watched these doomed people. No compassion or empathy. No guilt.

As an Outrider, he'd been created to blend in with Earth's inhabitants. For sixteen years he had lived among them, but he'd never been one of them. He'd been homeschooled in a remote farmhouse in Ohio, his days spent poring over science texts and lab equipment. Limited television, internet, and music. Little contact with anyone except for a few other Outriders and his albino guardian, Frost.

Two months ago, Frost had sent Lynxx into position. His job was to observe the effects of the First Wave on the inhabitants of New York and to take notes on how quickly they died from the Red Fever.

He glanced up from his notebook as a pale girl in jeans and a white top hesitantly approached him. She looked in her mid-teens. Her shoulder-length auburn hair shone in the sunlight, and her green eyes appeared frightened.

What did this one want?

Since his arrival in New York, he'd found that his regular features and toned physique had attracted the attention of both males and females. Most had wanted a relationship with him, either physical or emotional.

All the males had been disappointed, and many of the females.

The auburn-haired girl paused before him. She took a deep breath, leaned up, and kissed him.

He stiffened, about to shove her away.

Instead, to his surprise, he found himself gathering her into his arms and crushing her mouth with his own. Her lips felt sun-warmed and soft, and a faint scent of jasmine wafted from her skin. Something about this female—a vulnerability, a fragility—reminded him of a glass figurine in danger of shattering.

He was kissing one of the walking dead.

As his mouth pressed against the girl's lips, she trembled in his embrace, and his cheeks warmed beneath the heat radiating from her body.

Something stirred within him. A foreign emotion. Human.

He felt ... curious ... about her.

Who was she? Why was she in the park? How did someone so frail survive in the wilds of New York City?

And why did he almost enjoy kissing her?

After several long and confusing moments, he pulled away from her, muttered "Interesting," and walked off.

He crossed to a new viewing spot further down the tree line. Once he settled into the shadows again, he glanced at his watch.

In a few hours, the First Wave of the apocalypse would arrive.

Lynxx labeled the auburn-haired girl in the park "Subject 77."

She joined a long list he'd made since his arrival in New York: men, women, and children of various nationalities, jobs, or classes of society. Some subjects had addresses, but he didn't use names. He preferred numbers and descriptions: *Subject 19, the homeless old man in Borant Alley, Brooklyn; Subject 34, the bus driver in the Tannic Apartments, Queens.*

After the girl left Central Park, he made discreet inquiries among the teens watching another tug-of-war match.

"Yeah, Kassia ... Kassia Madison. She lives down the block from me," a boy said, his avid gaze locked on Lynxx's face. "You want her address?"

"Yes." He wrote her details in his notebook.

"She's got leukemia, you know. It's one of those bad types that'll croak her sooner rather than later." The boy spoke with a cold calculation, as though hoping the girl's illness would make Lynxx transfer his attention to him instead.

Lynxx noted this new information. Leukemia. So, she was already seriously ill. Most of his other subjects would die over the coming weeks, but there was no way this girl would survive the apocalypse for more than a few days.

His pen hovered next to the number he'd given her: 77. Then he jotted down her estimated death date: Day 4.

53

SUBJECT 77, THE GIRL with leukemia, was still alive on Tuesday, Day 5.

During his wanderings around the red-hazed city, Lynxx paused outside the Harriet Beecher Stowe High School in the Bronx.

For a long time, he stared at the empty building. Never again would it ring with life and laughter. His guardian, Frost, had warned him the death rate would start skyrocketing from Day 6 or 7.

Even now, people weren't too worried. They still thought that life was semi-normal. They still believed they had a future. Everyone was aware of the red mist in the air, and they saw the tiny multicolored plants that speckled the ground and buildings. However, no one realized—yet—that the mist and the plants were relentless forms of death.

At a sudden cry, he looked around.

Subject 77 sat on the sidewalk, supporting the head of a blond-haired girl who had collapsed. A friend crouched beside them, face panic-stricken as she pulled a wad of tissues from a bag.

Blood streamed from the blonde's nose and down her yellow top. She had The Bleeding.

Frost had mentioned this variation several months ago.

"Most will die from the Red Fever," his albino guardian had explained. He'd licked his wormlike lips in eager anticipation.

"Their symptoms will be the same. They'll fall unconscious, their throats will close up, and they'll expire."

"They'll die quickly?" Lynxx had asked.

"Unfortunately, yes. After all these years, after all this work, I deserve a longer, grislier spectacle. You know, like a movie. *The Texas Chainsaw Massacre* is barely eighty minutes long. Morons! It should've been at least four hours."

Lynxx wasn't surprised at Frost bringing horror movies into their conversation yet again. The few hybrids he'd met at the farm had behaved like model Outriders: obedient and emotionless soldiers. But his guardian had always been more emotional. He reveled in gory movies and enjoyed watching people getting hurt. Perhaps, Lynxx surmised, it was something to do with being an albino, an object of stares and whispers whenever Frost had moved among humans.

His guardian stared at him with bloodshot eyes that reminded Lynxx of raw meat. "Why do you care if they die quickly?" Frost asked.

"I don't. It's just less messy if they go fast."

"If you don't like mess, then you won't like The Bleeding." Another anticipatory lick of his wormlike lips.

"What's that?"

"Some people will bleed heavily from their noses, then fall unconscious and expire." The man smirked as he gazed into the distance, as though visualizing a gory scene from one of his favorite slasher movies. "I guess it doesn't matter how they die, as long as they do."

Outside Stowe High, Subject 77 looked up from her fallen friend, saw Lynxx, and shouted at him, "Hey! Call an ambulance. Hurry."

He jotted down some notes. *Day 5. Subject 77 is still alive.*

Her voice rose in desperation. "Call an ambulance. Help us."

She shows no sign of the Red Fever, an unexpected result in one already seriously ill before the Mist. Pocketing his notebook, he turned and walked away.

"Jerk!" she yelled at him.

Lynxx didn't react. Didn't look back at her. If she realized he was a part of this apocalypse, even in a small way, he was certain she'd yell much worse things at him.

Deep in his stomach, a tiny knot formed and tightened.

He ignored the strange sensation.

Instead, his thoughts shifted to the oncoming fall of humanity.

How ironic. For centuries, humans had bragged about "survival of the fittest." They'd preached that it was the natural order of things. The way of the world. Life.

They were absolutely right.

54

Five weeks later, it was New Year's Day—and the city was almost dead.

Lynxx stood outside the Hayden Planetarium. He'd never visited the world-famous attraction before. A shame. He wished he could've compared its artificial star-filled heavens with the night skies back in Ohio.

Now, of course, New York's artificial lights were permanently darkened, and its veils of pollution were finally thinning. For the first time in centuries, the night skies above Manhattan were lit with thousands of diamond-bright stars.

He walked to the corner of Columbus Avenue and West Eighty-First Street. From here, he scanned the deserted sidewalks and the empty buildings. A hush filled the midday air, as though all of New York's sounds had died along with its inhabitants.

It wasn't true, of course.

He could hear the faint cries of birds in the red sky. The scrape of windblown trash along the pavements. The occasional gunshot. The rumble of a distant vehicle.

Some humans—a fraction of one percent—had survived the Red Fever. Back in Ohio, his guardian, Frost, would already be gathering information on the problem, resentful at having to analyze new data instead of watching *Evil Dead* again.

Lynxx scanned his surroundings.

Although humanity was dying, the terras were thriving. In this section of Columbus Avenue, many buildings remained untouched. Others had vines climbing their walls, their leafy fingers clawing fresh territory each day. A scattering of bony green stems poked from the curb. Tendrils strangled two trash cans. A mesh of plants smothered a parked car.

The terras were spreading faster than he imagined and—

A scream sliced the silence, coming from an alley on his left.

He frowned at the annoying interruption to his thoughts.

More screams shredded the air, shrill with pain and terror. They spiraled upward, then stopped.

Lynxx hesitated.

He crossed to the alley and peered around the corner.

Halfway down the narrow passage was an orange-haired man wearing a tattered cloak made from the skin of a zebra. His long, frizzy locks fluttered in the breeze as he kneeled next to a young woman on the ground—stabbing her over and over again with a huge hunting knife.

Blood flowed.

The female shuddered, then lay still in a dark pool of death.

The man with the zebra-skin cloak began carving chunks of flesh from her abdomen.

Lynxx stifled his startled gasp. In the past month, he'd come across several partially eaten bodies in side streets and lanes. He'd thought the people had been killed by wild animals, but what if this man had slaughtered them for their flesh and then left the remains for animals to feed on?

The murderer jammed pieces of flesh into a plastic bag. When it was full, he sliced a small chunk from the woman's thigh and shoved it into his mouth. As he clambered to his feet, Lynxx glimpsed a gun wedged in his belt.

The man licked blood off his fingers. Clutching the bulging plastic bag, he disappeared down the alley, his zebra-skin cloak flapping in the wind.

Lynxx surveyed the mutilated body.

Thousands of cans sat in kitchens throughout the city. Deer, pigs, and other edible animals roamed the streets.

There was plenty of food to eat in New York.

What had driven this ZebraMan to cannibalism? Had he always been crazy? Or had he been driven insane by the mass dying of his family, friends, everyone he knew?

Lynxx walked away, detailing the event in his notebook.

He looked up as a car roared down Columbus Avenue. As a white Chevy sped past, he glimpsed a familiar face at a window.

Subject 77.

Over the past few weeks, he'd stopped by her apartment several times. It had always been empty. Eventually he'd given up, assuming she'd died elsewhere.

Interesting.

It was over a month since the Mist, yet the girl with leukemia was still alive. She was one of the rare few people resistant to the Red Fever.

Down the street, the Chevy screeched to a halt, then reversed toward him.

Lynxx hurried inside the nearest building. He didn't want to talk to these walking dead. He couldn't answer their frantic questions about how to survive, what to do, where to find other people. Most of all, he didn't want to feel ... uncomfortable ... at the anguish in their eyes and the desperation in their voices.

When the sound of the Chevy faded away, he went outside and watched the car shrink into the distance.

No, he wasn't interested in talking with these leftovers. But he *was* interested in how long Subject 77 would survive. It would give him something to do, since all the other people on his list had expired in their expected time frames.

He gave a faint smile, satisfied in his new course of action.

Subject 77 would become his own experiment.

55

Lynxx needed to follow the white Chevy containing the girl.

Time to mind-blend again.

He had been practicing this skill for the past few weeks, using it to help fill the increasingly empty hours as his subjects had died.

He was already an expert at mentally remote-pushing any animal that tried to attack him. Thankfully, remote-pushing could be performed while his mind remained in his own body.

Mind-blending, though, was a much harder and more complex feat. It involved his mind completely leaving his non-conscious body and entering an animal's mind to take control of it.

When he'd first begun developing his mind-blending powers several months ago, just after his sixteenth birthday, Frost had told him, "Outriders cannot mind-blend with humans, with a few exceptions."

"What exceptions?"

"We can briefly mind-blend with infants—and adults with severely weakened minds, like someone injured or in a coma." The albino's bloodshot eyes glinted with malice when he spoke about humans in comas.

"That's not much use," Lynxx had said.

"Exactly."

"Can we remote-push humans?"

"Occasionally. However, it's incredibly exhausting. It's usually not worth the effort."

"That's unfortunate."

"It's much easier to remote-push—and mind-blend—with animals."

"Scientifically, it would be more valuable to mind-blend with humans than animals."

"It's the ability that's important, not the hosts," Frost said.

"I understand."

"Here's another important thing. As a hybrid, you can *sometimes* sense other hybrids if they approach you while they're mind-blended with an animal."

Lynxx thought of the various Outriders who'd visited Frost's farmhouse in Ohio over the years as humans. "Strange."

"What?"

"We can't sense Outriders when they're in their human form, right?"

"Right."

"So why can we sense them when they're mind-blended with animals?"

"We can *sometimes* sense them. Not always. Sometimes hybrid minds give off vibrations when they're mind-blended with animals. The closer the mind-blended hybrid-animal gets to a regular hybrid, the greater the vibration." Frost paused. "But there's a much easier way of identifying a hybrid that's mind-blended with an animal."

"How?"

"The animal's eyes will turn silver."

"Always? Or just sometimes?"

"Always."

"Curious. Why do they turn silver?"

Frost shrugged. "There's some scientific explanation, I suppose." He scowled as he went on, "Also, you need to be aware that rogue hybrids exist."

"Rogue hybrids?" Lynxx stiffened at the bizarre concept. "What are they?"

"Hybrids who've been infected by their years of living among people. They embrace their emotions and their humanity. Many even fall in love with humans."

"That's unnatural."

"We're allowed to kill these rogue hybrids." Frost licked his lips, excited by the idea of killing. "But the pleasure of killing them is fleeting. I prefer to punish them with a lifetime of pain and misery."

"How?"

"Simple. I slaughter the humans they love."

Now, Lynxx raced across Columbus Avenue, into the boutique Branson Hotel. He'd moved here a couple of weeks ago. He knew he could've stayed in one of the many luxury apartments that lay empty in Manhattan, but those places contained their dead owners' photos, clothes, and personal effects.

He felt more comfortable with the blandness of a hotel.

Inside his suite, heavy drapes covered every window, except for one in the living room. On a stone ledge outside, a pigeon pecked at the food he'd placed there this morning.

Perfect.

Like all hybrids, he could only enter an animal's mind if it was within twenty yards or so.

Lynxx lay on a couch and closed his eyes.

He pictured the nearby pigeon, braced himself ... and mentally pushed.

His mind shot through a cluster of gold starbursts, as though he were rushing through space. His consciousness arrowed onward, ripping through a thick gray wall. Finally, he landed in a familiar sensation: a mixture of basic thought processes and animal instincts. As usual, he felt smothered and claustrophobic, but this soon passed.

Then he was there, centered in the pigeon's mind. In control. The unpleasant insertion was over. Now came the next step.

Lynxx stretched his pigeon wings, launched himself from the ledge ...

... and flew.

He allowed himself a few moments to cruise the currents of air. The sensation was pleasant, and his view of the empty streets and buildings of New York below was informative.

However, his focus quickly returned to Subject 77. He needed to find where she lived so he could monitor her as she died.

Wings beating, small heart pumping, he flew toward a pair of eagles, seeking his favorite host. *There!* One eagle had golden feathers slightly darker than those of his female companion.

The closer pigeon-Lynxx got to his target, the more the pigeon's mind struggled against his control. His host's fear of being eaten swelled into a throbbing urge to retreat. He pushed back against the bubble of its consciousness and continued on.

A few yards from the golden eagle, he threw his mind forward in another leap. More starbursts and thick gray walls. And then he was inside, centered in the eagle's mind. This time, his host struggled less than it had during earlier mind-blends. It seemed more accepting of its familiar mental intruder.

Through the golden eagle's eyes, he watched the pigeon fleeing back to the safety of its roost, blurred wings beating the air in its panic to escape.

Time to find Subject 77.

A little while ago, the Chevy had been heading toward Lower Manhattan. Taking a gamble, eagle-him flew along Columbus Avenue. He realized 77 and her driver could've changed directions, but he headed south anyway.

Within minutes, he spied a lone vehicle crossing the Manhattan Bridge. His eagle vision, three times sharper than his human eyes, allowed him to identify it.

A white sedan, probably the Chevy.

Excellent.

He followed the vehicle into Brooklyn, where it eventually ended up at Brooklyn Grace Hospital. Circling overhead, unseen and unheard, Lynxx watched 77 and her male companion enter the emergency department.

Why were they at this hospital? It didn't have any medical personnel anymore. Were they looking for someone? He shook off his questions. Their motives weren't important, and his own curiosity was irrelevant.

For the next forty minutes, he circled the main building, glancing through windows and open doorways as he followed the pair. They seemed to be searching for someone or something.

At a startled cry, he looked over. A chimpanzee was scrabbling up a drainpipe to the hospital roof.

What was going on?

Ignoring some mites biting his skin, eagle-Lynxx flew to the open window. Inside, a massive grizzly was rising onto its hind legs, claws raking the air. Its roar promised a bloody death for the terrified girl and boy huddled at the back of the open-plan office.

Lynxx mentally groaned. This beast was going to ruin his experiment. He'd wanted to see how long it'd take 77 to die from her leukemia or some other disease, not from having her guts ripped out.

Only one thing to do.

With a fearsome screech, he swooped through the open window. In a few flaps of his large wings, he crossed the room.

The grizzly was only a few yards from the two humans.

Subject 77 was wielding a chair before her like a shield, frightened yet determined. The auburn-haired girl even took a step toward the upright bear, refusing to retreat from the oncoming battle.

Her male companion shuffled further into the shadows, a knife gripped in his trembling hand.

Lynxx circled the bear and attacked. Like most eagles, his host had a strong beak, but its blunt talons and weak legs were almost useless for fighting. However, through sheer mental force, he powered his host's legs into a brief burst of strength and ripped into the bear's back.

The grizzly roared. Whirled toward eagle-him.

He darted away. Circled around. Attacked again.

Finally, with a bellow of rage and pain, the bear thundered from the office and down a stairwell.

Lynxx scanned the room. In a trash-littered corner, some rats scuttled for cover. Good. He had backup animal hosts in case 77's knife-wielding companion tried to stab him.

He fluttered onto a desk and stretched his wings to their six-foot width, blocking the pair in the corner. Like all scientists, he needed to observe his subject, mentally logging her appearance and behavior.

The girl, 77, was staring at him, stunned. Chest heaving, she struggled to catch her breath. Her face was paler than he remembered from their kiss in Central Park, and she was thinner. The leukemia seemed to be like an internal fire, slowly burning her health away.

The boy gasped at eagle-him. "WindLord."

"What are you talking about, Jase?" asked 77, still shaking.

"It's WindLord, the golden eagle from the Bronx Zoo."

"Why are its eyes silver?"

He tensed. They'd noticed his silver eyes. Then Lynxx relaxed. The humans couldn't know that the golden eagle was mind-blended with a hybrid.

"No idea," the boy, Jase, replied. "They used to be black. Maybe they've turned silver from eating terra plants or something."

"Are you sure this is WindLord?"

"Positive. One of my buddies worked as a volunteer at the Bronx Zoo. A couple of times, I watched him clean WindLord's aviary."

How strange to name an eagle. Still, humans did a lot of strange things.

The boy looked at eagle-him. "How are you doing, eagle? Listen, I need to get out of this room. Take off, bird, so I can leave."

As Jase addressed him directly—*why on Earth does this coward think a bird can understand him?*—Lynxx continued studying 77.

Despite the bravery she'd just shown with the bear, she seemed to be holding herself together with adrenaline and fear. Her lovely green eyes stared at him in confusion, and in their depths he thought he saw a fire of determination, unusual in someone so gravely ill. What was keeping this leukemia-stricken girl alive? A desire to survive? Or a need to find a loved one? Since the Mist, Lynxx had learned that self-preservation and love sometimes drove humans to extraordinary acts of selfishness—or selflessness.

Interesting.

From her fragile body and pale skin, he guessed 77 had only a couple of days left.

He estimated her new death date as Day 42.

56

To Lynxx's increasing surprise, Subject 77 was still alive beyond Day 42.

And she continued to show no symptoms of the Red Fever.

Every morning, he'd leave his body in his locked suite on Columbus Avenue. Once he entered the golden eagle's mind—WindLord's mind—he'd fly to the Bronx apartment where the couple was staying. WindLord-him would perch in a tree until they emerged.

From there, he'd follow them from the air as they checked various places. He'd learned that the girl was looking for her missing relatives: cousin, twin sister, father.

He doubted she'd find any of them alive.

From snippets he'd overheard, the couple's relationship seemed stressed and distant. In fact, the boy, Jase, was treating 77 with deliberate coldness.

On Day 47, eagle-Lynxx was in his usual tree outside their apartment when it happened again. For the fourth time that week, he felt as if hundreds of ants were crawling through his mind.

He recognized the warning. Back in his Branson Hotel suite, his non-conscious body was starting to stir. He needed to return to it as soon as possible, otherwise his body would stagger around the hotel rooms like a dazed drunk, slamming into furniture and possibly hurting him.

According to Frost, some Outriders had suffered ugly deaths when their bodies had prematurely awoken during mind-blends.

Beating his large wings, Lynxx rushed back to Columbus Avenue. The moment he landed on the ledge outside his living room, he mind-leaped back into his own body. He lay on the couch shaking uncontrollably, fighting a wave of nausea.

Why was this happening so much lately?

What was he doing wrong?

Frowning, he examined various possibilities. Finally he arrived at a logical conclusion.

He'd been overdoing the blending with WindLord.

The large eagle needed a lot of effort to control for hours at a stretch. And he'd been manipulating the bird for days as he'd followed 77 on her futile searches for her family.

He needed to take more breaks from the blending. Rest between the sessions. Or blend with a smaller bird, like a pigeon or sparrow.

But he preferred WindLord.

The eagle's huge wings allowed him to cruise at high altitudes, keeping track of 77 when she was traveling in a car. Also, most other birds and animals wouldn't attack an eagle. Lastly, WindLord had become semi-tame after his many mind-blends; it would be a lot harder trying to control a new eagle each day.

A few minutes later, his body stopped shaking and his nausea eased. Standing, he shoved a notebook into his shirt pocket and hurried from the hotel.

Outside, Lynxx watched a pair of eagles wheeling in the sky, their outstretched wings silhouetted against the pink clouds. WindLord was probably one of them. How did the golden eagle feel when he—an intruder—finally released its mind after their blends? Did the bird feel better with him gone? Happier? Free?

He shook his head. WindLord's feelings didn't matter. The creature was merely a tool.

He rode his Harley into Central Park, to a grove of trees near the Pond. Yesterday, as WindLord, he'd heard Jase and 77 discuss their plan to search this area today.

Leaning against the trunk of a maple tree, Lynxx waited.

Finally, midafternoon, the pair arrived on motorcycles.

Keeping to the shadows, he followed them.

In Sheep Meadow, they ran into a group of survivors near a field of *Sinachus exTerrus*—or, as he'd heard someone call them, glow-lotus terras. Subject 77 and Jase talked with the survivors, who'd already lost two children to the deadly plants. A few minutes later, a boy that Lynxx had met a few times before, Asher Weston, persuaded the group to help him burn the terras.

As the glowing plants screamed in the flames, a cloud of locusts erupted from them. Driven by panic and smoke, the insects swarmed over 77 and a young woman, Sophie.

Lynxx frowned as 77 cried out in fear. She stumbled around, beating at the bugs that crawled over her face and body. He wished she'd be more careful. If she tripped and fell into a patch of unburned flowers, she'd be dead within moments.

His experiment would be ruined.

When she kept screaming and flailing, he felt a flicker of ... something.

No time to analyze the emotion.

He sat against the trunk of a tree and braced his mind. Calling on every scrap of his mental strength, he somehow remote-pushed the scores of tiny insects that were attacking 77.

As one, the swarm of locusts rose into the air, whirled left, and disappeared.

It worked!

Lynxx slumped wearily against the trunk, then staggered to his feet. The multiple remote-pushing had left him feeling blurry, as though he'd just whacked his head on the ground.

Subject 77 stumbled forward and knocked the woman, Sophie, into a patch of unburned glow-lotus terras. The plants' needle-sharp leaves speared the fallen woman's body, pinning her to the ground as though she were a paper doll studded with floral drawing pins.

Clutching the tree trunk for support, Lynxx watched the next events occur like falling dominoes: 77's distress and guilt.

The other survivors' rejection of her.

Jase leaving with the group.

The girl's abandonment.

Keeping to the shadows of the trees, Lynxx followed 77.

Dejected, she returned to her Honda motorcycle—and found that her possessions had been stolen. She stared at the looted saddlebags, her shoulders sagging as she struggled not to cry.

After a couple of minutes, she trudged to the Gapstow Bridge in Central Park and climbed onto the footbridge's wide side. Face strained, green eyes haunted, she sat gazing at the poisonous pink terras floating on the waters below.

What was she doing? Why did she keep staring at those flowers with the fascination of an arsonist staring at flames?

Lynxx jerked in realization.

Subject 77 was giving up. She'd fought and battled to stay connected to other humans, but she'd lost. She was alone. Afraid. And broken.

From the way she was studying those deadly blossoms, she was also about to ruin his experiment.

He had to stop her. But how?

A swell of operatic voices suddenly filled the air.

Lynxx froze, stunned. He pictured the doors of a church being flung open, freeing the heavenly sounds. Naturally, that was impossible. These days, churches were empty shells where hope had died along with the priests and parishioners. The only things now sitting in the pews were piles of gray decomp-dust.

The beautiful singing seemed to soothe 77. A faint smile lightened her face and she gazed into the air, enthralled, as though actually seeing the notes flowing overhead.

Finally, the music trailed into silence.

Would she still jump?

Lynxx didn't wait to find out.

Although still weak from remote-pushing the scores of locusts, he sat on the ground, leaned against another tree trunk, and scanned for a host. He needed something small that didn't require too much mental strength.

Nearby, a squirrel ran along a branch.

Perfect.

He mentally leaped. Plunged through starbursts. Ripped through a new wall of grayness. Centered himself.

This new mind felt tiny, but it didn't matter. He still fit. And he was still in control.

On squirrel feet, he scampered to the footbridge, onto the wide parapet, pausing a yard from 77.

She looked at him in surprise.

"Hello, little cutie," she murmured. "What are you doing here?"

Stopping you from killing yourself, he chittered in response. Of course, she didn't understand him.

"Huh! Your eyes are silver too, just like that eagle, WindLord. Weird."

Inside the squirrel's mind, Lynxx gave a mental shrug, unconcerned. He knew 77 had no idea that hybrids could mind-blend with animals and temporarily change their eyes to silver.

Heck, she had no idea that hybrids even existed.

They sat together, gazing at the Pond. Lynxx could tell that the presence of this small, bushy-tailed squirrel somehow comforted her. Was she really that lonely? Maybe her imminent death would be what humans called "a blessing."

After a few minutes, he felt his hold on the squirrel slipping. An invisible bubble swelled larger and larger, trying to shove him out of the small animal. He focused. Pushed back. Held the bubble in one spot, his control shaky.

His own body was too far away to leap into. He couldn't let his mind be ejected from the squirrel, since there were no other potential hosts nearby. He had to hold on for a bit longer.

Besides, the girl needed company.

He glanced at 77 again. She was smiling at squirrel-him and, to his surprise, he realized she had a lovely smile for one so stressed and sick.

Would she decide to live?

He hoped so.

His mental grip wavered as the invisible bubble again swelled. Its shove was stronger this time. Or his control was getting weaker. If he didn't return to his body now, his mind could be forced out of the squirrel. With nowhere to go, his consciousness would simply disappear.

He'd be no use to 77 if he was dead.

With a flick of his fluffy tail, he whirled and scampered away.

57

SOMETHING WAS COMING.

As Lynxx leaped from the squirrel's mind and back into his own body, he felt the small animal's fear. It wasn't just fear of him. The creature was sensing the approach of something bad. This was why it'd been so desperate to get rid of him. It wanted to flee and hide, and he'd been forcing it to stay on the footbridge.

Lynxx sat against the tree trunk as his human body regained consciousness. He saw the squirrel darting into a hole in the oak. Lizards and frogs and other small creatures were also disappearing into crevices and burrows, seeking safety.

Something was coming.

What?

Would it affect him—and 77? They were both outside which, according to the animals, was the wrong place to be.

He gazed around. Saw nothing unusual.

Above him, a sunset-glazed sky appeared serene and beautiful.

At a movement in a tree, he looked over. The eagle, WindLord, was perched on a branch, its golden head rotating from side to side, as though seeking a sheltered spot.

Quickly, before the eagle flew out of leaping distance, Lynxx rested against the tree trunk again and threw his mind into his favorite host.

No time to waste. He sensed he only had a short period before his weak hold on the bird's mind slipped and he was ejected.

Powering his wings to their limit, WindLord-him flew upward, higher and higher until he was soaring above the skyscrapers. From there, he could see something headed toward the city—a greeny-yellow mass of clouds, bubbling as though boiling.

A strong wind gusted in a southerly direction, its foul breath ruffling his feathers. His extra-sharp eagle smell identified the stench. It was the same as the one in the field of glow-lotus terras. But this one was stronger.

Locusts. Millions of them. Hidden in the roiling greenish clouds. Agitated. Afraid. Trapped.

Around eagle-him, the air pressure surged and dropped and rose again as the strange storm advanced.

Hundreds of invisible ants again crawled through Lynxx's consciousness, and his mind felt as if he were slowly slipping.

His hold on WindLord began to weaken.

There were no other birds to leap into, as they'd all fled the oncoming storm.

Lynxx tightened his grip on the eagle, aware he could only hold on for a few more minutes. He dived toward the ground, mentally kicking himself. Why had he risked his life for 77? Wasn't impulsiveness a human trait? Obviously, he was slipping in more ways than one.

During his frantic descent, his acute eagle vision saw some of the city's inhabitants in the streets and parks below. The animals were all scurrying for shelter, their survival instincts triggered by the abnormal vibrations in the air.

The humans remained oblivious.

How was he going to convince 77 to take shelter? His subject was already on edge. No way would she listen to him, even if he were back in his own human body. Several weeks ago, she'd kissed him in Central Park—and he'd walked away from her. Days later, outside Stowe High, her friend had collapsed with a bleeding nose, and she'd begged for his help. Again, he'd just walked away.

As he flew over Central Park, he saw 77. She was still on the Gapstow Bridge. Still alive.

Relief surged through him.

A short distance beyond the bridge, on the other side of a clump of trees, he noticed someone heading north toward Gapstow Bridge. Dressed in dark coveralls, the person had a machete slung over one shoulder and a rifle over the other. His hyper-sharp eagle eyes saw through the grease that covered her face, and he recognized features identical to those of Subject 77.

Extraordinary.

Was this the twin that 77 was so desperate to find?

The girl with the machete suddenly stopped.

She turned and headed south, *away* from Gapstow Bridge.

58

BACK IN HIS OWN human form, Lynxx forced his weakened body into a run as he cut through the park. An outstretched branch snagged his baseball cap. No time to stop and get it. He kept running.

Keeping to the trees, he circled in front of the girl with the machete and rifle. At the edge of the meadow with the burning glow-lotus terras, he hid behind a thick shrub.

As he waited, he nudged his sunglasses up his nose again, wiped the perspiration from his face, and tried to stop his body from shaking. If he appeared in front of ... Olivia? ... sweating and puffing, she'd probably think he was about to attack her.

He dropped his black jacket and red plaid shirt to the ground, leaving on his white T-shirt. White should help Olivia trust him. After all, wasn't white the color of the good guys?

Footsteps crunched on the path.

Calmly, he stepped onto the grass, pretending not to notice her.

From the corner of his eye, he saw the girl spot him. She jerked to a halt, hand darting to the revolver in her belt. She scanned her surroundings for danger, then studied him with a wary expression.

Casually he turned—and pretended surprise. "Oh. Hello."

Frowning, she remained silent. Suspicious.

He noted her outfit. Functional navy coveralls with lots of zippered pockets. Hunting knife strapped to her thigh. Pistol shoved into her boot. Hair tucked out of sight beneath a black woolen beanie. Rifle and machete slung over her shoulders.

This girl was a fighter. A warrior.

And even though her face was grimy, her features were identical to Subject 77's.

"What happened here?" she asked, surveying the burning glow-lotus plants. "Were these non-terrestrial plants?"

Lynxx controlled his trembling body. "Yes," he replied, somehow keeping his tone calm and nonthreatening. *I'm harmless*, he thought, relaxing his posture. *I'm harmless.* "But most survivors call them *terras* these days."

"I hate that word. It sounds like 'terrors.' If I link the emotion of terror with the plants, it'll weaken my ability to deal with them."

So she wasn't just physically strong. She was mentally strong too, just like Subject 77.

"*Terra* is short for *non-terrestrial plant*," he said, stating the obvious.

"I know."

Ignoring a bead of sweat that slid into his eye, Lynxx glanced at his watch. He'd left 77 a few minutes ago. Had she jumped onto the poisonous flowers by now? Or was she still standing on the Gapstow Bridge, debating her fate?

This warrior-twin was his best shot at keeping 77 alive.

Without thinking, he said, "My name's Rock." He frowned, unsure why he'd used his old name, the one his guardian had given him at birth.

She silently sized him up. Finally, she replied, "Olivia."

He gave her a friendly nod. Then, his eyebrows knotted in exaggerated worry, he looked up at the sky. "You should get to safety, miss. There's a bad storm coming."

She glanced at the clouds, which were ablaze with golds and oranges and crimsons. "It's just a sunset. A beautiful sunset, our first in weeks. Hopefully, it means life is getting back to normal—or as normal as it can be after the Mist."

Lynxx stifled an impatient sigh, searching for a way to convince her. He'd heard that people connected more with those who gave them valuable information. So he warned her, "There's nothing normal about life in New York. This place has death around every corner."

Her grip tightened on the butt of her revolver. "What are you talking about?"

He spread his hands before him, showing he was unarmed and harmless.

"I'm from Canada," he lied, aware that Canadians were supposed to be safe and harmless. "I got caught here after the Mist. Since then, I've seen some bad things. Terrible things. I'd scoot back to Vancouver in a heartbeat, only I've heard the terras are worse in the countryside. I probably wouldn't make it home."

Home. The word echoed in his mind, a hollow sound devoid of warmth.

Face shadowing, she nodded. "Yeah, there are some huge terras in the countryside. They're awful."

"Things are awful here too. There are bikers—Wilders—who grab up young girls. Two weeks ago, some Wilders even tried roasting me over a burning car. Luckily, a couple of other guys saved me."

Horror flared in Olivia's green eyes, which were almost as beautiful as 77's eyes.

He went on, "The terras here aren't as big as those in the countryside, but stacks will kill you in seconds. Others will digest you alive over several days. And then there are the cannibals."

"The *what?*"

"I can't believe it either. Lately, bodies have been turning up all around the place, each with huge chunks of flesh carved from it. It's rumored that some guy in a zebra-skin cape is responsible:

ZebraMan." He glanced at the sky again. "Plus there's a strange storm coming. A little while ago, I was checking on things ... through a telescope. In the distance, I could see a mass of greeny-yellow clouds that look like they're boiling. You need to find shelter right away."

Olivia inspected the sky. "Okay. Thanks for the warnings." Hand still gripping her revolver, she turned to the south again.

Wrong direction.

Lynxx struggled to appear calm. "You should get your sister to safety too. She doesn't look well."

"What?" She whipped back to him, eyes wide with shock.

Casually, he gestured to a northward path winding through the trees. "That girl on the Gapstow Bridge, isn't she your sister? I mean, you look like twins and all."

"When did you see her?"

"A few minutes ago."

Olivia's voice faltered. "I've been searching for her ever since I got to Manhattan." She paused, as though unable to believe that her sister—frail and sick with leukemia—had survived the Red Fever.

Then, face haunted by fear and hope, she raced up the path.

Keeping to the trees, Lynxx followed her.

From the shadows, he watched the twins' joyful embrace on the footbridge.

"Via!"

"Kass!"

Their behavior puzzled him.

How could these girls, in the midst of an apocalypse, still feel happiness and hope at their reunion? Why was the discovery of a single loved one so important to them, so vital for their ... souls?

And what exactly was a soul?

Puzzled, he followed 77 and Olivia as they left the park and clattered down some subway steps, into a railway tunnel. Here, he shook off his irrelevant questions about human relationships and souls. He focused on keeping 77 in sight, while keeping himself out of sight.

After parking his body in a dark spot in the tunnel, he gathered the last of his energy to mind-leap into a nearby bat. On silent wings, he trailed the girls to an underground bunker about half a mile from Grand Central Station.

Olivia pocketed a hand-drawn map and aimed her flashlight into a small partially furnished room. "This is our new home, Kass," she told 77. "We'll probably be here for a while. When the storm's passed, we'll fix it up and get some fresh blankets, books, and pictures. That way it won't be so bleak."

Subject 77 leaned tiredly against her sister. "I don't care how bleak it is, Via. As long as we're together, any place we live is home. Dad always said, 'Home is where the heart is.' "

Inside the bat's mind, Lynxx gave a mental frown.

Home. That word again. It seemed to mean so much to people. Why did it hold such emotional weight?

Strange.

Lynxx watched 77 and Olivia enter the bunker. Neither girl flinched as rats scurried away from their flashlight beams. They didn't blink at the spider-infested cobwebs on the boxes of supplies. They ignored the animal droppings scattered across the floor.

Instead, both girls seemed content to just be together ... be a family.

Definitely strange.

Wearily, Lynxx used his bat radar to navigate down the midnight tunnel, back to his non-conscious body.

Tomorrow, when the storm had passed, he would resume his experiment.

It was Day 47.

Subject 77 was so weak and sick that she'd probably be dead by Day 60.

But to his surprise, he found himself hoping she'd still be alive.

59

Lynxx dragged the carcass onto Broadway and left it in the middle of the leaf-littered street.

Hurrying to the curb, he hid inside a bus almost covered with harmless terras known as velvet-vines. A mesh of soft green leaves veiled the windows, providing small gaps to peer through. He crouched in the shadowy interior, waiting.

Olivia Madison had told her sister that she'd be taking this route today, so he knew she'd be along eventually.

Five weeks ago, the two girls had moved into the subway bunker. Since then, he'd mind-blended with WindLord and other creatures, and occasionally shadowed Olivia on her daily trips to the surface.

Today, Day 81, he had needed to be in his own body to hunt the deer.

Sure enough, just before 8 a.m., Olivia drove down the street. She pulled up a few feet from the carcass. Rifle in hand, she slipped from her pickup truck and studied the hollowed-eyed buildings alongside the road.

She removed her woolen beanie, swept up an escaping clump of auburn hair, and jammed her beanie on again.

Senses alert, muscles tense, she scanned for movement. Listened for furtive footsteps. Braced for a trap.

Nothing.

The morning was soundless and still. No one else was around.

She crouched beside the dead deer, frowning at the gunshot wound in its furred forehead. Lynxx was worried that she'd decide the animal's death was too suspicious and would retreat empty-handed.

But her desperation was stronger than her caution.

Using a small pulley attached to her pickup, she heaved the carcass onto the cargo bed, then sped off down Broadway.

Lynxx left the bus.

He knew it'd take Olivia all day to deal with the deer. After gutting it, she'd hack off a haunch to keep, and then she'd trade pieces of the remaining carcass with small groups scattered across the city. Some people would offer vegetables grown in their hidden gardens; others would barter cans of food or fresh fish from the Hudson River.

Lynxx gave a faint smile. His experiment had become far more interesting and time-consuming than he'd expected.

No need to hurry, he told himself as he rushed back to his Branson Hotel suite. He didn't have to wolf down his cereal, but he did anyway. Lots of time to read a few chapters of his latest mystery novel, if he wanted.

Instead, he threw himself on the couch and closed his eyes.

Time for his triple mind-leap. First into a pigeon, followed by a bat in the subway tunnels and then, lastly, into the white mouse's mind.

Finally, he was there.

In the bunker.

With her.

Kassia.

A couple of weeks ago, he'd decided to mentally refer to the girl by the full-length version of her first name. "Subject 77" was awkward and too long; "Kassia" was much nicer.

"Mousy!" Kassia's eyes lit up as he scurried into the middle of the crowded bunker, squeaking loudly. Rising from her cot, face soft with concern, she lowered her hand to him. "Where have you been?"

Napping behind some boxes of tools, he silently answered, scampering onto her palm. *My mouse host thinks that sleeping in a dirty, cobwebbed corner is acceptable behavior.*

He settled onto her lap as she picked up her novel. At first, he thought she wasn't going to do it. That she'd forgotten him. She stared into space for a few minutes and, as a scientist, he wished he could read her mind, experience what she was thinking and feeling.

Kassia jerked out of her memories. With a sigh, she stroked his furry back.

As Lynxx's tension eased, she said, "Okay, Mousy, where were we up to? Oh, yes, page seventy-five." In a gentle voice, she read aloud from a Harry Potter book that Olivia had brought home.

Home.

He still didn't understand the full emotional weight of the word. However, after weeks of visiting Kassia in her bunker, he was beginning to grasp the meaning of the quote *Home is where the heart is*.

His own heart didn't live in this bunker, of course. It was firmly lodged in his chest. And his "home" in the technical sense was back in Frost's farmhouse in Ohio, where, on the occasional summer day, he had wandered through the swaying fields of wheat and corn, studying the vegetation.

Or maybe his home was now in his hotel suite on Columbus Avenue, with its immaculate rooms and stylish furnishings.

And yet he preferred being in this cramped, musty bunker with Kassia.

She was a most interesting subject, he thought. After eighty-one days, she was still alive—although he was partially responsible for that.

He told himself that he would've let her die if she'd shown symptoms of the Red Fever.

But she hadn't.

During her time underground, though, other things had tried to kill her: a lack of leukemia meds, infections, the flu. Loneliness.

Like any good scientist, he'd handled each threat to his experiment as it had arisen. In the afternoons, when he was back in his own body, he would check medical facilities and apartments across New York. Whenever he found some of the drugs she needed, he would place them inside buildings scheduled to be searched by Olivia the next day.

A few times, he'd provided the twins with fresh meat.

Olivia was good at many things. Searching. Fighting. Keeping other people at a distance. Taking care of her sister.

But she was a poor hunter. He suspected it was because, deep in her heart, she hated killing animals.

Three weeks ago, Olivia had been injured by a terra.

Two days later, he'd killed some wild rabbits and left them out for her to stumble across. He remembered the relief on her face as she'd "found" each one. Although bewildered by the rabbits' broken necks, she'd quickly bagged them, then staggered back to the bunker, where Kassia had cooked a nourishing stew.

Today, he'd decided to add some red meat to the girls' diet. Venison would give Olivia more energy for hunting animals and evading the human predators in Manhattan.

If her sister didn't stay alive, Kassia might again lose her own will to live.

Every day, Kassia was left alone for long hours in the bunker. At first, she had cleaned and organized their new home. She'd stuck posters to the walls and stashed excess supplies in a nearby storeroom. But when she'd eventually run out of things to do, and the days had begun to inch past with glacial slowness, she had become anxious. Depressed.

That was when he'd decided to lighten her loneliness with a companion: Mousy-him.

He'd needed a creature easy to control for a few hours each morning. Rodents were the perfect size. However, he figured she'd be disgusted if a flea-ridden brown rat or mouse entered her home. So he'd mind-blended with a tame white mouse with a ripped pink ear, black front paws, and a pink nose.

It had worked.

She'd quickly befriended Mousy-him, cleaned him, fed him her choicest canned cheese, and read aloud to him every day. She stroked his fur as they shared novels of different genres: romance, young adult, fantasy, mystery, and thrillers. Growing up under Frost's rigid guardianship, Lynxx had only ever read science texts and manuals. He'd no idea that novels could be so pleasing.

Often after he returned to his human body, he found himself bringing novels back to the Branson Hotel and poring over them with a curiosity that left him puzzled. He was just keeping busy, he told himself. Studying humans through their stories. Trying to understand them. Seeing what made them tick.

And—in Kassia's case—discovering what kept her alive.

60

Hisses ...

Lynxx warily looked around as he walked through a wide tunnel of trees.

It had been a month since he'd left the deer carcass for Olivia to find. To fill his afternoons, he'd begun experimenting with terras, hoping to use them for medicinal purposes. Yesterday, he'd found some rare crimson-sun terras in this park, and he hoped to find some more today.

Once, this area had offered pleasant groves of trees, comfortable benches, and paved pathways alongside the Hudson River.

Now, the benches were overgrown with vines, and the walkways were ruined by layers of gray terras that crunched underfoot, releasing a putrid odor with each step.

Ghost-white webs covered parts of the tunnel of trees. They stretched between the top branches, creating a filmy roof that dappled the ground with shadows. Lynxx realized these "webs" were actually flat, translucent terras that were crawling with hundreds of spiders, some of which dropped onto him every now and then.

In the tunnel, hisses filled the air, soft with menace.

What was making the creepy sounds?

"Rock."

He froze. That voice. The memories. The work.

Slowly, he turned.

A plump, bald man with ice-white skin and the red eyes of an albino emerged from behind a tree.

Lynxx's eyes narrowed.

Frost.

His guardian.

Here in New York.

Frost brushed several hairy spiders off his clothes with the casualness of someone brushing off crumbs. As usual, he was dressed in expensive garments. Today's outfit of tailored white pants and white silk shirt echoed the image of an overfed Hollywood director on his way to dinner.

Except every restaurant in this city was as dead as the stores, the homes ... the people.

Behind his dark sunglasses, Lynxx's eyes narrowed, wary and watchful.

Looking left, Frost raised his hand in a theatrical gesture. A skinny biker pushed through a wall of web terras and stepped forward, moving like a robot. Lynxx recognized the man as Viper, a member of Fang's gang.

They made a strange pair, he thought. A bald, overweight man in classy white clothes, and a lean grubby biker with stringy hair and a mustache.

"What are you doing here, Frost?" he asked. "I thought you were in Ohio."

"Really?" The man flicked more fat spiders from his silk jacket. "I've been in New York for a while."

The biker, Viper, stood statue-still, staring into space with glazed eyes. He didn't flinch when a huge tarantula dropped onto his head, crawled down his neck, and disappeared beneath his dirty shirt. No reaction at all, Lynxx noted. Was this Viper drugged? In a trance? Crazy?

He forced his attention back to his guardian. "Have you been following me?"

"Why would I spend my time doing that? I was merely inspecting some terras in the area when I saw you enter this delightful tunnel."

Delightful? Lynxx winced. In the overhanging branches, scores of ragged web terras shifted and swayed in the breeze, occasionally raining spiders onto the trio below. He shoved away a fat huntsman that plopped onto his shoulder. "Why are you here, Frost?"

"For work, of course."

"Of course." Lynxx lapsed into silence. In the past, he'd never questioned his guardian's actions. He'd simply obeyed his orders. Tended the experiments. Read the manuals. Worked.

Now, after being independent for several months, he viewed his guardian through fresh eyes.

In their sixteen years together, Lynxx had never received a shred of warmth from his guardian, even when he'd slaved for days over experiments. On many occasions, his tests had gone wrong, leaving Lynxx's skin bleeding or burned. Yet Frost had never shown the slightest concern or regret.

They'd had a distant relationship—like a stern teacher and an obedient student.

The albino regarded him with his creepy bloodshot eyes. "Have you been doing your job, Rock?"

"Of course. And my name's Lynxx now."

"Ahh. That's right. I keep forgetting. Lynxx. Bizarre choice."

"It's better than Rock."

At birth, every hybrid was given a short, hard name in keeping with the hybrid's mixed origin. Names like Rock, Axe, Hammer, Nail, Gravel, Steel, Ice, Snow, and so on, were popular choices, since they were based on emotionless and inanimate objects.

His albino guardian's name—Frost—had been chosen because of his frost-white skin.

On Rock's sixteenth birthday, in a rare flash of independence, he had insisted on changing his assigned name. He'd always admired the lean, cat-like grace of lynxes, their golden eyes—so like his own—and the way their gold-brown fur allowed them to blend into the background, just like he was supposed to do. As an afterthought, he'd added an extra "x" to his name, to separate him from the Earth-animal and to indicate his extra-terrestrial origin.

Frost nodded at the web-veiled tunnel of trees. "Things are progressing nicely, *Lynxx*, don't you agree?"

Lynxx peered over the top of his sunglasses. *Nicely?* This park looked like it'd been ripped from a nightmare.

More hisses arose from within some draped shrubs, soft and furtive, and his skin prickled with alarm. What was making the sounds?

Frost licked his fat lips as he waited for a reply.

Again Lynxx's skin prickled, although this time not from the strange hisses.

He felt chilled by the predatory glint in Frost's eyes.

Last week, while searching for one of Kassia's favorite novels in a bookstore, he'd met a timber wolf with that same deadly expression in its hungry eyes. During that incident, he'd been able to mentally remote-push the wild beast away.

But he wasn't strong enough to mentally remote-push Frost.

"Yes," Lynxx finally replied, keeping his voice casual, "the terras are spreading faster than I expected. I'm puzzled, though. Isn't the First Wave supposed to take decades to change the existing vegetation? At this rate, the planet will be ready within a few years."

"Good. Hopefully the Second Wave will arrive a lot sooner than expected."

"Really?" Lynxx hid his dismay. "You told me that wouldn't occur for decades." He certainly didn't want to be around when it happened.

"It all depends on how soon we can dispose of the remaining humans. After all, that's why we're here."

"In New York?"

"Alive."

Lynxx jerked in shock. "I thought we were created as Outriders: persons who prepare the way for the arrival of a greater force."

"Is that how you regard yourself? As a *person*?"

Lynxx ignored Frost's questions. "Are you saying you want to eliminate the human survivors?"

"It's our job."

"Not mine. I studied Earth's vegetation. I worked out what makes various Earth plants successful. I provided samples." He drew in a steadying breath. "Once the Mist arrived, my job was to record the demise of New York's citizens. That's all."

"You used to be a model soldier. You were emotionless, unquestioning of orders, a potential killer."

"I've never been a soldier or a killer. I'm an Outrider. A scout."

"Is that what you tell yourself?"

Lynxx remained silent. He didn't want to think about the past. He preferred to focus on the present—and his experiment with Subject 77: Kassia.

Although physically weak, she showed surprising mental strength. She would push herself to cook for Olivia even when she was ill. She'd highlight parts of books and read the snippets back to her twin at night. She'd make jokes, discuss movies, talk about happier times with friends and family. Her conversations were all designed to ease her sister's stress.

Sometimes, Olivia would return with injuries from a terra or a Wilder. As Mousy, he'd watch Kassia rush to bathe and bandage her sister's wounds, murmuring comforting words as she worked.

The twins treated each other with concern, kindness, respect, and love.

With humanity.

But wasn't humanity weak? Lynxx asked himself, confused. Weren't the Outriders and their creators the strong ones, the winners in a world that was crumbling beneath the terras?

Frost studied him, his lips pressed in a tight smile. "I haven't received any reports from you lately."

"What's to report? Nearly everyone's dead."

"True. So how do you spend your days?"

"I try to survive," he hedged. "It's not easy."

"There are ways to make it easier. You could always join forces with me."

"No, thanks." With an illogical amount of pleasure, Lynxx told his guardian, "I've found my own way to survive. I trade information. Sometimes I tell survivors how to kill certain dangerous terras. In exchange they give me canned food."

In total, he'd received three dozen cans. Most of it was food the survivors didn't want. Roasted scorpions from Thailand. Lambs' tongues. Canned fish mouths.

Seriously, who'd eat that stuff, even in an apocalypse?

"Go ahead, Lynxx, do your little trades. The survivors can kill terras all day every day, but in the end Earth will be like *Titanic*." When Lynxx looked puzzled, his guardian explained, "After *Titanic* struck the iceberg, the ship took on water, which the engineers desperately tried to pump out again. But the water kept coming. The levels kept rising. And no matter how hard the engineers and pumps worked, the ship still sank."

Lynxx fell silent. Had his experiments on Earth's vegetation been a small part of the iceberg that was sinking this planet?

He felt a vague stir of something. Guilt?

"We have a visitor." Frost looked at his motionless companion.

Eyes still glazed, Viper raised his right arm out at his side and held it there, motionless.

A loud squawk came from behind.

A black vulture with a red beak flew down the leafy passageway, massive wings beating a path through the air. The bird descended onto Viper's outstretched arm as if it were a perch. Two sets of sharp talons stabbed the man's flesh, dripping blood onto the ground.

Viper didn't flinch. However, the hand at his side balled into a fist, whitening his knuckles.

Frost's tongue flickered across his fat lips, as if excited by the dripping blood.

Cocking its featherless head, the vulture watched Lynxx with eyes that were bright with menace. He'd seen this bird several times before, either flying down deserted streets or soaring in the sky. Always alone. Always watching.

His glance slid from the frozen Viper to Frost, who was staring at the vulture with a strange expression on his face. A slight smile hovered at the corner of his lips.

"It's you," he gasped at Frost. "You're controlling both the biker and the vulture."

"I'm rather good at it, aren't I?" Frost bragged.

"You said we can't mind-blend with humans, with rare exceptions."

"I'm *remote-pushing* the biker. So much easier than mind-blending. At least with remote-pushing, my mind gets to stay in my own body."

"I thought we couldn't easily remote-push humans either."

"We can't. Not unless they're mentally impaired, or they're babies. This idiot here is high on dope terras, which makes him vulnerable to remote-pushing. Care for a further demonstration?"

"Not really." Lynxx glanced at his watch: 10 a.m. He was going to be late.

Back in the bunker, Kassia would be waiting for Mousy-him. She didn't realize that the rodent only ever responded to her calls when *he* was in control, or when the critter was hungry.

Left on its own, the white mouse would never spend hours on Kassia's lap, listening as she read from a book. It wouldn't think of scampering up to her shoulder to smell her soft hair, nuzzle her silky cheeks, settle on her warm palm.

These actions were a part of his experiments, he told himself. To understand humans and their emotions, he had to study them.

"Worried about the time?" Frost's smile echoed the menace in the vulture's stare. "Do you have somewhere to be?"

Unease fluttered in Lynxx's chest. He sensed he shouldn't let Frost know about Kassia. "I'm fine."

"Good." Frost spread his plump white hands again in a curiously threatening gesture. "Let's have some fun."

Abruptly, from their hiding spots in the tunnel of trees, the hisses increased.

Grew louder.

Closer.

61

THE GROUND CAME ALIVE on either side of Lynxx.

Long thin shapes slithered from the bushes and trees, into the open. Scaly bodies. Pointed heads. Forked tongues.

Rattlesnakes.

Large and small. Aggressive and docile. Patterned and plain.

Lynxx knew most rattlers preferred living in rock crevices or holes in the ground. But these snakes were living in the undergrowth.

He suspected they hung around because of the rat-rods. Resembling upright poles, these black terras had sweet-scented leaves that attracted rodents like flakes of metal to magnets. When touched, their wide leaves snapped shut around the rats and mice, trapping them for eventual digestion.

He hated rat-rod terras, but snakes loved them. They seemed to view the leaf-wrapped rodents as some sort of ready-made Happy Meals.

As the serpents wriggled toward Frost, their scaly bodies scraped across the dried leaves that carpeted the ground.

Lynxx glanced at the evil-eyed vulture perched on Viper's arm. "How can you remote-push the biker and all these creatures at the same time?"

"As I said, the biker's mind is weakened by drugs. And snakes are easy to control." Frost's lips widened in a smirk. "Watch this."

Lynxx stood still as a massive brown-and-green python emerged from the bushes. It coiled itself around his legs and slithered up his rigid body.

A large pointed head drew level with his own.

Stomach twisting, he stared into the snake's gaping mouth. Saliva dripped from its fangs, and its forked tongue flickered against his skin, tasting him.

Its breath felt hot and fetid on his face.

He struggled not to throw up.

"Interesting," he said with forced calmness. "I've never been this close to a *Python reticulatus* before."

"Snakes are fascinating, yes?"

"Most intriguing."

Lynxx knew the python wrapped around his body wasn't poisonous. However, it was large enough and strong enough to squeeze him to death.

Desperately, he tried to mind-blend with it, but instead of a flexible gray wall, the snake's mind was encased by a steel-hard case. He was being blocked by Frost. He couldn't even remote-push the serpent away. He was totally at Frost's mercy—although he doubted his guardian possessed such a human quality.

Nearby, three rattlers crawled up Viper's stiff body. One wrapped itself around the biker's waist like a belt. Another ringed his neck, its tail shaking in a faint clatter. The third encircled his outstretched arm, ignoring the huge vulture still perched there.

Even though Viper didn't move a muscle, his frozen eyes glinted with terror.

"Enough," Lynxx snapped. "Call off your pets." His guardian's behavior was inhuman. "The biker's about to have a heart attack."

"So? He's a dead man walking, anyway."

Lynxx winced with guilt. He remembered thinking a similar thing about Kassia when she had kissed him in Central Park months ago. What had he called her? *One of the walking dead?*

How could he have been so ... unfeeling?

Frost's round, ice-white face creased in disappointment. "Aren't you having fun yet, Lynxx?" He flicked a fat finger at the python.

The snake squeezed tighter and tighter until Lynxx could barely breathe. For the first time, he understood the danger he was in. For decades, his guardian's sadism had been repressed by the need to blend in with human society. But with the eradication of most people, Frost had finally allowed his darker side to openly emerge.

The albino was more than an avid horror movie buff. He was an outright sadist. Wasn't sadism one of the worst human traits? "Family" ties meant nothing to the man. Loyalty, compassion, and affection were meaningless terms.

Which meant that Frost could kill him on a whim.

Fear flooded Lynxx, but not for himself.

Kassia.

Over the past few months, he'd worked hard to keep her alive. If he died, who would find the meds she needed to survive? Who would keep her company during the long empty days when Olivia was away hunting? Who would care for her the way he did?

His fear exploded into shock.

Care?

How could he care for Kassia?

Yet how could he not?

She was intelligent, determined, sweet, and loving. Even in the dim bunker, when she smiled at Mousy-him, he felt as if the sun were shining. And when she laughed, something deep within his heart stirred into life.

He cared for her.

And yet she had no idea he even existed. So much had happened in the past few months. She'd probably forgotten all about the stranger she'd kissed in Central Park so long ago.

The python tightened its coils again, squeezing his chest and lungs, choking the breath in his throat.

Lynxx's fear for Kassia flickered like flames within him. Gasping for air, for life, for *her*, he fanned the fire until it turned into a white-hot blaze of determination.

He closed his eyes. Focused. Pushed against the python's steel-encased mind.

He heard Frost's low growl. The hisses retreated as the rattlers were mentally released and slithered back to their hiding spots among the bushes and shrubs.

He kept pushing.

Eyes still closed, he felt a gush of air and a brush of feathers as the vulture, also mentally released, fled down the tunnel.

The sound of running footsteps indicated Viper's escape as well.

He knew that Frost was releasing his prisoners so he could center his mind in the python.

Lynxx made one last ferocious push, and the serpent's mental steel case shattered beneath the weight of his desperation.

He was inside. Mind-blending with the snake.

Go, he ordered it.

The huge python relaxed its deadly grip.

Lynxx mind-leaped back into his own body and gave a fierce remote-push.

The snake slid down his body. Slithered away in a rustle of fading hisses.

Gasping for breath, Lynxx rubbed his sore chest. He was still alive. Now he needed to stay alive so he could see Kassia again.

Shaking, he turned to Frost, readying himself for the battle of his life.

To his surprise, his guardian was regarding him with icy amusement. "Not bad. Of course, if I hadn't been remote-pushing so many critters' minds at once, I could've crushed you in an instant."

"Why would you?"

"As an experiment, of course." At Lynxx's frown, the albino gave a theatrical laugh and clasped his ward on the shoulder. "I was just playing, boy."

"It didn't feel playful. It felt deadly serious."

"Why would I harm you? You might be useful again one day. Besides, we're family."

Lynxx suspected that the cold-blooded rattlesnakes had more sense of family than this man.

Frost looked around. "Anyway, I must get my biker buddy back. Any idea which way he ran? My eyes were closed when the ingrate took off."

Lynxx remembered the sounds of footsteps heading south. He pointed north. "That way."

"Excellent. You and I will catch up later. Actually, much later."

"Why's that?"

"I'll be busy helping some other Outriders set up a compound in Washington Heights."

Lynxx had visited that area ages ago, before the Mist. Many of the brownstones had been quite beautiful, and he'd liked the cafes and delis. Of course, a lot of the streets would look very different now. "What type of compound?"

"A settlement for hybrids and our recruits."

Lynxx felt a stir of curiosity. "Recruits?"

"Weak-minded humans who are easy to control and desperate enough to join our group. They'll be doing all the drudge work. Not everyone is suitable, of course. Most people are too strong-minded or ask too many questions; those humans will become test subjects in our experiments." The man gave a cold smile. "Speaking of test subjects, I need to get going. Otherwise my biker buddy will escape."

Shaded by his dark sunglasses, Lynxx hid his alarm. Test subjects? Experiments? Was Frost hoping to wipe out the surviving humans? Fortunately, Lynxx knew the albino didn't have the scientific skills needed to make this happen. In fact, he doubted that anyone left on Earth—human or hybrid—could develop such a specialized virus.

Good.

He watched Frost move northward through the tunnel of web-draped trees.

When his guardian was finally out of sight, Lynxx sagged forward, almost weak-kneed from the revelation he'd hidden from Frost—

—and himself, until now.

He cared for Kassia.

He didn't think he loved her, even though he had no idea what love felt like. But the warmth that filled him whenever he thought of her was definitely real.

He had feelings for Kassia.

He wanted her to live, not for any experiment or clinical trial—but because his own world was happier and brighter with her in it.

Heading south, he hurried down the dim tunnel of trees, eager to feel the warm sunlight on his skin.

At the snap of a branch, he jerked to a halt.

The girl was almost hidden by some tall bushes. A pair of green eyes, identical to Kassia's, stared at him with horror.

Olivia.

She was almost at the end of the tunnel, too far to have heard his conversation with Frost. But from the way her rifle shook as she aimed it at him, she'd seen enough to leave her trembling in fear.

62

Lynxx's heart thundered.

He'd planned to reconnect with Olivia one day, but not like this. Instead of a safe environment, he was standing among trees webbed with terras and shrubs infested with rattlesnakes. He'd wanted her to see him as harmless, not as someone who associated with sadists, or who'd survived being squeezed to death by an enormous python.

Slowly, he moved toward her.

She stepped out from behind the bush, aiming her rifle at his chest. She wore her usual outfit: dark coveralls, black beanie, grease-smeared cheeks, machete slung over one shoulder, gun tucked into her belt, knife strapped to her thigh.

"Stay there," she snapped. "Don't come any closer."

He held up his hands, showing he was unarmed. Harmless. "Don't shoot, Olivia."

Green eyes darkening with suspicion, she asked, "How do you know my name?"

"We've met before, a couple of months ago in Central Park. I warned you about a terrible storm that was coming. Did you find your sister?"

Scowling, she studied his dark sunglasses and brown clothes. Her rifle wavered as her brow knotted in memory. "Stone? No, Rock."

He almost told her his new name—Lynxx—but something stopped him. "Yes."

Her fierce expression softened a fraction. "You helped me find my sister."

With a friendly smile, he pretended ignorance as he asked, "And you both got through that storm okay?"

"Yeah." Olivia's face hardened with suspicion again. She jerked her rifle at him. "Move. You and I need to have a talk, but not here." She threw a wary glance at the web-covered trees and the shrubs with their hidden snakes and hisses.

Lynxx kept his hands in the air as he left the leafy passageway. He crossed to a grassy area next to the Hudson River, followed by a grim Olivia.

Rifle still trained on him, she asked, "What was that all about?"

"What?"

"That scene with the weird albino in the tunnel of trees."

If he admitted the truth—that he and Frost were hybrids sent here to assist and report on the First Wave—he guessed she'd put a bullet in his chest the second she realized what he was.

A hybrid.

A being born of two worlds, belonging to neither.

A minor participant in the apocalypse.

"I don't know," he finally replied.

"Try again. Who was that guy? And what the heck was going on with those snakes?"

"His name's Frost. He's dangerous."

"Dangerous like you, right?"

"Look, I don't know what was going on with those snakes." The lie slipped easily from his lips. Wasn't lying a human trait? "Maybe the snakes ate some terras that made them behave weirdly."

"Weirdly? We're talking about a massive python that wrapped itself around you."

"I know. I was there. I thought it was going to kill me." This wasn't a lie. Even now, he fancied he could still feel that thick scaly body slowly squeezing the life from him.

He shuddered at the memory.

Perhaps his shudder convinced her more than his words, because she lowered her rifle a little, saying, "That guy and the snakes freaked me out."

"Me too." Sensing he'd made a fragile connection, he pressed his advantage. He needed to convince Olivia to stay away from Washington Heights. He couldn't tell her that Frost and some other Outriders were setting up a compound there and were hunting for test subjects. Thinking quickly, he found fresh lies sliding from his lips. "Look, Frost's not the only new danger in this city."

"What are you talking about?"

"I've just gotten back from Washington Heights. You need to warn everyone you meet that the area is dangerous. It's a red zone. People should stay away from it." How strange, he thought. He actually wanted to warn the other survivors in the city about the danger. When had he started feeling the slightest concern for anyone other than Kassia and her protector, Olivia?

"Why's it a red zone?" she asked.

"Because of the super-lethal terras growing there. They—" He stopped. Looked behind her.

The air was shifting. A basketball-sized object hovered a few feet away, its opaque surface flickering with rainbow colors.

Jellyfish terra.

Fast, accurate, and deadly.

63

"Run, Olivia!" Lynxx cried.

A long jellylike tentacle burst from the object. It shot toward the girl. Lassoed her neck. Yanked her backward.

She staggered, her finger jerking on the rifle's trigger.

A deafening blast rang out and the hot breath of a bullet whizzed past Lynxx's cheek.

Olivia tumbled to the ground, screaming. She scrabbled at the noose around her neck, but the jellyfish terra's poison burned the fingertips poking from her cut-down gloves, and she pulled her hands away.

She had only minutes left to live.

Lynxx ran. Dropped to the ground beside her. Wrenched at the spongy tentacle.

It tightened its grip, digging into Olivia's neck and choking her screams into a gurgle. Her bulging eyes pleaded for help.

"Hang on," he cried as she writhed on the grass. Ignoring the poison burning his hands, he again tried dragging the tentacle from her neck. Its stranglehold tightened.

His mind raced. What could he do? How could he save her? Since the Mist, he'd worked out ways to kill some terras, but jellyfish terras hadn't been on his list.

Sunlight glinted off the barrel of her rifle lying nearby.

Maybe ...

Lynxx leaped to his feet. Shucking off his backpack, he pulled off his brown shirt, folded it in half and shoved it over her face. "Keep this here," he told her. "It'll protect your skin. Close your eyes. Don't move until I tell you it's safe."

She pressed the shirt against her face.

Bare-chested, he nudged his sunglasses up his nose, protecting his eyes. Then he snatched up the rifle, aimed it at the floating ball, and pulled the trigger.

A thunderous blast shattered the air.

The jellyfish terra exploded into pieces. Several clumps fell onto the shirt covering Olivia's face. Others splattered Lynxx's naked chest, burning his skin. He brushed them off, ignoring the angry red splotches they left behind.

He dropped to his knees beside Olivia again. This time, the tentacle-noose around her neck broke away at his first yank and, disgusted, he threw the thing across the grass.

"Are you okay?" he asked, lifting his shirt from her face and tossing the poison-splattered clothing aside.

She gasped for air, eyes bright with terror and pain. A long thin cut encircled her neck, as though she'd been partially garroted.

When she lifted her hands to her throat, Lynxx gently pushed them away. "There's still poison in your wound. I need to wash it out."

From his backpack, he pulled out a bottle of water and poured it over the bleeding line around her neck. The liquid stung her wound and she gasped but lay still, enduring the fresh pain.

Next, he removed her fingerless gloves and washed her hands, then his own.

Lynxx dug around in his backpack again and withdrew a clump of precious crimson-sun terra leaves. In the past few weeks, he'd set up scientific equipment in his hotel suite so he could continue his experiments. Only this time his focus was terra plants, not people. While many terras were dangerous, others were harmless. Was it possible, he had wondered, that some terras might have medicinal value?

Often, Olivia returned to the bunker with injuries. Sometimes, the sisters' small supply of lotions and ointments helped her cuts and burns; other times, they were useless and she'd have to wait weeks until her wounds healed. He knew Kassia's twin needed something more effective than the standard treatments. So far, the crimson-sun terras had shown promise in healing injuries.

"Hang on, Olivia." He crushed the rare leaves in his palms, gently layered them over her wound, then tied a bandage around her neck.

From her sigh of relief, he guessed her pain was easing.

"How's that feel?" he asked.

"Better," she croaked, slowly sitting up.

Around Lynxx, the air rippled like a pond disturbed by a tossed rock.

He spun about, scanning for another jellyfish terra.

Nothing.

The air continued to ripple.

Strange. What was going on?

Olivia's voice trembled. "What happened to me?"

Lynxx pointed at the jellylike chunks on the ground. "Jellyfish terra. They look like jellyfish, only these are terra plants. They have one main tentacle and several smaller ones."

Fingertips resting on her bandaged neck, she gazed at him in confusion. "They're plants?"

"Yes. They're not common. But they're lethal."

He glimpsed something out of the corner of his eye.

Turning, he frowned.

Across the grass, a pair of legs poked from behind a distant bush.

64

"Wait here." Shouldering his backpack, Lynxx took the rifle and headed across the grass.

Olivia struggled to her feet and followed.

An old man lay behind a bush. His age-fogged eyes stared sightlessly at a bloated red jellyfish terra hovering above him. A fat tentacle connected his body to the terra like an umbilical cord.

"Is he dead?" she whispered.

"Definitely," Lynxx replied, noting the man's gray skin. "Their poison kills within minutes. The terra then floats above its victim, absorbing nutrients as its tentacle burrows inside, feeding on blood and organs." He pointed to the man's abdomen, where a long thin shape burrowed beneath the skin.

Olivia paled. "That could've been me." Her words trembled into silence.

"This thing's had its last feed." Lynxx took her arm and moved them both back to a safe distance.

He blasted the jellyfish terra into oblivion.

Thick red chunks and soft blobs splattered the area, along with a foul odor.

Wincing at the smell, Olivia gestured to the crimson splotches on the grass. "Is that blood?"

"Yes. His."

She gagged, about to throw up, but her face quickly hardened again as she refused to submit to her weakness.

During the past two months, Lynxx had always visited Kassia in the bunker during the day, when he knew she'd be lonely. Often, though, he'd found himself returning in the evenings as well.

As Mousy, he would listen as Olivia told Kassia about her day on the surface, describing her hunts and searches for supplies. Reluctantly, Olivia also told Kassia about the human predators that sometimes tried to hunt *her*, and she detailed the various terras that had injured her. These incidents were used to educate Kassia—and to emphasize the importance of being careful whenever she left the bunker.

Lynxx knew Olivia would tell Kassia about these jellyfish terras, the snakes, and his guardian, Frost.

Olivia staggered away from the man's body.

He caught her by the elbow. "You need to get home and rest."

She gave a weary nod, then touched the bandage at her throat. "Will I be okay?"

"Yes. However, you'll probably be left with a nasty red scar."

She shrugged. Since the Mist, her concern for her looks had been eroded by her struggle to survive. "At least I'll live. I need to, because of Kass."

Playing dumb, he asked, "Is Kass your sister? The girl I saw back in Central Park?"

"Yes."

"She looked sick the day I saw her. Is she better?"

Olivia hesitated, then gave a weary shake of her head. "She's slowly getting worse. She's got leukemia."

"I'm sorry."

"Me too."

Around Lynxx, the ripples grew a little stronger. Was something coming closer?

Or was it just his imagination?

Still, he sensed a sudden need to hurry.

He gestured to the slash on Olivia's neck. "Wash the wound every day for a week. Cover it with antiseptic cream and a bandage."

She looked at him, grateful, her green eyes an echo of Kassia's beautiful eyes. "Thanks." She nodded at the ugly red splotches on his bare chest. "Are you going to be okay?"

Belatedly, he pulled another plastic bottle from his backpack and poured the water over his chest, rinsing off the poison. "I'll be fine."

Why hadn't he washed off the poison sooner? He'd been so focused on helping Kassia's sister that he'd forgotten about his own injuries. What was wrong with him?

Deep within him, he felt another strange flicker, almost a stir of ... what?

"Your hands are blistered," she said.

"They'll heal."

"You're hurt because you tried to help me."

"We both survived. That's the main thing."

"True." Shaking her head in disbelief, Olivia muttered, "Jellyfish terras swollen with blood. Can things get any more disgusting in this place?"

Lynxx suspected they could—and would—but he kept quiet.

As they glumly headed across the grass, she asked, "Do you have any more of those leaves you used on my neck, Rock? They'd sure come in handy."

He shook his head with genuine regret. "I've been looking for crimson-sun terras over the past week, but I've only found a couple of plants. I used their leaves on you today."

"What? You put non-terrestrial leaves on my neck without telling me?"

"If I hadn't, you'd be dead by now."

"Oh. You're right. Thanks."

They stood at the railing that edged the Hudson River and looked across the yellow water.

In the distance, the Statue of Liberty loomed against a red-tinted sky, her upheld torch symbolizing freedom and triumph.

He wondered whether the remaining people in New York realized that Lady Liberty was now a lie, a sad reminder of a past era. The terras would continue to flourish throughout the city, reducing the survivors' freedom with each passing day. There'd be no triumph for humanity. They'd already lost.

However ...

His eyes narrowed in memory.

Yesterday, he'd been down at a dock area when, amazingly, a helicopter had landed nearby.

At first, he'd thought some remnant of the armed services had survived. Then he'd recognized two of the four passengers who'd emerged from the cabin.

One was Asher Weston. The other was Colonel Powell, an Army officer he'd met several times over the past few months.

Curious, he had parked his body in a safe spot and leaped into the mind of a pigeon, then into the golden eagle WindLord. From the air, he'd followed the pair to Weston Tower.

Eventually, Asher and Powell had arrived at the rooftop gardens. WindLord-him had hidden behind some thick plants, listening as they'd discussed the situation in New York. Eventually Powell had stuck out his hand to Asher.

"Let's do it, son. Let's join forces and start a real resistance movement."

Lynxx thought their determination to fight the terras was ambitious, noble—and doomed.

Still, he'd felt a surprising stir of admiration for them, along with another unexpected emotion: envy.

He envied the camaraderie of most humans. The way they looked out for each other. Their sense of family and community.

Sure, the Wilders were vicious scum only interested in violence, drugs, and alcohol. Most people, though, helped and supported each other through disasters.

As he and Olivia headed down the walkway beside the Hudson River, Lynxx had a sudden idea. "Do you know a black Army guy named Powell?"

"Yes. Why?"

"He's just merged forces with a group living in Weston Tower. Why don't you and Kassia join this group?"

Kassia would be safer in the tower than in that dank subway tunnel.

Maybe he'd join the group as well. That way, he'd finally be able to talk to her in person—as himself and not a pea-brained mouse. He and Kassia could sit together in the rooftop gardens, discussing books. They could share meals. Work in the farms.

Maybe become a couple.

The possibilities were endless and exciting.

Olivia shook her head. "I've already tried joining Colonel Powell's group. I told him I wanted to bring along an ill ... friend ... but they don't allow in sick people."

"Did you explain that Kassia isn't contagious?"

A nod. "It didn't matter. They won't waste their limited meds on people with incurable conditions."

"Maybe they'd change their minds if you told them she was your sister."

"They wouldn't. Colonel Powell was firm about their policy. Anyway, I don't want people knowing that I have a sick, vulnerable sister who's alone during the day. There are Wilders out there who might go looking for her."

"True. I—" Around Lynxx, the ripples suddenly increased, almost vibrating through him. This time, he knew he wasn't imagining things.

He jerked to a halt on the sidewalk.

And waited.

65

THE VIBRATIONS GREW STRONGER, as if a breeze were rushing through Lynxx.

He looked around.

The trees were motionless. Scattered pieces of paper lay still on the walkway. Not a single leaf blew across the grass.

His confusion shifted into understanding. The vibrations were mental, not physical.

Was an Outrider approaching them, mind-blended with an animal or bird?

"Are you okay?" Olivia asked him.

"I'm fine." He scanned the area, seeking the source of the ripples.

A large dark shape swooped from the sky, settled in a nearby tree, and peered at him.

He recognized the vulture with the red beak. It was the same one that his guardian, Frost, had mind-controlled back in the creepy tunnel of trees. Its eyes were no longer black. They were now a bright silver, cold and sharp as a blade.

The silver eyes meant the vulture was mind-blended with a hybrid—in this case, probably his guardian.

Why was Frost watching him?

When the vulture shifted its silver glare to Olivia, Lynxx realized his guardian was checking where his loyalties lay. Again, why?

The answer suddenly flashed through him. Frost possessed human traits like sadism and rage, and he was also controlling. He had always hated humans and wanted Lynxx to remain isolated from them—physically, mentally, and emotionally.

Lynxx turned away from vulture-Frost, trying to conceal his alarm. He needed to hide the fact that he knew Olivia.

On the walkway, the girl looked at him, wide-eyed. Despite the grease smears on her cheeks, her face was still lovely as she said, "I'm grateful that—"

"I didn't kill you," he harshly ground out, aware he couldn't let her finish that sentence. He guessed she'd been about to thank him again for saving her from the jellyfish terra.

"What?" She stared at him, shocked.

Lynxx ignored his shame and distress. Told himself he was saving her life.

Indicating his bare chest, he snarled, "You ruined my favorite shirt. The next time you get in my way, scum, you'll be dead." Was that too brutal?

On the branch, the silver-eyed vulture spread its wings and squawked in delight. Vulture-Frost obviously approved.

Face paling, Olivia's hand darted to the revolver in her belt.

Good. Let Frost see that she was afraid of him.

She gasped, "What are you talking about?"

"Shut up. I don't want to hear another word from you." He stormed away, as though disgusted by her presence.

He could feel her stunned gaze on his back.

Worse, his skin crawled beneath the vulture's scrutiny as Frost watched him stomp down the walkway. Lynxx longed to go back and ask Olivia for forgiveness—but he knew he'd be signing her death warrant.

Wings flapped overhead as vulture-Frost flew north, probably resuming his search for the biker.

As the rippling air settled into stillness, he exhaled in relief. His guardian was gone. Should he go and apologize to Olivia?

No.

If Frost suddenly returned and saw him talking to her, the man's suspicions could blaze into rage.

He forced himself to keep walking down the path, sickened by his treatment of Olivia.

Yet he was also relieved.

Kassia and Olivia were safe—

—for now.

66

The white hairs on Mousy-Lynxx's body prickled.

After yesterday's meeting with Frost in the tunnel of trees, he'd been on high alert. He'd watched for his guardian everywhere, regularly stopping to check the air for ripples.

Nothing. No ripples. No silver-eyed vulture. No sign of Frost.

Eventually, his alertness had simmered down into wariness.

Right now, though, the danger he was sensing was personal. He was already near his daily limit in this rodent's body. He'd hung around waiting for Kassia to visit her underground mushroom farm. Usually she went every Friday morning, but today she'd lingered to finish her novel, and now it was after lunch.

Lynxx knew his time was running out. He needed to do a reverse triple mind-leap from Mousy into a bat, then a bird, and finally into his non-conscious body slumped in the Branson Hotel suite. Any minute now, his body might wake up—but if his mind wasn't there, he could accidentally injure or even kill himself.

He sighed and stayed in Mousy's body.

He couldn't let Kassia go into the subway tunnels alone.

"Snack, Mousy?" She placed a piece of cheese in front of him.

As Lynxx, he hated canned cheddar, but Mousy-him loved it and would eat the disgusting stuff all day, if allowed. Strange.

From the top of a stack of boxes, he watched Kassia move around the crowded room, humming as she prepared for her weekly outing. The prospect of leaving the bunker always gave her a temporary burst of energy.

When Kassia wasn't looking, he scampered across to Olivia's locket, which she'd left behind this morning. The long slash on the girl's neck, caused by the jellyfish terra yesterday, had made her skin too sore to bear the necklace's weight.

With his mouse nose, he pushed its tiny clasp, then pawed the two brass sides apart. One held a photo of the twins' parents. The other held a small portrait of Kassia, which he studied with avid eyes. She looked healthy and lovely. Her auburn hair hung to her shoulders in thick shiny waves, her beautiful green eyes glowed, and her smile was warm and happy.

Clearly, the picture had been taken before the Night of the Red Mist.

Lynxx bent to the locket and kissed her photo.

A few minutes later, he used his nose and paws to close the locket again.

"What do you think, Mousy?" Kassia pirouetted like a model.

Good. She was keeping her promise.

Last night, Mousy-him had popped by to check on Olivia. As expected, Kassia had been in full nurse mode, tending to her sister's injured neck, then cooking her favorite canned meal. Olivia, still upset from the day's events, had made Kassia promise to arm herself more heavily on her short trips from the bunker.

Now, he ran his gaze over Kassia's beefed-up appearance. Jeans. Shirt. Revolver in belt. Pistol in boot. Hunting knife strapped to thigh. Woolen beanie hiding her hair.

Kassia smiled, one side of her mouth quirking in a distinctive uplift that he always found appealing. "Do I look badass, Mousy?"

Luckily, his silver eyes were too small for her to see his sudden worry. Despite her weapons, she was still easy prey. Over the past two months, the leukemia had burned away most of her energy and health, leaving her body fragile, her face pale, and her eyes weary.

Mouse tail flicking in agitation, he paced the top of a cardboard box. Her meds were becoming harder to find each week. He couldn't cure her leukemia or make the drugs she needed. Could he find something else to prolong her life?

The rare crimson-sun terras were successful at healing some injuries in humans. Could another terra slow down or even stop Kassia's disease?

"Okay, time for the Dynamic Duo to rock and roll." Gently she cupped him in her palm and raised him closer to her face. "You're a funny little mouse, aren't you? Sometimes your eyes look black. Other times, they look silver, like today. Strange."

Lynxx gave an uneasy squeak. He disliked these weekly outings. And now, after yesterday's meeting with Frost, he disliked them even more. He wanted Kassia to stay in her bunker, safe from his guardian.

"Shh, Mousy. I know the subway is creepy, but we'll be fine. We always are."

She popped him into a shirt pocket over her breast, left the bunker, and closed the door behind them.

67

Kassia moved down the tunnel, her flashlight carving a cone of light in the blackness.

Mousy-Lynxx stood up and, gripping the top of her pocket with his black front paws, scanned their surroundings. His eagle host, WindLord, had incredible vision, but Mousy's eyesight was poor. He could barely see anything in the dimness. Luckily, like all rodents, his sharp sense of smell helped even things up a little.

His pink nose twitched in disgust at the stench of bat droppings and urine. Honestly, couldn't the critters pick just one place to use as a toilet instead of everywhere?

His rodent skin quivered as a ripple of air flowed over him. His guardian, Frost? Panic stirred in his small chest. But it was just a downdraft from a bat.

For the tenth time that morning, he wondered if Frost had somehow followed him—unseen and unfelt—from the Branson Hotel to this subway. Was the man watching him right now? Was he blended with one of the bats that clung to the roof? Lynxx knew the phrase "as blind as a bat" was wrong; all bats had vision, even in the dark.

"Don't worry, Mousy." Kassia ran a gentle finger over his furry head and ripped pink ear. "We'll just deliver the food, then go home."

Shortly after Kassia had moved into the bunker, she had set up a large mushroom farm in an old crosscut. Since the fungi had thrived in the moist dark air, her crop was always larger than she and Olivia could eat. Each Friday, she'd take a bag of mushrooms plus some other food to the only other inhabitant of this tunnel: an old man who lived further down the track.

By the time she arrived at the man's bunker today, her breathing was labored. After catching her breath, she knocked on the closed metal door. "Hello, Mr. Isaac?"

A gruff voice rasped from within. "Who is it?"

Mousy-him snuffed in disgust. The old guy knew it was Kassia. She was the only one who knocked on his door every Friday like clockwork.

"It's me, Kass Madison. I've brought you some more mushrooms. Plus a couple of pounds of venison."

"Leave the stuff outside."

"Okay." She placed the bulging burlap sacks on the ground and retrieved the two bags she'd left last week. As usual, they were empty.

"Well," she muttered to Mousy-him, "he's still eating the meat and mushrooms we give him. Maybe one day he'll even open the door to me. Or at least thank me."

Lynxx snuffed again. *As if!*

A metallic clang rang in the distant blackness.

Kassia paused.

"What was that?" she whispered, aiming her flashlight up the tunnel. The beam illuminated the tracks for a hundred feet or so before being swallowed by darkness.

Another clang.

Through the fabric of her shirt, Lynxx felt Kassia's heartbeat increase a little at the strange noise.

In the several weeks that he, as Mousy, had accompanied Kassia on her Friday mushroom collections, the tunnels had always held the hushed silence of ancient caves. The only sounds had been the squeaks of bats and rats, and the steady drip of water from overhead crevices.

A third clang. Louder this time.

Kassia hesitated, then knocked on the metal door again. "Hello, Mr. Isaac?"

"Who is it?"

She gave a long-suffering sigh at the same-old question. "It's me. Kass Madison. Again."

"What do you want?"

"I heard something in the tunnel."

"So?"

"I was hoping you could come with me to check it out."

"Not today. I'm busy."

Frowning, Kassia studied the distant darkness again. This time, the fingertip stroking Lynxx's furry head trembled a little. She gulped. "Okay, Mousy, it's just you and me, the Dynamic Duo. That noise is probably just the wind blowing down a vent or something. We need to check it out, though, just in case."

Why? he wanted to shout.

It could be a trap. His guardian, Frost. Or bikers. Or even one of the wild animals that roamed Manhattan like it was their new hunting ground.

Kassia's hand touched the revolver tucked into her belt. Reassured by its presence, she cautiously set off along the tracks.

Whiskers twitching, Mousy-Lynxx balanced on his hind legs as he peered over the top of her pocket. He sniffed the air, analyzing each smell for danger.

Dead decaying snake on their left. Disgusting but harmless.

Old human feces. Also disgusting but harmless.

Decomp-dust. Ditto.

Mold. Mud. Rancid water. This place was infested with foul smells, he thought. So far, though, nothing was particularly alarming.

After a couple of minutes, Kassia followed the clangs into a tunnel that branched off from the main one.

A crashed train lay further ahead.

Kassia paused several yards from the crumpled front car, puffing.

Lynxx twitched his mouse whiskers. *Let's go home.*

Another clang, louder, came from further down the tunnel.

"We have to keep going, Mousy," she whispered. "Sure, I can hide in the bunker, where I'm nice and safe. But Via sometimes wanders up and down these lines, making sure everything's okay. If I don't find out what's causing that noise, she could walk straight into danger, just like she did with that jellyfish terra yesterday."

Lynxx fought back his frustration.

His nose twitched at an odor of death.

He sensed something terrible awaited them in the train.

With every cell in his—Mousy's—body, he longed to return to his own body at the Branson Hotel so he could rush back into this tunnel, as himself, to protect Kassia and deal with whatever was making those sounds.

But he knew the trip would take too long.

She could be dead by the time he returned.

68

With difficulty, Kassia climbed into the tilted train.

As she aimed her beam down the first passenger car, a horrified gasp snagged in her throat.

The sloped interior was a mess of snapped seats, cracked floor, smashed windows—and more than a dozen bodies. Some lay twisted and maimed, their decaying flesh gnawed on by rodents and other vermin; Lynxx assumed these people had died in the crash. Others, possibly injured and unable to leave, had waited for help that had never come. Eventually, they'd perished from the Red Fever and had turned into decomp-dust.

Kassia staggered down the sloping floor, moving from car to car.

Everywhere, pieces of people's lives lay among the bodies and dust piles.

Women's purses. Men's glasses. Children's toys.

Lynxx also saw laptops, cell phones, and tablets. These devices had once connected their owners to millions of people via a worldwide web.

These days, survivors lived in tiny patches of isolation, cut off from faraway humans, and ignorant of happenings in other areas, states, countries. While some people had banded into groups, he guessed that with the loss of their families, friends, and their wonderful linking web, each person felt more alone than ever before.

Lynxx's situation was the opposite. All his life he'd felt alone and it had never worried him. Then he'd met Kassia and everything had changed. *He* had changed. Now, whenever he was with her, even blended inside a rodent, he felt ... connected. Alive. Happier.

"You okay, Mousy?" Kassia whispered as she climbed from the last toppled car, onto the track.

Relieved she was safely out of the death train, he gave a soft squeak. *Yes.*

Kassia shined her flashlight back at the rear car, murmuring, "I thought the noise might've been coming from inside the train, but—"

Another clang rang out from somewhere ahead.

It sounded close. Maybe a couple of hundred feet away.

Mousy-Lynxx's nose twitched at the coppery smell of blood.

Fresh blood.

Kassia needed to turn back. *Now.*

Frantically, he pawed at her shirt, as though trying to dig through the material. Would she realize he was attempting to warn her about something?

"Settle down, Mousy," she whispered, heading along the track.

He rolled his tiny eyes. *So much for that brilliant warning.*

They reached a narrow passage that connected their tunnel to another one on the far side of the bedrock. He'd read that maintenance workers had once used these corridors as shortcuts between the various lines running beneath Manhattan.

A faint yellow light glowed at the end of the passage.

Let's go home, Kassia!

She switched off her flashlight and moved through the dark passage, running her fingers along a wall to guide herself.

Beneath her shirt, Mousy-Lynxx could feel Kassia's heartbeat racing in her chest.

He stiffened as a familiar sensation filled his mind. Hundreds of invisible ants were crawling through his consciousness.

No. Not now.

As he'd feared, his body at the Branson Hotel was starting to wake up; if he didn't return soon, he could stagger blindly around the suite, injuring or even killing himself.

But he couldn't leave Kassia alone in this black place with its stink of fresh blood.

He hardened his mind. Ignored the crawling ants.

When she gingerly peered around the end of the passage, Mousy-Lynxx leaned from her pocket and peered around as well.

In the new tunnel, a flashlight on the tracks highlighted a man swinging an axe. He was hacking at something in the shadows. Every so often, his blade would strike the metal tracks with a loud clang.

Lynxx felt the breath freeze in his mouse throat. The wild-haired adult was wearing a ragged cloak made from a striped black-and-white skin.

ZebraMan.

Weeks ago, he'd seen this wacko in an alley, hacking flesh from a woman he'd killed. Since then, Lynxx had tried finding the cannibal several times, but the creep obviously hid between his hunts, feasting on his forbidden meat in private.

Kassia took a hesitant step forward, about to introduce herself to this survivor.

She had no idea how dangerous he was.

He had to warn her.

More and more ants crawled through his consciousness. Time was running out.

Leaving Mousy slumped in Kassia's pocket, he threw his mind upward, into a bat. His new host struggled against him, and his mind-blend wavered, weakened by the crawling ants. But his fear for Kassia flared into a brief burst of strength. He shoved the bat's mind into a mental corner, locking it in a case like the one Frost had created in the python.

Bat-Lynxx flew across to the flashlight lying on the tracks. With his tiny, clawed feet, he kicked it to the side.

The beam shifted from ZebraMan and onto the object he was chopping up.

A man. Possibly.

Dead. Definitely.

The light revealed blood puddled around the mutilated body and splattered on the tunnel wall. A severed hand poked from a pile of hacked flesh.

Bat-Lynxx flew to the roof.

Shock exploded on Kassia's face. With a horrified gasp, she staggered back into the narrow passage.

ZebraMan must've heard her gasp, because he spun around, eyes slitted, axe raised.

Lynxx flinched as the ants scurried even faster through his bat mind. Somehow, he still managed to mentally remote-push a dozen nearby bats into action.

As one, the bats dropped from the roof and swarmed around ZebraMan. Leathery wings slapped the lunatic's face. Tiny talons ripped at his fuzzy orange hair. A couple of bats even pooped in his eyes. ZebraMan shrieked. Swung his axe blindly at the flying attackers. Struck air.

The bats continued swirling around him.

Swearing, ZebraMan wiped the feces from his eyes, then flung his animal-skin cape over his head, protecting his face. He dropped to his knees and shoved bloodied chunks of flesh into a plastic bag.

Bat-Lynxx watched from the roof, disgusted. *Psycho.*

Once the bag was full, ZebraMan grabbed his flashlight and fled down the abandoned tunnel, away from the one where Kassia and Olivia lived.

Lynxx rushed back to Kassia.

She was hurrying down the narrow corridor, light still off, and Mousy huddling in her shirt pocket. She used a hand to guide herself along the wall. When she turned into the tunnel, she switched on her flashlight and, ashen-faced, ran toward the crashed passenger cars.

He knew she'd soon be safe in her bunker.

Unfortunately, if he wanted to live, he had to get back to his own body. *Now.*

Bat-Lynxx hated leaving her, but he had no choice. He'd be no use to her dead.

Reluctantly, he flew past Kassia, down the long tunnel, toward his hotel.

With each tired flap of his wings, he wrestled questions without answers. Would ZebraMan go looking for the person who'd seen him hacking up a body? Or would he simply move his murderous activities to another spot? After all, Lynxx told himself, it was easier for the psycho to hunt humans on the surface, in the sunlight, rather than in the black underground.

But what if ZebraMan preferred to hunt in darkness?

What if Kassia became his next target?

69

OVER THE NEXT WEEK, Lynxx mind-hopped from animal to animal, searching for ZebraMan.

He cruised the skies as the eagle WindLord, scanning the city below. He scoured inside buildings and subways as bats and rats, trying to pick up the man's scent. He roamed the streets as a wolf, then as a deer and an antelope, using the animals' speeds and silence to travel into spots inaccessible on a noisy motorcycle.

Lynxx knew ZebraMan would see other people as threats or prey. However, the psycho wouldn't suspect that an animal was stalking him, just as he stalked humans.

Nothing.

No sign of the freak.

He was disappointed, yet not surprised. New York had millions of places to hide. Searching for one particular person was like trying to find a needle in a Mount Everest-sized haystack.

After a week, he realized he was wasting his time. And energy. Mind-blending for hours each day with a range of new and unwilling animal hosts left him exhausted and ill. Each evening, he'd lie in his hotel suite, nose bleeding, throwing up from nausea.

These long mind-blends left him so sick that he needed all night to recover, which meant he didn't have any energy left for visiting Kassia as Mousy. As the days passed without visiting her, he felt more and more alone.

Finally, he put his futile searches on hold.

And returned to the subway bunker.

To Kassia.

When he scampered onto her lap, she gave a delighted smile and stroked his white fur.

"So you've come back, Mousy. I've missed you."

I've missed you too, he thought, quivering at her nearness.

For the past week, being away from her was like being underwater, in danger of drowning. But now that he was with her again, he felt as if he'd battled his way back to the surface and could breathe again.

She was like air to him.

As Kassia read a novel aloud, he nestled on her lap. He knew her loneliness was so intense that she needed to pretend her pet mouse could understand her.

The thing was, he understood her in so many ways. He understood the extent of her strength as she struggled to stay alive each day. He understood her longing to help Olivia, and her frustration with the disease that kept her weak. He understood her joy in simple pleasures like reading old novels, poring over pictures of paintings she'd never see in person, writing in her journal of places she'd never visit, and talking to a white mouse as though it were her friend.

At the end of a chapter, she smiled down at him. "Good book, isn't it?"

He hadn't been paying attention to the story. He'd been listening to the sound of her voice, which flowed over him like honey, sweet and gentle.

He gazed up at her mouth.

Incredibly, he'd once kissed those perfectly formed lips. It had been a lifetime ago when she'd approached him in Central Park on Day Zero. For the thousandth time, he remembered how soft and sun-warmed she'd felt. He'd been kissed before, of course. He'd even explored his human sensuality with a few eager and pretty girls.

But not one of them had ever stirred the slightest flicker of emotion within him.

Why was he drawn to Kassia and not to her sister Olivia? Or to any of the other girls he'd met?

What made him long to kiss her again and again, as himself, and not some idiotic mouse?

Since Day Zero, he'd spent numerous nights reliving that moment in Central Park when he'd embraced Kassia. Even now, months later, he could still recall the warmth that had heated him like a fire during their kiss, and he could still feel the way her body had melded against his own, as though they were one.

He longed to embrace Kassia again. As a human. He wanted to gather her into his arms, run his hands across her hair, kiss her lips.

He wanted to talk to her as a human, share jokes and laughter, cook meals together, watch movies, read books, and spend time as a couple.

But for any of that to happen, he had to keep her alive.

Lynxx cut his visits to Kassia from three hours a day to one.

Logically, he knew he should stop visiting her altogether so he could devote himself to his research. But, emotionally, he needed a daily dose of her in order to breathe, to live.

He moved into the seventeen-floor Ferguson Complex, around the corner from Grand Central Station. The lower floors of the Complex held offices and apartments.

Half of the top floor, though, was a huge laboratory once used for making fake perfumes and synthetic hormones. The facility was stocked with an impressive range of scientific equipment, connected to a powerful generator in the basement. Even better, the lab opened onto a massive glasshouse, perfect for growing plants.

Still watching out for ZebraMan—and Frost—Lynxx traveled around Manhattan. After collecting a wide range of terra specimens, he started his experiments.

He hoped to find something to cure Kassia's leukemia. However, since that was unlikely, he sought a plant that would put her disease into remission. The odds of a cure or remission were both tiny, but desperation drove him to try anyway.

Five weeks into his research, he stumbled across a terra with potential benefits. The *Lobelien exTerrus*, or Lazarus-vine terra, was a fast-growing climber with fragrant flowers and turpentine-scented leaves. When crushed, its juice could heal burns or cuts. Even better, the stamens in the middle of the huge purple blossoms carried a pollen with unusual properties.

He needed test subjects.

His mind-blends with Mousy made him reluctant to experiment on other mice. Instead, he collected scores of rats and infected two dozen with a flu virus he'd found in another lab. Then he separated them into various groups for treatment. Most of the terras had no effect on the flu. Surprisingly, though, the rats that smelled the Lazarus flowers recovered quickly and completely.

He stared at the pages of results. Could the stamens or other parts of the Lazarus plants be developed into a drug to help Kassia? Unfortunately, that kind of research could take weeks or even months to achieve results. Months she didn't have.

Lynxx decided to use what he had for now. He needed to keep Kassia alive while he worked on his more complex experiments.

The trouble was, first he'd have to face Olivia again ...

... as himself.

70

Lynxx waited outside Empire Tower, pacing the footpath.

As Mousy, he'd heard Olivia tell Kassia that she was going to search this building for meds today. If she'd found the bottles he'd placed at dawn in one of the main offices, she'd be in a good mood when she left.

Hopefully, she wouldn't shoot him on sight.

Earlier today, he'd dressed in the same white T-shirt he'd worn when he'd first met Olivia in Central Park and had told her where to find Kassia. He'd even put on the same sunglasses, hoping they would remind her of how grateful she'd been that day.

Now, he watched Olivia exit the front door. She was smiling.

Good. She'd found the meds.

When she noticed him standing at the bottom of the steps, her smile vanished and her hand darted to the rifle slung over her shoulder. "What are you doing here, Rock?"

"Waiting for you. I saw you go inside an hour ago."

She frowned at the bundle of huge Lazarus blossoms he carried. "Go away. I don't date weirdos." Obviously, she still remembered their meeting in the park beside the Hudson River, when he'd saved her from a jellyfish terra—and had then done a Jekyll and Hyde and threatened to kill her.

"Let me explain."

"Get away from me." Unslinging the rifle from her shoulder, she hurried down the steps and along the sidewalk.

Lynxx knew better than to follow.

He cried out, "The flowers are for Kassia."

She stopped. Whirled to face him. Pointed her rifle straight at him.

"What are you talking about, Rock?"

"You told me she was sick. These flowers might help her."

Suspicion warred with desperation on her face. Rifle still trained on him, she moved closer. "Why should I believe anything you say?"

"That day at the park beside the river, I wasn't threatening you. I was saving your life."

"Yeah? How?"

"Remember that albino? The one who loved rattlesnakes and pythons?"

She shivered. "I still have nightmares about that weird scene."

"Me too," Lynxx answered honestly. "Anyway, he used to be my guardian. He's one twisted, sadistic son of a—"

"Got it."

"That day in the park, he wanted me to work for him again. When I refused, he was furious. He was hiding in the shadows, listening to us talk." He didn't mention that Frost had been mind-blended with a vulture.

"So?"

He hesitated. He couldn't tell Olivia about the hybrid Outriders and their ability to remote-push and mind-blend with animals. Such a confession would guarantee a bullet in his chest. "There aren't many people left. Frost believes if he keeps me isolated from other people, I'll eventually become so lonely that I'll work for him again."

"And what? Does he think I'm interested in you? I barely know you."

"He doesn't care. You saw him. He's crazy."

"Yeah. He's definitely crazy. Maybe you're crazy as well."

Lynxx allowed genuine regret to saturate his words. "I'm sorry for how I behaved that day, Olivia. I was trying to make him believe you weren't a threat to him, that you were someone I hated."

She considered his claim. Her gaze darted from his worried face to the blooms in his arms. Finally, desperation won. She lowered her rifle but didn't shoulder it.

"Okay, maybe you're not a murderous nutcase after all. Tell me about these flowers. How can they help Kass?"

"They *might* help her."

"How?"

"I've been experimenting on rats, making them sick. And every time, these terra flowers have made them well again."

"These are terras?"

"Yes, but they're harmless."

"They're still terras." She turned, about to walk away.

"True. They could still help your sister. Remember the crimson-sun terras a few weeks ago? They helped after you were almost strangled by that jellyfish terra."

She stopped. Turned back to him. Lifted a finger to the red scar encircling her neck. "You're right." Longingly, she gazed at the purple flowers. "What would I do with them?"

"Just take them ..." He stopped, about to say *home*. "... to your place." When had he started thinking of the subway bunker as his home? Lately, he was only there for an hour a day. Then again, the quote was *Home is where the heart is*.

"Really?" Olivia asked, interrupting his thoughts. "I don't have to boil them or turn them into a soup or something?"

"No." He pointed to the long stamens in the middle of the blooms. "I think the pollen on their stamens might help her."

When she hesitated, he pulled a single blossom from the bunch. "Look, I'll prove they're harmless." He shoved his face in the purple flower and inhaled deeply. "See, I'm still alive." Then he crushed some stamens and petals on his cheeks and mouth, rubbing them in as though washing himself with the pieces.

When he finally lifted his head from the mashed flower, Olivia's lips twitched in a smile. "You have purple and yellow stains all over your face and sunglasses, Rock."

He shrugged. "Would I rub this flower on me if it were dangerous?"

"I guess not." Finally, she shouldered her rifle. "Okay, I'll try them."

"It's important you don't tell Kassia about their potential medicinal value. And definitely don't mention that they're terras."

"Why not?"

"Studies have shown that many sick people temporarily feel better with a new treatment, even if they're only given sugar or water instead of meds. It's called a placebo effect. If Kassia believes these terras might help her—but they turn out to be useless—it's possible she'll think she's getting better. Later, she'll crash back to her original condition, or even worse."

"I don't like lying to my sister."

"If she sends my research in the wrong direction, will you like watching her die?"

Olivia fixed him with a hard glare. "Okay, you win." She snatched the Lazarus blooms from him. "If these flowers harm Kass, though, I'll hunt you down and kill you."

He knew she meant it.

71

THE NEXT MORNING, AS Mousy, Lynxx was relieved to see an improvement in Kassia.

Her eyes were brighter and her skin was slightly pinker. When she went to give Mr. Isaac his weekly mushrooms and meat, she moved with a little more energy, and her breathing wasn't as labored.

She loved the purple "roses" that Olivia had brought home, and often buried her face in them, inhaling their heady scent—and their pollen. However, the medicinal effects faded as the cut terra flowers died.

A week later, Lynxx arranged to run into Olivia again.

"The flowers helped Kass for a few days," she told him. "Then she slipped back."

"How's she today?" he asked, pretending ignorance. Of course, he'd already had his precious hour's visit with Kassia this morning. He knew she was no better overall.

"About the same as a week ago," Olivia answered.

"No worse?"

"No. I guess that's good."

He adjusted his sunglasses. "Maybe the flowers can keep her leukemia stable until I develop something more permanent."

Hope flared in her eyes. "Can you do that?"

"I'm going to try."

"Why? You don't even know Kass."

How wrong she was.

Quickly, he thought of an answer. "It's obvious these Lazarus plants—these terras—are here to stay. Maybe some good can come from them. Certain species might be able to help your sister, and others as well. Since the Mist, factories no longer make medicines and drugs. Perhaps some terras can help people instead."

To his surprise, he realized he meant what he'd just said.

Over the past few weeks, he'd occasionally mind-blended with various animals, using them to study the new resistance cell at Weston Tower. Each member seemed to have an assigned role. Fighter, soldier, hunter, fisher, teacher, farmer, mechanic, guard, and so forth.

As he'd watched the people working as a community, he'd begun to wonder about his own role in life. His top priority would always be Kassia and, to a lesser extent, her sister Olivia. Lately, though, he'd had the feeling that other areas of his life had become too ... small.

He needed to do more. Be more.

Were the medicinal terras his answer?

Maybe after he'd found a treatment for Kassia's leukemia, he could move on to other terras. He might be able to help people with other diseases and conditions.

Excitement stirred through him, and suddenly his future felt ... larger.

Olivia sighed. "You're right. We have to use what we've got and pray it works. Where can I find some more flowers?"

Lynxx led her to a small courtyard beside Grand Central Station. Its internal walls were covered with green Lazarus-vines that were studded with purple blossoms and small pear-like fruit.

"So far, this is the only place I know where the *Lobelien exTerrus* grow. We have to be careful not to pick all the mature flowers too quickly."

She stared longingly at the purple blossoms. "What should I do?"

"Only take three flowers once a week. That way, the other buds will have time to grow and open."

"But they don't last for a whole week. Kass only feels better for a few days. Then the effect fades away."

"At least she'll live, even if she's still unwell some days. If you use all the flowers too quickly, before I can find a more permanent treatment, she'll have none for the months ahead. And if she doesn't get any more meds or flowers, she could die."

Her sigh held a sad resignation. "I suppose you're right."

Around him, the air rippled faintly.

Frost.

Still far off but approaching.

He couldn't let his guardian see him with Olivia again.

Lynxx glanced at his watch. "I have to go. I need a sample of mold from inside the subway. Then I have to start some experiments."

"Sure. Sure." She seemed anxious not to hold up his work. "If you find a treatment for Kass, how will you let me know?"

The ripples were growing stronger. Closer.

Hurriedly, he said, "I'll leave a note in the sandstone planter outside Empire Tower, giving you a place and date to meet me." He looked up, searching for the silver-eyed vulture, but the courtyard only allowed a glimpse of the red sky. "If you need me, you can leave a note there as well."

"Okay."

Lynxx sensed the seconds ticking down to zero. "Gotta go." He bolted across the courtyard, through the employees' dining area, into the concealing blackness of the passages beyond.

Heart racing, he leaned against a wall and drew in deep steadying breaths.

Had he made it in time?

Or had Frost, in the vulture, glimpsed him with Olivia?

Had he just signed the girl's death warrant?

Lynxx passed an agonizing night in his apartment at the Ferguson Complex. Fear destroyed any chance of sleep.

Hours ago, when he'd finally left Grand Central Station, he had used a different exit, sensing it was dangerous to be seen anywhere near the courtyard and Olivia. Was her body there right now, lying in the dark? He longed to check but knew he couldn't. He couldn't even risk popping into the bunker to see if Olivia had made it home. Frost might be watching.

The next morning, as WindLord, he flew across the courtyard, bracing himself for an unbearable sight. He almost expected to see Olivia's body sprawled on the pavers, flesh ripped to the bone by the vulture's talons, eyes gouged from her sockets, face mangled beyond recognition.

Nothing.

No blood.

No body.

Still, he didn't breathe easy until he arrived outside the bunker, leaped into Mousy's mind, and saw Kassia having breakfast with her sister.

He'd dodged a bullet—this time. But as long as Frost was around, he'd have to limit his meetings with Olivia if he wanted her to stay alive.

72

The city was getting worse.

In the month since Lynxx had shown Olivia where to collect her weekly Lazarus terra flowers, he'd kept away from her.

Each morning, Mousy-him would spend a blissful hour with Kassia. Later, he would experiment on terra specimens in his lab.

Sometimes, when he was on the streets, he sensed Frost nearby. Looking around, he'd see the silver-eyed vulture watching him from a tree or building. Lynxx always made a point of ignoring the bird, and eventually his guardian would grow bored and fly off.

He suspected that his guardian regularly flew over the city, checking things out.

Lynxx knew that many places around Manhattan had hardly any terras.

In other areas, the terras reigned. They climbed the walls of skyscrapers. Covered roads and sidewalks in leaves. Smothered parked cars in vines. Within a decade, he suspected that every manmade object in the city would disappear beneath these layers of non-terrestrial vegetation, as though they had never existed—and as though humanity had never existed.

One afternoon, he came across Asher Weston and Harlem in a plaza near Rockefeller Center. Before the Mist, this place had contained lush plants and fountains that had provided an oasis of nature amid the tall buildings.

Now, terras thrived everywhere.

Lynxx paused at the edge of the plaza, watching the two resistance fighters use flamethrowers to burn a patch of terra vines. Harlem, lacking confidence, handled his flamethrower as though it would explode in his face. Asher, ever the leader, tried to encourage Harlem with praise, but the boy bristled at every comment as though he'd been insulted.

Lynxx frowned. The pair seemed to argue a lot. And yet they occasionally joked too. They seemed to be starting to become friends.

Lynxx had never had a friend, and he envied this pair's squabbling relationship.

As the wind blew burned leaves over him, he grabbed one and examined it. Sighing in annoyance, he stalked across to the duo, who were standing near a tall, squarish tree.

Switching off their flamethrowers, they watched his approach.

"Are you two really as stupid as you seem?" Lynxx snapped.

"Whoa," Asher said, brow rising. "Hello to you too."

"See, Don Q?" Harlem rolled his eyes. "I told you he wasn't grateful that we saved him from those Wilders. We should've let them roast him over the burning car."

Lynxx faced Harlem, his tone disdainful. "That day, I had things under control."

And he had. As he'd hung over the makeshift bonfire, he'd closed his eyes and mind-leaped into a pigeon, then the eagle, WindLord. He'd scooped up an enormous king cobra and had been waiting to drop it among the bikers at the right moment. This distraction would have allowed him to leap back into his own body, climb the rope, punch out the driver, and shimmy down the extendable arm of the boom fire truck.

As a backup to the cobra-eagle strategy, he would have remote-pushed the grizzly bear that had wandered into Barr Street. Plus he'd had a couple of other ideas up his sleeve.

However, he hadn't needed any of them, thanks to Asher's crawlers.

Flamethrower in hand, Asher looked at Lynxx's black outfit: T-shirt, leather jacket, and jeans. "So, you finally took my advice about ditching your country gear. I almost didn't recognize you."

Lynxx shrugged and gestured to the boys' scarlet fire-resistant coveralls. "I see you guys are going for a trendy but functional look."

Asher sighed. "What do you want? We've work to do."

Lynxx surveyed the smoldering climbers. "Why are you wasting your time burning harmless velvet-vine terras?"

"Velvet-vines?" Asher's eyebrows shot up. "These are poisonous devil terras."

"They appear the same. But people with a high IQ—like me—know that velvet-vines have four tips on each leaf. Devil terras have only three, like a devil's trident or pitchfork."

Asher and Harlem peered more closely at an unburned section of leaves. They groaned.

"Meanwhile," Lynxx continued, enjoying their embarrassment, "you two firebugs are only a few minutes from certain death."

"What?" Asher and Harlem spun around. Scanned their surroundings. Frowned in bewilderment.

With an impatient sigh, Lynxx pointed to the squarish tree next to them. Its branches were covered in leaves dotted with tiny bubbles. As they watched, the bubbles grew larger and larger.

Harlem gasped, "Freakin' heck!"

"It's a swarmer terra," Lynxx informed them. "In about ten minutes, those bubble bulbs will be the size of baseballs. That's when they'll burst and release swarmer seeds into the air. The seeds will only have thirty minutes to find nice warm bodies to burrow into. For their victims, it'll be an ugly and agonizing death."

Grasping his flamethrower, Harlem slowly backed away. He stopped when Asher didn't move.

"Can we kill it?" Asher asked Lynxx.

"If it's alive, it can die."

"Nice answer, Yoda. I need specifics."

Lynxx gestured to the flamethrower. "They're not fans of fire."

"Thanks." Asher beckoned to his colleague. "We can burn them, Harl."

"Before you start," Lynxx said, "I need a favor. After all, I just saved your life and your sidekick's life."

Harlem glared at him. "Who are you calling a sidekick?"

Distracted, staring at the bubble-encrusted swarmer tree, Asher asked Lynxx, "What favor?"

"I'm aware you use solar power at Weston Tower."

"How do you know that?"

"Irrelevant." Last week Lynxx had mind-blended with a series of small animals to investigate the facilities in Weston Tower from top to bottom. "Anyway, I need to print off a few dozen posters, and I want some of your members to stick them around the city, warning people."

"About what?"

Lynxx told them how he'd seen ZebraMan carving up the flesh of his victims. He also described the other mutilated corpses he'd found around the city over the past few weeks. "I'm positive it's the same wacko." He gave them a detailed description of the psycho, then finished with, "ZebraMan needs to be stopped before he kills anyone else." *Like Kassia or Olivia.*

As Asher and Harlem exchanged alarmed glances, he asked, "Will you put up the warning posters?"

Asher nodded. "Of course."

"Good. I also want a meeting with you and your leader, Colonel Powell."

"He's *Commander* Powell now."

"Whatever."

Harlem folded his arms. "Why do you want a meeting with him?"

"Do I snoop into your business?"

"Probably," the boy replied.

True. During Lynxx's clandestine visit to Weston Tower, he'd counted twenty-three electronic devices in Harlem's tiny room. *Talk about obsessed.* Then a sudden realization had tempered his harsh judgement. Maybe Harlem's collection was like a security blanket to him. A reminder that he was no longer a hungry kid wandering the streets, alone and afraid and penniless.

Asher spun back to the growing bubbles. "Is this meeting with the commander important?"

"Very."

"Okay. Come over at eight o'clock tonight. I'll tell the guards at the gates to let you in."

"Good." Lynxx watched the pair train their flamethrowers on the squarish swarmer terra tree. Within seconds, it was engulfed in fire.

As he strode across the plaza, the crackle of the bubble bulbs rang in his ears, and the stench of the burning seeds filled his nostrils. Ignoring the death rattles of the swarmer tree, he fingered a tiny photo deep in his jacket pocket.

Tonight, after he made his two copies, he wanted to discuss an important matter with Asher Weston and Commander Powell.

73

THAT EVENING, LYNXX PATTED his jacket pocket, checking the items were safely inside.

They were.

He'd just used the color copier at Weston Tower to print off the warning posters about ZebraMan, plus the two photo enlargements he wanted. Back at his lab, his own printer had run out of ink, and he didn't have time to search for fresh cartridges.

Now, he accompanied Asher into Commander Powell's office.

The wood-paneled walls, plush carpet, and long mahogany desk indicated this used to be a spacious conference room.

These days it was a crowded war room.

Boxes lined the tops of cabinets. Others cluttered the floor. A pile of guns stained a plush couch. Two flamethrowers lay beside a marble coffee table. A glass-fronted mini-fridge held medical supplies instead of expensive champagnes and wines. Heavy drapes covered the floor-to-ceiling windows, hiding any lights from watchers in the night-swathed city.

Charts and maps of New York covered the main wall. Some displayed the locations of various buildings. Others marked the homes of survivors outside the Weston Battalion. One showed the city's suburbs broken into numbered zones, and he was relieved to see that Washington Heights—where Frost and other hybrids were setting up a compound—had been colored scarlet and labeled the Red Zone.

Good. Olivia had obviously passed on his fake warnings about the "super-lethal" terras in that area.

Behind his desk, the commander motioned Lynxx and Asher to a pair of seats. A framed photo of a middle-aged black woman and two teenage boys stood beside a pile of folders.

The former Army officer sat back in his mesh chair, his face expressionless as he listened to Lynxx's request. Then he replied, "Hey, I'd love to have Olivia join our cell. In fact, we've invited her several times."

Asher picked up a stained machete from a seat. "She's always refused." He hefted the weapon in his hand, assessing its weight.

Powell leaned forward, elbows resting on the long table. "Doesn't Olivia have a sick friend whom she wants to bring into the cell too?"

Lynxx noted the word *friend*, and he remembered that Olivia didn't want anyone knowing about her sick sister. She wasn't ashamed of Kassia; she just wanted to protect her.

"Yeah," Asher told Powell. "I think her friend's got leukemia."

"In remission?"

"I don't know, sir."

The commander turned to Lynxx. "Is Olivia's friend in remission?"

Caught off guard, he hesitated.

Powell said, "So, that's a no."

"I didn't say that."

"You didn't have to."

Desperately, Lynxx said, "She *is* in remission. She's been that way for months."

Powell studied him with sharp eyes. "You're lying." Face hard, he leaned back again. "We can't accept the friend."

"But—"

"It's non-negotiable." The furrows in the middle-aged man's forehead deepened. "We don't have enough meds for our existing members, and they're generally healthy. We can't take in a terminal girl who would exhaust our meds within a few weeks. I'd love to have Olivia join us, but the cost is too high." He rubbed his temples, as though weighed down by the pressures of caring for hundreds of people every day. "The needs of the many outweigh the needs of the one." He turned to his lieutenant. "Your thoughts, son?"

"I agree with you, sir," Asher said regretfully, placing the machete back on the seat. "I wish we could take in everyone, no matter how sick, disabled, or old. But we can't. Our cell would collapse within weeks."

Lynxx sighed. He knew that arguing would be useless.

Curious, Asher asked Powell and Lynxx, "Have either of you ever seen Olivia without her black woolen beanie, sunglasses, and grease on her face?"

The commander shook his head. "No. She could walk in here wearing civvies and I wouldn't recognize her."

Lynxx thought of his daily visits to the bunker, always timed so the girls were up and dressed before he leaped into Mousy's mind. Olivia had the same beautiful eyes and hair as Kassia. However, he doubted that her skin was as soft as Kassia's, and although her smile was nice, it never warmed him the way Kassia's did.

He pretended ignorance. "I've no idea what Olivia really looks like." These days, he lied as easily as a human.

"She's one mysterious girl." Asher's voice held a thread of interest.

Lynxx stiffened in his seat, as protective as a brother. He knew Olivia was lonely, and he would welcome anyone who'd make her happy. But first he had to make sure the guy was good enough for her.

Still, from everything he knew about Asher Weston, the resistance fighter was more than decent. He was brave, resourceful, and committed. Lynxx had seen the respect people gave him, both in the garrison and on the streets. He'd watched Asher fight the terras with passion and determination. He'd noticed the way he cared for people and helped them.

And he'd sensed the relationship Asher had with his commander—almost like a father and son.

A flicker of envy shot through him.

From what he'd heard, Asher and Powell had only met in the past few months. Yet they'd already built a close relationship based on mutual respect and trust.

To his surprise, Lynxx realized that he not only envied Asher Weston, but he also liked and admired him. Perhaps one day they might even become friends.

Maybe the guy *was* good enough for Olivia—although he couldn't be sure Asher's interest was personal. Perhaps he was just keen to add another fighter to his team.

Commander Powell cocked his head at Lynxx. "Where are your weapons? Did the guards at the gate confiscate them?"

"I don't have any," he replied.

"Good grief, boy. Are you crazy?"

With a grin, Asher said, "I've often wondered that myself."

Lynxx gave him a brief smile. "Ditto. I've seen you battling the terras. You must not be interested in growing old."

"Hey," Asher bristled, "you're welcome to join us any time. Killing terras is good for the soul."

Soul.

Recently, Lynxx had looked up the word's meaning in a dictionary. It meant "the spiritual part of humans, as distinct from the physical part." In some novels he'd read, the villains were regarded as "lacking a soul" if they didn't care about right or wrong, or if they were unable to feel love or guilt. By that definition, Frost was the perfect example of a soulless person.

But did every Outrider lack a soul?

"How about it, Lynxx?" asked Asher. "Want to join Harlem and me on a hack-and-slash mission tomorrow?"

Lynxx dragged his mind back to the conversation. "I prefer to fight with my brain, not my brawn."

"These days, there's a place for both kinds of fighters." Asher's words held a grudging respect.

Yes, Lynxx thought with satisfaction, he and Asher could become friends one day.

Powell's sharp stare remained fixed on him. "Why don't you carry any weapons, boy?"

Lynxx hesitated, unable to admit the truth.

When he'd encountered trouble in the past, he had always handled it his own way. Wild animals were remote-pushed aside. If there were one or two hostile people, he'd mentally remote-push nearby animals or objects, distracting his attackers. Even when he'd been ambushed by the pack of Wilders and hung over a blazing car, remote-pushing animals had always been more effective than using guns.

He gave a careless shrug. "I must've forgotten them."

"Take my advice, boy. These days, forgetful people are dead people."

"Got it."

Asher raised a brow at Lynxx. "Are you ready to join us yet? You'll be safer in Weston Tower than out on your own. We can set up a lab for your research on the terras and maybe even give you a couple of assistants."

Lynxx felt a sudden flare of excitement. For weeks, he'd only had an hour's contact each day with Kassia, and that was as Mousy-him. The rest of the time, he worked by himself—and the loneliness was increasingly hard to bear. The thought of joining a resistance cell was highly appealing. He could still visit Kassia each morning. Then he could spend the rest of the day working with his lab assistants.

He'd be part of a community.

Have friends.

Belong.

74

Lynxx hid his excitement at the thought of joining the Weston community. "I thought you didn't like me, Asher."

Asher suppressed a smile. "Well, you can be an ungrateful pain-in-the-butt, and at times you're weirdly cold and distant."

Lynxx rolled his eyes. "Please, don't spare my feelings."

"However, we'd work on humanizing you."

Humanizing.

Asher had been joking but, with a jolt, Lynxx realized that was exactly what was happening to him. Over the past few months, he'd been turning away from his emotionless hybrid side and embracing his humanity. The slide had been so gradual that he hadn't noticed it. But Frost had noticed the change when they'd met in the tunnel of trees—and his guardian hadn't liked it.

That was why he'd been watching Lynxx.

If Frost knew that his ward had joined the Weston Battalion, he would kill some of the resistance members simply to show his disapproval.

Lynxx's excitement shriveled into disappointment. He couldn't risk people's lives just so he could have the company he craved. Powell was right. *The needs of the many outweigh the needs of the one.*

Forcing his face into a neutral mask, he told Asher, "I'm not interested in joining your cell." A lie. "I work better alone."

Another lie. He hated working alone. Longed to be part of a community. Knew it wouldn't happen.

His shoulders slumped.

At least he could still look forward to seeing Kassia each morning.

Asher shrugged. "Pity."

Lynxx remained silent.

Commander Powell picked up some papers from a pile on his desk. "Well, you've used our copier and heard our answer about Olivia. Is there anything else?"

Suddenly reluctant to leave, Lynxx moved to a wall displaying a dozen large photos. Each showed a different terra, all dangerous. Hades plants. Glow-lotus terras. Boulder terras. Strangler vines. Cathedral-dome terras. Tentacle plants.

He gestured to the photos. "There are many more lethal species throughout the city, you know. And new ones are popping up every day."

"We know." Distracted, Powell scribbled some notes on a report.

Moving along the wall, Lynxx stopped at a plaque bearing about thirty names. "What's this?"

"Our Honor Roll," Asher said. "It lists the name of every person in our cell who's died fighting the terras."

Lynxx moved on to a roster of resistance fighters, noting their daily assigned areas and the targeted terras. "Why are you waging this war?" he asked, confused. "You can't win."

Commander Powell looked up from his paperwork. "No one expects to win. It doesn't mean we stop fighting."

His words triggered a strange flicker within Lynxx.

No one expects to win. It doesn't mean we stop fighting.

Over the years, Frost had kept him isolated from the world and normal people—and his own humanity. Although his guardian had relished bloodthirsty horror movies, he had fostered Lynxx's cold, analytical side. Questions were forbidden. Reasons were never given. Emotions were crushed.

Lynxx had robotically obeyed his guardian's orders. He'd made endless lists of Earth plants, along with their strengths and weaknesses. He didn't know if any of his information had been used in planning the apocalypse. But what if it had? He needed to atone for some of the damage he might've caused.

It doesn't mean we stop fighting.

Maybe it was time for him to *start* fighting.

Within him, he felt another strange flicker. It almost felt like invisible wings fluttering inside his chest. Perhaps it was determination. Or guilt.

Whatever, he knew he needed to help the other side ... the human side ... now *his* side.

Lynxx looked from Commander Powell to Asher. "I agree that we should keep fighting." His voice held a conviction he'd never felt before. "I still can't join your cell. But I think I can help."

<h1 style="text-align:center">75</h1>

WindLord-Lynxx soared above Manhattan.

ZebraMan remained elusive. Nevertheless, Lynxx regularly swept the city from the air, just in case he got lucky.

Today, he'd been checking the streets and parks far below for a couple of hours. No sign of ZebraMan. It was time to head back to the Ferguson Complex, to his own body and his work.

Last week, after he'd used the copier at Weston Tower, he'd proposed a deal to Commander Powell and Asher. He would continue to research ways to kill the various terras, and he'd share his results with the Weston Battalion. In return, they would provide him with fresh food, other supplies, and fuel for his generator.

Thankfully, they had accepted his terms.

No more cans of rattlesnake meat, pork brains, or roasted crickets with eggs. He'd miss the canned bread, though.

On Lynxx's left, a flock of pigeons changed direction as they noticed eagle-him. He shook his feathered head in frustration. He wasn't going to eat them, but they didn't know that.

He started flying back to the Ferguson Complex, then changed his mind. Before returning to his lonely lab, he wanted a few minutes of fun.

Months ago, when he'd first mind-blended with birds, he'd regarded flying as a mechanical activity, a means of getting around. These days, he found it hard to believe he'd ever been so ... emotionless.

For the past few weeks, at the end of every aerial search of Manhattan, he allowed himself a brief period to revel in the pure bliss of flying.

Now, he surrendered to the joy of powering his wings up and up, toward the warm thermals that flowed like unseen rivers in the sky. Air surged beneath his feathers and the wind gusted past his eagle face. When he reached the thermals, he stretched his wings and glided on the currents, sweeping and soaring in delight.

The weights of his earthbound life vanished. His cares and worries disappeared. He was a part of the sky. Merged with the air. Free.

Too soon, memories of his responsibilities crowded back. As a familiar heaviness pressed on him once again, he dropped out of the warm air currents and descended toward his lab.

With a silent sigh of regret, he dragged his attention away from the incredible views of Manhattan—and saw a familiar figure in a large plaza below.

Olivia.

What was she doing out here?

Earlier this morning, as Mousy, he'd seen her vomiting into a bucket in the bunker. She'd gotten food poisoning from something she'd eaten last night. Fortunately—or unfortunately—Kassia had been too sick to touch her dinner.

"Via, please stay home and rest today," Kassia had told her sister that morning. "I can do without my meds for a little longer."

"Okay." Pale and nauseous, Olivia had tumbled back to her cot.

But now, a few hours later, she had come aboveground. Lynxx shook his eagle head. Talk about stubborn. She must've decided to try to find some meds for Kassia after all. But from the way she was staggering across the plaza, she was clearly too ill to be outside.

And too ill to realize that she'd just turned herself into a target.

WindLord-Lynxx swooped down to his lab and mind-leaped into his own body.

His rooms at the Ferguson Complex were only a block from the plaza. With any luck, he'd reach Olivia before any wild animals, wild humans, or terras got her.

Too late.

Lynxx, in his own body, crouched behind a dumpster at the end of an alley beside the large plaza. Peering over the metal container, he watched a man wearing a zebra-skin cloak slink across the pavers. The psycho was headed straight for Olivia—his silver eyes glinting with menace.

Sick again, she had crumpled to the ground, grasping her stomach, eyes closed, oblivious to the approach of death.

Lynxx's mind raced in an agony of panic and anger at himself.

Stupid. Stupid. Stupid.

In his rush from the lab, he hadn't grabbed a weapon. He'd never needed them before, preferring to remote-push potential attackers away from himself.

However, he couldn't remote-push the person now sneaking toward Olivia. True, ZebraMan was a psycho who'd probably lost his mind, anyway. But today the wacko's silver eyes indicated the psycho was mind-blended with a hybrid—almost certainly Frost.

How was that possible?

Hybrids couldn't mind-blend with humans, with some exceptions. Was this one? Did ZebraMan's insanity leave him vulnerable to a mind-blend?

Lynxx could feel the mind-blend vibrations rippling through the air and washing over him in foul waves. Fortunately, these ripples were one way. As long as he stayed in his own body, Frost wouldn't know that his ward was watching from the shadows.

What could he do? How could he help Olivia?

He scanned the plaza. Nearby, a flock of pigeons pecked at some scattered seeds on the pavers. Further off, a lion hunkered in the shadows, studying a skunk nibbling on a tuft of grass. At the far side of the plaza, a giraffe grazed on a wall of vines, unconcerned about the distant lion, apparently confident it could kick any attacker to death with its sharp hooves.

He shifted his attention back to the two people in the plaza. Could he race up behind ZebraMan and tackle him to the ground?

Bad plan.

ZebraMan would hear him coming, withdraw the gun tucked into his belt, and shoot him.

Lynxx didn't want Olivia to die. But he didn't want to die either. He had too much to live for: Kassia.

Spreading his animal-skin cape in a dramatic flair, Zebra-Man circled the fallen girl.

Olivia opened her eyes, saw the man, and shakily reached for her revolver. "You. I was warned about you."

"Were you, my sweet?" ZebraMan snatched the gun from her fingers. When she tried to sit up, he punched her in the head, slamming her back to the pavers. As Olivia lay there, dazed, he grabbed her other weapons—backup pistol, knives, machete, rifle—and dropped them down the center hole of a trash bin, out of sight and out of reach. Only the wooden butt of her rifle poked from the bin.

ZebraMan yanked off Olivia's sunglasses, revealing her green eyes. Then he pulled the woolen beanie from her head, freeing her long auburn braid.

"Just as I thought. A pretty girl trying to pass as a boy. Why, my dear? Afraid of attracting someone like me? Someone who wants to sniff the aroma of your blood, taste the sweetness of your flesh, watch the life fade from your beautiful eyes?"

Lynxx was certain these corny but terrifying words were coming from Frost, not ZebraMan. The psycho, ZebraMan, had always struck him as a slice-and-dice kind of guy, not the type to rave on about warped needs. That was pure Frost. His guardian was so twisted by his hatred of people that he'd inserted himself into a psycho's mind just to experience the pleasure of killing a human without dirtying his own hands.

Desperately, Lynxx scanned the area, searching for a way to reach the man unseen, but the huge plaza was free of bushes and trees. No matter which direction he came from, Frost would see or hear him coming.

ZebraMan-Frost twisted his hands together, as though stopping himself from lurching forward and slashing the unarmed girl to death. Lynxx guessed that Frost was savoring Olivia's weakened condition, and feasting on her pain and fear like a glutton gorging at a buffet. No doubt her eventual slaughter would be his dessert, carefully delayed until the end for his ultimate pleasure.

"You're such a fine specimen, my pretty. Your blood will create beautiful patterns on these pavers."

Olivia raised herself onto one elbow as she glared at the weirdly dressed man. "Get away from me, you silver-eyed freak. If you touch me, I'll kill you." Her weak voice left her threat hollow.

She reached for her weapons. Felt air.

Fresh terror flashed across her face.

"Kill me with what, sweetmeat? Your puny little hands?" ZebraMan-Frost smirked at the trash bin with its protruding rifle butt. "Weapons all gone. Too bad. So sad."

Lynxx sensed that the seconds were ticking down to disaster. Any moment now, Frost could surrender to his swelling craziness and throw himself on Olivia. He'd hack her to pieces, watching as her blood made "beautiful patterns" on the pavers.

If Olivia died, Kassia could lose her will to live and follow her sister to the grave.

No. He couldn't let that happen.

"I've heard that human flesh tastes like chicken," Zebra-Man-Frost said. "Pity. I'm not a big fan of chicken."

Through his panic, Lynxx struggled to remember what Frost had told him about mind-blending. He knew hybrids couldn't sense each other when both were in their own human bodies—or when both were in the bodies of animals.

But what if a hybrid like Frost was mind-blended with another human? Could he sense the approach of another hybrid mind-blended with an animal?

Maybe.

Maybe not.

From beneath his cloak, ZebraMan withdrew a huge hunting knife. Its death-sharp blade glinted in the sunlight. Kneeling beside Olivia, he slowly raised the weapon.

Lynxx was out of time.

And options.

76

Lynxx slumped behind the dumpster and leaned back against the alley wall. Leaving his body, he mind-leaped into a pigeon pecking at some seeds.

He could still feel Frost's ripples.

ZebraMan's knife paused midair. He stopped. Whirled around. Glared at the flock of pigeons.

Yep. Frost had sensed that a mind-blended hybrid was nearby, but he didn't know which pigeon held him.

Lynxx changed plans. He did a series of quick mind-hops, keeping his exact location in doubt. He mind-leaped into another pigeon. Then into a rat scurrying across the plaza. Another pigeon. The skunk. Back to the pigeons. Skunk. Pigeons. Skunk.

He created numerous sets of ripples that collided into a mess.

Enraged, ZebraMan-Frost glared from the pigeons to the skunk, then back at the pigeons. "Lynxx? Is that you?"

With a massive effort, Lynxx mind-leaped across a twenty-five-yard gap—longer than the usual range for a mind-leap—and into the lion that had been stalking the skunk.

Saliva dripped from ZebraMan-Frost's mouth as he scanned the plaza. "Lynxx! Where are you hiding?"

Lynxx clamped an invisible steel cage around the lion's mind.

Go!

The animal bounded forward.

It bolted across the plaza on soft paws, its tawny mane waving in the breeze. The silent four-hundred-pound mass of death headed straight for ZebraMan, whose attention was still focused on the pigeons and the skunk.

For precious long seconds, Frost didn't feel the animal approaching from behind. Then, suddenly, he must've sensed a new and stronger set of ripples.

ZebraMan-Frost whirled around and saw the lion. Silver eyes widening in shock, he raised his knife again.

Lion-Lynxx bounded forward and slammed into ZebraMan, knocking the blade from his hand.

He felt Frost trying to leap into lion-Lynxx, but his guardian's mind struck the mental case he'd erected within the animal, and it bounced out again.

Lynxx sank his lion teeth deep into ZebraMan's throat. With a soundless scream, the psycho struggled against the massive jaws crushing his windpipe. Lynxx could taste hot blood filling his mouth, trickling down his chin, onto his mane.

The man's struggles grew weaker and weaker. Hopefully, Frost would die along with his psycho human host. If his guardian died, Lynxx's ties to the Outriders would be cut. He could put his past, and his actions, behind him as though they'd never occurred.

To his dismay, he felt a ripple as Frost mind-leaped from the dying man, into a pigeon flying overhead.

Frost had mind-blended with the bird.

The silver-eyed pigeon flew away.

Lion jaws clamped around ZebraMan's neck, Lynxx shook the body, watching for movement. There was none. The psycho was dead. Relieved, he opened his mouth and dropped the maimed body to the ground. The man's blood seeped onto the pavers ... creating ugly patterns.

A strange sensation whispered through Lynxx, a dark and unsettling feeling. It took a few moments to identify it.

Guilt. He actually felt guilty about killing a human being.

But if he hadn't done it, he told himself, Olivia would've died. The killing had been justified. Necessary.

So why did he feel guilty?

Furred chest heaving from stress and fatigue, he turned to Olivia.

She was standing a short distance away, eyes narrowed, rifle aimed at him.

Lynxx looked around, desperately seeking another creature to leap into, but every bird and animal in the plaza had disappeared, scared off by the lion's savage attack.

This is it, he thought, stomach knotting. If Olivia killed the lion, he would also die since his own body was out of range and there were no animals nearby to leap into.

Kassia.

Even though he wasn't in his own body, Lynxx felt as if his heart were breaking. He couldn't bear the thought of leaving Kassia. Not now. Not when, after all these years of existing, he was finally alive.

She filled his world. Gave it life and color and warmth.

And now he was about to be blasted into a cold and lonely oblivion.

Unless ...

Olivia was ill from food poisoning. Her head probably throbbed from being slammed onto the pavers, and she was still in shock from ZebraMan's attack. She was weak enough for him to try something he'd never attempted on a human before. He wasn't even sure it would work.

He threw a sharp mental message into the girl's mind.

Don't shoot the lion. It won't hurt you. Let it leave.

She hesitated. Brow knotted, she lowered her weapon a few inches.

Lynxx held his breath. Had she received the message? Or was this just a coincidence?

Olivia shook her head, then resumed her stance. Front-on position, arms tucked in for stability, one foot in front of the other ... but she kept her rifle lowered.

Again, he remote-pushed.

Don't shoot the lion. It won't hurt you. Let it leave.

She stiffened. Glanced from side to side. Frowned at lion-him.

Eyes glazed with pain and confusion—and resolve—she lifted the rifle and aimed it straight at him.

77

PANIC CLAWED AT LYNXX. *Olivia's going to shoot me. My remote-pushing isn't working.*

He knew the lion must be a terrifying sight to her. The large beast was standing over the body of a man whose throat it had just ripped open. Lion-him could still taste the coppery tang of blood, and his snout and mane were stained red, adding to his savage image.

Only one thing to do.

One chance at life.

Lion-Lynxx sank onto his haunches and lowered his furred body to the ground. Sitting with his dark forepaws stretched out, he retracted his claws into his soft pads.

Olivia's finger curled around the trigger.

Lynxx lowered his lion head close to the ground, trying to show that he wasn't a threat.

Don't shoot the lion. It won't hurt you.

Her finger froze on the trigger. "What the—?" Blood trickled from her scalp, where ZebraMan had slammed her head against the pavers.

Lynxx could see the hesitation in Olivia's eyes. She had just watched lion-him rip into ZebraMan. It didn't matter that the dead psycho was going to kill her. All she saw was an unprovoked attack on a human by a wild beast. Naturally, she'd fear she was next.

Slowly, Lynxx lowered his head even more, until his blood-smeared snout was buried in his thick mane. Silver eyes round and beseeching, he stared at the girl.

His pulse raced. Fast. Too fast.

In front of him, Olivia faded away and the image of Kassia appeared. She was smiling down at Mousy-him, one side of her mouth quirked in that cute way he loved so much.

His racing pulse slowed a little, soothed by her appearance. At least, at this moment of his death, Kassia would be the last thing he saw.

But to his distress, her image faded away.

Olivia was staring at him. "What *are* you? And why do you have silver eyes?" Her questions slid out on a hush of wonder. She moved her finger away from the trigger.

Quickly, before she realized what she'd done, he edged backward, crawling away from her. He tried to send her another message: *The lion won't hurt you. Let it leave.*

All he wanted was to get back to where he belonged.

To Kassia.

"Why are you leaving?" she asked, trembling. "Why aren't you trying to eat your kill? Did you do all this just to ... protect ... me?" She shook her head, as though throwing off that last crazy thought. Still, she lowered the rifle again.

When his crawling had put a wide gap between them, lion-Lynxx rose to his feet. Silver eyes still wide, tawny head still lowered, he continued backing away.

Olivia watched his retreat, never taking her gaze off him.

When Lynxx finally reached the alley, he gave his host a massive mental push, thrusting the lion into a run that would carry it a block before its mind settled down again. As the animal bolted past the dumpster, Lynxx mind-leaped into his own slumped body.

He clambered to his feet. Keeping out of sight, he watched Olivia grab the rest of her weapons from the trash can. As she staggered across the plaza, in the opposite direction to the lion's exit, he guessed her thoughts were a whirlpool of confusion and unanswerable questions.

Sticking to the shadows, he trailed Olivia until she disappeared down a subway entrance. He considered mind-leaping into a bat and following her, just to make sure she got home all right. But it was too risky. What if Frost returned and caught him protecting Olivia?

With a sigh, he turned away from the subway entrance and headed toward his lab.

Suddenly anxious, he patted his jacket, making sure the enlargement he'd made at Weston Tower was still in his pocket.

It was.

He pulled it out and gazed at the four-by-six-inch portrait of Kassia.

Weeks ago, as Mousy, he'd nudged open Olivia's locket one morning in the bunker. He'd bent and kissed Kassia's tiny photo, then used his paws to scrabble the photo from the locket. Gripping the picture with his teeth, he'd scampered through a hole in the wall, into the tunnel; here, he'd hidden the picture in a crevice until he was ready to retrieve it later, as a bat.

Later, with Commander Powell's permission, he'd used the copier at Weston Tower to make two enlargements. He ran his fingers over the picture, smiling at Mousy's teeth marks on a corner. He'd framed the larger eight-by-twelve-inch photo for his lab, so he could see Kassia during his lonely hours of research. He'd tucked the smaller six-by-four-inch photo into his jacket pocket, to keep him company on his trips around the city.

Maybe one day he'd even have a framed photo of Kassia, Olivia, and him on his desk, just like Commander Powell's family portrait.

Photo in hand, Lynxx leaned against a brick wall, studying Kassia's happy face. Hopefully, one day she would smile like that again. When the time was right, he planned on forming a friendship with Olivia that would lead to him meeting Kassia as himself. Maybe he and Kassia—

A chill surged through him, colder than an Arctic wind.

He stood there, struggling to absorb the shocking revelation.

Numbly, he tucked the picture back in his pocket.

A little while ago, Olivia had almost shot him. Amazingly, he was still alive—and yet, in a sudden leap of understanding, he realized he was about to die.

Dazed, he rode his motorcycle to Central Park.

To the place it had all begun.

78

Alone, Lynxx stared at Sheep Meadow.

On that long-ago Thanksgiving Day, he'd first met Kassia here. The green fields had been crowded with people, and sunlight had glinted on her beautiful hair as she'd nervously walked toward him, gathering the courage to kiss him.

Now, Kassia spent most of her days alone in a dank subway tunnel. And Sheep Meadow was an empty expanse of blackened glow-lotus terras.

On the Gapstow Bridge, he kept his hands away from the footbridge's parapet, which was covered by a thin layer of gray vegetation. Rust-moss terras looked soft and inviting, but they scraped the skin like crushed glass, plus they ate into metal and concrete.

Months ago, as a squirrel, he'd scampered along this parapet toward a distressed Kassia. Chittering, he'd sat beside her, providing a few precious minutes of companionship. And up there, over the Pond, he'd soared as the golden eagle, WindLord—and had spied in the distance the one person Kassia needed to stay alive. Her twin sister.

Now, in order to keep Kassia alive, Lynxx knew he had to cut himself out of her life.

Today, he'd been lucky.

But his luck had just run out.

His guardian, Frost, had felt ZebraMan being attacked by a mind-blended Outrider—who he'd guessed had been his rebellious ward. Determined to confirm that Lynxx was a traitor, Frost would blend with a variety of animals and start trailing him every day. Lynxx knew the psycho would keep far back so his vibrations wouldn't be felt.

Aware of this, Lynxx could continue to avoid Olivia as much as possible, but their paths might accidentally cross again.

The moment Frost saw Lynxx talking with Olivia, he'd know that Lynxx had been the hybrid who'd protected his victim today. Even worse, he'd know that Olivia was important to Lynxx.

Frost's revenge would be terrible. He would stalk either Olivia or Lynxx back to the subway bunker. There, he'd undoubtedly slaughter both girls—not just for fun, but as a punishment for his ward.

Icy fear unfurled within Lynxx.

He couldn't let anything happen to them. He cared about Olivia.

And he was in love with Kassia.

Love.

The word swelled in Lynxx's mind, its heat burning away his former chill.

A surge of clarity sent him staggering forward. Ignoring the abrasive rust-moss terras, he grabbed the side wall of the footbridge, steadying himself as the truth blazed through him.

He loved Kassia.

She was in every breath he took. He felt her presence when he gazed at a sunset. She sat with him when he read a novel late at night. In bed, he could close his eyes and touch her soft skin, hear her gentle voice, feel her warmth.

He knew he would love her for the rest of his life.

Right now, she would be treating Olivia's scalp wound, listening in horror to her tale of almost being stabbed to death by a psycho and eyeballed by a weird silver-eyed lion.

Kassia.

Because of Frost, he couldn't even risk returning to the bunker as Mousy to say goodbye to her.

He could never see her again.

Pain filled him, so intense that he wondered how he'd bear it.

He felt as if he were dying. Not physically. Emotionally.

A short time ago, he'd saved Olivia's life—and had destroyed his own. In that one incident with ZebraMan-Frost, he'd lost everything: his home in the subway bunker, his family ...

... and Kassia, the love of his life.

Lynxx glanced at the poisonous flowers that floated on the Pond below. Their heady perfume promised a quick end to his pain. Shuddering, he turned away from the lethal blossoms and lifted his gaze to the endless red skies.

Minutes passed as he struggled with his bleak future.

Kassia had been ripped from his hopes and dreams—but he still wanted to help her survive.

He would continue working on a treatment for her leukemia.

Alone.

Plus he'd promised Asher and Commander Powell that he'd find ways to kill other dangerous terras.

To protect the Weston Battalion from Frost, he'd have to keep Asher and every other person at an emotional distance as well. He'd have to continue behaving as if he were cold, remote, and detached from humanity.

He couldn't even leave the large photo of Kass on his lab bench, in case Frost snuck in and saw it.

As Lynxx's grip tightened on the wide parapet, the rust-moss terras scraped his skin with the sharpness of ground glass. Lifting his hands, he stared at the blood seeping from his palms.

It was like watching his own heart bleed.

Was this what it meant to be human? This blend of pain, despair, longing, and love?

He finally recognized the strange sensation that he'd felt stirring within him over the past few months.

His great love for Kassia had awakened that most elusive thing of all.

His soul.

And now he had to live with it.

Alone.

KASSIA

79

DAY 232—July 13

ONE MORNING, SIX MONTHS after Olivia and I had moved into the subway bunker below Grand Central Station, my sister prepared for her usual trip to the surface.

"What are you doing today, Kass?" She squeezed past me, looking for her favorite gun. Our bunker was beyond cozy. It was crammed with two cot beds, a small portable cooker, and stacked boxes of clothes, books, toiletries, and equipment, plus bottles of water and a few cans of food.

"It's Friday, so I'm taking some mushrooms and venison to Mr. Isaac." I ignored a twinge of nausea. My leukemia meds were running low, and I was trying to stretch them out by only taking them every second day.

"Be extra careful in the south tunnel, Kass. I heard a strange noise in it yesterday."

"What did it sound like?"

"A high-pitched cackle."

My throat tightened. "It can't be that psycho in the zebra-skin cloak. You said he was dead, Via."

"He's been dead for weeks," Olivia assured me, finding her revolver. "Like I told you, I saw a lion rip out his throat." She tucked the gun into her belt, within easy reach. "Besides, the cackle I heard didn't sound human."

"So it was an animal?"

A shrug. "What else could it be?"

Sighing, I touched the empty breast pocket of my shirt. "I miss Mousy. I always felt safer in the tunnels when he was with me."

"He was three inches long, sis. He couldn't protect you from anything."

"I know. But I still miss him. Do you think I'll ever see him again?"

"Hope so. You really loved that white mouse."

"I think he loved me too." I passed her a huge hunting knife. "Be careful up there."

"I always try to be." She strapped the blade to her thigh. An ornate gold locket hung around her neck, once treasured for its photos of our parents and me. Strangely, my photo had disappeared sometime over the past few months, but she still had the one of our parents. As usual, she tucked the locket out of sight, next to her heart.

Olivia pinned up her long auburn braid, pulled on a woolen beanie, and smeared the last of the black grease over her face. Huge goggles, fingerless gloves, and loose coveralls added to her masculine image. In certain areas on the surface, she'd found that appearing to be a boy helped deter unwanted attention from male survivors. When that didn't work, her gun was a backup deterrent.

She forced a smile. "I've got a good feeling about today. I think I'll find some more meds for you. Oh, and I need to get another jar of black grease. I've just used the last of it." She paused, her expression wistful. "I remember when I wore makeup on my face, not disgusting thick grease."

"I remember clean clothes and showers and electricity." I sighed, filled with a sad longing for our old life.

"Summers at the beach," she added, slipping into our well-worn routine.

"Hanging out at the mall."

"Going to the movies."

"Surfing the internet."

"Chatting to friends on social media."

"Another world," I murmured. "Another time."

"Yeah." Then, in an overly cheerful voice, she told me, "I won't forget your flowers."

"Thanks."

Every Friday for the past few months, Olivia had returned from her hunting trips with three huge purple roses. I'd bury my nose in the satiny petals, inhaling their heady scent, and somehow I'd always feel better for a few days.

"Anything special you want me to bring home, sis?"

"Just books. Please don't stay aboveground any longer than you need to, Via."

"No chance of that." Olivia's green eyes shadowed, as though visualizing the dangers of aboveground Manhattan.

As always, I longed to go with her. Watch her back. Help her.

Of course, that was impossible. My weakened condition and slowed reflexes would probably get us both killed by the first dangerous terra we met.

I inspected Olivia's gear before she left the bunker.

Empty sacks for food, water, and medicines—check.

Tools for breaking into stores and apartments in her new search area—check.

Guns and other weapons in case she encountered any wild animals, wild humans, or dangerous terras—check.

I hugged my twin goodbye, then wiped a glaze of sweat from my forehead. By all that was fair, someone as ill as me should've joined the billions of fatalities last year. But fairness had been extinguished along with most of humanity, and I was still alive. For now.

However, unless Olivia found some more meds, I soon wouldn't be.

After she left, I trudged to Mr. Isaac's bunker and left some bags of mushrooms and venison outside his closed door.

Next, I cleaned our room, read a book by the light of an oil lamp, made a canned-ingredients dinner, and watched the clock creep past midnight, then beyond dawn.

My anxiety rose with each passing minute.

I tried to convince myself that Olivia was okay. *She'll be back soon. She's had to shelter somewhere overnight. She'll be back later this morning.*

By midafternoon, I finally admitted an awful truth: something must've happened to her. An accident. Or worse.

Fear fluttered in my chest like a trapped moth. I'd lost so many people since the Mist. Was Olivia next?

My sister was the only person left that I loved in the world. The thought of her lying injured and bleeding somewhere was unbearable.

The thought of me venturing alone through the streets of a desolate and hostile city was terrifying—

—but I had no choice.

When I was younger, I'd been afraid of the needles used in my chemotherapy sessions. My father had stuck a quote on my bedroom mirror that had helped ease my fears. *Courage doesn't mean that you don't get afraid. Courage means that you don't let fear stop you.*

No way would I let fear stop me now.

I couldn't wait any longer. Although I'd promised not to go aboveground, I had to find Olivia.

After leaving a note in case she returned while I was away, I shoved a first aid kit into my backpack. Then I gathered some other items, strapped on a caver's helmet, and left the bunker.

Outside the closed door, I was surrounded by a blackness that felt thick and tight, as though I'd been swallowed by Death.

The breath snagged in my throat and I rushed to switch on my headlamp. When a slice of the underworld reappeared, I breathed a little easier and set off.

My light gleamed on the train tracks that led toward one of Grand Central's platforms.

As the tunnels rang with my footsteps and the hollow sounds of loneliness, I rubbed my goosebumped arms, feeling as if I were the only inhabitant left in the city.

I wasn't, of course.

Somewhere in the streets above, my sister—*please be okay, Via, please, please*—and other survivors were living in a post-apocalyptic New York.

I hadn't been aboveground for six months.

Where would I even start my search for Olivia? Were the Wilder bikers still around, still hunting women? What other frightening changes had taken place?

And how could a weak, sick girl like me survive up there ... alone?

Trembling, I forced myself onward, into the darkness.

Don't miss *Ashes Falling*, Book 2 in the *Girl on Fire* Series. Available now.

******IMPORTANT NOTE: The rest of this series—books 2, 3 and 4—will focus on Kassia's viewpoint only.***

Billions are dead. Humans are now an endangered species.

Six months after the apocalyptic red mist, Kassia emerges from her subway bunker beneath New York, desperate to find her missing sister.

After she is almost killed, Kassia links up with two strangers. Asher is a charismatic leader in the local resistance, while

Lynxx—a loner—is both brilliant and mysterious. Both boys help Kassia as she struggles to survive in the changed world.

However, a series of frightening events soon jeopardizes her new life and an unexpected romance.

Get your copy today!

THANK YOU

Thank you for reading *Girl on Fire*. I hope you enjoyed the book. If you did, I would be very grateful if you would tell your friends and consider leaving a review online—it can be as short or long as you wish.

Not a fan of writing reviews? That's okay. A rating (where you just leave stars) online is also much appreciated.

Reviews and star ratings are like life buoys. They help my book float on the surface of a gigantic ocean of books. From there, other readers can see it.

Without reviews and star ratings, my book will sink out of sight, dropping to the pitch-black bottom of the ocean. This is a graveyard for books.

Please help save a book today.

Happy reading!

Eden Hart

ALSO BY EDEN HART

The complete *Girl on Fire* Series:

Girl on Fire Book 1

Ashes Falling Book 2

Embers Burning Book 3

Phoenix Rising Book 4

About The Author

There are several authors named Eden Hart, who write in a wide variety of genres.

So far, the only books I've written are the 4 books in the *Girl on Fire* series.

My dystopian post-apocalyptic novels focus on compelling characters caught up in extraordinary events. They are laced with romance, action, sci-fi, and suspense, and aim to create immersive worlds that stir the imagination and enthrall the reader.

Along with writing, I'm passionate about travel. I've explored the crater of a mildly active volcano in Hawaii, abseiled down cliffs in Australia, trod the ruins of Pompeii, breakfasted with an orangutan in Asia, and crawled through the tunnels of an ancient subterranean city in Turkey.

Some of my less enjoyable experiences include flying on a broomstick-like ultra-light, having a ten-foot snake draped around my neck, and traveling in a plane whose engine burst into flames over the Indian Ocean.

Books are now my preferred way of adventuring!

I love hearing from my readers and can be found at:
Facebook Page: "Eden Hart - Author"
Email: EdenHart77@outlook.com
Website: www.edenhart.com.au